Book Two of The King's Renegade

BURDEN

A Vatan Chronicle

by

L. Steinworth

In memory of my mother

The strongest person I knew.

AUTHOR'S NOTE

One can view a work of art and arrive at their own conclusions about what the piece's mood and meaning is, but they can't ever truly know the artist's intent. This realization gripped me hard ever since I began painting 'Burden' in 2014. As I layered on a series of brush strokes, I was compelled to tell the story hiding behind the character's hood. And so, I wrote.

CONTENTS

VATAN

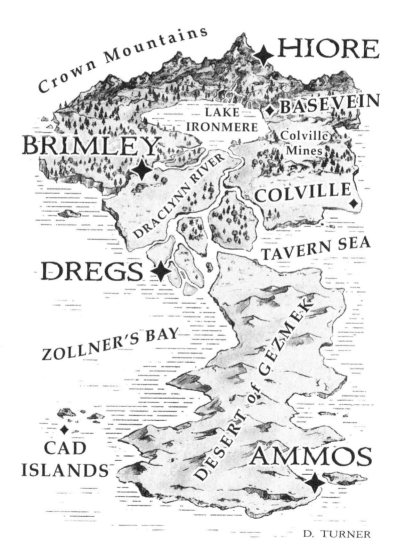

Crown Mountains

HIORE

BASEVEIN

LAKE
IRONMERE

Colville
Mines

BRIMLEY

DRACLYNN RIVER

COLVILLE

TAVERN SEA

DREGS

ZOLLNER'S BAY

DESERT of GEZMEK

CAD
ISLANDS

AMMOS

D. TURNER

CHAPTER ONE
COLIN

"Today should'a been spent celebrating my engagement," Colin whined, slumping into a stiff armchair. He let the hard wood dig into his ribs, uninterested in comfort. He'd watched the Ammosian ship sail in, his heart fluttering in anticipation of finally meeting his love—his future. Princess Mayli.

They had written for months, counting the days until they would be in each other's arms. But when the ship finally docked, the princess wasn't aboard. Instead, her mother, Queen Margaret of Ammos, stepped off. Pursed lips and hardened eyes scowled as if he were some mangy mutt crossing her path. In truth, she judged his family as far worse: illegitimate royals leeching off Vatan.

And then, she'd refused him her daughter's hand.

Glasses clinked as his cousin Briar plucked a bottle of mead from the bar cart nestled in the corner of the study. "Aye, but now the three of us can celebrate that you're *not* getting married!" He popped the cork, eyebrows wiggling.

Dominick, Colin's brother, lifted a glass. "Cheers to that." Suited in his doublet, one button undone, he looked as refined as their father, despite not yet being of age to be crested.

"Just cause you and Nick don't wanna wed, doesn't mean I don't," said Colin.

After filling Dominick's glass, Briar's lopsided smirk fell. "I want to... Just not to Evelyn. She's pretty, but has proved to be kind of a bitch."

"Good." Dominick closed his eyes, breathing in his drink. He stretched his legs out and crossed his feet at the ankles. "Ya finally see it."

"Yeah, well Mayli is one too." Briar offered the bottle to Colin.

Colin wet his lips. "I shouldn't."

"It's just honey," said his brother after taking a sip.

"He's right." Briar took a long gulp and sighed, eyes fluttering in pleasure. "Refreshing, really. It will do ya good."

The familiar sweet smell of lavender and honey wafted beneath Colin's nose as Briar placed the bottle in his hand. He'd tamed his habit when the prospect of marrying the only eligible princess in all of Vatan was his. Now, Mayli was anyone's but his, thanks to Queen Margaret's greed.

With nothing more to lose, Colin drank.

The bittersweet bite crawled down his throat. He coughed at the fermentation.

"There's my cousin!" Briar said, patting his back.

Colin shrugged him off. "Yeah, yeah. May's not a bitch though. We loved each other..." He took another sip.

Dominick laughed. "Loved? Ya never even met the princess, Col. At least Briar did and can back up his claim. She wouldn't let it go the day he shot that log."

Briar stabbed a finger toward Dominick. "Shut up."

Dominick laughed, leaning back in his seat. "Still got that splinter stuck between your teeth."

Briar swept his tongue over his gums in search of it.

Colin stared at the amber liquid as if glimpsing the golden sands of Ammos within the ripples. "We met on paper."

"Letters can't give you a good time in bed." Briar winked.

Colin threw him a look. "And tangling in the sheets can't reveal their heart."

Briar playfully shoved Colin at the shoulder. "What do you know about that? Been sneaking off to the brothel without me?" He waggled a finger.

"I don't do that," Colin said, shaking his head at the concept. He wiped his face. "Nah. May and I? Our letters were heartfelt. Real. We know what we have. How could her mother deny us this love?"

"Sure, sure. But more importantly, how can Queen Margaret deny us royal status?" groaned Dominick.

Briar tapped his chest. "That's right. Does she not understand that, unlike herself and the other self-declared royals, we actually *are* descended from kings?"

Colin sipped, shrugging. "Maybe she's right and our fathers aren't really sons of King Edune."

"Don't say that," snapped Briar. "We are royal."

"There's no denying *you* are," said Colin. "Your mother was Trisha Colte, so being the king of Dregs is still within your birthright."

"True..." Briar considered, cradling his chin.

Raising the bottle, Colin peered through the glass to determine the mead's remains. A single drop rolled inside. He let it fall onto his tongue. He blinked slowly, feeling the drunken haze hit him. "But me? I'm... I am nothing."

"Come on..." Dominick walked to a section of books. He pulled one and started flipping through its pages. "Somewhere in here has to prove our father's blood, Col."

Colin sneered. "Oh, in those old documents Granda stole? Or did Da forge 'em with his artistic expertise?"

The rumble of a cleared throat echoed in the study. In the doorway stood his grandfather, arms folded and scowl deep. "Your fathers are royal, and don't ever question your bloodline again."

"Dean!" gasped Briar, yanking the empty bottle from Colin to hide behind his back.

"Don't think I don't know what you three are up to." Shaking his head, Dean walked to the library wall and withdrew a key. He inserted it into a hole in the wood. Disguised by books, a hidden cabinet popped open. He drew out a long-necked bottle and arranged three short glasses. With care, he poured a splash of clear liquid into one.

Before Dean could set the bottle aside, Colin grabbed the glass and downed the contents in one gulp. He flashed his tongue at the rancid burn that followed, slamming his fist on the table as if that would lessen the pain.

"Damnit, boy, that dune ale was for your father." Dean plucked the glass from his hand and shook his head upon seeing it dry. He set it down and refilled it. "At least tomorrow you'll be too incapacitated to embarrass this family further."

Colin stared at his empty hand, then recoiled his fingers. "Not much more I can do when Margaret is here waving silk n' sword in yer face accusing us of bein' illegitimate. You've made us fools."

"I did not risk my life crossing the Desert of Gezmek with two stray, entitled boys just for good fun! King Edune pushed Liam and Jamus to me when the stairs collapsed in the quake. After his sacrifice, I made an oath to protect his sons no matter what trials lay ahead. No matter how drunk and intolerable their own would become."

Dominick and Briar exchanged guilty looks.

Colin stomped forward. "I may be that, but at least I'm not a thieving liar!"

"We are a family of honor and valor. And it's time you understood that—" Dean raised his hand to discipline him.

"Don't you hit my nephew and call it valorous," said an authoritative voice. Prince Jamus walked in, a stern glare held on Dean. Light armor clung to his frame, mud was caked on his boots, and the fragrant smell of horse emanated from him. Despite his rugged appeal, his gait was smooth, clothes fine, and hair just as blonde and well-groomed as Briar's, honoring every bit of his royal title despite anyone's objection.

Dean lowered his hand to cover his shoulder in respect. "Your Highness."

Jamus eyed Colin with the same disappointed look he'd thrown at Dean. "You know better than to drink."

Colin stepped back, dipping his head.

Walking past, Jamus leaned in, speaking in a friendly whisper. "Don't worry. I won't tell your father."

Colin raised a smile, but Jamus had already moved on to meet Briar at the desk. "Besides, I suppose this one is to blame? Thought you were to keep an eye on your cousins?" He tousled his son's hair, ruining the perfect combed wave, making ends stick up in every direction.

Whining, Briar ducked and threw his hands up, brushing through his locks. "Da!"

Jamus laughed, deep and mighty, but it quickly faded when Dean crossed his arms and cleared his throat. "What news do you bring, Jamus?" asked Dean.

He sighed and shook his head. "The gossip in town isn't good. Already there are those believing the lies and causing disturbances. Seems like some contest our story in here too." Jamus took a glass of dune ale, looking at the three of them.

Colin hunched his shoulders. "Queen Margaret brought evidence. It's compelling."

"All it proves is that Gezmek is still alive and well. Maybe even your other grandparents."

Dominick turned the book he'd been flipping through around. He pointed to an illustration of King Edune raising matching dual sabered blades over his head: one a sword, the other a dagger. Both shone silver. "Uncle's right, look. The knife that Prince Arkello gave Queen Margaret to prove he'd come from Gezmek? It looked just like this and your sword, Galavant."

Jamus coiled his hand around his saber's black-jeweled handle at his hip. "Yes, I remember the dagger. I always thought the jewels were blueberry candy. Tasted more like iron." He showed his tongue, where a small nick on the side left a depression.

"Anyone can forge a weapon," Dean grumbled. "And don't call that man a prince. His story is an Ammosian fable to discredit us to keep their claim on independence. Otherwise, this Arkello fellow would have come along, not wander back into the sands. They are trying to prevent us from taking back Vatan, and depriving you boys of marriage will do just that."

Jamus sat at the desk. "Maybe instead of criticizing, we talk with him. If this young man can answer some questions only Liam and I would know about Gezmek, then perhaps we could join him on his upcoming expedition and go back home! You always wanted to go to the desert, did you not, Colin?"

Home? Colin stared at the illustration of his great grandfather. Giant dunes surrounded the stone-carved palace as if King Edune rode a ship across a golden ocean. "We really could go to Gezmek?"

"We are home." Dean slammed the book shut, meeting Colin's gaze. "Even if some did survive the quake and storm, there's no way they would be alive today or could've managed to live almost thirty years underground. Let alone resurface."

Jamus leaned back in the chair, crossing his ankle over a knee. Tapping his fingers together in a wide spread, he smirked. "Are you forgetting how stubborn us Densens are?"

"Never." Dean looked at Jamus as if sharing an untold joke. "What I doubt is Queen Margaret's willingness to let Vatan merge and be ruled as one again. This will bring war if we aren't careful. Which is why King Liam is in conversation with the queen at this moment."

While Dean kept his attention on his conversation with Jamus, Colin coiled his hand around the bottle of dune ale. Undetected, he slipped it under his cloak. Nudging his brother, he gestured toward the door. Dominick shook his head, nodding to the conversation his family was having with great interest. Finding Briar looking on with a bored expression, Colin jerked his head again, inching toward the door. As Jamus and Dean discussed Vatan's future, Briar followed after.

"I think Dean and Arkello are both telling the truth," said Briar once in the hall. "Because then you could have everything, Col."

"I have what I need." Colin pulled the bottle of dune ale from his cloak.

"You thief." Briar laughed, snatching it. He sipped, face souring as if he'd been punched in the gut. "Shit, this stuff is awful."

Colin laughed, taking it back. "It's worth the effects after a hard day." Arm around his cousin, they swaggered into the great tower and collapsed on a bench at the bottom of the spiraling staircase. Closing his eyes, Colin raised the ale to take another fiery gulp.

"Colin Densen, that better not be what I think it is."

Already defeated, and feeling the delayed effects blooming from the shot he'd taken in the study, Colin sheepishly peered up and raised the bottle above his head for his father to take.

King Liam descended, his long blue cloak following behind like a waterfall. Sunken eyes, droopy shoulders, and hair pulled slightly from his ponytail, his father looked like he'd crossed swords and fought for a kingdom. Without lashing out, hitting, or even looking at either Colin or Briar, he took the bottle and sipped. Despite the harshness Colin knew of the ale, his father's stoic face remained unfazed.

Colin swallowed nervously. "What did the Queen of Ammos say?"

"Nothing good." He handed the bottle back.

Dread mixed with the alcohol burbling in the pit of Colin's stomach. "Will there be war?" he asked.

His father stared at him, eyes unusually soft. "Margaret went against our verbal agreements for you and Princess Mayli to wed. She's initiated a war, yes, but that is a battle we have already lost and cannot even begin to fight for. I am sorry, Son."

Hope escaped with Colin's next breath. His head spun as if his world was crumbling around him, and not just due to his intoxication. He felt as if the tower had fallen, destroying any further chance he had to live.

"What do you mean?" Briar shook his head. "I thought we had more troops than Ammos?"

"Ammos, sure, and I know how to get past their silks, but not when they bring in their allies. We cannot fight the steel and arms of Hiore." Liam walked to the stair's base, heels clicking once on the tile before muting on the blue rug before them.

"What about Dregs?" asked Briar. "Uncle Olivar could help?"

Liam laughed, sad and lonesomely. "No. No, he won't. I am afraid we have no say in this matter, boys. Which is why the queen was kind enough to bring the news personally. She's a bird perching on a blade's point—nothing can hurt her."

Colin's hands turned to fists. His teeth grit together. Jaw feeling as though it were to crack, he threw his mouth open and yelled, "How can she walk into our home like this? Destroy everything we have worked to achieve? How is it that, despite everything, we still aren't enough in their eyes? True heirs of King Edune or not, we have proven ourselves just as worthy as all those other self-proposed royals!"

His father placed his free hand on Colin's shoulder, squeezing the royal crest tattooed upon it. "Because it takes more than one generation to build a kingdom." He patted him and walked off toward the study.

Colin's heart rate continued to elevate, his rage battling the calming remedy the dune ale offered. He tilted his head back. His head spun as his eyes followed the stairs coiling around the old grain silo encased in the tower. Finally, they found a landing where the dome capped it. He glared as another flight past that, Queen Margaret was surrounded by comfort in her suite, pleased at Brimley's impending ruin. Off-balance, he swayed. "Mayli's not a bitch—Margaret is."

Briar wrapped his arm around Colin. "Come on, Col. Let's get ya to bed. I'm not carrying your heavy ass up six flights."

He stumbled, allowing Briar to lead him up the steps like a horse to its stable. The door leading to the guests' floor swung open, and a young servant emerged in a flurry. He bumped into Colin, breaking him from Briar's weak embrace.

"Oie, ya nearly threw us down!" Briar growled, looking back over the rail. "What's the rush?"

"I'm sorry!" The servant bowed, placing his hand on the left shoulder. Orange silk swooshed forward, displaying a falcon with three stars embroidered on his cape.

Colin squinted at the bright outfit. "You're a servant to the Ammosian queen..."

"That's right! And I've been sent to find Prince Colin!" The servant pointed between them. "Do you know where I could find him?"

"Ya just have..." Colin snarled, taking an unintended sip of dune ale. He pointed with his grip around the bottle's neck. "And if ya have a message from *Margaret* my reply is...fuck 'er."

"Uhm." The servant bobbed on his toes. "I was told to say that after talks with King Liam, Queen Margaret wishes to discuss the prince's future with her daughter in the privacy of her room."

"My future? With May?" Colin swayed. His loose sense of self was fading beyond reach, dune ale threatening to take its full effect. Memories collapsing. He furrowed his brow at Briar for assurance. "Bri, I'm drunk..."

Briar caught him and pointed up the stairs beyond the servant. "Sure, but ya always speak truthfully when intoxicated. Here's your chance to show 'er how ya feel!"

Alden's conté crayon snapped.

Pulled back to the present, Alden frowned at the broken tip and line it created. Crumbled pigment littered the page. With a sigh, he blew. The air clouded, dusting the room with blood-red powder as it revealed his drawing.

Long wisps of hair curled around a pointed face and falling hands. A silken scarf hung loosely. Feathers danced all around. Smokey eyes were wide and curious about her melancholic world being torn asunder. A grim line split her lips.

Alden used his blade to sharpen his crayon, but even with the finest edge, Alden couldn't recreate her smile.

"May, I'll make this right..."

CHAPTER TWO
HER LADY DAMGARD

"I feared I'd never see that smile again."

Mayli jerked from the open porthole and faced the door. Poised with shoulders back, chin raised, and dual scimitars strung at his sides stood her royal guard, Charli Damgard. Sleeves unstrung and removed, his dark skin and toned muscle displayed his noble Ammosian tattoo on his right shoulder. He covered it, bowed, then rose with a knowing grin through his freshly trimmed goatee.

How long has he been standing there?

Creaking, the ship pitched over a wave. Mayli gripped the oval hatch for balance as water splashed in through the window. She closed her eyes, willing her stomach to cease its dance with the ship. When she opened them, specks of rainbow shimmered across the captain's quarters like shooting stars. Her gaze followed the wondrous reflection until she spotted a vase centered on the table; the etched crystal sparkled in the sun's rays. In it, a unique tropical flower leaned—just so—for her to see the orange bloom. Beside it, dinner awaited, complete with a bowl of grapes.

A while then... She giggled.

"Or ever hear that sweet laugh," Charli said, exhaustion heavy in his voice. Although he had washed clean the grime from her rescue, a streak of blood still stained his ivory cape from battling Shadowen thieves in the Cad Islands.

Mayli rolled her eyes and walked to the table. "I've never known you to fear anything, Charli."

"There's plenty I fear," he said.

Mayli lifted the flower to breathe in its alluring fragrance. A sweet undertone kissed the air, contrasting with the sharp Ammosian cuisine below. Spices from home stained the dish yellow. Red flakes dusted the top. Steam warmed Mayli's face as she moved closer. "Like what?" she asked.

"Aside from losing you?" Charli pulled her chair out for her to sit. "Desert storms, cold tea, or...a rock in my boot."

"A rock?" Mayli sat.

"It could cause a misstep. In battle, that is certain death."

"Is that why you check your boots so often?"

Charli tapped his boot to her chair as if to rattle any stones loose from the tread. He grinned. "One can never be too sure." Taking the flower, he kissed the top of her head.

Mayli waved him off. "You fear a pebble but not my father's warning?"

Charli returned the flower to its vase, then traced his finger along the underside of a petal. "Is Bakhari here?" His eyes lifted slowly.

"No..."

"Then I have nothing to fear," he said, plucking a grape from her bowl.

"You are too brave."

Charli sunk into the chair across from her. "It doesn't take bravery to fight for you, Princess. I will always protect you. Your father knows that, which is why you're here, safe with me."

Safe.

The word seemed to still the ship's rocking like the sea after a storm. She was going home. Alive. Mayli reached across and touched his hand. He squeezed back as if to help her believe the truth. She smiled at him. "Thank you."

"You aren't wearing that dress I left out for you." Charli's voice took on a sultry tone. His fingers weaved between her own. "I thought you might thank me with that on?"

Turning, she eyed the frilly garment upon the bed. Loops and lace left little for the imagination. Brows raised, she pulled her hand free and tucked it into folded arms. "I'd hardly call that a dress."

"Same could be said about the rags you're wearing." He scrutinized her attire with a sneer. "Are the holes in the sleeves intentional?"

Mayli stretched forward, demonstrating how her thumb in the hole kept her sleeve from climbing up her arm. "Keeps it on." She brought her glass of water to her lips.

He smiled. "I'd rather see it off."

Mayli choked on her sip. *He's acting as if nothing has changed...* She wiped her mouth then put the glass down. "Father said we can no longer be together."

"As we both acknowledged, your father isn't here..." Charli took her hand once more and leaned in. "We could—"

Mayli pulled away from his nearing kiss. "No!"

His eyes fluttered open. "No?"

"I mean. I'm just...hungry, and tired, and a bit over-whelmed." She lifted the kabob and ate directly from it.

Charli narrowed his eyes. "What happened to you out there?" he asked, offering her the fork.

Fingers greasy, Mayli set the kabob down and accepted the proper utensil. Stabbing a piece off the metal skewer, she pulled it off and bit down. She chewed slowly, ensuring she kept her mouth shut before she overshared or showed any more questionable manners.

The urge to tell Charli everything as she usually would caused her heart to ache. To recount her abduction and how one of the thieves went rogue to save her. Her adventures traveling to the mill, the cabin, and then—of all places—Brimley Castle. How she hunted, cooked, and cared for not only herself but a stranger—a perceived enemy. She could go on about how Prince Briar found them and secured safe travels... Until the draclynn diverted them to the Cad Islands.

She was sure Charli would likely find her tale of fighting amongst pirates to be one of great interest and worry. But mostly, Mayli wished to talk about Alden, her hero—her rogue. And how vigilant he'd been to save her. How he'd pleaded for his uncrowned king's innocence, trying to make her understand Colin still loved her. But even if Alden hadn't asked to stay anonymous, she knew discussing charming men in conversation with another wasn't advised. Mayli swallowed and shrugged. "I was captured by Shadowen thieves. They took me to the Cads. I escaped and found you."

"But—"

Mayli forced more food into her mouth and spoke with it full. "It is as simple as that, Charli."

Silence fell between them.

The ship crested on a wave, and Charli's dark complexion gleamed in the setting sun. Radiant pale eyes, the color of new glass, offered transparency as if waiting for her to tell the tale in its entirety.

Trapped in his gaze, Mayli wavered. "I—"

Charli rested his chin on his fist and eased in. "Go on."

Mayli shook her head free from the enchantment. "I am really okay."

"Princess..." He inched forward, the earnestness in his eyes pleading for her trust. "You know confiding in me has always helped."

"Maybe so, but I just need time to process things on my own right now."

"On your own?" Concern hung in his voice. "Do you think that is wise?"

She dipped her head, hair shielding her face as she debated her ability. Last she was alone with her feelings, she'd fallen deep into a fog. Surrounded by smoke and shadows, she'd clung to Charli's hand to guide her out. But in the past two weeks, his steadiness was gone, leaving her to find a path of her own, leading her places she had never considered. "Just...for now."

"As you wish." The table bumped as Charli dismissed himself, spilling rice from her plate. Giving her space, he positioned himself by the window with arms folded behind his back. A guard once more.

Lungs tight from the strain between them, Mayli chewed her lip. Unwilling to resume the discussion, she breathed out the tension and returned to eating her dinner. Rich and flavorful, the homey spices were a relief from the squirrels, rabbits, and goose she had cooked in Brimley. She was almost home—she could taste it.

Charli made a curious noise, his head moving as if something had caught his attention.

Mayli rolled her eyes, not falling for his game to start talking. Instead, she sipped more water.

A gasp came. Then an excited "Ooh" as Charli poked his head out the window.

Huffing, Mayli turned. "What is so interesting out there?"

Pulling his face out from the porthole, he frowned. "Oh, just rough waters... Seaweed. A flying fish."

She blinked at the idea of such an absurd creature.

Charli chuckled. "Dolphins."

Fork clanging to her plate, Mayli hurried to his side, worried the draclynn had returned. They bumped hips as she stuck her head out of the ship. Water swelled alongside the barnacle-infested wood. Fleeting currents swirled. A long strand of kelp floated aimlessly by. Something did splash in the water—a seagull. Just as she stepped away, two gray dolphins burst into the air. "Oh! You are right!" She shot up on her toes as they disappeared under the ship.

"You think I'd lie to you?"

"No..." She grinned as more arrived. "I am just glad it is not another draclynn!"

"Another?" He cocked his head.

Mayli hunched. *He pulled at my tight lips after all.* She bit them. "I just...heard the rumors."

"You're telling me! It's all the people on that drunken island would talk about. Captain Scraggs this. Draclynn that. It was as if I was battling the beast itself trying to fight for information on you." His thick brow furrowed. "Do you think Scraggs is a captain or a bosun?"

"He wears a fancy hat, so he's definitely a captain."

"Interesting perspective." Charli scratched his head in thought. "I'm sure he was the bosun, then became captain. Maybe after slaying the beast?"

"You might be right." She snickered.

Another dolphin jumped. It splashed and twirled, spiraling with others swimming just below the surface. Mayli raised her hand, shielding the sun to better watch their playful dance.

So free...

"What's this?" Charli took her wrist. He unhooked the thumbholes and rolled back her sleeve. Shades of yellow and green bruised her skin, markings left behind from the bonds thrust upon her by Alden.

"Nothing to be concerned about..." She pulled back.

Charli leaned in, his pale eyes widening. "I should have been at your side..." Cradling her small hands, his voice trailed off.

She shook her head. "I'm sorry. It was my fault you lost your position as my guard."

Thick arms wrapped around her, warm like the sun and as sturdy as the ground. "Don't worry. I will earn that honor back so you never need to endure such hardships again." He pulled her head in to rest on his wide chest.

The scent of sea and damp wood filled her nose. Still, Charli's characteristic metallic undertone of iron and sword oil lingered. She clutched deeper to find it and hold onto the beacon of familiarity after weeks of uncertainty.

I'm truly safe now... Mayli settled in.

Hypnotizing circles meandered along her back as Charli massaged. His touch eased tension, broke knots, and soothed her body. Mayli's heart quickened. He pulled her tighter—an embrace that promised he'd never let her go again. His chin dipped, brushing their lips together as he spoke against her mouth, "Oh, Princess. I missed this." He kissed.

Face burning, Mayli stilled. She trembled, conflicted.

Alden's lips were here just this morning.

Charli lapped across her. Tongue full and dominating, begging her to part for him. *But Charli did come all this way just for me. The least I could do is offer him this small reward.* She kissed back. *Besides, we left on a similar note...* As she opened her mouth, his kiss deepened.

Mayli faded into the moment—her body acting on impulse, desperate to find that shred of peace after the death of her mother and betrayal of her fiancé. Unable to relate to her heartbreak and gloom, her friends had faded one by one, until the only person left by her side was her guard, obligated to or not.

Charli had always made sure the archery range was

supplied, the bath house made private, beach outings shaded, and bouquets plentiful. To her surprise, he proved to be more than a guard. He was a man—a friend. One who was kind, sympathetic, and supportive. As their bond grew, conversations lasted long into the night. Eventually, she felt free to speak about her life. Unlike her friends, he listened.

Tongue working passionately with Charli's, Mayli relived their first kiss.

Angry tears clouding her eyes, she had fled the court—and her father. Despite her pleas for more time to grieve, he refused to call off the new suitors. Charli had followed as she sought refuge in the flower garden.

As they stopped, Charli pulled her into his shoulder to cry on as he often would allow. Instead, Mayli pushed their boundaries in a fit of angst. She pinned him to the wall, shaking ivy leaves and white flower petals around them. Her mouth went to his, sloppy and broken, begging for some kind of release other than tears.

Charli had needed no persuasion to indulge in her lustful demands. He pressed back, just as eager, fusing their lips. What melded was something she knew wouldn't hurt her. It wasn't love. It wasn't hate. But freedom, rebellion, and power. And with it, came safety from within the fog.

Their private moments continued. In the halls, courtyards, baths, guard towers. Her room. His. Anywhere they had privacy to become undone. Finding pleasure in her body supplied Mayli with momentary happiness, where nothing else mattered. Courtly life, politics, matchmaking, recent deaths, and even her desires became a faded memory when they coupled.

In recent months, her father had found them together in bed, no thanks to her brother, Jair, ratting them out. To their shame, Charli was stripped of his position as her personal guard. However, unable to deny his unrivaled skills in arm-to-arm combat, Charli was recommissioned to serve directly under the king where her father could keep a watchful eye on him. Powerless to convince anyone otherwise, Mayli was sent to visit Prince Gavin of Hiore to court him without distraction. To her relief, she never made it to the mountainous city, and instead met someone who didn't just protect her within the shrouds she lived in, but parted them.

Alle...

Pressure along Mayli's waist drew her attention to where Charli's hands had drifted. One on her thigh, lifting her dress. Another fondling her breast. Her breath tempered. His kiss intensified. He cupped between her legs, fingers teasing. Instead of finding her usual sense of arousal, Mayli's abdomen twisted in knots. The strange discomfort pulled her from his kiss with a gasp. "Charli—"

"Princess..." Muscles taut and heavy, he pinned her against the wooden wall with the ship's roll. Teeth tugged at the linen around her neck, tearing the hem. "This ugly thing needs to go."

Once more, her body objected. Hands became fists. Lips pinched together. She winced. "No..." She blinked, surprised at her quite objection—her reactions to his usual well-received affection. *No?*

"I'll work around it then..." His kisses slipped to her collarbone.

The sickening swell tightened inside her, and Mayli clasped a hand over her mouth. *Is this how Alden felt when I came on to him? His pained looks. His plea to be anywhere but near me?* Needing space, Mayli pushed against Charli. "Stop!"

He eased off with a suck of air and rested his arm above her, still trapping her to the ship. His eyes danced back and forth playfully, then furrowed as he thumbed her cheek. "You're crying."

Mayli shook her head. "I...can't do this."

"Can't? Princess, we are finally together after *a month*. Those looks you kept giving me around the palace even around your father..." He nosed closer and caressed her ear with his mouth. "I know you missed me too."

"I have..." Mayli hunched her shoulders, shielding herself from more kisses.

"Then what's the real problem?"

Wiping her face, Mayli shook her head. "I told you. I am tired, Charli. Overwhelmed and hurt. I...I want to be alone tonight."

"Alone?" Charli scoffed. "Are you really telling me to leave?"

Shame blushed her face. "I-I'm sorry."

The air in the room changed. Heavy. Foreboding. It pressed on her lungs and against her throat, suffocating, demanding her to change her mind. She couldn't.

His hand slid down the wall clapping on his thigh. He clicked his tongue. "Fine." He sighed, hanging his head.

Mayli clutched her hands to her chest, feeling her heart working to relax, but it only hurt more than ever.

Charli eyed her up and down, observing every tell. His lips twitched to smile but fell. He rubbed her shoulder, then stepped away. "When you need me, you know where I'll be."

Mayli turned to the open window as he walked away, the cool ocean breeze soothing her. She stood firm until the latch clicked shut. Once alone, she blinked away a sea of tears, gazing beyond the endless blue.

Her heart ached. Not from the confusing moment with Charli, not from the challenging time in enemy lands, sailing, or even from mourning her mother, but from demanding more from Alden. A man whose sole purpose was keeping her safe, all without asking or needing anything but her understanding in return.

How foolish of me. I'm Alden's enemy as much as Colin is mine. She put her hands to her face. *Alden must hate me...*

The memory of Alden's mouth opening for her and indulging in their last kiss pressed into her forethought. It was wholesome. Wishful and honest. *That wasn't resentful.* Their first kiss burst into her mind too—initiated by him amid the draclynn's attack... It held promise and sorrow as he held desperately on before letting go to save her life. *It was desire.*

She pictured them cuddled together in bed at Thielen's Lodge. Legs intertwined. Hands bound. Despite Alden's polite efforts to not get emotionally involved, Mayli realized he truly wanted her as much as she did him, and not just out of angst. It hadn't been that he was repulsed by her as she'd just felt with Charli, but rather his honor to her and Prince Colin.

When Alden had broken free from their farewell kiss, leaving her alone on the street in the Cad Islands, he'd stolen something. Something she thought she'd kept locked so tight, no one could ever steal and hurt her again: her love.

That thief... She smiled.

CHAPTER THREE

NEW QUARTERS

"You're stealing from my room!" a woman shouted through the atrium, her tone piercing Kira's ears.

Leaning over the railing, Kira glanced to the floor below. Held in the arms of two Yellow-Coat guards was a woman with red hair, braided in fine ribbons. Her dress was a glamorous creation of silk and lace and her attitude was just as entitled. Baroness, Evelyn Alwell.

"You can't do this!" she exclaimed, watching two servants carry an overstuffed trunk from her chamber. It swayed in their arms as they began down the stairway, following a parade of other movers. "This has been my home for years!"

"This is now *my* home, *my* castle, Evelyn," said King Briar, stepping into view with his royal guard. "*I* determine who resides in it. And that excludes you."

Two more servants left the room. One held a half-full crate while the other left empty-handed having removed the last of Evelyn's possessions.

"I've done nothing to deserve this!" she cried.

"You haven't? Are you sure?" Briar drew in a hissing breath through a smug grin. "Because according to this guard here, you caused quite the stir last night with Lady Kira in an attempt to make me a fool."

"Me?" Evelyn said, mocking an aghast tone. Evelyn raised her chin, showing off a beautiful welt on her cheek she'd tried to cover with makeup. "Kira is the one you need to look out for! She attacked *me!* Look at these bruises!"

"A well-deserved mark," said the taller one of the guards. From under the helm, Kira could see a growing smirk within a new beard. *Alden.* He kept a tight hold on the baroness. "Evelyn and her friends lured Kira out. Once secluded, they pounced, making a ruin of her dress. I saw it all. Watched with great admiration when Kira kicked her ass."

Evelyn threw her head up to look at Alden, eyes quivering in horror. "You!"

Briar chuckled. Lifting a ledger, he began fingering down the page. "If attacking Lady Kira last night wasn't reason enough for my decision, it says here that you haven't paid for room and board in...mmm, two years?" He tapped a line then returned her stare, one eyebrow climbing high.

"It was paid." She tried to take a step forward but was held by the guards. "I can pay!"

Briar pinched his lips together and shook his head. "Yeah, unfortunately sleeping with the king is not going to be an appropriate type of payment anymore, Ev."

Kira blinked at the revelation. *So it wasn't just Olivar's captured women he coaxed.*

Evelyn cheeks turned red. "But—"

Briar held up his hand. "I'm not as desperate as my uncle was, and I know your tussles in bed aren't worth the coin."

Giggling erupted around the atrium. Kira glanced around, spying nobles on each floor who had stopped to watch the drama. Evelyn looked up too. Meeting Kira's gaze, she narrowed her eyes to glare. Growling, she whipped her head back to Briar who had chuckled along with the crowd. "You know nothing!"

"I know more than you seem to give me credit for. Including exactly what you're capable of." Briar stepped forward, his playful demeanor hardening as he pointed at her. "I'm not the same naive prince you tried to fool into marriage or get me knocked off my horse. I'm your king. And I won't tolerate any games. Especially ones relating to Lady Kira. Is that clear?"

Evelyn's mouth hung open, her spirit falling as well. "Where will I go? I don't own an estate." Evelyn asked breathlessly.

Briar shrugged. "I don't care. Find another man to manipulate into showering you with gifts you don't deserve. But I expect to see you in court when sessions are in. You owe a debt and work is to be done."

Her head dipped, submissive. "Of course, Your Majesty."

Briar addressed the shorter guard holding Evelyn's other arm and gestured to the stairs. "Earl, I can trust you to escort the Baroness of Dregs from the castle, right?"

Squirrel, as Kira now recognized with his freckles and lanky arms, clicked his heels together and dipped his chin, his oversized helm slipping over his brow. "Yep!"

Alden released Evelyn's arm, leaving her other arm in Squirrel's grasp. She kept still, staring at Briar with defeated eyes. Then, to Kira's surprise, she dropped into a bow, her hand covering the Dreggen crest upon her shoulder. Rising, she turned enough to hide the tear falling down her face from Briar's view. Yanking herself free from Squirrel, she rushed down the stairs on her own, joining the line of servants taking her possessions out of the castle.

"How embarrassing," whispered a noblewoman to Kira's side.

"She doesn't own an estate?" Another laughed inside their huddle.

More gossip grew. "She slept with King Olivar? Gross."

Closing her eyes, Kira pushed from the railing and took a deep breath. Looking up she saw the nobles had silenced their chatter to eye her. Keeping her chin even, Kira walked toward the stairs. As she passed the nobles, a few untied bows on their dress to let them hang free to mimic the look of Kira's dress after her fight with Evelyn. Just when Kira thought they were mocking her, the women smiled and bowed.

Flustered by their pledge, Kira hurried down the stairs and nearly bumped into Alden and Briar as they came around the corner. She ducked into their quiet conversation, looking between their smug grins. "As satisfying as that may have been for you two, you didn't need to shame and displace her so publicly."

"Sure I did. Everyone needs to know what the consequences are for disrespecting you," Briar said, taking a step back to enter the ransacked room. He put his hands on his hips and looked around, nodding with a grin. "Besides, Alden needs new quarters to lie low."

"I wasn't planning on staying," said Alden.

"That's before you found out I had become king." Briar walked to a built-in desk in the corner and wiped at a smudge of loose powdered makeup left from Evelyn's beauty products. He dusted his hands and leaned against it. "Look, this room is perfect. It's got a desk and south-facing light, capturing the view of the ships just like you prefer."

"I don't think it's wise for me to be around so many nobles for very long. I could be spotted," Alden grumbled.

"Oh please. That beard and Yellow-Coat is more of a disguise than your body transformation."

Alden touched his flat belly.

Kira eyed him. When she first saw Alden, he had been a thicker man. His face was fuller and clean-shaven. His arms were wide and without form. His gut bulged. While Alden had been larger than most when she met him, he still hadn't held to the rumors of the heavyweight, long-haired, drunken young adult Vatan remembered Prince Colin by. She never questioned his identity until a year after they met. Alden had reshaped his past life into the man he was today by taking daily runs, refusing alcoholic drinks, and skipping meals. Although his old bad habits had changed along with his appearance, some of his new ones seemed just as damaging.

Alden let his hand slip to the newly mended dagger at his side which had replaced the King's Blade after giving it to Mayli. "Still, I need to solve Queen Margaret's murder. And with Princess Mayli's kidnapping, there's a good chance that whoever is involved could be the culprit. So, I should be out in the city to look for signs of the Shadowen Thieves Guild, confront Pierz, and get answers. Not locked away again in some stone room." He gestured to the door.

"Yes, but...if Pierz captures you..." Briar looked between them. "Either of you."

"I'll just tell my *guild leader* I've been spying on you." Kira poked Briar's chest.

Briar winced. "Yeah, that makes me uncomfortable."

Kira rolled her head. "Come on. Learning secrets is what we are best at! Like about your late-night rendezvous with William."

He shifted his eyes to Alden then back at her. "You know about that?"

"You keep coming back to bed smelling like horse." Kira waved her hand. "A bit hard not to notice."

Briar laughed, shaking his head. "Right, apologies."

"I'm only teasing. I know the rides clear your head and you

come back with the right solutions. William is one smart horse."

"I'm not afraid of Pierz," Alden said. "I'm afraid of not doing everything I can to solve this. Because I'm afraid of being guilty myself. But mostly, I am afraid that Mayli could still be in danger."

"Alden." Briar sighed. "You said she is safe with Charli, meaning we'll hear news of her arrival home any day now."

"Yeah, but her enemy could still be out there!" Alden gestured vaguely.

"Which is why I've allowed investigators and inspectors from every kingdom to be on the prowl. And, with them about, it would be good if you stayed out of sight. Here. Where no one can get you."

With a groan, Alden toured his new room. He paused at the window, observing its view. Kira followed his gaze and saw the docks, busy despite no new trade ships arriving. A crowd bustled around a departing vessel. It was painted black and red aside from patches of new wood: *The Lucky Fish,* as she had learned from the rumors and Alden's tale of his journey.

A waft of Evelyn's peach perfume hit Kira's nose as Alden sat on the plush mattress nestled in a wooden frame. It was larger and looked much more inviting than the cot he'd had in the tea shop. She was glad to see he'd no longer have to shiver in hole-ridden blankets, especially with the stone fireplace on the far wall. He would be protected by guards and friends, just like a proper king.

Despite the luxuries he deserved, Alden frowned.

Kira sat, joining him at the hip. "Your cousin is right, Alden. So you can relax a little." She bumped against him playfully.

He swayed with her for a moment before bumping back with a challenging smile. "I will admit, it is nice here."

"Just wait until breakfast comes. The assortment for just

one sitting is more than we would see in a week. And the doughnuts...!" Kira licked her lips, imagining the soft fried treat. "I think I could live off those alone."

Alden sighed, leaning back on his arms. "I won't have the appetite if I'm not working on something."

"Do you ever have an appetite?" Kira teased as she leaned in closer to Alden.

Allowing her to lean against him but ignoring her comment, Alden looked at his cousin. "Maybe I can page through some documents from your uncle, Bri?"

Briar's face contorted, lip hitched, and a brow raised. "Unless you consider Olivar's finances engrossing, you won't find anything useful."

"I'm sure anything related to the late king of Dregs is gross." Kira shuddered at the memory of the disgusting man eyeing her up as if she were a piece of meat while she was locked in the tower with a flock of other women. "I can't believe Evelyn willingly slept with him."

"I'm not surprised by anything she does anymore," Briar said, walking toward them. "But my uncle wasn't involved with the queen or Mayli. Dregs stayed neutral during the war. He couldn't care less about Ammos."

Kira peered up as Briar stood over her and Alden. "Neutral doesn't mean they weren't an enemy. It's no secret Olivar hated your family."

"True." He offered his hand to her.

"Why is that by the way? And how? You're so..." Kira accepted his hand and stood. Taking a step back she gestured at Briar. "You."

Briar self-consciously examined himself and tossed his hair. "Isn't it obvious?"

"No," she giggled.

Alden sighed from his position on the bed. "That's cause Olivar was upset about the death of his sister, Trish."

Kira lost her wry smile. Looking at Alden for a moment then back to Briar. "Your mum?"

Briar rubbed his nose, folding his arms across his chest as he looked away. "Like a blood-wet babe could be such a monster."

Kira furrowed her brow. "You lost your mother as you were born?"

"Yeah. And Olivar never forgave me for it. But really, I think her death was just his excuse to finally exile my father."

"Prince Jamus? Why?"

Briar walked to the window and rapped his fingers on the sill. "Their feud had started well before my parents married. He didn't believe in marrying for love like the days of Vatan—just duty. So when my mum ran off to marry Jamus, that broke the treaty Olivar had been trying to form with Prince Gavin of Hiore. So, after my mother died, we were no longer welcomed." He pulled himself from the view and leaned against the desk.

"Where did you go?" asked Kira.

"Brimley. With us," said Alden, rolling forward to rest his elbows on his knees.

"Aye," agreed Briar. "Alden's mum, Queen Lily, and his grandmother, Mary, worked to raise him, his brother Dominick, and me while his grandfather, Dean, and my father, Prince Jamus, helped raise the kingdom of Brimley with King Liam."

Kira watched Alden stand and join Briar, gently patting his cousin's shoulder before leaning against the desk too. Over the last two years, Kira had watched and admired their close bond from afar. Spying through portholes of Briar's ship, *The Albatross*. Briar had always taken care of Alden. He provided him with extra coins to get by, clothes, and always tried to make him eat a hearty meal. Once he even offered Alden women, but Kira hadn't stuck around to find out if he accepted. Briar kept his cool when Alden would be in a mood and worked to calm him with reason. Kira adopted similar tactics. Their bond had confirmed Kira's intuition that Briar was a good, trustworthy man, allowing her the confidence to find and trust in him when she realized he hadn't been in on King Olivar's schemes. "No wonder you two are so close."

"We may be cousins, but Bri is more like a little brother to me." Alden elbowed him with a genuine smile.

"Watch it, I'm a crested king now so you're more like my little brother." Briar pushed back, teasingly.

Alden's playful smile subsided. "I'm still the king of Brimley. And I'll sit on the throne of Vatan as soon as I solve all of this."

"Of course, you will," Briar said cheerily but Kira noticed a hint of skepticism.

As if sensing it too, Alden pushed from the desk, walking aimlessly.

Briar lifted his palms. "Would it help if I send carriers to fetch your things from Colville?"

Alden pivoted his next step with bright eyes. "Really? Think they could bring Rek too?"

"I'll make sure your cat comes along." Briar looked at Kira. "And I'll have them grab your things as well."

"I didn't have a lot. Everything I've needed I'd just take and use in the moment..." Kira said, spotting a ring lost on the bed. She slipped it on, admiring the golden twist. "But there are some clothes I'd like, might as well get everything."

"It's decided then." Briar clapped his hands together and rubbed them as he stood. "By next week, you'll both be all moved in. Until then, please try to relax, Alden?"

Kira laughed, watching Alden as he started wiping the desk clean from Evelyn's makeup. "I'm not sure he knows how," she said.

CHAPTER FOUR
ARKELLO'S WOES

Summoning the courage to take on the day despite her lack of sleep while sailing, Mayli threw on the black cotton dress Alden had bought for her in the Cads. While it wasn't Ammosian Silk, it was soft, warm, and fit perfectly along her body. She secured a belt at her waist then looked at Alden's blade. Its hilt was wrapped in worn and fraying leather as though it had been made as a repair. Carefully, Mayli pulled it from the wood sheath. Hints of lavender reflected within the blade's sheen. It was sharp—deadly—but that's not how she viewed it. It was a beautiful parting gift so that he may continue to keep her safe. But she was safe. Guarded. On her way home. Knowing Charli would take offense if she held it, she gave it a quick hug to her chest before placing it in her bag of belongings she had collected during her travels.

The Brimleyn cloak lay on her bed. Its dusty blue color no longer threatened her and instead now offered security knowing there were some from the fallen kingdom who cared for her. Mayli pulled the linen around her and buckled the clasp under her chin. She tossed her hair out from under but shuddered as it felt slick with grease and dirt. She was sure it looked just as bad. Snarling, she reached to search for her scarf. Mayli froze—it was gone. Left swirling in the winds, high over the Cad Islands. Withdrawing her hand, Mayli brought her hood up instead.

Ready for the day, Mayli pushed the door to the captain's quarters open and walked through a small kitchen with a few platforms for beds. She crawled up the ladder to the deck above. The sunny, salt-laced air invited her to take a step toward the railing, but as a burly man in a deep hood hurried by, Mayli flattened herself against a crate. Over the man's shoulder hung a waterlogged net stuffed with fish. It swayed with his footsteps, the fish slapping against each other in protest. A water droplet fell on her nose. The briny stink snuffed the sweet sea air, and Mayli raised her arm in an attempt to stifle it with her sleeve. She ducked around the deckhouse for a fresh breath. There, another crewman came her way, jerking his head for her to move as he dragged a large, empty cage behind him. She retreated, only to bump into a hard body.

"Careful there, Mayli," came a muffled, rough, yet youthful voice.

Sweeping hair from her face and stumbling back, Mayli smiled. "Sorry, I—"

Layers of black stood before her like night had fallen over the brisk morning. A long flowing cape rose from the floorboards to a deep hood, hiding the man's identity with a silk ebony scarf. A matching gloved hand tugged the covering free. Stepping forward, the features of his face caught in the light revealing a square, clean-shaven, white-dappled chin. His sun-damaged complexion masked the features of an attractive man. The unique coloration spread up his face until it fell into the shadow of his hood. Although unseen past a pair of blue-tinted goggles, Mayli knew dark eyes lurked beneath. "Arkello Densen! *You're* here?"

He pulled the eyewear into a brush of chestnut hair, leaving a smudge of black paint clouding around his eyes. Thick lashes lowered. "Charli didn't mention me after whisking you away?" His cheeks caved into his jaw as he smiled. The act would have reminded her of Briar if the tingling sense of danger hadn't been roused within her.

"No, but then again I didn't invite much conversation."

"You two not talking?" Arkello held his hood as the wind picked up. "That's...different."

A glimmer under Arkello's cloak flashed, drawing Mayli's attention to an array of blades.

I should have kept Alden's blade on me after all...

Mayli scanned the ship for her guard. There were plenty of crewmen, several dressed in dark layers like Arkello's—members of his original crew from Gezmek—but Charli was nowhere to be seen. Her gaze fell back on Arkello, standing smugly. "What's different is you being on board Charli's ship!"

Arkello swiftly leaned in, his wild eyes capturing hers. He smiled with poorly aligned teeth. "This is my ship, milady."

Mayli's jaw dropped. "Yours?"

"Yes. Mine." Righting his back, Arkello walked past her, trailing his hand along the sun-worn wood.

Mayli grimaced as brittle pieces flaked away. "Why is your ship so ugly if you're supposed to be royalty?"

"Ugly?" Arkello's face soured, matching the vessel's aesthetic. Glancing down, he peeled a fleck of black paint from the chipped railing. He smiled as it caught in the breeze, swirling and climbing up the patched sails. "I used everything I had to buy *The Rotting Barge*. He's beautiful."

Heavy steps approached from around the deckhouse. "She's called *Her Lady Damgard*."

The mass of muscle and blades that was Charli returned much-needed air to Mayli's lungs. He was bare-chested aside from his gold-encased pendant necklace. A sash wrapped around his waist to secure his scimitars. Mayli's heart found its rhythmic pace with his steps as he shot her a smile.

"Oh, please..." Arkello held his ground despite Charli's large presence demanding clearance. He looked him up and down in disgust. "Just because you commandeered my ship, doesn't mean you get to flaunt so much skin while on board. Put a shirt on."

Charli scoffed. "Don't tell me what to do."

Mayli stared as Charli squeezed by to take position at her side. "You commandeered the prince of Gezmek's ship?"

Arkello set his hands on his hips. "Excuse me, *noble*, I'm the prince of Vatan."

"Need I remind you that times have changed while you've been living underground with your lost kingdom of Gezmek? I am royal just as much as you are now." Mayli lifted her chin. "Or have you forgotten?"

"I haven't forgotten, I just choose to not recognize the new *kingdoms* and their so-called royals." He waved his hand, dismissing her to look over the waters.

Charli chuckled, addressing Mayli. "I loaned him the rest of what he needed to buy it so we could search for you. And I only suggested renaming the ship to something you would be familiar with, Your Highness." He bowed.

She smiled at his respect. "Well, it was a wise choice. I knew it was yours right away."

"Mine!" Arkello snapped, pointing to himself.

Charli looked over the edge. "She's got my name on it."

Arkello grumbled. "Not for long! Once I pay you back, he will be named *Arkello's*..." His voice trailed off, and he tapped his sun-bleached chin in thought.

"*Woes*," supplied Charli with a sardonic grin.

"*Arkello's Woes?*" Gazing at the shore, Arkello's face grew sour, lips pressed into a tight line.

Despite Charli's continued laughter, Mayli frowned, unable to find humor at Arkello's apparent affairs. *What if it was true? That somewhere hidden among layers of golden dunes was his home. Gezmek. And his family—the true heirs of Vatan... If alive, could they confirm the Densens' story.*

As he claimed, Arkello's life had been one of suffering. Born underground, he had been trapped in the stone-carved palace of Gezmek where food was scarce, dangers of kanavaurs present, and his people malnourished from lack of sun and resources. In recent years, the sands had shifted, presenting an opening. Sensing freedom, the newly crested prince and his people had climbed out. On the surface, they worked diligently to rebuild while the underground continued to be a safe palace for them to reside. As animals were herded and desert crops farmed, their health improved and numbers increased. However, after only one year, a raid from nomads caused another collapse, blocking their passageway to the surface.

Sealed off, Arkello was determined to lead a party into the desert for help. Constant exposure from the sun's harsh rays had permanently scarred his and his crew's skin, leaving it to heal in white patches. Thankfully Charli and his mother, Madam Nive, had been exploring the desert as part of their training and found the lost prince near the point of collapse. Arkello was brought back to Ammos where he learned that the city-states his family once ruled were no longer theirs to command. Ever since, Arkello as Prince of Gezmek had made it his mission to return home and reclaim Vatan. He'd even sold the King's Blade, a precious family heirloom, to her mother so he could afford an expedition to find and free his people. Each attempt proved futile.

"*Arkello's Woes...*" Mayli repeated with a somber nod.

"It does have a ring to it." Arkello peered from beneath his hood. His eyes held notes of sadness—a familiar gaze she'd seen before in Alden. He straightened and grinned lazily. "Doubt I'll have many more of those after this, though."

Mayli tilted her head. "Why's that?"

"Well, when I was in the Cads, I met a nomad who had information about Gezmek's whereabouts. And once we get to Ammos I'll be able to settle my debts and fund a proper expedition there." He gazed at the sand-barren shore, hope and determination warming his face.

"Is my reward what brought you out?" Mayli asked.

His brows bunched, looking back at her. "Excuse me?"

Mayli lifted her chin and spoke with authority. "How did you know I was in the Cads, Arkello?"

"Your brother mentioned it was the perfect place for illegal business, gathering information, or conducting hostage negotiations." Arkello shrugged. "Turns out, he was right."

Mayli put her hands on her hips, tightening her tone. "And what illegal business were *you* attending to?"

"None. Besides, I'm the prince of Vatan, nothing I do is illegal."

Arkello's cocky smile sent chills down Mayli's back.

Charli wiggled a nearby steel cage. "The undocumented transport of live merchandise from Ammos is definitely illegal."

Arkello laughed. "So arrest me, *Damgard*."

"Live merchandise?" Mayli paled as her attention was drawn to the coops, kennels, and cages stacked throughout the ship. She stepped from the crate half shrouded in cloth that she leaned against. *If Charli hadn't been on board, would one of these have been for me?* She shuddered. "You never export people, right?"

"People don't usually offer value to me. No. Just kittens, birds, bugs... Those kinds of live things."

"Kittens?" Charli threw back the cloth, exposing the empty cage. "They were full-grown desert cats!"

Arkello leaned against the cage, sticking a finger in as if to play with what was once inside. "I will miss them..."

"Not me." Charli rubbed his hand where a thin red line revealed an old wound. He showed Mayli. "Not as friendly as they might look."

"If you weren't such a brute, maybe they would trust you." Arkello pushed off the crate and held on to a fixed partition. "Brace yourself."

Before Mayli could comprehend the meaning of his statement, the ship pitched. Air whooshed through the corridors as the bow splashed into the sea. She stumbled. A sickening feeling swelled inside her stomach. *Not again!* Quickly, she pushed past the men to grip the side rail. Mash from breakfast flew from her as she wretched and coughed. As another wave hit, she expected Charli or even Arkello to rush to her side, help brace her, pat her back, or even just hold her hair as she retched again. Instead, they kept their distance as if privacy was needed. She frowned at their lack of concern. *Even my rogue had been more chivalrous.*

"You okay?" Charli called.

Mayli spat a sour clod. "Do we have any Brimleyn tea?"

Charli scoffed. "You are specifically asking for that foul water?"

Tainted spit stained her cloak as she dried her hair with it. "Yes, it helps keep me at ease..."

Charli approached. "I knew you hated it, so I didn't bother," he said.

"It's not so bad with cream and sug—" Mayli hunched over the rail as the ship bucked once more. With each slap to the sea, her stomach tightened. A dolphin broke the surface and twisted. So did her gut. Needing to look upon something solid,

Mayli gazed at the golden horizon. The steady line where the dunes met the sea worked to ease her queasiness. Soon, her stomach settled, and she was able to look farther out. When the ship reached its peak on the next wave, something sparkled in the distance. Raising on her toes to keep it in view, she gasped. "Charli?"

He broke his conversation with Arkello. "Yes, Princess."

"Do you have a spyglass?"

He shook his head.

Arkello pulled a long segmented device from deep within his black robes. "What do you see?"

Mayli put it to her eye. The lands flashed and glinted. There was a white spray, black, then ultramarine. The sky. A bird. Three lines. And then once more the sea. Feeling the sickness arise, she thrust the spyglass into Arkello's chest and folded over the edge in anticipation. Nothing came.

"Anything?" Arkello asked, eagerly.

Without looking up, Mayli pointed. "I saw...a light? Something metal? Or glass?"

Charli put his hand on her, his touch warm and stabilizing. His voice was just as soft. "Likely a mirage."

"No, it seemed man-made." She held her fingers up to mimic. "It had three shining pillars."

Arkello's white-scarred nose touched the brim of his hood. He stepped one foot to the shroud and wrapped his arm around the ropes. His head jerked as the object blinked. "Splitting sands..." He yanked the spyglass to its full length.

Hand shielding the sun, Charli squinted. "What is it you think you see now?"

Pointing energetically, he handed the spyglass to Charli. "See the yellow sheen between those two dunes? That is no mirage. That... That's a marker toward home. Just as the nomads described!" He beamed like a child.

"Home?" Mayli perked up. "Ammos?"

"No, Mayli Drake." A mischievous grin pulled at Arkello's lips. "Gezmek."

"Gezmek?" The word escaped her like a dream.

Charli put the scope to his eye. "Are you sure? We have gone over your maps, Gezmek is said to be more inland."

Arkello was already high above deck. Hollering and whooping, he threw his head back, hood falling away, revealing his short hair. He spun and pointed to his onlooking crew. "Hard-a-starboard!"

Bodies moved at his command. Ropes whistled as they loosened. The sail caught wind and the ship jerked to the right. Using the momentum, Arkello swung to the deck from a long rope. He rushed to a crate, flinging it open. Inside, bundles of glass orbs rattled. He pulled them out frantically. One rolled to the stern, nearly falling overboard through a break in the rail. A mesh in the crate's lid held long black and red flags. Arkello retrieved one and began fastening it to the buoy.

Charli strode over. "What are you doing?"

Arkello finished one, sat it down, and selected an anchor. "Land maps lie as the desert breathes."

"Excuse me?"

He threw a side glare at Charli. Shaking his head, he took out a sketchbook from inside his coat. He showed a well-rendered illustration of three pillars. "Remember? That nomad told us they put up monuments like that, marking the boundary of Gezmek. They will lead us home. We could—"

Charli slammed the lid shut and put his foot on the crate. "That nomad would tell you anything for your coins. We stick to the plan."

Arkello scurried to his feet, waving a flagpole in Charli's face. "It's proof right there his word was good. Come on, Damgard, you know opportunities like this are far too rare!

We've been searching and studying how to find Gezmek for years so we can each get what we want. And now that we have something tangible you want to back away? We can forgo the plan!" He whipped his arm out, forcing Mayli to hop back.

Charli snatched the flag. "I'm not risking it."

Arkello stepped forward. "There's no telling how long the marker will stay within view before the sands swallow them again. We must move now." He swiped Charli's foot off and opened the crate.

Charli used the flagpole to slap Arkello's fingers as he reached for another buoy. "Remind me how many times I saved you from becoming lost out there following such illusions so ill-prepared."

"Enough..."

"So do you really expect me to risk the princess's life because you saw a glimmer in the distance?" He narrowed his eyes.

Arkello opened his mouth to argue, but seeing Mayli—as if remembering she existed—he shut it.

Mayli folded her arms.

Arkello brushed his hand over his exposed head and down his marked face. He held it there for a moment, then let his hand fall to his shoulder. With grace, he bent into a deep and formal bow royalty rarely showed to another. Submissively, he spoke softly. "Mayli, as the Princess of Ammos you have the final say. But consider this; you've been lost for only a few weeks whereas I've been gone for years. Please, allow me just one full day to survey the shore and sky to chart the stars and mark the shore for our return. This may be my only chance to help reunite me with my family before it's too late."

The sincerity in his groveling voice tugged at Mayli's heart. *His humble bow contrasts the self-righteous personality he flares. He even addressed me as Princess. He's desperate.* She glanced at her guard for guidance. Charli held a stern yet unbiased expression, leaving the decision to her. Looking back at Prince Arkello, she touched his hand that covered the hidden crest of Vatan. "I will not stop you."

With surprising speed, Arkello popped from his bow and hugged her. "Thank you, Mayli Drake!" He flashed a toothy grin before dashing away, barking more commands at his crew and snapping gloved fingers.

Mayli blinked, the pressure easing from his tight and sudden embrace, realizing it had been the first time he'd ever touched her.

Charli stepped forward. "We don't need to go. I can ensure we sail straight home," he said, cracking his knuckles with his gaze on Arkello.

A litter of flags, poles, and buoys shifted at her feet as the ship turned toward land. Mayli grabbed a flag, stroking the fabric. "One more day won't affect me, but it could hurt innocent lives. I won't be the cause of that anymore," she said, fastening it to the buoy as Arkello had done, then grabbed the next.

CHAPTER FIVE

THE DESERT

A light whistle sang in the distance. Plumes of dust danced over dunes scalloping the desert. Dry air raked against Mayli's face, peppering it with sand. While waves lapped the shoreline, occasionally crashing down in violent bursts, the land remained stable, inviting Mayli to relax. However, her guard blocked the way.

Mayli shifted from side to side, looking for a way around his bulky frame. "Let me off this ship!"

Charli matched her steps, blocking the ladder leading to the rowboat. "No."

Mayli huffed, waving her hand. "Yes. Now."

"Princess, we should stay on board while they work. You've done more than enough to help Arkello by piecing together those markers. It's almost dark. We should retire inside."

"But I've never been to the real desert." She inched to the left. "Just let me—"

Taking her by the shoulders, Charli ushered Mayli back an arm's length, stilling any further movements. "That's because the Desert of Gezmek isn't safe."

She tapped his bare chest. "Well, isn't that why I have you?"

Charli pressed her hand to his skin where his pendent lay. Around it, she felt the quickened beat of his heart and the warmth of his dark tan skin. His head dipped to her eye level. "It is, but I do fear losing you again."

"You won't." She leaned in, batting her eyes. "We are together, this time."

"Cute," Charli said. "But flattery won't work."

"Logic then?" She held her vomit-covered hair. "I'm seasick. Don't think I'm spending another moment on the water when there's perfectly sound land an arrow's flight away."

"I would hardly call the shifting sands solid ground, Princess."

She flicked her hair over her shoulder, nearly whipping Charli with it. "I'd rather have sand in my hair than puke. Now, need I remind you that my father removed you from serving as my personal guard? Therefore, I order you to move aside." Mayli used her firm, royal tone while swishing her hand.

He remained as imposing as a stone barrier.

Mayli huffed, lowering her shoulders, and offered a defeated sigh. When he, too, relaxed—fooled by her obedience—Mayli scurried under his arm. She grabbed the ship's side and swung onto the rope ladder. The rush of rebellion sent her several steps down, grinning with delight.

"Don't slip or you'll fall," Charli warned from high above.

Mayli's stomach curdled. Slowly, she glanced at the water. The distance seemed to double as a wave sunk into a trough. She let out a tight whimper. *I'm much higher than I thought...*

The ropes shook, and Mayli held on tight. When it settled, she took a breath and continued, taking each step slowly. Eyes closed, she did her best to not think about the swirling water, the menacing breeze, or the great height. As she lowered further, her foot dangled in the air, finding nothing to touch.

Struggling to open her eyes, Mayli bravely peeked.

Prince Arkello coiled a rope in a small rowboat patched with mismatched boards. Deep blue water surrounded it. Arkello's amused eyes judged her. "Scared of heights?"

"Of course not." Her voice rattled with the ladder against the ship.

"Then jump."

She sucked in a breath and willed herself to move. Instead, she clung tighter.

"Hm." Arkello dropped the rope to offer his hand.

"I've got it...I..." Mayli yelped as her foot slipped. She fell against the ship, holding on dearly to the ladder as she hung.

"Do you like hanging there, or do you have a fear of heights?" teased Arkello. He rested his hands on his hips, letting her struggle. "Which is it?"

"Heights," she admitted.

"Okay." Arkello took her boot, allowing her to regain balance on the last step. Once she was steady, he offered his hand once more.

Unable to brave the leap herself, she accepted the prince's offer. He held tight, respectfully helping her down. The small boat rocked, and she collapsed into a bench. She scooted far from him, hugging her knees in.

He chuckled. "That's all right, Mayli. Fear keeps you alive, as long as you believe you can overcome it."

The ladder waved and smacked against the ship's hull as Charli descended. Arkello lifted a hand, offering him the same generosity. Ignoring it, Charli dropped in, making the rowboat rock precariously.

Mayli held fingers to her lips, willing everything inside to behave. She closed her eyes. *Just a little further. Almost on land...*

Charli's heavy arm wrapped around her as he sat. "You almost fell."

"I managed."

"Not without help. So how can I guard you, Princess, if you do not listen to me?"

"I know." She faced the shore. Light reflected from the golden sand, as peaceful as a painting Alden might render. "Don't worry. I'll just lie out and relax in the sun. Nothing dangerous about that."

Arkello paused rifling through supplies and turned his nose up. "You do that for pleasure?" Disdain carried in his voice.

She smiled awkwardly at his weathered face. "In...moderation?"

Arkello shook his head. "The sun is the most dangerous thing out there, so if you insist on torturing yourself, and revealing skin like Charli here, at least use this." He tossed a soft leather tube.

Mayli caught it in her lap. "What is it?"

"A shield against burning. Learned how to make it from the nomads."

Pulling the cork, a strong aroma of coconut caught in her nose. Smiling, she squeezed. White cream coiled into her palm. The silken texture glided smoothly as she applied it.

Charli thumbed at her cheek, wiping a glob free. "You may tan, Princess, but we must go back to the ship before the sun sets."

Mayli groaned. "I didn't sleep well last night."

"That's because I was not beside you." His words sent a tickle of nerves down her neck, and she flushed.

Seemingly unbothered by their closeness, Arkello took his lotion back. He applied generous amounts on himself, leaving white streaks. "We will be setting up tents. One can be erected for you two if you wish?"

"Yes!" Mayli clapped.

Arkello reached across, offering the tube to Charli.

"No." Charli pushed it back.

Mayli dropped her arms and glared. "Why not?"

"Because royalty should sleep in a proper room with a bed and door."

"I've slept in worse over the last few weeks, Charli." She glared at him. "Like ships."

"There are no nauseating waves this close to shore, so you can sleep soundly."

Mayli blew out a long exhale, accepting his logic with a nod. "Fine."

Arkello shrugged. "Makes no difference to me."

His crew pushed off from the ship, beginning their short voyage to the Desert of Gezmek.

Mayli dipped her hand through the passing blue surface. Despite the peaceful look, the sea bit back, cold and wintery. She shook free of the freezing water and held her fist tightly to her chest.

Charli took her hand, soothing the chill. "The seasons are shifting along with the water currents."

"How is it you always have an explanation for things?"

"I read." He let her hand go.

"Is that why you're always in that stuffy library?" She wrinkled her nose, imagining the musty smell.

"Yes, but that's mostly for your benefit. If you won't read them, I am happy to teach. You'll be queen one day, and a simple fact could be the difference between life and death."

"Like what?"

He nodded to the approaching shore. "Why do you think nomads wander Vatan instead of settling in Ammos or any other kingdom?"

Mayli squinted past the looming dunes, imagining a

caravan of nomads riding sand striders. "To find lost treasures?"

"In a sense." Charli rubbed his hands together. "But it is because they are loyal to Vatan, and do not recognize the lands divided."

Mayli turned to her right. "Does that mean they are loyal to you, Prince Arkello?"

Arkello kept his gaze focused downward as he fingered through a small pouch. He chose something and popped it in his mouth. "To an extent," he said, chewing.

"How so?" She leaned in to peek at what he had.

He gave her the bag. "Most rightfully acknowledge me as the true heir of Vatan but won't agree to seek out the capital."

Mayli pulled the string open, finding an assortment of roasted seeds, nuts, and dried fruit inside. "Why?" She selected a slice of dried orange and nibbled.

Breath whispered against Mayli's ear. "Reavers," spooked Charli.

Arkello smiled with confirmation as he slid his goggles over his eyes.

The boat slowed. Although several strides from shore, one by one the crew disembarked. Arkello whipped his cloak around his neck and hopped out. Water splashed around his knees.

Cool droplets sprinkled Mayli, but she didn't flinch, eyes focused on the mysterious golden sands. Another eerie whistle cried in the distance as the wind blew. Sheets of sand flew from the dune's peak, coiling like a phantom claw. She hugged herself.

"Still wish to go to the desert, Princess?" Charli said smugly.

She glared at him. "You're just trying to scare me."

"Reavers are scary. As are sand mites, kanavaurs, and—"

"Rocks in your boot?" she teased.

"I'm serious," said Charli. "You are much safer with me aboard *Her Lady Damgard.*"

"You mean *The Rotting Barge*?"

"*Arkello's Woes.*" Arkello pulled a cluster of flags from the rowboat.

Mayli giggled, but Charli's face stayed grim. He gestured at Arkello. "Will you tell her about your trials out there?"

"All right, Mayli. Truth is..." The prince dipped his head, leaning down to Mayli's level. She stared at her reflection and the endless dunes behind her in his goggles. He flexed a devious smile. "The desert isn't that bad."

She beamed at Charli triumphantly. "Ha! See!"

"Arkello..." Charli growled.

The prince waved him off, then directed Mayli's view over the landscape. "I spent a month lost out there. Long days and nights living off what the desert provided. Which wasn't much. In all that time the worst danger I faced was the one you're already challenging." He touched his face, then pointed up.

The sun shimmered in praise, and Mayli felt as though it grew hotter on her skin.

"And, while there are superstitions of reavers, the only reason I haven't found Gezmek is that nomads still value coin. And of that, until recently, I've had very little."

Charli narrowed his eyes. "Not helping."

"And neither are you." Arkello tossed a rope. "Anchor the boat to shore and unload some equipment. The faster we put up these markers, the quicker we'll leave so you can return your princess and claim your reward."

"I'm not your crew or your subject." Charli handed the rope to a passing member. Waving Mayli up, he stood. "Come on, then."

Mayli clapped then began unlacing her boots. "Thanks, Ark!"

"Really, I have *you* to thank. This wouldn't have been possible without..." He waved the flag in the air, trying to find the appropriate words. He frowned. "Well, without you."

"Putting those together was the least I could do for your efforts in finding me." She pulled her feet free from the tight binding and stretched her toes.

"Charli is the one who hunted you down," Arkello said, covering his mouth and nose with his scarf.

"A combined effort," Charli said as he stepped into the water.

Mayli set her boots and socks aside then bundled her cloak and dress in her arms. Delicately as she could, she stepped into the cold water. Shivers rippled through her. "Brr..."

Charli looked her up and down. "You knew it was cold. I could've carried you."

"You need to start letting me do things on my own, Charli. I'm nearly twenty—not the helpless girl I once was." She trudged to the beach, focusing on the hot air to keep warm. Soft sunbaked sand squeezed between her toes. The grit worked to ease the tension in her feet from long days traveling with Alden.

Charli's finger traced her chin, brushing a spiral of hair from her face as the wind shifted. "I know you're a woman. Which is why I care for you." Charli's hand lingered on her neck.

Her mouth dried like the desert as goosebumps rose from his touch. She craved the familiar interactions, the seductive whispers, the looks that said more than words. Fighting the distractions, she unclasped her cloak and whipped it into the air, giving her space. It fluttered down. "Then don't disrupt my light." She sat in his shadow.

"Yes, Princess," he said almost mockingly, then stepped away.

Sensing he'd moved a respectful distance, she lay upon her

cloak to lounge, taking comfort in the soft cushion of sand. The warm granules enveloped her like a soothing bath. Soon, her legs thawed from the water's chill. It warmed a smile, and she eased her eyes closed, glad the tantrum in her stomach washed away like the water off the shore. *Safe*, she mentally declared while pulling out a toasted almond from the bag and popping it in her mouth.

A coolness fell over her, the sound of shifting sand stirring her awake. Mayli groaned, rolling from her belly to her back. "Charli... You're blocking my sun, and it's almost set!"

Confused by a soft and hesitant touch padding at her side, Mayli opened her heavy eyes. Silhouetted by low rays, a sharpened shape took form, and it wasn't Charli.

Six appendages, each almost her size, towered above. A segmented body jutted up like mountain peaks. Too many eyes to count blinked in erratic succession, festering with hunger as white tendrils twisted around a chittering beak, one outstretched and exploring her body.

Mayli screamed.

The beast hunkered to the ground, screeching as well. Mayli kicked furiously, sand exploding as she worked to create distance. She scurried to stand, but slipped, tangling in her cloak.

Shouting erupted. Footsteps raged toward her. Something flashed. A new shriek sounded, sharp as a baby's cry, then something warm and slimy sprayed.

A new shadow stood over her—tall, barrel-chested. One of Charli's dual scimitars shimmered with a clear oily substance. He pointed with it. "Mayli, get to the boat."

Nodding, she tried to find her balance along with her breath. As she rose, so did the creature, slow and cautious.

Dressed in his silk robes once more, Charli stepped forward, blades at the ready. "Go, *now!*"

At the raise of his voice, a bloom of tendrils—minus one that lay severed on the ground—uncoiled in a brilliant display. Like a gas lamp, they began to glow. Mayli stared in awe.

"Whoa, whoa! Stop!" A black blur rushed past, cloak swooshing. Arkello put his back to the creature and held his sword outstretched to Charli.

"Are you insane?" Charli pointed with his blade. "That's a kanavaur!"

"It's a hatchling—a baby," Arkello hissed. "So lower your blades."

Charli huffed out his words, "You think I care how old something is if it's attacking the princess?"

"It wasn't attacking her..." Arkello stepped towards Charli.

"Bullshit. It had its grimy mauler on her." Nose snarling, he took a step back, waving his sword. "I had to cut it off before it killed her."

Killed me? Chills danced down Mayli's back.

Sand shook from the kanavaur as it rattled its segmented body. Tendrils curled in, fading their luminous glow.

"See, already it's calming down." Arkello looked at Mayli, keeping his voice calm. "Do you still have the mix?"

"Wha—?"

"The bag of fruit and nuts I gave you?" He opened and closed his palm, impatiently.

Mayli touched her side where the kanavaur had been rummaging and pulled the snack bag out.

"Thought so. Toss it over." She did and he caught it, turning his back on them.

"What are you doing?" Charli hovered over his shoulder, pointing his sword out. "We need to kill that thing, not feed it!"

Arkello pulled his scarf down and goggles up as he squatted

in front of the young kanavaur. Its eyes darted between them as its beak clattered nervously.

"Shh, it's all right." Arkello outstretched his hand offering a cashew. When still it hesitated, he tossed the nut.

The beast flattened into the sand as the treat came flying. It bounced off its head, causing each eye to wince. When no danger followed, a curious coil reached forward. Finding food, the glow finally subsided.

"That's right... It's okay," Arkello cooed, shuffling forward. He shook a variety of fruits and nuts into his palm. Arm outstretched, he offered the selection. "Want more?"

"Don't!" Mayli warned as Charli raised his sword.

Arkello waved his arm. "It's fine, they aren't—"

Just as the creature was about to select one, Charli threw his attack. A ring of metal pierced the air as Arkello twisted his knee in the sand to clash his saber with Charli's sword. Both men glared past their kissing blades.

Mayli blinked, impressed by the prince's speed.

"Back off." Arkello stood, driving Charli's boots into the sand as he pushed him back. "A kanavaur is only a threat if you are."

Teeth grinding, Charli pressed his weight down, forcing Arkello two steps back. "Don't you tell me a kanavaur is harmless! I've watched them mutilate men in the arena."

Arkello scoffed. "Out of defense! Trial by combat is an Ammosian fear tactic to keep crime down, silk production up, and money flowing."

"And to expose criminals!" Charli barked.

"Do not be so naive. There is no such sagacity from a creature—only instinct. After being starved and sent into a roaring crowd, anyone in that ring will be perceived as a threat *and* lunch. Trial by combat is purely for exploitation, entertainment, and murder."

"You admit it yourself. They will eat us!"

"Oh please. Kanavaurs are much like nomads. They will eat meat only out of necessity. They are mostly vegetarians, grazing on roots, vegetation, or whatever nutrients they can pull from the desert and sea."

Mayli put her hand on her guard's arm. "Charli, maybe he's right."

"I told you to get to the boat!" he snapped, muscles tensing.

"But look." She pointed to where the creature's body hid. From under the sand, white tendrils blindly searched. Finding a fig, it pulled it under. Light munching sounded from underground. "It likes fruit."

"See." Arkello twisted off of Charli's blade and knelt beside the creature. Dusting sand away, its eyes blinked one after another as they became exposed. Arkello offered a piece of orange, and it rose from the ground. Chittering softly, it ate directly from his hand. Smiling, Arkello fed it another. "There you go, little friend."

"Little friend?" Charli mocked.

"Prince Arkello..." called a crewman. He waved a flag from a nearby berm. "We've got a nest over here!"

"More?" Arkello leapt to investigate.

Mayli and Charli exchanged looks as the hatchling scurried after Arkello as if he were its mother. Once he was out of sight, Charli glared at Mayli. "You could have been killed."

She stood, pulling her cloak from the sand, and shook it out. "Some guard."

"I had matters to discuss with Arkello. It was only for a moment. You shouldn't have even been out here! See how dangerous the desert is now? We are going back to the ship."

Mayli turned to walk towards the gathering of crew members with Arkello at the nest. "I think the prince of this desert and his crew have things under control. I mean...look at that thing. I've seen dogs more frightening."

Below, the kanavaur sat loyally at Arkello's side. The prince stroked its bug-like head without fear. Before them lay a cluster of large, membranous eggs in a ditch. Long legs folded, twitching inside each translucent shell. Coiled tendrils drifted in the yolk. One egg lay empty, split in two. The casing glistened in the sun, still wet from its recent hatch. Crewmen worked to pluck eggs free and lay them in a net.

Arkello patted one. "Good find men. These will fetch a fortune with Mr. Vaurus, and we'll be back home in no time."

Charli pulled Mayli's hand to leave. "You've seen it, now let's go."

Mayli yanked herself free from Charli's grasp. "Why are you so afraid?"

He leaned in close. "You know why."

"Did you get a rock in your boot when fighting with Arkello?" Mayli walked down the slope to the nest.

He huffed, following. "Why are you being so difficult?"

"Because it is just a baby." She neared the kanavaur. A few of its eyes held at her while the others kept on Arkello, Charli, and the other crewmen. She shuddered.

"Maybe..." Charli said, positioning himself between her and the creature. "But we don't want to be around when the mother beast finds we disturbed her nest."

Arkello stroked the hatchling as it frisked his pocket for more snacks. He fed it one. "Nah. Mamas don't stick around."

Charli scanned the horizon. "What about the father? Surely he's lurking."

Arkello watched his crew secure more eggs within the net. "Dead."

He crossed his arms. "How are you so sure?"

Arkello turned his head, offering only his chin. "After mating, mama eats him to have the energy to lay."

Mayli's mouth dropped. "That's horrible!"

Charli raised his brow. "What about protecting her young?"

"She has." Arkello slashed his saber at the empty egg. Miraculously, his blade skidded off without any tear in the clear membranous covering.

Mayli gasped. "That's like silk!"

"It *is* silk. Where do you think your fine dresses come from?"

Twisting her mouth, she realized she'd never given it thought. "But Ammosian Silks can't be cut, so how can they hatch? Let alone be used to make anything from."

Arkello pointed at the kanavaur. "Mucus from kanavaur's tendrils have the toxicity to break down the fibers. It—"

Mayli's eyes shot wide. "It was on me! Get it off!" She used her cloak to scrub, but the sticky substance clung to the hairs on her arm like glue.

Charli rushed to aid, piling sand on her arm. He scrubbed hard, using the grit to break off the remains. "Shit, Arkello, *now* you tell us?"

A roll of mockery came from the prince. "You know she's fine. Only when the tendrils glow is it a problem."

"They *were* glowing!"

Arkello yawned. "And whose fault is that?"

Realizing Charli's efforts were unnecessary, and her arm feeling worse than before, Mayli folded it with her other. "How do you know so much about them, Ark?"

"One doesn't live under or in the Desert of Gezmek, and be an heir of Vatan, without learning how to survive it."

A flash of light emitted from one of the eggs.

"Hey!" Arkello snapped. His eyes shook wildly as he pointed his saber at the crewmen handling the net. "Cause those to hatch, and I will feed you to them! Those eggs are more valuable than your lives!"

The men stopped their roughhousing, easing the net to sway more softly. The nervous egg continued to pulse a moment longer before fading out. Once steady, the crewmen carried the cluster to the rowboat.

Mayli shivered. "If you are so against exploiting kanavaurs, then why are you rounding them up to sell?"

"Because"—Arkello met her gaze—"in order to save my family and reclaim what is mine, I have to do whatever it takes."

In that moment, Arkello resembled Alden. Focused. Pained. Determined. Even his eyes pinched with the same concern. However, a cruelness harbored within, suggesting the true threat in this desert was Prince Arkello Densen. As if to agree, a distant, wet scream cut through the dry air.

Shouts of alarm roared over the dunes.

Charli pointed his scimitar at Arkello. "I knew that mother beast would be back!"

"That wasn't, ah—" Arkello's voice stuttered as he looked past them. His head shook and eyes widened. A bemused smile twisted on his lips. "No way..."

Turning around, Mayli's back tingled. Tips of curling horns grew from the dune's crest. The heavy mass had a mane of jagged feathers that waved in the howling wind. Two thin legs walked it forth. Another similar creature arose. Then another. More appeared silhouetting the twilight sky in a horrifying display. *Reavers.*

In the grasp of one, a crewman struggled, his limbs flailing to beat it off as he cried in pain. A long swordlike claw withdrew. The body slumped, tumbling down the dune with a trail of blood following in its wake.

"*Charli...*" Mayli rasped.

"Princess, it's really time to get back to the ship."

"Yep!"

He seized her in his arms, cursing with each fierce step as he carried her. "Damnit, damnit, damnit."

Daylight gone, Mayli strained to see a reaver stalking over a berm toward Arkello. His kanavaur jumped in front to defend, its tendrils rising. A fierce glow burst around them, illuminating Arkello as he stood with his arms out as if to reason with the creature. The reaver and kanavaur dove at each other, creating a tangle of feathers and claws. Shadow and light. Descending the dune to the water's edge, the fight disappeared from view.

"Arkello!" Mayli stretched her hand out as if she could grab him from the nightmare.

Charli stopped to glance back. The light grew brighter. Someone screamed. He shook his head and kept going towards the ship.

"You're leaving him?" Mayli gasped. "Isn't he your best friend?"

"Yes. To keep *you* alive."

"But he needs help or he'll die!" Mayli shook her head.

Charli clenched her tighter. "If you're living, Princess, then someone else is always dying for your cause."

From the corner of her eye, she watched black shadows effortlessly traverse on the sands and cut through more men. The unguarded screams across the desert rang in her ears—clanging of steel, thumps, and grunts. Her guard's heavy breathing and the thunder of his steps drowned out all else.

Mayli hid her face in the protection of his embrace. "I'm sorry. I should've listened to you..."

"Yes. You should have." Anger held in his tone.

Suddenly, Charli's muscles grew taut. He twisted. A sharp ring pierced Mayli's ears. Braving a look, she fell weak seeing a dark form held back by Charli's scimitar. Two ribbed horns loomed high like a crown. Black feathers hissed in the wind.

Huge hollowed sockets from a dead, skull-like face stared at her without any eyes. Mayli opened her mouth to scream, but fright rendered her speechless.

Charli tossed Mayli from his grip, in favor of drawing his second blade.

Tiny grains racked across her skin as she fell, banging her head. Sand spilled from her hair as she rolled upright. "Charli!"

His blades swung upward, but the creature maneuvered effortlessly in the dark to dodge. It jabbed, forcing Charli to leap away, but not before sending an attack across the reaver's arm. As if hitting steel, it ricocheted off.

"Oh no..." Mayli gasped.

Charli tried again to no avail. Spying Mayli still collapsed on the shore watching in awe, Charli pointed his blade. "Princess —to the ship!"

Given the opening, the reaver thrust a jab into Charli's chest.

"Charli!"

Protected by his silks, Charli endured the hit. Still, he lost his footing in the uneasy terrain, falling to one knee.

The creature raised its claws but before it could deliver a killing strike, a howl traced the landscape, calling the creature's focus to the dunes.

In its hesitation, Charli slashed his scimitar at the creature's knee, toppling it. He rolled out of the way, and within the same heartbeat, gripped Mayli's hand. "Had enough of the desert yet?"

She ran into the sea with him. "...Yes!"

Splashing through the water, they hurried to the rowboat waiting just offshore. Charli took her by the waist and helped her on board. He cut the anchor rope and gave a running start before hopping in. Mayli rummaged for an oar, finding it under a bench. Charli ripped it from her grasp and drove it through the water, steering it toward the ship.

Mayli shook her head, holding her knees in. "That wasn't folklore or men in suits..." She rocked back and forth.

"Men in suits?" Scoffed Charli. "Where did you hear such a thing?"

"A...friend mentioned it," she said, sounding foolish.

"Rumors like that can get you killed...like it did Arkello."

Mayli sat frozen in fear, hardly registering what Charli said as a kanavaur egg blinked in the moonlight in front of her. Each of the many eyes looked around in wonder through the milky shells. She swallowed, watching the occasional bioluminescence glow within. "Are they going to hatch?"

"No. You're safe now." Despite his sentiment, an angry snarl plastered his face.

Tears of guilt streamed down her face. She leaned forward, wrapping her arms around herself. "I am so sorry."

Charli ignored her as he rowed, splashing dark water with each powered stroke. The night cooled. The sky blackened. Once they reached the ship, he secured ropes to the rowboat's front and back. He tugged on one. "Hey! Raise us up!"

A head crewman popped over the side. "What's going on out there?"

"Reavers." Charli gestured back. "Now let us up."

"Where's the prince?"

"I have the princess!"

Mayli rose on her toes.

"We only take orders from Prince Arkello."

"Did you not hear the screaming? We are all that's left. He's dead."

The deafening silence over the dunes indicated it was true. No longer were there cries of pain or suffering. No creepy calls howled in the wind. No luminous glow. Even the sand had stopped dancing in the breeze, its whistle hushed.

"So..." Charli pointed to the beautiful white and orange script curling on the old wood. "So now you'll listen to the one whose name is painted on this ship."

"Would that be you, Damgard, or Her Lady?"

They all stared at her.

Mayli turned to the desert. Though unseen in the black of night, she knew bodies littered the sand. Arkello, his crew, maybe even the kanavaur hatchling. Any one of them could have been her. She was in no state to lead or rule. Even something as simple as a ship.

"Charli." She sniffled. "Take me home..."

CHAPTER SIX
ALL DONE

Hot from activity, soft fur clung to the perspiration on Briar's skin as he stretched across the bed. White tufts of mink tickled his cheek. Blankets tangled between his legs, and a pillow supported his side. He lay sprawled, catching his breath. His body tingled as a gentle finger swept through his disheveled hair, coaxing out a purr.

Kira lay beside him, sprawled just as leisurely in nothing but an extra-large knit sweater she'd been overjoyed to see when the carriers arrived from Colville. Its wide collar slipped over her tattooed shoulder threatening to expose her plump breasts hiding just underneath. She petted him once more, drawing his gaze up to her face. "You are like a cat."

He curled his lips into a feline grin. "Cute? Cuddly?"

She clapped his thigh, hopping out of bed. "Lazy."

Playfully grabbing her sweater, Briar tugged Kira back into his embrace. He nosed over the perfectly illustrated lines of his kingdom's crest. "Oh, I don't know... I was plenty busy moments ago."

Dark eyes twinkled as if wishing him to go on, but her brow

tested. "As honored as I am to tussle in bed with you, Your Majesty, it's midday."

"It can't be already." He kissed one of the stars flanking the draclynn design. "We have time for more."

Kira wiggled free, shrugging the sweater over her crest as she stood. "See for yourself." Tugging a rope, she drew open the black drapes cloaking the windows.

Briar threw his hand over his eyes as the sun charged into the room. It glinted off the bed's polished wood, forcing him to further squint and look away. The heavy drop of clothes lured him to brave the light. Adjusting to the day's bloom, he lowered his shield and gulped.

Kira stood bare in the window. Bold shadows accentuated every bend, tight muscle, and curve. She looked out over Dregs with confidence...like she knew one day it would be hers.

Ever since Kira broke into his room wearing nothing but a sheer nightgown, Briar, to his gleeful surprise, hadn't seen her in much else when in private. From her trials with Reyn throughout the years, He had assumed Kira would be a woman he'd never touch. Especially after his uncle, the late King Olivar Colte, had imprisoned her.

True to her nature, Kira escaped the king's clutches. Chaos ensued in her wake. His uncle died. And Briar claimed the throne.

With his newfound power, he'd honored the documents Olivar had made, proving the ink on Kira's shoulder made her a noble. The inking had, after all, been observed by a noble of each kingdom and a king. Her nobility was a partial lie of course; as it claimed she belonged to the Harlow family, who had all died in the Brim War three years past. However, with the scatter of refugees, no one could dispute she wasn't a lost heir. With the title came the deed to the Harlow Estate, clothes, a horse, and a chest of gold—all more than anything Briar's uncle ever gave to him.

Due to the king's bloody demise, the king's chambers—now Briar's—had needed to be cleaned and prepared before he could move in. So, on the first night of being king, Briar returned to his loft. He'd fully expected Kira to have fled, but she'd remained—waiting for him just as he hoped. Content to sleep in the straw-lined cells of the guardhouse below, Briar had offered her his bed. To his surprise, Kira had refused.

"Kings don't sleep in dirt and hay," Kira had said, moving to the stairs. "I'll go."

Briar lifted his hand, halting her. "Nor do noblewomen."

Kira snorted. "What's your point? I'm not noble." She shoved his arm away.

"You are. We just went through this." Briar pointed at the roll of documents on the table. Kira had refused to look, still pretending they didn't exist. He stepped in. "My uncle wanted nothing more than to deprive me of the throne. That meant he didn't want anyone challenging him that any heir he created was illegitimate. Those papers and your tattoo claim you as noble. It is so."

"See, you said it yourself. I'm illegitimate. Now let me go sleep in the hay like the commoner I am."

Briar swiftly moved to block her path once more as she neared the railing. She seemed nervous so he took a step down and bowed, covering his royal-crested shoulder in deep respect. "Regardless of what you or I think of your ink, you deserve a good night's sleep after what you've been through. You look exhausted. Take the bed, I'll sleep below. You can lock me in if you wish."

Her tired eyes trailed to the heavy piece of furniture suffocating the room. It was layered in soft furs and blankets, though old as well as lacking quality. She peered back at him and spoke nonchalantly. "It's big enough to share."

Briar's cheeks had heated at those words. No woman in three years had freely suggested such an act thanks to his royal Densen name being associated with frauds and killers. Thankfully, it hadn't stopped whores at the Binx & Drinx from taking a fierce sum of his coin in exchange for a mediocre hour despite his efforts to please and swoon. Yet, that night wasn't for pleasure. *Not with Kira. Having a man near her is the last thing she'd want. Sleep. We are just going to sleep,* he had reminded himself. Nodding with a lump in his throat, he agreed. "I'll be honorable," he had promised.

Without any further debate, Kira had walked to the bed choosing the side nearest the window. Folding back the bedding, she slipped in. It consumed her as she pulled the fur so high that only her eyes peeked out. They closed dreamily.

Seeing her settled, Briar took a step down to escape.

"Don't 'cha dare go down in the hay, *Your Majesty!*" Kira had flung the blankets back and rolled to face him, eyes alert and glaring.

"Kira..." he whined, neck rolling.

She patted the overstuffed pillow beside her. Her voice tamed and spoke in an alluring tone, "This is far too comfy for anyone to pass up." She nestled back in.

She's not wrong.

Tempted and defeated, Briar removed his leather jerkin and draped it over the rail. He kicked his boots off then tugged free his socks. Heart racing to such a point he knew sleep would never come, Briar padded barefoot to the bed occupied by a woman who had chased him from it with a bloodied chair leg earlier that night. After slipping into the sheets, he rolled to his side, keeping as close to the edge as possible to offer as much room as possible.

Silence lay between them.

His brain sought to dream, but each train of thought jour-neyed through dangerous grounds. A gorgeous woman, dressed in *his* shirt as a sleep gown, rested but an arm's reach away, yet was completely untouchable. He could hear gentle breathing escaping her open mouth. He could feel the bed move with her as she shifted to get comfortable—feel her warmth under the covers. He visualized her curvy body, her skin, her beautifully inked tattoo, her...scars. He winced. Kira would never tell where they came from, but Briar knew enough about the abuse she'd endured. *She'd likely stab me if I even look her way.* Shamed for allowing his thoughts to deviate, Briar settled further into his pillow. When finally he'd convinced himself that just sharing his bed with a woman he fancied was doable, Kira had burst into a fit of rolling laughter.

"What?" Briar mused, eyes fluttering open.

She slapped her hands to her face, muting snorts and giggles. She shook her head.

He flipped to face her, a smile growing at the sound of her happiness. "What's so funny?"

She split her fingers to look at him. "I can't unsee your nude sword fighting."

"Sweet kings, Kira. Have you been thinking of me naked this whole time?" He raised on his elbow.

Kira continued her humored tantrum, nodding hysterically.

Laughing himself, Briar swung a pillow at her. "Quiet your thoughts, mine are loud enough."

Kira had effortlessly blocked and in one continuous motion, stole his pillow to fling it back. He dodged and it sailed across the room, disappearing over the balcony. Together they scram-bled to their knees, hands poised to continue their battle.

Briar wiggled his fingers. "You should know, before I was king, I was guard captain."

Kira raised a pillow jestingly. "You gonna arrest me?"

"Might."

She smirked. "Try."

Before she could swing, Briar had flung his quilt over her head. While she was caught in the snare, he dove for the last pillow guarded behind her. Collecting it, he rolled over, ready to attack. But Kira had pounced with the outstretched blanket like a monster. Pinned and trapped, she tickled him mercilessly. Briar laughed in a fit, losing the strength to defend himself. When he had called her name, the blanket tugged off. He braced, expecting another down assault, but something just as soft connected—her lips...

"Hey!" Clothes slammed into Briar's hardened lap, jarring him to the present as Kira snapped her fingers. "Get dressed."

Groaning, Briar fell back with the bundle. Pain throbbed from the tender hit. "I should have you arrested for assaulting a king..." he hissed.

"As I recall, you tried that once already, and I wasn't the one who ended up shackled to the bed." Kira, now dressed in a simple black outing gown, piped in yellow, set her lip brush down and met his gaze through the reflection of the vanity mirror. A flirty red smirk twisted.

He grinned gayly as he finished reminiscing over the events after their first kiss. She hadn't been afraid or timid as he'd assumed. Instead, each passionate action was directed by her—him being the cautious one. He let her control him, consume him, and yes, cuff him to the bed, making a very memorable first day as king.

"Briar. Don't cha make me throw your armor at ya too." She raised a weave of chain mail.

Rolling to his feet, Briar threw his hands in the air. "I'm up!"

Kira eyed his arousal. "I see that. Now come on and get dressed. I'm starved for lunch!"

Sighing deeply, he collected his trousers that had fallen and stepped through, buttoning himself inside. As he continued to dress, memories and fantasies faded with each article added. Briar fussed with the stiff fabric of his new formal overcoat.

Fingers traced along his neck as Kira straightened his collar. His head ricocheted from the tickle. A few locks fell in his face, and he went cross-eyed to look at the tuft. She looked at it and then continued adjusting the coat. Briar raised a brow. "Aren't ya gonna nag me 'bout my hair?"

"Nag?" Kira ran her hand through, messing it further. "Why would I?"

"You've already harassed me to get dressed and ready. And Fredrik always goes off about my hair."

Kira stepped back. "Do I look like your man-in-waiting?" Mouth drooping and eyes cast upward, Kira mocked the man's loose face and upturned nose.

"Ugh, no!" Briar dragged his hand over her face to wipe the haunting image away.

"Then you'll find no judgment from me about your good looks." She tousled his hair from one side to the other. "Besides, I like it. It shows you have nothing to prove."

"Really?" He flicked it from his eyes, admiring himself in the mirror with a charming smile.

"Yep. This is all they need to see." Kira's firm yet precise hands unbuttoned the flap on his upper sleeve. As she rolled it, the royal crest of Brimley became exposed. A fresh line of jagged yellow designs crowned it, signifying Briar as the king of Dregs. Kira pinned the fabric back, then leaned her face against his warm, tattooed skin, smiling at him through the mirror.

Briar wrapped his arm around her, teasing to untie her shoulder flap. "Yours too."

Kira shied her face into him. "No..."

"Come now." Briar peeled her off. "Why are you still so nervous about that? It's been weeks."

Her eyes grew wide as she gazed up at him. "Because, Briar, I'm a fraud. And if anyone found out, you'd be the one in trouble. Being with you is risky enough."

He laughed. "Kira, I'm the king of Dregs, and heir to Vatan, you think I'm intimidated by a little trouble?" He squinted.

"No..." She lowered her gaze.

Briar stepped in front of her and lifted her chin with his knuckle. Big brown eyes blinked back, and he explored them, searching for truth. "Then what are you really so afraid of?"

She absently touched his shoulder and took in a breath. "Embarrassing you."

"That's impossible." Briar shook his head. "There's no one who can embarrass me more than myself."

She rolled her eyes.

"I mean it. So, that excuse is gone." He fluttered his hand. "Next?"

Kira scoffed. "You're not going to give up, are you."

"Nope. Not until there's a reasonable answer as to why you won't feel confident showing your crest."

"Maybe I just don't feel worthy. Worthy to be considered noble, or live in a castle, wear nice things, or..." Her voice caught then weakened.

"Or what?"

"Or have you." She fiddled with her long fingernails.

"Kira," Briar said firmly. He cupped her face in his hands urging her to look at him. He squared his stance, settling into a firmer position. "You are worthy of all of those things *and* more."

She scoffed, dropping her hands and rolling her eyes. "No, I'm not."

"Yes. As worthy as any queen." Briar traced her pronounced

collarbone leading to her neck. "To prove it, I have something for you."

"You think you'll win a thief over with gifts I could just as easily steal?"

Kira spun a ring on her finger—Evelyn's. He never questioned Kira about it though, feeling no sympathy for his ex. He'd bought it once upon a time anyway.

From his pocket, Briar drew out a long, thin golden chain. A golden pendant with three rare, blue, tear-shaped gems. It twinkled in the afternoon light. "I think you'll appreciate not needing to live so precariously." He gave the clasp to his other hand, wrapping it around her neck. As he brushed aside her hair, Briar smiled seeing Kira shiver at his endearing touch. The necklace clicked together, and he turned her at the shoulders to observe.

The three gems glowed like they knew they belonged there, knew they were made for a powerful woman. He cradled them in one hand then tugged slightly, leading her in for a kiss. He gave it tenderly, and her plump lips moved against him to offer one back. When she broke away, he grinned with a flushed face. "You're so lovely..."

"Thank you, Briar." She touched the gems with genuine appreciation. "Even without the gifts, I've never felt so adored."

"It is a shame none have appreciated or celebrated you properly." He stroked her face. "I promise to make up for that."

She shied away. "That's not your responsibility to make up for."

"No matter. It is a burden I am honored to take on."

"Oh! So I'm a burden now?" She folded her arms and gave a sassy grin with a sway of her hips.

Briar scooped Kira into his arms, squeezing a yelp from her. He spun, making her hold tight. "You are a bit heavy," he said, carrying her to the bed.

"Briar!" She laughed and thrashed playfully. "We can't make love all day!"

He set her down on the soft mattress. "We can't?" He traced his hand up her leg.

"You promised me lunch at your favorite place!" She smothered a pillow onto his head, knocking him back to lie down as she rolled on top of him. Stray wisps of her hair fell onto his face as she leaned over him.

Briar remained still. With all their playing, he respected her limits. He sighed, staring up at the timber ceiling. "I did, didn't I?"

She gave a peck on his cheek and slipped off, shaking the wrinkles out of her dress. "Yep."

He rolled to standing and elbowed his arm out for her to take. "Then why are you dawdling?"

She whacked his arm before hooking hers inside it with an endearing laugh.

Carriage wheels rolled like thunder over the wet cobbled streets. To Kira's surprise, the cabin didn't rock or sway like the wagons she'd journeyed on in the past but instead glided with ease. Her head kept level even as the carriage dipped into a mud-filled pothole. A cry of protest rang out as water splashed a group of soggy-footed commoners clustered under an awning brimming with yesterday's rain.

Kira released the golden curtain, hiding from their shaking fists. She remembered being the one doused by the carriages of nobles and spitting back curses as they had. But here she was, laced into an elaborate gown she'd stolen, and accompanying royalty—though, aside from her attire and transportation, that wasn't something new. For the last two years, she'd stolen whatever she needed and been at a king's side—only now for the last month, it had been with the king of Dregs.

Seated beside her, Briar held a giddy smile—one a child might wear. His always-present joy was not what she had expected or was used to seeing from a king. Alden had always been so melancholic, making the moments he flashed a smile worth more than all the stolen treasures. She'd always tried to lure them out, desperate to find what brought him happiness. To her surprise, it had been a challenging task. Most at ease by himself, her presence had seemed to sour Alden's mood. She had, after all, been intrusive, always inserting herself in his personal space, asking questions, following him about, and lingering as closely as possible to feel safe. In time, her persistence earned her a close friendship with him, and she had mastered all the little things to coax Alden to smile, like enjoying the same blend of tea as him (Brimleyn with orange peel added), posing for him to draw (just seductive enough that he could enjoy privately later), playing pranks (although he preferred it when Squirrel was the target, rather than himself), and, her favorite...platonic cuddling.

It wasn't until Kira learned of Alden's secret identity as the uncrowned king of Brimley, Colin Densen, that she truly understood his hesitant nature. She couldn't blame him for being skittish with so many accusations against him. Murder. Fraud. Cowardice. She had been just as judgmental and insulted the Brimleyn king without even knowing it was him time and time again. So, figuring out what would make him smile the most, Kira worked on the bigger picture: clear his name, and heal his heart. That endeavor had brought her here, into the arms of another king.

Kira leaned into Briar, and his firm muscles softened, creating a pillow for her to relax into. Alden had always been tense, as if she'd nestled against a warm stone—no matter how many times they would sit or lie together. Although Alden and Briar were cousins, their contrast of light and dark personalities made them seem almost unrelated. If it weren't for their matching noses, structured jaws, and prideful attitudes, she'd consider it was possible they weren't. But, unlike Alden, Briar was relaxed, happy, and as Kira gladly learned, a really great kisser. Most of all, Briar was entirely open with himself with no secrets to hide. It made it easy for her to fall into a relationship and let go of her crush on Alden so he could someday have his princess.

"That's a stylish dress, Kira." Briar leaned heavily against her, his hand tracing the hem. "Have I seen that before?"

"You like it?" She looked down at her outfit. Yellow piping rimmed the contours of her breasts, while angled sections alternated black until at her waist a bloom of yellow spread like a flower. "When I saw another wear it, I knew I had to have one. You know how the trends go around here."

"I don't follow the trends so much, but I do know what accents your beauty well." Briar nuzzled into her neck, kissing around the necklace he'd given her.

Kira blushed. "Oh please. I'm not beautiful."

"Don't argue with your king," he said, unfastening a button that choked too high around his freshly shaven neck. He nosed closer, then waited for protest. She rarely gave him any but always appreciated his quiet ask. Welcomed, he brushed his lips with hers.

His kiss given ever so softly, Kira bit for more. Her demand was rewarded with a long and determined kiss. He moaned pleasantly as Kira brushed her hand through his thick shaggy hair, knocking off his crown. A hand slipped under her dress, playing with the frills of her undergarments. Keeping it cupped around her behind, Briar pulled Kira onto his lap. She trembled, being given the power and pleasure to be on top of a man—not trapped below. Briar put his other hand on her hip, gently holding her as she fished for his belt.

"We have arrived, Your Majesty," announced the driver as the carriage came to a halt.

Halfway unbuckled, Kira and Briar smacked apart. She chewed on her lips, rolling her head back to look at the ceiling with a groan.

Briar chuckled. "We can finish up here if you like." His thumb snuck between her legs finding the seam of her ever-dampening cloth.

She shuddered at the well-placed touch. *Damn if he isn't persuasive.* She kissed him once more, teasing him just the same with a brush of her fingers as she fixed his belt back together. She tightened it with a tug before rolling off. "Dessert will have to wait. Are we at your favorite place you promised to take me to?" She looked out the window, eyes searching.

Briar sighed deep, the disappointment lingering. After licking his thumb clean, he placed his hand on the door and flung it open. "It sure is!"

Kira stepped onto the street with expectations of grandeur. What stood before them brought an internal wince. *What a dump.* Yellow paint curled from window trim, patches of wood hung haphazardly on hinges with single nails. A gutter over-flowed from a drizzle that seemed to fall with Kira's mood. The wraparound porch teetered on angled stilts, looking like if she were to glare hard enough it might fall into the river below.

This can't be it. Assuming the fine establishment Briar was going to take her to would be on the other side of the street, Kira turned around. The buildings there, however, were somehow even worse. Chickens pecked in the street. Tattered drapes acted as a roof where part of a building had crumbled. A few blocks down was the central island's guard tower and Briar's old home. She turned her gaze to him.

His smile grew even bigger as he stepped from the carriage and beamed past her. "Ah... The Binx & Drinx!"

Above the door swung a wooden sign. It was in the shape of a shield and depicted a black cat arched over a golden stein. Poor illustrations were painted on the window, displaying their selection of local breweries' ales and lager—nothing imported. Discarded tankards collected on the porch's rail. A pile of trash moved in the corner—*or is that a homeless Brimleyn?* Kira stepped from it. "I thought we were going somewhere nice for lunch."

Briar took her hand, helping her dodge a questionable pile of pale chunks soiling the dirty road. "I promised to take you to my favorite place."

"You have odd perceptions of what beauty is."

"Come now, you know I don't have such shallow views as to judge something based on outer appearances."

"Ah hah, so I'm not beautiful!"

He pulled her into his arms. "Don't twist my words, Kira Harlow. Your beauty is unmatched."

Kira laughed, looking at the disheveled building. "I would hope so!"

Briar palmed his face. "Kira..."

"Okay. But I get to pick our next outing. Perhaps a proper eatery? One worthy of this dress?" She lifted it out of the mud.

"Oh, so there will still be a next time after this?" He helped her up the steps. "Glad I haven't embarrassed you too much yet."

"I'm not embarrassed. Just wondering if they serve food here?" She sniffed but only found the river's muck catching in her nose.

"Of course they do, that's why we are here. Lunch." Briar

hooked his arm around Kira's side, walking her through the veranda. He paused as their royal knight opened the broken-hinged door. "Thank you, Sir Tarek."

"That's Sir Exten," Kira corrected.

Briar paused in the doorway and looked back at his knight. Exten dipped his helm to agree. Grinning at Kira, Briar's blue eyes danced in fascination. "I'm usually good with names but they're twins, by face and armor. How did you know that?"

"Exten is left-handed." Kira gestured at the man's scabbard hanging at his right hip.

"You made note of hand dominance?"

"Yep. It's the first thing I do when I come across someone. Knowing how they use their weapon allows me to use it against them." She fingered the pommel of Briar's sword hooked at his side. "Which is how I was able to best you."

"Ha. I let you win our little sword fight back then." Briar took her hand. "But good instinct. Although I doubt you can find a way to best my royal knights. Even I haven't yet."

She observed the man clad in armor. The Hiorean suit was well-tailored, with many rivets and plates allowing a full range of motion. A weave of mail detailed in a V-like pattern skirted his legs above Ammosian Silks. Even his feet were protected in pointed steel. Kira twisted her lips. "In a match against someone like him, the best thing to do is avoid at all costs." She hopped inside.

"Ha! Precisely why Sir Exten is accompanying us. His presence should allow us some privacy." Briar followed.

Kira held her breath as the Binx & Drinx smelled as terrible as it looked. Char and grease from ovens fought with the tinge of foul ale lingering in the air. Stale breath wafted from laughing drunkards. The wood siding reeked of rot where the building sat too close to the passing river waters. Normally, she'd feel right at home, but after weeks of a pampered life, the shock was overbearing.

"You need to leave," grouched a woman's haggard voice.

Expecting the request to be directed at her, Kira shot her attention to the bar. Tending it, a burly woman with arms as thick as her neck shook her head at a pair of raggedy men.

"We haven't eat'n in days!" begged one. His accent was thick and undeniably Brimleyn.

"I already told you two, and all those other mangy brim noses cluttering the streets: I don't do charity. There's been enough harassment and thieving by you lot!"

His companion, just as thin and famished, rubbed his stomach. "We aren't trying to steal or take handouts." He extended his bony arm. A few copper coins glimmered weakly in offering. "Whatever this will get us. It is all we have left. A scrap. A dribble of broth. Anything!"

The barmaid slapped his hand. "I said, leave!"

Coins burst into the air, showering the room. The first man caught a few while the other scampered to collect a fleeing copper as it rolled toward the door.

Briar lifted his toe, trapping the coin. The desperate man reached, but upon seeing the polished leather boots he glanced up. His eyes widened as he seemed to take in the other fine furnishings of Briar's attire. His cape. His sword. His crown. Mouth gaping, he stared at the royal tattoo presented on the king's right shoulder. "Y-Y-Y-Your Majesty." He touched his nose to the grimy floor submissively.

Briar scowled at the barkeep. "I see your hospitality is still as friendly as ever, Binx."

"Piff!" Binx wiped her counter as the other Brimleyn scurried to bow. "I don't see why I need to be when there are so many now looking to take advantage. Already, I've lost a keg, and then one of my girls failed to show up for work. Likely scared of what diseases this lot carries. There are more fights than ever. Soon I'll need to hire security. So, Briar Densen, seeing as you're to blame for my problems, don't you think for a moment that I'll be treating you differently than I once had."

At the mention of his name, the crowd's whispers tingled like heated knives behind Kira. Whispers of their king being outside the castle, followed by mentions of her. Her throat caught, and her skin itched. Subconsciously, Kira tugged at her shoulder's covering, ensuring her fraudulent tattoo was well-hidden.

"Sorry to hear about your troubles, Binx, but beggars don't typically offer coin." Briar released the copper from his boot, allowing the man on the floor to snatch his life savings. Briar stepped to the side and walked to the bar. "I know you hold a grudge after what happened when your husband served in the war, but these people are not your enemy, and I know quite well that yesterday's pottage is no more than a copper. But they will have whatever they like. I'll cover."

The Brimleyns' eyes sparkled as their jaws drooped. Briar gestured for the Brimleyns to take a table. They dipped to bow again, then hurried to sit, nearly tripping over their loose bootstraps.

"I expect your outstanding tab to be paid off too."

"Of course." Briar plopped into a worn stool at the bar, his smile returning. He looked around as if he'd finally returned home after days of adventuring. Spying Kira still hunkered in the doorway beside Exten, Briar swooped his arm. "Kira, come meet Mrs. Binx! She's what keeps me coming back to this tavern."

"Bullshit." Binx turned to grab a stein from a hanging rack. "It's the drinks you sought."

With Exten in tow, Kira met Briar at his side, leaning into his embrace. "Binx seems to know you well." She laughed.

"Damn right," said Binx. "I've been feeding, tending, and picking his ass off the floor far too many nights over the past years. By now, you'd think he'd call me mother."

Briar leaned in and winked. "Ah, but Mother & Drinx doesn't quite have the same jolly cheer."

"Nor do I." Binx rested her puffy-eyed gaze on Kira. "What's your name, honey?"

"Kira."

"Yeah? You're cute enough. How much do you charge?"

Kira raised a brow. "Excuse me?"

"As I said, I'm down a girl. Not even so much as to collect her last pay." Binx sucked on her teeth, looking Kira up and down. "With your bust, you'll earn twice her earnings, I'm sure."

Briar's grip tightened around Kira as he laughed awkwardly. "This is Kira *Harlow*. She's with me of her own accord..."

"Noble ladies already wanting you back?" Binx turned away and began pouring a stream of yellow from a keg into the stein. "My gals will be fretting over that, Briar."

Snickering rose from the back corner. Kira turned to see a flock of three scantily clad women whispering behind yellow and black fans. Ribbons were loose around their bosom and hair, tempting the eye. One winked at her as another blew a kiss to Briar.

Oh... She cocked her head to the king, smirking. "Now I see why you really like it here."

"You got a smart one, son. Don't disappoint her," Binx called over her shoulder to Briar. She turned from the keg once the stein was filled and clunked it on the bar. Briar quickly brought it to his lips, hiding his blush. Dusting her hands, Binx looked at Kira with impatience. "So, what will it be, Lady Kira?"

"Tea. Brimleyn. Cream, sugar, and make sure it is very hot."

"Brim tea has been a popular choice as of late... I suppose I'll need to add it to the menu..." Binx whined, pouring another stein of lager. "Until then, I can offer you what he's having."

"Oh. Thanks..." Kira said, accepting her stein without question.

"Sure, hon. Now what to eat?"

Briar gazed through a window opening that separated the dining hall from the kitchen. A cook worked to cut strips of meat from a goat with a skilled blade. "Binx, can you prepare a veggie plate?"

"No meat?" She huffed. "You on some sort of Gezmekian diet now that you're king?"

Kira leaned in, rolling her eyes. "It's for his horse."

"Ah!" A smile grew for the first time on Binx's thick face. "My favorite client. William shall eat like a king."

Briar tapped the bar. "That's perfect. Prepare it as such. Oh, and with hummus! And then we will have the mutton pies."

"Sure, but we won't have hummus until my shipment from Ammos arrives in a few days." She walked to the window, relaying their order to the cook.

Briar's face lit up and he turned to Kira. "Say, why don't we go shopping when the trade ships dock? I know all your things just arrived from Colville, but the market is an exciting place when fresh goods come in."

"Shop for clothes?" She looked down at her dress. It was nice, no doubt, but it didn't quite fit. As with most of her wears. Either they were altered from what she'd stolen, or gifted from Briar. "I've never done that. Sounds fun."

"Didn't you buy this dress?" He tapped at the frill.

Kira just smiled, blinking innocently.

"Kira..."

She leaned in to whisper. "I *may* have borrowed this from the laundry."

Briar laughed. "You are trouble."

"Best have a couple of guards keep their eyes on me when we go to the market then." She winked.

"You know it, and I'll be one of them in case an arrest is in order." He kissed her ear—teeth nipping the lobe as if promising discipline.

"You need to be able to catch a thief first." Kira slipped from his encroaching fingers on her leg. Taking her stein, she walked backward. "Let's go sit at the booth."

Briar kept planted on his stool with a frown. "I always sit here," he said, fixing his arm into a worn dip and grinding the stein in a depression marked on the bar.

"I see that, but I always sit in a corner where no one can listen to our conversations or watch me." She tilted her head toward the gathering mass.

The crowd stiffened as their king looked their way. Some faces peeled from the windowpanes. Several heads bobbed to see over those in front, while others hid. A few brave eavesdroppers slipped through the door, filling the mostly empty tavern. More than a few cheeks grew rosy, and several onlookers sheepishly waved. When Briar lifted his hand in response, they grew giddy with acknowledgment. He rose from his stool. "The way they gawk, you'd think they'd forgotten I used to live right down the road."

"It's rare to see the crested dining at a common tavern. Or even out at all. Especially royalty." Kira led the way to the corner nearest to the river.

Briar sunk into the booth and slid to the window looking out. "I don't see why it should matter. I've always been their prince, and no one gave more than a fleeting glance when I walked the town. Most moved away. I didn't expect it to be any different."

Kira sat beside him pointing at Exten, where an invisible

barrier kept people a lance length away. "You hold power now. With it comes respect. And attention."

Briar twisted the stein in his hands. "That will take some getting used to. I was joking before, but perhaps Alden has the right idea, always dressing as a guard when he's out and about."

"Right? How many times have I walked past him without noticing?"

Briar chuckled. "More than you know."

"Hey, just know I'm the one who taught him how to be sneaky."

Briar leaned back. "Noted."

Kira looked down at her stein. Frothy and rich with a yellow glow, the lager promised a refreshment. Without the worry of the guild bearing down on her and accompanied by a crowned king, she reached for it. Sipping, Kira winced. Although smooth, a revolting bitterness assaulted her mouth. She set it down. "I understand Binx's sign now. It tastes like cat piss."

"Really." Briar drew a healthy gulp. He bobbed his head admittedly. "Yeah... I guess it does. But it was all I could afford as an outcast prince, and I guess I grew to like it."

"And Alden had made me into a tea snob who hates booze." She rested the drink on the table, she watched the ripples calm and settle. "Do you think he will ever hold power again?"

"That's for him to decide."

"Then I'm sure it will happen." Kira cozied into Briar's side. "I think he is more determined now than ever."

"I think your friendship with him over the years has a lot to do with that," said Briar. "And I think I realize why now. You two are...quite close."

Kira pulled away slightly, flicking her eyes up and down his body. "Is that jealousy I'm detecting, Briar Densen?"

His frown proved it.

Briar stroked her fingers with the back of his own. "I know he adores you. And seeing you two hanging off each other makes it hard for me not to be."

Kira rested her chin on Briar's shoulder, pouting her eyes up at him. "We are just friends!"

His brow tested. "I don't see you cuddling that close to Squirrel."

Scoffing at the absurdity, Kira sat up. She opened her mouth only to slowly close it with a bite of her lip. "Oh. Yeah, I see how that probably looks now. But we've been like that for years, ya don't need to worry. Alden has never come onto me."

"And I wouldn't expect him to, but I'm not one to share..." Briar took her hand, holding it tight as if she might slip away.

Looking at it, Kira smiled. "You don't need to. I'm yours. I promise." She squeezed back.

A wave of relief sighed from Briar as he wrapped his arm around her. "Good. You can trust the same from me. But it has been nice to see how he's stayed sober and fit because of you."

"Maybe, but being with Mayli has given him a spark in his eyes I've never seen."

Briar chuckled. "Oh, I've seen that look before."

"Oh?" Kira wiggled her shoulders. "Do tell."

Briar nodded. "It wasn't until Princess Mayli wrote to him that he started to take his role as prince seriously."

"Wait." Kira waved her hands, eyes fluttering. "Mayli, wrote to *him* first? I thought princes were to do the courting."

"Gender is irrelevant, but they must be crested to send letters. And I'm sure every crested man in Vatan *had* written to Princess Mayli—even me." He smiled sheepishly. "All but my cousin, despite his ink, and I think that stood out to her."

"Go figure he'd be the one playing hard to get."

"That wasn't it. Pressure from his father to be the next heir to Vatan pushed Colin to become lost in his habit."

"His habit?"

He raised his stein. "Boozing. That and overeating. It's how he grew a belly, and quite honestly, intolerable. But then, he found purpose."

"Mayli," Kira said.

Briar sipped. "Yep. Love. Which made his father so proud to see him reanimated that he invited Mayli to Brimley so that they may officially propose. That had him going on runs with me. Learning it took more than exercise to lose weight, he adjusted his diet and tossed the bottle. Soon he began joining me and his brother in classes, picked up sword fighting, and dancing."

"So wait..." Kira leaned into the table. "If Alden quit drinking to impress Mayli, does that mean he wasn't actually drunk on the night of Margaret's murder?"

Shame snarled on Briar's lip. "I may have been a bad influence that night."

"You?"

Briar rubbed the back of his neck. "I convinced him to drink a bottle of mead with us that night."

"Oh..."

"Then he took a shot of dune ale."

"Uff."

"Yeah. We were fools." He hung his head. "Then after Brimley fell and we were on the run, I suggested we drink our sorrows away, but he said that wasn't him anymore. That he was *all done.*"

"All done..." Kira let the words roll in her mouth, then blinked. "Wait, like *Alden*?"

"Yep. I teased him with the name at first, but for him, the words became a promise—an oath. He said when people called him Alden it was a reminder of the life he had put behind. That he wasn't going to make those mistakes again."

Kira sighed. "He really isn't the same person anymore, is he?"

"Although his habits have changed, he's exactly who he's always been, Kira."

"And who's that?"

"A lovelorn prince."

CHAPTER SEVEN
THE LOVELORN PRINCE

Alden lifted the last article of clothing from a patched canvas sack and folded it neatly. Looking over the array of his belongings delivered from his room at the Five Leaves in Colville, he set the tunic inside his dresser with the rest and smiled. Briar's most trusted men seemed to have collected everything, from his clothes to his supply of Brimleyn tea, excess armor, art supplies, and his extra set of throwing knives. They even followed his careful directions to his secret stash where he kept notes on the guild and thoughts on the mystery behind Queen Margaret's murder.

Sitting back down at his desk, Alden dragged his elbows on the surface and pressed the heels of his palms to the recesses of his eyes. He rubbed, welcoming the mild pain and wishing the allegations against him would just disappear. For the last three years, he had spent nearly every night reading, long days studying, and countless hours regretting but still, the suspension remained.

A soft nudge pressed against him, bumping a wet nose across his knuckles. Tiny black paws marched on loose papers, crinkling them. Alden didn't mind—there was no room for his cat to sit, and besides, the notes all seemed meaningless. "Nothing. How, Rek? After so long, how can I not remember what happened after being invited to the queen's chamber? Or find any evidence that I didn't do it? And even with the princess being kidnapped, I still have no idea who hired the attack or if the events are related."

Rek's white chin disappeared into the blackness of his fur as he yawned. His one good eye remained squinted, matching his blind one.

Purrs erupted.

Alden smiled.

Glad his friend had endured an eventless journey along with his possessions, Alden reached to pet him. When he had first found Rek, the cat had been but a heap of wet fur on the side of the road leading to Colville. It had mewled softly, drawing Alden to investigate. Wagon treads crossed a mud puddle beside it.

Blood dampened its face, its eye swollen. For a moment, Alden had considered putting the injured cat out of its misery. However, the thought of killing anything after being accused of murder had hung heavily on his heart.

"You got into a bit of a trouble there too, didn't ya..." Alden had said, cradling the cat. It lay weakly in his arms as he wiped its head clean. Tiny claws strained to cling to him. Alden hugged it close, feeling the need for company after being kicked out of his grandparent's mill just as much as the cat needed him. "We'll fix this wreck."

"Mrea," the cat mewed.

"You like that? Rek?"

Rek purred.

Caring for something, Alden felt free to share the details of his life with the one-eyed cat. Over the years, Rek had learned

Alden's true identity as Prince Colin Densen, heir of Vatan. He knew Alden was wanted for murder and blamed for the kingdom of Brimley's demise. He knew that if the killer wasn't found Alden could never live a life outside of shadows—never be able to share a life with anyone other than a cat. Rek knew that despite the accusations and bloodshed hammered down from Ammos, Alden still loved their princess, Mayli Drake. Rek was also acutely aware of Alden's harbored feelings for the thief he'd met in Colville: Kira. He understood how neither women were options Alden could rightfully consider, nor anyone else, as he was branded as an outcast royal. And only Rek knew how close Alden had come to searing off that tattoo months ago to be free. Thankfully, he'd meowed loudly as a voice of reason, and soon after he was on the mission to kidnap and rescue the princess.

Rek's ears perked as laughter echoed from outside Alden's door. It was loud, thus familiar. *Squirrel.* At Alden's request, the young teen boy was allowed to continue serving as a Yellow-Coat guard with him so he may stand at his door. The boy would have found a way even if Briar refused—his loyalty always prevailed. Regardless of their bond, Alden continued to keep his identity secret from Squirrel. Not that he didn't trust him, but he didn't think the boy would handle the reveal well having lost so much because of him.

Despite the door being locked, it suddenly creaked open. Alden groaned. "Squirrel, I told ya not to let anyone in..."

"I didn't!" His maturing voice cracked.

Alden dropped his hands to the desk and threw a look at the yawning door, mouth opening to argue.

"I let myself in," said Kira as a bold black and yellow dress swished into the room. The skirt of the gown dusted the floor in her wake where the front was cut higher, showing off firm legs laced in matching stockings and just a sliver of skin across her thigh. Black leather boots paused just a half-step past the door. "If that okay?"

Alden retired his sour glare for a welcoming grin. "Noble life has changed ya."

Kira closed the door before Rek could escape. She scooped him up and cradled him like a baby, swaying naturally from side to side. "That so?"

"Yep." Alden leaned into his cushioned chair. "Now you're asking permission to invade."

"Is that what you think about my presence? An invasion?"

"Has it ever not been?" He smirked.

Her head cocked as she sent her eyes to the ceiling in thought. Teeth chewed her red-painted lip. Face set with foundation, cheeks rouged, braids neatly woven, and an elegantly embroidered sash purse hanging around her hips, Kira was as elegant as any princess. *Maybe more than Mayli.* As a thief, her strength, wisdom, and cunning personality had already won his admiration the day she pinned him to a dusty loft. But now, as a member of the court—not the thieves guild—she drew admiration from all, even other kings.

Rek pawed at the three blue gems hanging from Kira's neck, making them sparkle in the firelight. Alden inhaled deeply, recognizing the charm. It had belonged to his aunt, Princess Trish. Not even Briar's ex—whom he'd spoiled rotten, had received such precious gifts. Yet it lay like the Stars of Gezmek on Kira's chest. Alden's lip twitched. "That necklace suits you."

"Does it?" She pressed her chin to her neck to look, rolling skin.

"It was one of the few things Briar has left of his mother's."

Kira lifted the necklace, eyes dazzled. "This was his mother's?"

"Mmhmm. Those gems are some of the so-called lost treasures of Gezmek. The same ones inlayed in the King's Blade,

Briar's crown, or his father's sword." Alden leaned into the arm of his chair. "His father had gifted it to her which is why he was able to keep it after her death."

Kira twisted it in her fingers, going cross-eyed. "Briar didn't tell me any of that when he gave it to me..."

"Nah, he wouldn't..." Alden followed the pendant as Kira rested it between the crease of her breasts. "But there isn't a ball tonight. Why are you all dressed up?"

"What, I can't wear nice things?" Kira kissed Rek's face then set the cat on the floor. She walked to Alden and pushed a pile of books aside. With a hop, she pulled herself up to sit on his desk. Crossing her legs, she flared out the layers of tufted fabric as if she sat upon a throne.

Alden pinched the fabric and lifted it curiously. "Well, compared to your usual attire, it's pretty outrageous for just walking about."

Kira tugged it back. "If ya don't like it, you can just say so."

He smiled. "I like it, Ki. I'm just teasing. Glad you are adjusting to life here." He leaned into his chair, crossing his arms.

"It does bother me to not have pockets." She tapped at her side. "Maybe I'll start another trend. Wanna be my designer?"

"Oh no." Alden waggled a finger. "If ya thought life in the thieves guild was stressful and cutthroat ya don't wanna get involved in the chaos of fashion design here."

Kira laughed. "I think I already have. Have you noticed that after the dance, women all over have worn loose ribbons and flyaway hair? They act like I was making some kind of statement that night. It's only a matter of time before they start wearing boots." She twisted her leather-bound foot around.

Alden shrugged. "You're someone to look up to."

"I must use my powers wisely then..." Kira slid her hand

back, bumping into a journal. She picked it up and started flipping through. Her face contorted as she thumbed over a line.

Alden snatched the journal before she could snoop any further.

"Why can't I read that? You think I'm a threat or something?"

Tucking the journal in his jacket pocket, he shook his head. "Ya know I like my privacy."

She ticked up a brow. "Still from me? After everything? After you know I'm on your side?"

Scratching fingers through his thickening beard, Alden blinked up.

"I still frighten you, don't I?" she asked.

"Kira, you—"

She uncoiled one finger at a time. "Stalked you, fought for you, harassed you, once mocked you as a king, stole your favorite sweater, and broke into your loft how many times?"

He opened his mouth.

She waved her open hand. "Don't answer that—you can't count that high."

Alden scoffed, looking at Rek as he jumped onto the table.

"Right, and I won over your cat!" She scratched Rek's head, summoning purrs. "I did all that up until you refused to undress... That and your ignorance of a commoner's life got me thinking; this guy's hiding something. I wouldn't be a very good Shadow Seeker if I didn't suspect you were at least crested...*Colin*."

"Don't call me that."

Her mouth hitched open. She closed it and gave a curt nod. "Fine. But ya know what I did with all that knowledge? Kept it. Not only that, but I then arranged for you to be front and center in Mayli's kidnapping in hopes of mending her misconceptions about you. I helped you two escape, then I lied to Pierz. After I fled the thieves guild, I managed to get crested, aided in a king's murder, helped crown another, and got myself in bed with him."

Alden's jaw tightened.

"So I get it, I can be devious. But I'd never do anything to hurt you. Only help." She leaned in to grip his shoulder and his chair creaked. "So you can trust me!"

He stared at her hand clenched on his arm. Touching another's crest was intimate. This was the first time she did so where they shared his secret identity. He didn't mind. With all Kira knew, he was shocked by only one thing. "You have my old sweater?" he asked, peering up at her.

Pulling away, Kira showed her teeth, offering a guilty smile while batting her eyes.

Alden laughed. "I assumed I had lost it in the Cads last year."

"Nope." Kira sat straight, the journal he'd just tucked away now back in her thieving hands. She flipped through nonchalantly. "You watched me steal it right off of you the night after we returned. I intended to give it back...but it reminds me of you."

That's right... After nearly losing their lives for Pierz's secret mission, he'd been so infatuated with wanting to share his love with her that he'd nearly forgotten the tattoo that he hid. While deep inside her, Kira had managed to remove his sweater and was attempting to unbutton his tunic to expose skin just like he'd done with her. As his body became exposed, panic had set in. *She's rallied off about her hatred of the Brimleyn royals before... Kira is a Shadowen. She will kill me! Turn me in! I can't. We can't...* With thundering anxiety poisoning his thoughts, Alden had fled her bed. A lost opportunity as that night she had seemed to learn his identity anyway. He sighed. "I completely forgot I'd been wearing it that night..." Alden said, rubbing the back of his head.

"I don't think I've forgotten anything from that night," she said softly, eyes averted.

Alden flushed, lowering his own gaze. Her hands lay in her lap, nervously touching her nails' long polished points. She'd painted them blue for Brimley. Alden smiled at that and reached to hold them. They were softer than he remembered, free from cuts and calluses and now were slick with a moisturizing cream that smelled of vanilla and daylilies—something new. He squeezed and found her eyes. "Kira, while your actions often made me want to scream, you don't threaten or frighten me anymore. You empower me. Always have."

Her smile twisted into a catlike grin. "Does this mean I get to keep the sweater?"

He smiled. "Sure."

"Really?" Her eyes grew, and he wanted to fall into them.

"Yeah. Besides..." He brushed his thumb over her fingers to caress her thigh. "I like that you still think of me from that night."

She lowered her gaze to follow the silken touch. Watching with heavy lids, her lips parted. Her chest grew with a tempered breath, raising the treasure of Gezmek to him. Heart beating for another moment bound with his old partner, Alden leaned closer. He slipped a finger under her dress's hemline, finding even softer skin.

Kira pulled her hands free from his hold and hopped off the desk. Tugging her socks up, she walked a few strides away. "So! I just had a lunch date with Briar."

Alden swallowed, staring at the spot where she'd just sat. A drawing of Briar he'd sketched remained on the journal Kira had left as if reminding him of who she chose to be with. Forcing a smile, Alden twisted in his chair to face her. "Oh yeah?" he asked, noticing his accent heavy with embarrassment.

"Yep," she said, walking to the door. "We went to his favorite place."

"The Binx & Drinx?" Alden flicked his eyes up and down her grand and alluring outfit. "Dressed like *that*?"

She spun on her heel. "Well, I didn't expect the king would take me to the mangiest tavern in the whole kingdom."

Alden chuckled, slouching an arm on the back of his chair. "I can take you somewhere nice if you like?"

Kira exchanged her joyous smile for a fighting glare. "Don't flirt with me anymore."

He sent his hands up, looking away. "I wasn't."

"And don't lie."

"Sorry..."

An awkward silence lingered.

Alden kept his head down, absently flipping through his journal. Each page sketched of Briar and Kira was a reminder that he'd missed his chance.

Kira sighed deeply, drawing his attention back to her. She stood at the door, hand on the knob. "Ya know, trade ships are arriving from Ammos soon. There's likely word from your princess by now. Best you stay focused on her."

CHAPTER EIGHT

AMMOS

Incense smoke beside a tall iron door twirled in wisps like ribbon dancers, beckoning her faster through the grand hall. Mayli hurried, each step closer to the familiar aroma of home.

A smiling guard pulled the door wide as Mayli rushed out onto the open-aired patio. Orange light bounced off silk canopies, illuminating the colonnade's carved plaster. Horseshoe arches bowed on the upper balcony. Delicately crafted tile mosaics sparkled on the walls. Palm trees stretched above the clay roof tiles and clapped for her arrival in the hot breeze. A white cloud parted, and the shadows within the semi-dome recess lit as if the morning sun was rising. Seated within, her father, King Bakhari of Ammos, crowned in gold and wrapped with silken grace, rose with open arms.

"Father!" Mayli ran across the rug-lined tile, her footsteps echoing over the shallow fountains to her sides. Her father jogged down the steps to meet her. She dove into his embrace, coiling her arms tightly around his sturdy body. The bitter, acrid scent of his pipes wafted closer, suffocating her. Despite the sting it left in her throat, she nuzzled deeper. "I missed you."

"And I you, Little Bird..."

After three weeks, the dam of her emotions broke. Tears spilled upon her father's white silks. All of what she'd gone through—too much to hide. The battling swells of fear, love, and loss poured from her in waves she hadn't let out since her mother's death. They splashed over to her father, his own body swaying with compassion.

"There, there," her father cooed.

Mayli sniffed and pulled back, wiping soggy eyes.

Cheeks balled with sympathy, Bakhari looked Mayli up and down. His smile wavered. "Look at what's become of you! They've brought you back a mess. And where's your mother's scarf?" He swept a tangled weave of hair behind her back as if searching to find the article.

Mayli touched her bare neck. "I lost it in the Cads."

"As in, the Cad Islands?"

She nodded.

Her father groaned, rubbing his forehead where a bead of sweat glistened. "Perhaps you would like to get cleaned up before we talk further? Some makeup and fresh silks will make you feel more like yourself."

Mayli touched her cheek. Despite being uncharacteristically free from painted beauty, her skin felt clean. Better than most days when she was forced to paint blemishes caused by the makeup itself. Regardless of being dressed in commoner's clothes, she took comfort and pride in having picked them out herself. Nothing screamed royalty, yet somehow she felt more powerful than ever. She smiled confidently at her father. "I'd like to rest beside you for a moment before I'm kidnapped again. This time by hairdressers, seamstresses, and servants." She raised a finger and winked.

A rumble of amusement rolled from her father. "Of course. I am sure you are exhausted. Come and sit." He turned to walk back up the dais. Four elegant chairs waited in grandeur. The largest, in the center, boasted an array of elaborate designs piped with gold carved into the dark wood, which itself had been milled from the now buried forest of Gezmek. It had been a wedding gift from the King and Queen of Vatan when Mayli's great grandfather married the queen's sister. Since Gezmek's demise, the throne's history carried great status for Ammos. Her father swept an embroidered cushion with his hand and eased into it.

Beside him stood a metal throne shaped like an arrowhead. Imported from Hiore, the steel shone like a mirror reflecting the inner patio. Jewels adorning the edges glimmered as if polished daily with tender and obsessive care. It had been three years since anyone had sat in it.

Flanking the king's and queen's thrones was a matching set made from a combination of both metal and wood. They were smaller and less detailed, but each had large metal arrowheads peaking the headrest. Blue gems glowed at their tops. Mayli sat in hers beside her father while gesturing at the other. "Where's Jair?"

"He's been gussying up. You know how much he prides his looks."

"You mean he didn't insist on going on an adventure to find me?"

"Oh, ho ho, he did!" Her father chuckled. "But I wasn't eager to lose the rest of my family so quickly."

The doors into the court rumbled shut.

Her father frowned deeply as he looked at the intrusion. "Damgard," he called in his kingly tone.

Three guards stood at the door. One Charli, the other two larger and clad in Hiorean plate and Ammosian Silks. An orange cape draped around their necks before cascading down their backs instantly identifying them as Ammosian Royal Knights and Charli's parents. Sir Dallion looked much like Charli although with an even darker complexion, and Madam Nive was pale-skinned from her Hiorean roots. They exchanged looks before his mother nodded for her son to go forth.

Charli glided from the position, but his steps were weighted. Since leaving the Desert of Gezmek, its prince, and half of *Her Lady Damgard's* crew behind, Charli was worn and sleep-deprived. Like Mayli, he was still dressed in the same garments from their travels, his sleeves torn off, clothes soiled from fish and seafaring muck. Hair had bloomed on his usually smooth scalp and face, dusting his dark skin in a rugged warrior's appearance.

Coming to the base of the dais he gracefully knelt to one knee. Bowing his head, he covered his exposed shoulder. "Your Majesty."

"Charli Damgard," the king's voice cracked through the dry air, commanding Charli's head to rise. They held each other's eyes in contest. When neither blinked, Bakhari cleared his throat. "I strictly forbade you to see my daughter after overstepping your obligations as a royal guard. To ensure I could monitor your devious acts, you were to be positioned at *my* side. Furthermore, I refused your request to search, yet you abandoned your post to seek her out anyway. This jeopardized my life—*your king*. Do you deny this treachery?"

Mayli whipped her head to Charli, blinking in surprise. *He went against orders?*

"I do not," Charli said.

Oh no.

The metallic draw of Bakhari's sword pierced the air. He took a slow step down. Then another. Charli held his position as the sword's point tapped his hand gripped on his shoulder.

Obeying, he lowered it, exposing the inked falcon to flare its wings. "Your actions aren't something I can easily ignore," said Bakhari, and Charli's muscles tensed as the sharp tip threatened to sever the crest.

Mayli's heart raced, thundering for her to scream. *A slashed crest would demote him from the guard. Removing him from the castle. Maybe from Ammos. From...me.* Mayli stepped from her throne and placed her hands on her father's arm, pulling at his stone-held posture. "Father, stop! He saved me! Please, you can't—"

"Mayli." The tone was deafening, leaving her mouth to hang open. Her father turned his head. "Perhaps had this man been at your side from the start, you wouldn't have endured such a horrible journey."

Her lips trembled. "What?"

"I won't risk that again." Bakhari arched the sword to Charli's other shoulder, his attention once more firm and kingly. "Sir Charli Damgard, you are relieved as my personal guard to resume your past duties."

Charli rose slightly, staying folded in his bow. "Thank you, Your Majesty."

"Sir? *Sir!* You *knighted* him?" Mayli's mouth gaped as she looked between her father and Charli. *Sir Charli.* Her eyes fluttered in confusion, trying to comprehend the swift passage of events. She waved her hands. "Wait, does that mean you're reassigning him back to me?"

Her father stepped back. "Yes. But need I remind you both that a door guard shall remain *outside* your door!" He crossed his arms.

The way her stomach flopped, Mayli wondered as if she were still out at sea. She bobbed her head slowly, processing the waves of emotion that just hit her, then shook it. "You won't need to worry about that anymore, Father. I promise."

With eyes observing every subtle detail on her face and no lies to detect, Bakhari's tight expression loosened. A fatherly smile grew from it. "Good. Now, Mayli, I've already sent for you to be brought a private bath, so do get cleaned up and well-rested before your brother comes along ordering you around like a servant."

"He does anyway," Mayli laughed.

Her father took a step back, giving way for her.

She skipped a step, landing at Charli's side. He winked past his cocky grin, and Mayli nudged him playfully in passing. The familiar swish and clang of his swagger lingered behind.

"And Damgard..." Bakhari called as they neared the fountains.

Charli turned at full attention, his hand over his crest.

"If you so much as look at my daughter in lust I will be sure to sever the Damgard lineage serving this family." The king pointed his sword between Charli's legs. "Understood?"

Mayli saw Charli's parents shift and straighten at the door.

Unthreatened, Charli bowed. "Yes, Your Majesty."

Bakhari sheathed his weapon. "Good."

Slowly, they funneled into the adjacent hall. After clearing her father's sightline, Mayli spun and walked backward. She laughed, spreading her hands out to show him off. "You're a knight!"

"Of course I am." Charli gave a championed smile and looked onward, chin high and mighty.

She shook her head, eyes wide. "I feared Father was going to sever your crest."

He chuckled, looking down on her. "Princess, I'm much too valuable. Your father understands that you require those strongest stationed close, and he needed to be reminded who that was. Me."

Mayli twisted around the corner leading up a stairwell,

walking backward up a step, and raised a finger. "Just not too close." Not wanting to discuss their shifting relationship, Mayli jogged to the covered deck above.

A pacing archer straightened to attention and dipped his head in acknowledgment, never letting his fingers leave his weapon. She smiled and continued along the balcony. Looking over the railing, Mayli saw her father watching from his throne, his smile content seeing Charli trailing at a respectable distance. She waved before tucking into her room at the end.

Charli took position beside her door. "You know where to find me."

"Thank you, *Sir* Charli," she said, slipping into her chamber.

Everything was as she expected. Clean, crisp, organized. Her bed was made with layers of orange silks with beautifully embroidered feathers in white thread along the edges. The carved wood seats of her lounge were polished and topped with plush, down pillows. The mosaic tile floor glistened. Birds sang within their cage. Her bow and quiver hung on the wall.

Crossing her spacious room, Mayli reached the only piece untouched by servants: her mother's iron vanity. Several hair-brushes, two hand mirrors, berets, ties, pins, powders, perfumes, and makeup cluttered it. Scarves of assorted colors draped from one corner to the other. Necklaces hung. The last letter from her mother sat framed.

"I love you, I miss you. Shoot true," she read.

A volley of pent-up sorrows came firing down, piercing her heart in a million pieces. She collapsed into her stool, crying from the pain and loss of her mother. Tears shed down her cheeks. Her hands shook. Crossing her arms, she wished she could feel her mother's hug, hear her sing as fingers brushed through her hair, and wished the gentle caress of her silk scarf still lifted her chin. Most of all, Mayli wished she never argued with her mother in the days before she left to Brimley.

Weak with guilt, her leg slipped. It bumped into something, and she lifted from her cocoon. There at her feet was the bag from her trip, brought up thanks to servants. Drying her face on her sleeve and holding in tears, Mayli reached inside.

First came the dress with the long sleeves and thumbholes —torn now from Charli's advances. She set it aside, noting to have it mended. Next, she pulled the casual yet formal shirts she scavenged from Brimley. Leaving them in her lap, she caught sight of the yellow and black Dreggen dress Briar had picked out for her. She lifted it and grinned. It was beautiful, even for a commoner. Last was the assortment of clothes she'd bought with Alden in the Cads.

Excited to see them all, she stood and folded each outfit over a tri-panel wood divider. She smirked as the dark style clashed against the bright glam of her room. Despite it, they comforted her more than any of the finery stored in her wardrobe.

Sitting once more, Mayli pulled the next item from the bag into her lap. A box. She opened the lid revealing the delicate dried rose. With care, she brought it to her nose. The smell was muted but still distinctly floral. She blushed remembering Alden's coy grin beaming at her after he'd stolen the flower from the man in red. She strung its stem through a loop of her vanity's intricate metal filigree in honor of his valiant efforts to steal her away and bring her home.

Looking back inside the box, she saw a wrinkled piece of paper. Mayli held her breath. *The drawing.* She picked it up and traced her thumb over the lines made by Alden's honest hand that formed her. He'd drawn her with eyes low. Lips too. Her hair seemed to dance freely, yet she was stuck in place. Mayli sighed. *Alden captured a vision no one ever wanted to see; the true and melancholic loneliness I feel.* Faint writing bled through from the back. She flipped it over reading the relaxed yet elegant script of an artist.

May, I hope someday you'll forgive me.

"Oh, Alden... I have," she said, tucking the drawing between the mirror and its frame.

Still aglow, Mayli looked to see a small twenty-sided die remained in the box, the number ten staring innocently up at her. *Oh no. I'm not rolling you again,* she thought, closing the box's lid.

Mayli pulled the last item from the bag: Alden's blade. She closed her eyes and clung to the knife feeling its weight just like when he had pressed it in her hands. As memories of that moment rushed back, Mayli's lips began to move. Her tongue lifted, gliding across her teeth to relive his kiss. It had been rough. Desired. Deserved...

"Wheel that into the corner, and be quick with it!" shouted a crotchety voice. "You've already let it lose too much heat!"

Startled, Mayli threw the knife into a drawer and slammed it shut. Crisp petals shattered from Alden's flower, littering her vanity as it rattled. She bit her lip at the destruction, then glared at the open door. Three handmaidens bustled inside with a deep copper tub, steaming water sloshing. Beyond followed an old woman pushing a tea cart. As if holding wrinkles in place, a scarf was wrapped under her neck and tied back and around her head.

"Lidia?" Mayli burst from her seat, running to her lady-in-waiting. She wrapped tight arms around the woman's boney body. "You're alive!"

Lidia patted her back. "You can't get rid of me so easily, Mayli Drake. Keegan did well to get me home."

Mayli pulled back. "Who is Keegan?"

"Your guard..." Lidia glanced at the doorway. "But I see that Damgard is once again assigned to you as well?"

Charli's smile vanished as he shut the door.

Mayli turned back to Lidia. "Father knighted him then awarded him the honor after he found me."

Lidia's one droopy eye widened. "Does this mean I need to keep a heavy watch?"

"No, Lidia. We are through."

Her brow tested.

"I've matured since."

The arch grew higher.

"Truly!"

"Good." Lidia took a teapot from her cart and poured the hot liquid into a delicate crystal cup. The smell of orange blossomed. "I don't want to be cleaning up those unsightly messes again."

Mayli flushed. "You knew?"

"My lady, believe it or not, I was once a young maiden such as yourself. After men and all their might." She wiggled her shoulders, fluttering her eyes. "I know exactly what activities go on between them."

Mayli shuddered at the idea of Lidia sashaying about. "Ew."

She pursed her lips. "How else do you think I earned the Seneschal's eye?"

"You two weren't arranged?"

"That was at a time when such things weren't necessary." Lidia looked at the closed door. "Anyway, I saw that guard was the only thing able to make you smile after your mother's passing. How could I deny you that?"

Ease sweeping over her, Mayli hugged Lidia. "Thank you, Lidia. You've been like a mother to me."

"Please, I can never measure up to such an elegant woman. And Queen Margaret wouldn't have allowed such risqué nonsense because she did believe in arrangements." She pulled back and offered Mayli the tea. "I am merely your lady-in-waiting, here to serve you."

Mayli accepted it and took a sip. The spiced citrus was soothing, yet now felt as though it lacked something. She pulled it away. "May I have some cream with this?"

"Cream?" Lidia's face seemed to weather as her nose bunched. "Whatever for would you want to ruin a good cup of tea with *that*?"

Mayli set it down. "It's nice. I grew to like it in Northern Vatan. It even makes Brimleyn tea smooth, and sugar sweetens it. It tastes completely different!"

Lidia's lips exaggerated downward as her brows grew tall. "Well here in the south, we don't use any."

"Don't use any? I'm sure the kitchen has some cream..." Mayli leaned forward as if to see past the door.

"I'm sorry, Mayli. We are fresh out; you'll have to enjoy tea as you once had." Lidia turned Mayli to the bath and tapped her rump. "Now let's get you washed up. You look and smell worse than the thieves who stole you."

Sheer floor-to-ceiling drapes swept the room as a handmaiden opened the windowed doors to her private balcony, spilling in the afternoon light. Overlooking the island's sheer cliffs, a scenic view framed Sandwater Bay and the city gripping the promontory beyond. Rolling orange dunes skimmed the horizon. Centered between the windows was her long-awaited bath.

Mayli watched rosebuds swirl on the water's milky surface. She dipped a finger in. *Perfectly warmed and oiled.* Excited, Mayli grabbed the hem of her dress and began pulling it overhead. Two handmaidens rushed to her side and took hold. They easily stripped her free. Mayli stood idly, blinking as the women continued to relieve her of her undershirt.

"Everything all right?" asked Lidia, folding a towel on a nearby stool.

"Yes, I'm fine..." Mayli sat on the edge of the tub, giving one maiden access to unlace her boots. "It's just that, I've grown accustomed to dressing and undressing myself for weeks now. I wasn't expecting the aid."

Lidia took the tunic from the handmaiden with disgust. "Well by the looks of this schmatte, that was quite apparent! It's a good thing you have us. We'll dispose of them." She walked to the trifold where her clothes hang.

Mayli outstretched her hands. "Don't throw them out!"

Examining the yellow and black Dreggen dress with a sneer, Lidia pulled it from the divider. "What reason would you want to wear these for?"

Mayli crossed her arms. "Doesn't matter. They are mine."

Lidia's sigh was loud and disapproving. "What shall you have me to do with them instead?"

"Cleaned and returned, of course."

"This one has holes in the sleeves." She lifted another between two fingers.

"I'm aware. Leave those, but please have the tear above mended."

Pursing her lips, Lidia strained to smile. "Right." She handed the clothes to a handmaiden, leaving her to collect each outfit.

"Thank you," Mayli said.

Freed from her boots, socks, leggings, and undergarment, Mayli twisted to dip a toe into the water eager to soothe away the aches and pains she'd been fighting to ignore. The warmth pulled her in, until, fully submerged to her chin, she sighed in deep pleasure.

Lidia sat at the stool behind her and took Mayli's hair in her hands. "How am I going to sort this mess?"

"I've been wondering the same..."

"Perhaps scissors," said Lidia.

Mayli jerked around. "I don't need to cut it, do I?" She bit her trembling lip.

Lidia's shoulders sank, looking at Mayli with pity. She waved her back around. "Dip. We will soak it even if it takes all night."

Sighing in relief, Mayli obeyed. Water crept in, already loosening strands with the soft fragrant oils. A light wave touched her lips, and she licked the ocean's salt. Despite it being a private bath, and one for royalty, freshwater was still too precious a commodity to use so extravagantly in Ammos. She closed her eyes. "Thanks for this. It must have taken many trips to the cove to collect."

"That's twice now."

"Twice?"

"That you've thanked me." Lidia took Mayli's arm and began scrubbing. "You really have matured."

Mayli flinched, splashing water. "Ouch! That's not dirt."

Lidia brought Mayli's bruised wrist to her eyes. Squinting, she gasped. "You're hurt."

"I'm fine." Mayli took it back. "Just don't scrub so hard."

Lidia continued more delicately. "Colin will pay for hiring those thugs."

"Colin?" Mayli spun, splashing water over the edges. "He hired the thieves?"

"Well, of course." Lidia shifted Mayli's shoulders forward once more and began weaving her fingers through her hair while another handmaiden continued scrubbing her skin with kinder hands. "Such circumstances don't just happen out of pure coincidences."

Mayli winced as Lidia's crooked fingers caught in a large snarl. "So it's still just speculation?"

Forcing her fingers through, Lidia yanked hair apart in snapping strands. Mayli watched in horror as Lidia pulled clumps of hair from her fingers and flicked them to a tray. "Yes, but don't you worry. Your father has been diligent to seek revenge."

Mayli captured a drifting rose. "I'm sure he has..." She cradled the water-soaked flower, thinking back on the revenge her family had already delivered to Brimley before collecting all evidence and listening to all trials. Before seeing the devastation firsthand, Mayli hadn't thought of what such decisions actually meant. Talking about how they destroyed their kingdom versus actually seeing it in ruin, or how easy it was to slander their people for being loyal when all they wanted was a home was all too disturbing. Her family's rash decisions based on assumptions were the source of so much pain. Now, she worried that perhaps, somehow, Alden and Briar were right—that Colin *was* innocent. So sure that Alden suppressed his own feelings in respect for the prince's rooted esteem for her. *Colin can't possibly still love me?*

Before her mother's death, Colin had always written to her with such adoration. He asked about her interests. Wanted to know about Ammos. Her family. Her. After months he finally opened up about himself. About his family. He expressed his worry about being an heir to Vatan and how he'd drank so much to avoid the burden of responsibility. How it had become a bad habit. Then he confessed how she gave him the strength to fight for it. There was always such a tenderness in his words that Mayli had been convinced they were destined to be together. That once together, they would make each other whole.

So when news of Colin's betrayal had come, Mayli didn't want to believe it. They said he'd done it out of protest for her denying their union. In the name of love? Mayli denied it, trusting in the person she thought she knew. The prince who didn't seek power. The noble who had no interest in hunting. The man whose love honored more than just himself. For a long while, Mayli argued with her father that Colin had to be innocent as claimed. But as the king and the court explained the series of events and Colin's drunken state, she was forced to accept what they said as truth.

The absence of her mother had been evidence enough.

Lidia's hands raked smoothly through her hair again and again, the motions now soothing. "There. No need for scissors after all."

Mayli let loose a sigh of relief.

Knees popping, Lidia stood. "Have a good rest, princess. Your father has granted you a night of privacy, despite your brother's protest."

"Thank you, Lidia."

Her warm elderly smile stretched across her face. "I like this new, considerate you."

Mayli matched her glow. "Me too."

CHAPTER NINE

CLOSED BORDERS

"**E**arl, stop calling me Your Lordship while I'm wearing this, Okay?"

Alden looked from his sketchbook to the two guards stepping through the castle gates into the plaza. Like Alden, they were dressed in the uniform of the lowest-ranking guards. Despite the Yellow-Coat disguise, a familiar saber and proud, bow-legged gait still revealed the identity of Briar and the twitchy movements of Squirrel.

Briar tightened the strap under his chin. "The point is for people not to recognize me as their king."

Squirrel sunk his helm on. "Yes, Your...Briarship?"

Irritation quivered on Briar's face, but upon seeing Kira lounging on the fountain's edge with her hand creating ripples in the water, he sprouted a smile and hurried his pace. "Hey, pretty lady!"

Breaking pose, Kira lifted and turned to face him. "Hey, you!" She leapt to her feet, shaking her hand dry.

Droplets splashed on Alden's page, blurring the fine lines he'd steadily placed. He wiped it dry, only succeeding in further smudging his work. Sketch half-complete and now ruined, he snapped his sketchbook shut.

Kira and Briar were a tangle of arms and body—lips fused. Squirrel stood awkwardly beside them, impervious to the public act of affection. Neither he, Kira, nor Briar seemed to mind the crisp air and haze puffing from each breath, but Alden felt the cold throughout.

He sent his gaze back to the fountain, wishing the rush of water would drown out the sound of their kiss. Thankfully bells chimed, and a low hum of an excited crowd overpowered the enthusiastic display of affection. As music joined the jolly calls of merchants peddling the last of their goods, Alden watched children chase down the hill in eager anticipation. Looking further, he saw masts of the trade ships peeking over rooftops lining the port as they sailed in. Locals migrated to the market with empty carts or thin bags in hand, eager to fill them with precious silks, spices, art, and tobacco fresh from the southern kingdom.

Kira finally pulled away from Briar, lips smacking. "Hear that? Ships are in! I'm so excited to shop for fresh Ammosian goods. Aren't you, Alden?"

"Sure," he said.

Briar wagged a finger at Kira. "And we are going to be buying clothes and food, not stealing them. Right, Kira?"

"How could I steal something when I'm surrounded by all you guards?" She spread her palms up to the three of them. She chuckled then placed her hands at her hips. "Speaking of, where's your royal guard?"

Briar gestured at Alden. "Right here!"

Alden rolled his eyes. "Funny."

Briar smirked, then addressed Kira more seriously. "Sir Exten is guarding the door to our chamber and Sir Tarek helped me sneak past Fredrik before resuming his post."

"You're king," said Squirrel. "Why do you need to sneak past anyone under you?"

"Because, those below often shout the loudest, and Fredrik has the most obnoxious tone. One which I could do without for the rest of my rule."

"Then why keep him around?" asked Alden.

"He's loyal, and your father respects him."

"Respected," he corrected.

"Right." Briar lowered his head. "Apologies."

"It's fine," said Alden. "But he has passed, so you shouldn't still feel obligated to maintain his wishes."

"Aye, but I like to keep his spirit alive." Briar raised his hand for Alden to walk ahead. "Anyway, let's go."

Alden shrugged and began his march toward the docks. "Hey, Kira, Squirrel..."

They looked at him attentively.

"Keep your eyes peeled for Shadowens."

"Shadowens?" Briar walked beside him. "You don't think they'd show their faces at such a busy time?"

Kira skipped just ahead of Alden, then turned to walk backward, locking eyes with him mischievously. "We did most of our business in a packed crowd versus an empty street. Didn't we?"

Alden nodded, staying in her shade. "Shadows follow the light."

Grinning, she spun around, letting her dress twirl and wrap around her knee-high boots. "And the light shines of gold," she said as sunbeams illuminated the elegant weave of braids laced in her hair like a crown.

Despite the treasure before him, Alden's lips fell into a deep frown. Past the cobbled streets surrounding the castle, dirt and stink lined the curb. Among the trash, people just as rugged gathered. Many wore tattered clothes, worn-out shoes, and strips of rope used for belts. A few donned yellow to honor Dregs, along with blue in support of their Brimleyn heritage—a brave display of support for their new king and himself, hopeful for unity.

Squirrel hopped over a pair of outstretched legs of a man sleeping in the street, the playful action contrasting sharply with the serious uniform he wore. "Were there always so many homeless in Dregs?" he asked.

Briar shook his head. "No, because before I was crowned they were banned. And since becoming king, I abolished the limitations and fees for those entering the city. Because of that, refugees have moved in."

"Not with much luck it seems." Squirrel frowned at a couple of kids who looked to be his age. They were mangy and huddled in a doorway like a nest of rodents. Much like how Kira and Alden first found Squirrel, having earned his nickname.

A girl broke from the group and walked barefoot to a pavilion filled with plums, pears, dates, and figs. Her clothes were threadbare, exposing her skin to the chill air. She held out a pair of dirty shoes in exchange for a bag of lush fruit. The merchant waved his hand, shooing the girl from his stand. As she left, he hurled a plump fig. It splattered across her head.

Alden tightened his fists.

Having also watched, Squirrel retired his playful mannerism and marched toward the merchant with a firm scowl, grip fiercely held on his bow.

Before he could reach the stand, Briar grabbed the boy's arm, yanking him back. "Leave it."

Squirrel bunched his lips. "But, as guards, aren't we supposed to help?"

Briar's helm glinted as he shook his head. "They have a right to turn away business."

"But she was attacked!" He pointed to the girl.

Fruit dripped off her face. A few passersby laughed as she worked to save every piece and sucked on her fingers as if they too could provide nutrients.

Kira shrugged. "She got a free meal."

Squirrel spread his arms out forcing them all to stop. "But you're their king, and that's not right."

Briar tugged at his uniform. "Dressed as a guard, I have to follow the laws."

"Then change more laws," said Alden, watching his people huddle in the streets.

"It's not so easy..." Briar pushed forward, waving his arm around. "I can't just make people forget a past that still hurts them."

"What past?" Squirrel looked back at the display of fruits, then waved his finger from it to the girl. "Did they know each other?"

"The war," Alden said.

"Oh. I forgot about that..."

Briar scoffed. "How could you forget about that? Aren't you from Brimley?"

"Ha. I dunno," Squirrel said, wandering away. His smile fell as soon as he was out of sight of Briar's view.

Alden hated that look. Squirrel was always a character, be it hyper and annoying, or centered and serious. Usually the latter. But when he lacked either, wavering into despair, Alden's heart crushed. Passing a silk merchant's booth, he gestured to it. "Ey, Squirrel, why don't cha pick out a cloak you'd like."

The boy's eyes came back to life as he looked up, staring in awe at the assortment of cloaks he'd just passed by. Running over, he poked the nearest fabric. It shimmered like rays from the sun, gold, and white. His grin grew wide in wonder—the past that haunted him shut away once more.

Alden exchanged a look with Briar as they neared the shop. "He hasn't really forgotten, ya know."

"Seems pretty absent-minded to me," scoffed Briar. "Does he ever remember anything?"

"Yeah, he absorbs more information than any of us, I'm sure. But whatever happened to him during the war was traumatizing. I try not to upset him, and when he does fall into a gloom, I redirect his focus." Alden shifted his shoulders to watch Squirrel leaf through a rack of limited choices. "Not much selection of color…"

"I apologize for our low stock," said a chalky voice. Elaborately embroidered silks shimmered yellow and orange as a tan man came forward. He bowed, covering his noble Ammosian tattoo. "It has been a fortnight since our last shipment. But in a half-turn, we'll have silks in every color imaginable. Fresh from Ammos!" He gestured toward the port where a crowd busied together in eager anticipation. Crewmen were just about finished securing the last few ropes to hold the first trade ship.

Alden turned back to the mercer. "Even blue?"

The mercer shook his head. "You should know, Ammos hasn't dyed anything blue since the war. But don't let that keep you from shopping! There are still plenty of fine wears. Heh heh, it looks like your friends have found something of interest!"

Alden watched as Kira pulled a pink cloak and offered it to Squirrel. Unfazed by the bright color, Squirrel wrapped it around himself proudly. His smile was so wide Alden couldn't argue with their selection. "How much for that cloak?"

"Eighty gold."

With a squeal of nerves, Squirrel hunkered down as if the fabric weighed of gold.

Kira pulled the hood off Squirrel, freeing him. "Seems a bit high for such an unusual color."

"My lady, our cloaks usually run for over one hundred pieces!"

"No way!" She stole a handful of gold from Alden's purse as he opened it. She counted them in her palm then offered it. "Most I will offer is twenty-one gold."

Briar snatched Alden's coins from her. "Don't insult the man. His pricing is fair. To suggest otherwise is still theft, Kira."

"Your guards are right." The mercer eyed Alden's coin pouch with glossy eyes. "My prices are more than reasonable."

Kira crossed her arms, muscles testing the sleeves of her dress. "Is it? Because that color was a reject from last year's trend, was it not? I imagine this has sat unsold for just as long."

The silk merchant wavered, looking from her to Squirrel, who twirled his arms to watch the fabric shimmer. He cleared his voice and straightened. "Silks are silks, and their armor-like quality still applies regardless of the color. You won't find fakes or half blends anywhere in my shop. Those are down the street." He pointed to another booth whose array of blue fabrics lured in a group of Brimleyns.

"Is that so?" Kira took out her dagger and walked to Squirrel.

"Woah, wait, Kira!" Squirrel shrieked, holding up his hands. "I'll give back your sock no need to get hostile!"

She lowered her weapon. "My sock?"

"Yes! I'm very sorry!" Squirrel bent low to bow.

"Why just one? Why—" She closed her eyes and took in a tested breath. "Never mind, give me the cloak."

"Awe." Squirrel clicked off the buckle and laid the shimmering mound in Kira's hand.

The shopkeep watched without protest as Kira positioned the dagger to catch on the garment's hood. In one strong thrust, she pushed the weapon into it. As expected with true Ammosian Silks, the blade slipped off without wounding the fabric. Sheathing her dagger, Kira nodded approvingly. "Okay, so it is real."

"As I said, mine are made true. I only sell silks imported directly from Taji Vaurus in Ammos."

"Mr. Vaurus?" asked Alden. "He's the one who handles the kanavaurs for trial, right?"

"That is he. As am I. Clide Vaurus. One of the five brothers, you see. Which is why my wares are of the finest quality and worth all the gold. Trending colors or not."

"I'll buy it." Alden handed over the required sum.

Kira rolled her head. "Okay, but really? This color? I was joking when I gave it to him." She let the cloak hang, looking at it with disgust.

Squirrel's eyes wavered. "You always do this, Kira!"

Briar pinched fabric, bringing it to Squirrel. "I don't know. I think green suits Earl."

The boy's eyes grew with praise at the king's compliment.

"Briar." Alden chuckled. "That is pink."

"Well, then pink looks good on him." Briar took the cloak from Kira and gave it to Squirrel. "He'll need such a cloak if he's going to continue being a guard."

A tight wheeze of excitement heaved from Squirrel upon receiving the gift and acceptance. Wrapping it around himself, he hurried to find a mirror.

Alden laughed more as the boy ran. The silk glinted from pink to yellow. A faint undertone of orange shimmered in between, but nothing close to green. He grinned at Briar, shaking his head. "You were never good in Da's art classes to get the colors right. Always painted the trees red."

"I don't have the patience to memorize the subtle differences in colors and what their names are."

"Yet you do well to remember each of your guard's names," said Kira.

"They matter. Colors don't."

"Perhaps you just can't see them?" Alden lifted three scarves, each one green. "Which one is red?"

Kira opened her mouth, but Alden threw a look to shush.

Briar looked between the trio, squinting. Rolling his eyes, he grabbed the one in the middle and shook it. "This one."

Alden restrained himself from laughing. "That's correct..."

Briar tossed it on the table. "I see just fine, thank you. Like how I know that will look good on you, milady." He stepped past Alden and hooked his arm around Kira's waist.

Heat crawled up Alden's neck. Kira held a scandalous white nightdress to herself. He swallowed. The lace was blue like her fingernails.

"You think so?" She tugged at the short hem.

Briar's hands toured the hourglass figure of the gown. "I know so. Much better than that big ugly sweater you've been sleeping in."

Alden drew his brow high. *She sleeps in my stolen sweater?*

Kira's eye twitched as if she was struggling not to meet Alden's gaze. She pressed her lips in a fine line as a blush began to glow. Refraining from looking, she stayed focused on Briar who did little to conceal his thoughts with a lick of his lips. Kira bunched the nightdress in her hands and smiled at him with a look just as devious. "I think you're right!"

Briar pulled her in his arms and leaned in for an arousing kiss—their lips falling together in sloppy strokes.

Uncomfortable, Alden turned to find Squirrel. Despite the bright pink cloak he now flared, the boy was nowhere to be found. Alden walked to a crate and stepped up for a better look. The crowd had tightened as the trade ships began hooking cranes to their goods. The nearest shop with bright tin toys surprisingly hadn't caught the boy's attention. "Squirrel?" Alden called.

Hand-in-hand, Kira and Briar walked to him. "Tell me, how did you lose him dressed like that?" asked Kira.

Alden continued to search. "You know how he is..."

Briar frowned. "I know I'm letting him act as a guard with us, but he can get into some real danger if he thinks he can push his own moral laws like before."

A distant scream echoed between the two-story buildings.

Briar threw his hand out. "What did I just say?"

They each exchanged knowing looks before Alden pulled out a short sword, Kira took off in the direction of the cry, and Briar drew Valor, chasing after.

Alden watched them both twist around townsfolk like oil in water. He attempted to follow, but the crowd tightened in their wake. Raising his sword in fear of piercing someone, he shimmied safely by. When he reached the other side, they were gone.

Alden's heart raced. "Ki?"

"Here..." her voice called from the next alley.

Bursting into the corridor, Alden bumped into a stack of crates. Wood crashed around him, spilling a sack of onions. One rolled to the boots of a Yellow-Coat guard. Squirrel. He held his bow in one hand and the arm of a cloaked figure in the other. Briar stuffed Valor back in his sheath with a groan. Kira walked from them, hands on hips and head shaking.

Alden lowered his weapon. "What happened?"

She rolled her eyes. "Absolutely nothing."

As Squirrel released the figure, they cupped his hand in theirs. "Thanks for scaring that thief away!"

"Lady, I think your scream did well enough for that," Squirrel said as if to compliment.

Orange hair spilled from the woman's hood as she pulled it off. Green eyes gleamed. "I think anyone secure enough to wear colors like that is not to be trifled with!" she said, earning a proud grin from Squirrel.

Kira thumbed back. "Go figure Evelyn Alwell would be the one causing a stir."

"Evelyn?" Alden repeated.

"Oh, it's *you*." Evelyn bounced her glare from Alden to Kira and then back to Alden. "You her personal guard or something?"

Briar laughed. "We all know Kira doesn't need a guard's help to kick you and your friends' asses."

"Why you—" She stomped forward, hand shaking in rage. Her pale and chapped lips opened then hung in awe. She blinked. "*Briar?*"

"Yo." Briar tossed his hand up, then let it drop to his side.

She closed her mouth and scoffed. "What are you doing out here dressed up as a guard?"

"I'm more curious about what you are doing lurking in the shadows, Ev?" He folded his arms tight above his chest.

"I wasn't! I was shopping before the ships unloaded, and then this—"

Alden smirked at Briar. "Coin must be tight if the baroness is shopping for deals."

Nodding, Briar exaggerated a deep frown. "The price to pay for assaulting my lady," he said, wrapping his arm around Kira.

Alden's smirk faltered. "Yeah."

Briar looked at Evelyn with a snide grin. "It must be difficult now that you can't use your status to seduce men into showering you with gifts anymore, huh?"

"I did not do that," Evelyn said through clenched teeth.

"Deny it all you want. It doesn't change the fact that you're a scheming bitch."

Evelyn stepped into a shaft of light. "You're an asshole, and you always will be."

Alden narrowed his focus as details revealed. She held her purse close to her body. A strap—torn. As was the lace on her dress. However, her gray cloak was faded, and the velvet bore bald patches. The rest of what she wore was black and concealing as if hiding herself. He moved closer. "Are you doing business with the Shadowens again?"

"*What?*" She thrashed her hands back and forth and leaned in. "No! And I never have! How dare you keep insulting me, guard! Do you have no respect for the crested?"

"I do." Alden placed his hand over his shoulder and dipped into a low, formal bow. He pivoted to Kira and Briar and lifted with a charming grin. "For those who deserve it."

Kira's cheeks burst pink even in the darkness of the alley. Briar's hostile smile quirked even further to the side, dimples pinching.

Evelyn balled her dress in her fists and marched between them. "Move aside and let me pass if you don't believe me."

Briar took her arm. "Stop. I'll humor you. What happened?"

Her nostrils flared and she yanked her arm free. "A beggar was sitting in this alley. I was going to give them a coin...but when I opened my purse, they tried to steal all I had."

"You, offering charity?" Briar scoffed. "That's the least believable lie you've told yet."

"It's not a lie! I may have been shopping for deals, but I am not so poor as to ignore a hungry child! Unlike you, letting hundreds starve! Some king..."

Briar raised his chin and glared, anger brimming to the surface. "Excuse me?"

Evelyn's eyes dimmed with regret. She lowered in stature and cupped her hands to her mouth. "I'm sorry, Your Majesty. I didn't mean to insult." Snarly red hair tumbled as she bent to a bow.

Alden frowned. As rude and deceiving Evelyn may be, she was right. Kept inside the castle, Alden hadn't been aware of the flood of Brimleyn refugees migrating into the city. Briar also said nothing. He had even withheld Squirrel from making a small difference with the girl and fig merchant. In a way, he understood; they weren't Briar's people. They weren't his responsibility. *They're mine...*

In the distance, a guard's bell chimed. It clanged eagerly with shouts and banging from the docks. Evelyn grew smaller, clutching her purse and looking out. "See! Thieves!"

"Let's go." Alden led the march, sword still ready.

In the streets, fists and knives were raised in the air. Voices loud and angry. A group of men had climbed aboard the nearest trade ship, wrestling with sailors as they defended their goods. A barrel crashed overboard. White splashed in waves along the dock, coating the dock with a sour stench.

Evelyn covered her nose. "What is going on?"

Alden ushered her back with his arm. "Looks like a riot."

The rotten odor wafted. "Over spilled milk?" She gagged.

Briar walked from the dark alley. His blue eyes seemed to turn to gray as he watched the chaos. "Sweet kings..."

Chaos broke out in front of them as townspeople started looting the silk booth beside them. They pushed and shoved, fighting over wares. The table overturned, summoning a horde of scavengers. A couple tugged on a yellow scarf. Another bundled hats and accessories into his arms. Taking notice of his greed, the two fighting over the scarf pounced to steal. From the corner of Alden's eye, a snarling thug eyed Evelyn's purse. Thrashing his sword, Alden kept the assailant away. "We have to get you ladies out of here!"

Kira threw a punch as a stray man tumbled out of the ball of fists and aimed one at her. Her knuckles smacked across his fat cheek, pivoting his mass back into the brawl. She shook her hand and grinned at them. "What, and miss out on the fun?"

Another barrel split open on the docks. A roar of both excitement and disgust boomed across the crowd.

Evelyn shook in fright. "I don't understand. There should be silks, coffee, and art. We export dairy, not import."

Another docking ship untied its tethers and began drifting back into the sea as a few rowdy men started to climb aboard. A tarp picked up in the wind, exposing a stack of lumber cut from the oak forest bordering Brimley. "These ships didn't make it to Ammos," said Alden.

"Think it was another draclynn?" asked Squirrel as he kept his bow drawn, warning others back.

"Sea beasts are myths," said Evelyn.

Squirrel shook his head. "Noh uh. He killed one while aboard *The Lucky Fish!*"

Evelyn threw a look at Alden. "You're Captain Bosun Scraggs?"

Alden drooped his sword arm and snarled at her. "Do I look like a pirate?"

"You sure act like one," she sneered.

Kira stepped back into the building's shade, sucking on a bleeding knuckle. She pulled her hand away and examined her nails. Noticing one had chipped, she bit off the rest and spat. "They wouldn't riot over a draclynn interfering with trade... No, this is far worse."

"What could be worse than that?" asked Alden.

Glass shattered nearby. A roar of fire exploded, igniting the lumber on board the trade ship. The crowd cheered, throwing more bottle bombs. Many more scurried to loot shops, ships, and any noble unfortunate enough to be caught in the commotion.

"We need to go," Briar said, pushing Alden into a run and wrapping his arm around Kira.

Swords out to protect Evelyn and Kira, Alden and Briar jogged with Squirrel in the rear pointing his arrows. Evelyn rolled her dress up, further showing off her worn leather slippers. Though they were still of high fashion, mud coated them, and a broken strap thrashed with each step as the chant continued to rage.

Is she just as poor as my people?

Briar turned the corner, leading them up the hill toward the castle. Kira took him by the hand, using his momentum to help her run up the slope. Perspiration beaded at her temple, and her hair was slightly damp.

"It's not that far of a run, Kira," Briar said, pulling her along as they neared the gatehouse.

Alden jogged beside them, not having broken a sweat. He smirked. "She could never keep up with my jogs, even when I was thirty stones heavier."

"Good thing too, 'cause you knew I could beat ya in any fight." Kira threw her arm into Alden's gut, making him stop and cough.

Briar slowed to a walk. "Perhaps I do need to get up early so we can go jogging together with Alden."

"No. Please don't torture me." Kira threw her hands on bent knees. She rolled her head up, heaving. She laughed, but her tone held serious. "Sleep in all ya want…"

Having jogged with a youthful stride, Squirrel blinked at Kira. "But, Kira, you've been able to run without fatigue before?"

Panting, Kira rubbed her belly. "It's just cramps…"

"Oh." He turned around, lifting his chin towards the harbor. The crowd cheered as the ship's mast lit like a match. Thick blooms of orange and purple smoke bellowed in the air, stuffing Alden's nose. He shook his head. "I can understand they are upset, but why burn the ships?"

Evelyn presented Briar. "Isn't it clear? Ammos is testing our new king's ability to rule. How his people react is an example of that."

Briar glared over his shoulder. "Are you saying I'm an unfit ruler, Ev?"

"I'm only stating the facts as I see them. Ammos asked for Colin in exchange for continued relations with Dregs. He refused."

Alden threw his focus at his cousin. "Is that true?"

Briar shifted uneasily as a chant began in unison.

"Turn in Colin! Turn in Colin! Turn in Colin!"

Alden paled.

Briar put his hand on Alden's shoulder. "Look, King Bakhari sent a letter after my crowning with demands. I simply called the Ammosian's bluff. They need our sustainable goods more than we needed luxuries. I didn't think Bakhari would hold a grudge more favorable than food for his people."

Evelyn scoffed. "Your cousin killed his wife. You expected him to be cordial after that?"

"Even more reason why we need to solve Margaret's murder," Kira said through challenged lungs.

"What are you talking about?" Evelyn scoffed. "Colin killed her, Briar just won't admit it publicly! Asshole probably kidnapped the princess too."

"Evelyn." Briar pointed his finger. "Shut up."

She raised her hands and turned away, eyes rolling. "Fine. But this is on you."

Squirrel bounced on his toes nervously. "Does that mean there's going to be more war?"

Alden frowned with Squirrel, unable to say anything to calm the boy's worry, his own fears brewing just as rapidly. "I don't know. But whatever happens, you'll be kept safe," he promised.

"Oie! You Yellow-Coats need to return to the docks and manage those riots. Guard Captain Thomas's orders!" At the castle gate, two guards were checking crests and ushering nobles inside for safety. The one who had shouted was dressed in a gray and yellow tabard, identifying him as the lieutenant. He pointed to Kira and Evelyn. "If you ladies are crested you may come in. The court is gathering, eager to hear what the king has to say."

Briar pinched and rubbed the bridge of his nose. "Of course they are..." He began walking forward with Kira and Evelyn.

The lieutenant stepped forward and tapped Briar's chest with the blunt end of his polearm, forcing him back a step. He directed south with it. "The riots are that way."

Glaring, Briar raised his arm with a pointed finger and opened his mouth, but hesitated seeing his yellow sleeve. Recoiling his hand, he chuckled. "Right. I'm still dressed as a guard... Hello, Lieutenant Carl. You said the nobles are expecting me?" Straightening his shoulders, Briar presented himself as kingly as possible and removed his helm. He grinned with arrogance.

Carl snarled seeing his orders still refused, then his face fell slack registering Briar's words and face. "Y-Your Majesty?" He fell into a bow along with the other guard beside him, heels clicking.

Briar smiled. "That's right. And can you give word that I'll address them in a few turns?"

"Yes, Sire!" The guards stepped aside, giving way to the bailey.

Briar broke from the group and started toward the stable. "You guys go on. I need a moment to clear my head with William before anything else."

Kira crossed her arms. "Is this really a time to spend riding?"

"Perhaps not. But I need his wisdom." He winked.

"Fine." She kissed him on the cheek and hopped away, pointing. "That's for William though."

Briar laughed, tapping the mark staining his skin red. "You'll have to give him one yourself, I'm keeping this."

She waved, following Evelyn through the bailey.

As Squirrel began to march back down the hill, Briar whistled him back. "Earl. I don't want you at the riots. Escort Kira, will you?"

Squirrel spun around and bowed. "Yes, Your Briarship!"

He sighed, waving him along.

"Thanks for keeping him safe," Alden said, following Briar to the stables.

"It is more of a precaution for myself. I can't trust him."

"Oh?"

"He took my favorite Noble's Dice I had won from Sir Stridan at the last festival," said Briar.

"Did he steal it, or did you roll low?" Alden teased.

Briar waved nonchalantly. "Doesn't matter, your thief friend too easily gets into trouble, and is too good at Noble's Dice to not be cheating."

Alden sighed, knowing all too well the sticky fingers Squirrel possessed and his good luck with gambling. "I'll talk to him."

"Good. And you should probably go to your quarters. See ya after the meeting." Briar patted Alden on the shoulder and entered his tack house, leaving him alone.

Alden watched as Kira and Squirrel disappeared into the castle. Instead of following, he leaned against the stone wall, collecting his thoughts. *The Ammosians didn't show up for Briar's crowning. And now they refuse to trade. Brimleyns are still hated, despite having a king of both realms. All because they blame me.* He massaged his forehead, wishing he could ease the painful reality. *How can I ever fix this?*

Briar came out a moment later with his saddle and tack. His face was grim, but a determined focus held in his brow.

Alden sighed. "You should have told me."

Briar jumped in fright, nearly dropping his bundle. Hand on his heart he looked at Alden. "Shit. Hey, look—"

"If I had known King Bakhari wanted me in exchange, I could have done something to prevent this..." Alden swung his arm to the chaos in port as a flash of fire lit the docks.

Briar slowly turned his head to look. He exhaled. "Right, that. I'm sorry. You weren't here yet and I honestly didn't think it would come to this."

Alden pushed off the wall. "So, what is our resolution?"

Briar waved his hand. "Please, you don't need to get yourself wound up in all this."

"Hard not to be when they are chanting my name. Besides, it is as you said, we are in this together. This is as much my problem as it is yours, Bri. I can't let this happen to you. I can't be the blame for another kingdom's downfall."

He sighed. "You won't. I just need to go for a ride, and I'll have an answer."

"Then I'll ride with you?" Alden took a step toward the barn.

"No." Briar moved to the side, blocking him.

Alden quirked his head.

Briar looked down. "Look, right now, I just need a moment. Alone. You understand, right?" He peered up.

Knowing all too well the clarity solitude brought, Alden backed off. "Sure. See ya in a bit." Alden bowed.

CHAPTER TEN

A LAND UNITED

Leaving William left Briar with more questions and concerns than it did answers. The decision made, though clever and the only option to keep his cousin safe, didn't feel right. It felt awful and roguish. Something Alden might understand, but not in this case. Not when his pride was concerned.

It doesn't matter. This is the decision of the king and one that will be honored, Briar reminded himself. Still, the pain cut deep.

Heralds scurried to attention, blaring horns as Briar pushed through the doorway into the grand hall. Nobles silenced their conversations and bowed in acknowledgment as he walked along the yellow wool rug leading to his throne. The armored clang of Sir Tarek—Briar looked behind him, spying a sword on his right hip—no, *Sir Exten*, followed in his wake.

Sinking into his carved wood throne, cushioned with pillows and a fur throw, Briar tried to relax his nerves. Still, the added comfort couldn't ease the latent hostility buzzing in the room. *Maybe having them wait so long was a bad idea.*

Briar watched as Kira took a seat at one of the two long banquet tables arranged in a V-shape pointing away from the throne. He smiled catching her wink, but upon seeing Alden and Squirrel guarding the main door he'd just walked blindly through he frowned. *He shouldn't be here for this...*

"Good evening, Your Majesty! I must have missed you leaving your room." Fredrik appeared before him with an outstretched and wrinkly hand.

Briar raised his arm to block his man-in-waiting before he could tuck a stray hair, straighten his clothes, or wipe something clean with spit. Without looking at the man's ugly long face he shooed him away with a dismissive hand. "It's fine."

"Yes, of course, Your Majesty. But perhaps I could fetch your crown? Or get you a change of clothes before the meeting? Some perfume?"

Briar glanced at the guard's uniform he still wore. His hair felt sweaty and matted against his head from wearing a helmet as he rode to the central guard tower and back. The smell of horse and ale wafted. *It doesn't matter. The people's opinions of me won't change.* He dismissed Fredrik with a wave of his hand. "They know who I am."

"That they do..." His fingers curled outward. "But if I may—"

Briar glared at the intrusive man before he could say or do anything more.

Fredrik placed his hand on his shoulder and retreated in a backward bow.

The room's low rumble of conversation grew louder as Guard Captain Thomas entered in a suit of leather, platemail, and dried blood, confirming the severity of the riot. He spoke a word with Alden then crossed the room to guard another exit. Trumpets blared once more, announcing all summoned were accounted for. Together, Alden and Thomas shut the doors, locking the room into silence.

Heat pricked at Briar's neck. A lump of nerves hardened in his throat like clay. Forcing it down, he straightened. All eyes were on him, both Brimleyn and Dreggen alike. Seeing the two kingdoms together, despite them being so divided, lifted Briar's spirits. *One step closer to Vatan. If only Liam could see this.*

Keeping his voice stern and confident, he spoke. "As I am sure you are all now aware, Ammos has sent our trade ships home without exchange. That is due to our trade treaty being terminated."

Immediately, a clamor of tongues arose.

"What will we do?" someone groaned. "Their finery and ivory are precious commodities that cannot be supplied elsewhere!"

A large fellow wiped his mouth. "That is right! Where will we get our spices?"

"I can't sleep without my dune ale," whined a bug-eyed woman.

"I need my smoke!" called another.

More worried queries rang out in alarm until Briar could no longer understand another word said.

Kira lifted a hand. To Briar's relief, many quieted and gave her their attention. She lifted her chin and held the audience captive by seemingly taking in each of their gazes. Like a practiced actress, she spoke with clarity. "A trade loss with Ammos is not to be feared. Should it have been one, our king would have done everything in his power to stop it."

A few heads nodded at her logic, Briar's with them.

She continued. "And the kingdom of Hiore remains a mutual ally. I am sure arrangements can be met for all Ammosian goods to transfer through them when their ships return through our port."

"Likely at a premium," huffed a woman.

A man dressed in shimmers of white and gold rose from the table. "So it will be another fortnight before I can complete my silken suit?"

"Yes, I'm afraid fashion will have to wait." Kira bobbed her head sympathetically, but her tone was laced with mockery.

Another clothier stepped forward and tossed her head. "Fashion never waits! My clients will be expecting my next statement any day now!" she said.

"We will just need to get a bit creative then, won't we?" Kira crossed her ankles, allowing one boot-hugged leg to slip out from her dress. Both clothier's eyes flicked to it, drawn in as intended. Several noblewomen hushed whispers to one another in curious desire.

Evelyn Alwell stepped from the crowd, stealing the room's attention from Kira to her. Many sneered at her worn clothing and exchanged gossip. She ignored them. "More important than Dreggen fashion is the people's ability to have enough money to be properly clothed and fed or sickness will be upon us all."

The male clothier bobbed his head. "That's right. How are they going to buy from me if my goods are being traded at a disadvantage? How will I make profit?"

Evelyn palmed her face.

Kira eased forward, drawing Briar to catch her eyes. They were dark yet warm, offering stability. "Your Majesty, I do believe you have a solution to all of this?" she said with confidence he wasn't sure he could match.

"Yes," said Evelyn, a bit louder than Kira as if competing for attention. "What are the Ammosian's terms?"

"I heard a chant that they demand Colin," said another. "Is your cousin what the Ammosians desire?"

Instead of more rumbles of gossip, the room stilled with understanding.

Swallowing, Briar looked over the nobles one by one. Some he knew well, some still just acquaintances. Many were loyal, others still appraised him as his uncle had—with hatred and scrutiny. Sweat from his palms began to dampen the arm rails of his throne. Then Briar caught the glint of Alden's eyes from under his helm as he lifted his chin. He nodded, more in reassurance to himself than to Alden. Ripping his gaze free, he addressed the room. "I have a solution," he began, but his throat hitched.

The hall remained quiet and attentive.

Kira's round eyes grabbed his, patiently awaiting his next words. Given strength, Briar forced his dry lips to part and recall the practiced words. "One which will ease the tension between my family's people, creating a stronger, more unified kingdom. This peace will be felt across Vatan. Reaching Hiore—reaching Ammos. Trade will no longer be a problem. Homelessness, hunger, and civil injustice will also be eased."

The crowd began to nod, their approval giving way for him to say the rest.

"To face this threat, we cannot be threatened. It is when we become self-reliant as one, regardless of accent, color worn, or city born, that we become powerful. So, as the son of Prince Jamus Densen of Brimley and Princess Trisha Colte of Dregs, I, Briar Densen, have signed into law provisions to ensure loyalties, trade, work, and homes to *all* of my people... Meaning, the kingdom of Dregs now spans across the city of Brimley and its territories."

The room roared with cheers and applause. Many nobles rose to their feet, shook hands, and clasped crests. Even the Dreggens turned to the Brimleyns in the back, welcoming them to join in the celebration—join in the union.

But Alden couldn't.

His fists were tight. Muscles tense. He began to perspire again seeing his little cousin take claim of what didn't belong to him. *City of Brimley? What the fuck? Is he trying to reclaim Vatan? He can't do that! That's mine. I...* Alden's lips parted in disbelief at the realization. That after the yellow ink framed Briar's Brimleyn crest as king of Dregs, his rank and power had succeeded Alden's own single-marked crest. *I have nothing...*

Armor creaked as his chest expanded to fill angered lungs. His throat swelled, preventing the scream he wished to tear through Vatan. The reality of what he was forced to swallow choked him further.

I am nothing.

An unseen weight crushed his body, and he leaned on a column for support. Lights began to spot in his eye. Voices became disembodied. Blurry figures drifted past him. A breeze cooled his damp face. His breathing came in tempered heaves. The air seemed to thin. His body sweat. Cheeks tingling and nose numb, he shook his head. "This can't be..."

A soft touch pressed to his shoulder. "Are you okay?"

He opened his eyes through a white haze. Someone stood before him. His ears rang. He shrugged them off—the motion weak.

His senses blurred once more.

A hand came to his chest, leaning him against the wall. "You look faint." It was Kira's voice this time, gentle and kind.

"I feel it," he admitted, head lulling to lean against her, in need of his friend's support.

She took his arm. "Come."

His feet moved, allowing her to lead. His knees met a chair, and he slouched into it. The motion further swirled his perception as if he were still falling. Fingers touched under his neck, relieving a strap. His helm came off and crashed to the floor, but the loud clang was drowned out by the scream of deceit in his ears. Snapping and pointing, Kira directed someone behind. A questionable moment later, a cup of water was pressed to his lips. Its coolness soothed embers in him, but still steam rose. He tipped his head back and groaned.

Kira began rubbing his back. "Calm down..." she soothed.

Alden lowered his head for her to massage. He blinked, finding his vision returning. Everyone was gone, including the servants and guards. The meeting tables were still set with chairs pulled back in disarray. The throne sat empty with even its fur blanket spilled to the floor. "Where's our king?" he snarled.

"I'm right here." Briar's voice came from behind.

Alden avoided looking, instead keeping focused on the person he could trust, Kira. "And everyone else?"

"Briar sent them away, giving us the room after noticing your reaction." Kira continued massaging the rock-hard tension in his neck, but it only knotted further. "You're lucky Squirrel had you. I don't think anyone else noticed... He's outside guarding the door now with Thomas."

Alden pulled away. "Who cares if they did... I don't matter anymore."

"Alden..." Briar spoke. "You matter."

"Fuck you."

"Uh... I think you mean, 'thank you.' Your people have a home now."

"My people? *My?*" He laughed distortedly then twisted in the chair, finally facing his cousin. "I don't have people anymore, Bri. You just stole 'em!"

Briar shook his head. "That's not what I did."

Pointing at the empty throne Alden raised his voice, uncaring if anyone outside the walls could hear. "Don't cha realize what you've just done? Ya stripped away any chance I had at reclaiming my life! I have nothing now, Bri. *Nothing.* Not you. Not May, not Kira, Brimley, or Vatan. My parents are dead, my friends along with 'em. My...brother. Granda can't stand me, and I'm sure Gran just pities me. Squirrel will turn on me just the same, but I guess there's always my cat, so there's that."

"You have to stop blaming yourself and thinking no one cares about you," said Briar.

Alden gestured around. "How can't I? Look at all that has been destroyed in my name! And now..." He sucked in a tempered breath.

Briar waited a moment then sat beside him. "Now what?"

Alden rubbed his hand through his hair and sighed. "I don't know what to do." His eyes became blinded with tears.

Kira took his hands in her own, their delicate warmth doing little to ease him knowing they held the heart of another. "Come on, Alden. I understand you're upset, but try to think clearly. Briar has supported you when no one else has. Sacrificed so much for you—"

"Nah he hasn't," Alden sneered, shaking his hands free. "He's sacrificed nothing. Ya think he made it a choice to be loyal to me? No. Ya think he chose to live in a stuffy loft and be belittled by his guards? No."

"I did."

"No." Alden turned to Briar. "Maybe I was naive to think you never wanted what I had, but in reality, you had no other option when Olivar was in control. But now that your uncle and aunt are dead and you're crested as a true king, ya took the first chance to claim everything from me, starting with Kira."

Briar's eyes rolled, but his jaw set. "Look, I won't apologize for falling in love with your friend."

"In love?" Alden gaped. Clenching his fists he leaned in. "It's only been a month, Bri!"

"Yeah, maybe, but from what you've said over the years I knew I could commit to her. Unlike you."

"Oh, sweet kings." Kira put her fingers to her temple, covering her eyes. "Don't you two argue over me... I'm not the point of this."

"You're right. It is about ruling." Briar dipped his head in an attempt to catch Alden's eyes. Ignored, he sat up. "As you know, King Bakhari wanted me to turn you in not only for the murder, but because he still fears you threaten Princess Mayli. He thinks you're behind the kidnapping, and I can't quite defend you on that as you kinda were."

Alden gritted his teeth. "Not my fault."

"Exactly. So, to protect you, me, Kira, and our people, to stop the riots, get the Brimleyns off the streets and into homes, and gain control of Vatan once more just as your father wanted, Brimley needed to be reclaimed. You couldn't do that. Not with everything set against you. But you suggested I change the laws. So I did by putting Brimley in Dreggen control. I took that leverage and fear away from Ammos. I gave purpose to the land. I gave our people hope. This is a political and humanitarian move. Nothing more. Please keep your trust in me."

Alden braved a look into Briar's blue eyes. They held no vendetta. Alden noticed then, he wore no crown. He hadn't even been wearing the proper kingly attire for the meeting, just the low-ranking guard uniform he'd worn all day, caked in sweat and dirt. Alden wasn't speaking to a king, but his cousin —his best friend. Briar, the man who had always guarded him throughout his life. A fragment of Alden's shattered heart held on to a thread of hope. "Can I trust you to sign my kingdom back when my name is cleared?"

Briar nodded. "Not only will I give you Brimley, but Dregs too. Clear your name, and I'll help you to reclaim Vatan. We will have a land united just as you and your father have always wanted. I give you my word, Colin. Trust me."

CHAPTER ELEVEN

FOUL TASTE

The rhythmic crash of waves upon a rocky shore loomed just beyond Mayli's conscious thought. Warm breezes swept in, carrying the fragrant aroma of roses. Cradled in soft silk sheets topped over a plush feather-stuffed mattress, Mayli felt as if she were drifting through a dream. One in which she was cared for, protected, and loved.

Only, she wasn't dreaming—she was home. *Really home.* Not on a ship, not in a shack, and not in the ruins of Brimley Castle. She was in Ammos, where luxuries filled her with peace, security, and ease of living. Where her family surrounded her with love and care. Where there were no thieves, dangerous monsters, worries of hunger, or imminent death.

Mayli slipped out from her bed despite the sun having only just lit the sky in an amber band. Yawning, she stepped into her favorite pair of padded slippers, cushioning her blisters, and shuffled along the smooth tile to her vanity. From a drawer of stationeries, she withdrew a fine-pressed paper, accented with tiny orange flowers. Then she dipped a quill into ink.

My Rogue,

I am home, thanks to you.

But as I reminisce, I can't help but feel guilty for my treatment of you. I mocked you, your kingdom, your king. I pushed to get closer than what you were comfortable with. It couldn't have been easy to help someone responsible for so much of your grief. For that, I'm truly sorry. I was naive, confused, and scared. Despite all of that, you stayed by my side.

I wish you still were.

Mayli paused, feeling the tear of separation between them. A princess and a rogue; love that could never be, like oil and water.

Pressing the quill down once more, Mayli continued her letter, scribing away her thoughts. Once finished, she folded it into an elaborate puzzle, creating an envelope. She struck flint to a candle and warmed a pool of orange wax. After dripping it, she laid a matching string across with a white feather and stamped it with her royal seal. She waved it in the air to cool then flipped it to finish the tie with a bow and addressed it to Briar, noted for Alden.

Excited chirps and a flutter of feathers roused as Mayli walked to her birdcage. The small flock of large white carriers hopped on pegs, spreading their long wings. They wore little silk vests, each colored to indicate which kingdom they flew to. Mayli opened the cage and selected the yellow-marked one. Well-trained, it waited on her arm as she stuffed her letter in the vest.

The bird peeped four times as Mayli opened the balcony. Smiling, she tossed the bird freely into the air. As she watched it fly north. She put her hand to her belly in awe. It had been years since her insides danced. *Not since Colin*, she realized.

Smiling, she walked to her wardrobe. Opening it, her lips fell expecting to see her clothes from her trip cleaned and returned as promised. Instead, rows of immaculate beauty lay in wait.

Mayli traced her fingers across the gowns. Their softness was like cream, inviting her to try each on, but none of the colors invited her mood to brighten with them. She paused, noticing a black dress hidden in the back. She pulled it from the cabinet and held it to her body. The midnight silk crossed in front making a low V across her back and ended at her ankles. *Have you been hiding in the shadows all this time?* Smiling at her discovery, she slipped it overhead and accented the look with a white leather belt sparkling with diamonds clasped on a pouch woven from feathers. Needing something around her neck to offer comfort and remembrance of her mother, Mayli pulled a matching black scarf from a drawer. Normally she'd wear thin-strapped sandals, but her feet were sore from weeks of travel, so she opted for staying in her slippers.

Mayli glanced at the vanity, finding her reflection in the mirror. Free from makeup or the prearranged dresses Lidia usually set out, she saw her true self. *Edgy.* Not the beautiful bird her father kept or the helpless damsel Charli saw. She saw Mayli Drake, the strong and determined Princess of Ammos, and she was proud to show it.

"Oh, you're up! Just in time for breakfast."

Mayli turned to see Lidia usher in several handmaidens through the door. They busied around her room, pulling dresses and arranging things in preparation to be gussied up.

Mayli waited for one of the servants to bring a rack of her commoner's wares. "Where are my new clothes?" Mayli asked as they opened her wardrobe back up.

"Oh, I'm sure your father would be happy to send for Mr. Vaurus if you wish," said Lidia, pulling out a much brighter and lively dress. "But this will do."

Mayli took a step back. "No, I mean the garments from my trip."

Lidia's face soured. "Those were tossed out."

"Tossed out?" Mayli gasped. "I asked for them to be washed and mended!"

"I'm afraid the servants in the washroom misinterpreted the instructions. Not surprisingly as no princess should possess such tatters. Now step out of that and put this on, I can hardly see you in that gloom."

Before Mayli could protest, the handmaidens were pulling at her belt and stripping her. Defenseless, she stood bare for a moment before a shimmering white and gold dress was draped overhead. To her relief, her chosen belt and pouch were strung back around. Then, a set of matching diamond-toed sandals with a lifted heel was set out expectantly. With a reserved sigh, Mayli stepped out of her comfort and walked into her role as princess. Keeping the momentum, Mayli shuffled to the door in an attempt to escape.

"Hold on now, you don't want everyone to see you like that." Lidia walked over to her, twisting a bottle of makeup open. Pulling off the brush top soaked in light brown liquid, she reached to apply it.

Like a dog's wet lick, the brush stroked across Mayli's cheek. She wiped her face, removing a smear of thick makeup. A greasy residue resided on her hand. She grimaced. "I don't want to wear this anymore, Lidia. My skin feels better without it."

"But we must keep up appearances. So much word is already traveling about your horrible condition when you returned home yesterday afternoon. We must do all we can to conceal the mess you've become." Lidia reached to reapply it.

"Mess?" Mayli pushed Lidia's hand from her face. She forced a steadying breath. "I had a bath already. I don't need to be cleaned up anymore."

"You need to be seen as a princess."

"I *am* a princess."

"Then you must not have anyone question it. Now, chin up. Vatan must see that you have not fallen."

"Vatan? It's just breakfast with Father and Jair..."

"Yes, and you mustn't let them worry any more than they have." Lidia managed to apply thick paste across her face. It felt heavy and sticky. The mucky smell wafted with each application. Mayli held her breath as Lidia took a red-stained brush and swirled it in a shimmering rose powder and dusted her cheeks. Still, she sneezed. Eyes closed, she felt a waxy pencil outline around them. Held captive, a handmaiden stroked through her hair while another sprayed a spicy perfume.

When Mayli opened her eyes, a stranger greeted her through a gold hand mirror. The woman who looked back was undeniably beautiful. Her eyes were smokey with dark liner and shimmers of orange on the lids. Her hair was silken smooth, shining in waves. Bruises, scars, and the dark bags under her eyes were all hidden. Despite the mask, Mayli knew the truth that hid beyond—the girl in the drawing that Alden saw.

"There." Lidia set the mirror aside and smiled victoriously. "That's the girl your father is proud of."

Mayli looked away, the tired compliments only making her feel low. "Yeah. Glad he will be happy..."

Lidia tucked a wave of hair behind Mayli's ear with a jeweled pin. Nodding once more at her work, Lidia turned to leave. "Hurry along, you don't want to keep them waiting any longer."

"Yes, Lidia."

Door clicking shut, Mayli folded into her hands. Mayli let her eyes wet, uncaring if they mucked up Lidia's fine work as a wave of emotion hit. *Already the pressures of court life are upon me —not a day or turn of sand wasted. No one cares that I need to process my pain, only that others think I already have. Again, I am left alone to sort the tangle of life on my own... The fog... Already, it's coming back.*

"How are you?"

Mayli popped her head up to see Charli freshly groomed, suited, and poised in her doorway. A new orange cape hung around his neck just like his parents. It trailed down his back signifying his new rank as a knight for his valiant efforts in returning her home. His soft eyes kept their focus on hers, waiting for an honest reply.

He cared. He's always cared. She smiled, glad for his friendship.

He walked into her room.

"Hey! You can't be in here!" She waved one hand, shooing him, while her other wiped her eyes.

Ignoring her, he kept walking. "I can if you need fresh flowers." He pulled Alden's dried rose from her vanity. A petal fell.

Mayli took the flower from him. "That...doesn't need to be replaced." She cradled it for a moment before tucking it back in her mirror.

"If you say so." His eyes glanced around her mirror, taking note of the drawing pinched between the glass and frame. He reached. "What artist disrespected you?"

Mayli pawed his hand away before he could touch. "No one, now get out before Father sees you." Mayli stood and pushed his muscled body, but he stubbornly held position.

He laughed. "Princess, do you really think Bakhari is going to be upset by my being here when your brother is with us?"

"Huh?" Mayli tossed her head around his bulk. Jair leaned against the wall with a smirk. He wore his finest suit, hair slicked back, eyes lined, and cheeks painted just as rosy as her own. She ran to him. "Jair!"

"Hey, Sis." Her brother pushed off the wall. He hugged Mayli and kissed her cheek. "Glad you made it home."

"As am I," said Charli, dipping his head forward.

Jair positioned himself between her and her guard, forcing him to take a step back. "Which is why I'm here to supervise."

Mayli raised a brow. "Supervise?"

Jair folded his arms. "I'm just ensuring whatever disgusting things I cannot unsee between you two already doesn't happen again."

Mayli laughed. "You'll kiss someone someday and see it's not so gross."

Jair picked up a silver tube from her vanity and pulled off the cap. He twisted it, and a stem of red-orange wax stuck out. He looked in the mirror and puckered his lips, applying it. "You implying I haven't been kissed?" He smacked them and winked to himself.

Mayli snatched the lipstick from him and closed the cap. "Lidia doesn't count."

"Ew!" He flashed his tongue and grimaced.

Mayli laughed and set her mother's lipstick back in its place.

"I may have never kissed someone, but when I do it will be someone I know I have the option to marry." Jair eyed Charli.

Charli's chest grew and his chin raised. "The princess has the option to marry me. I am crested after all."

"Crested, sure, but unless you're royalty, Father isn't interested," said Jair.

"Good, as I'm not interested in Bakhari."

Mayli shook her head at the audacity. "So who does that leave you with, Jair?" She folded her arms.

His mouth opened, then his teeth clicked together. Sealing his painted lips he smiled. "Obviously they have yet to be born."

"You'll be as old as Gavin at that rate. Forty years and still unkissed."

"Peh." He plucked the drawing from the mirror.

Mayli groaned. "Will you two stop touching my things?" She reached for it.

Despite being younger by a few years, Jair still stood a head taller. He lifted the drawing just out of her reach. "It looks exactly like you."

"It looks nothing like her." Charli snatched the drawing and put it back.

Jair cocked his head and held his chin. "I don't know. They captured that little mouth thing she does when she's upset."

Mayli folded her arms and sucked in her cheeks to purse her lips. Both Jair and Charli looked from her to the drawing, and back at her.

"Huh. You may be right, Jair," Charli agreed.

Mayli fluttered her hands between them as if they were a couple of flies. "Get out!"

Chuckling, Charli walked to the door and opened it.

The warm scent of stewed meat swept the palace, drawing her outside. She looked over the balcony onto the patio. Her father sat at a square tile table placed on the dais with each of her family's thrones around it. Her father's seat sat parallel to her mother's. A plate, bowl, glass, silverware, and napkin were set as if Queen Margaret were expected to join them at any moment.

Her father swooped his arm, his long sleeves swishing after. "Ah, there you are, Little Bird! Join us!"

Eager to stuff her face with a proper meal, Mayli hurried past the archers and down the steps. Jair chased after as they always had. Laughter filled her lungs, capturing a sense of normalcy for the first time in weeks. Rushing around the corner and bumping into each other, they scurried to touch their seats.

Having reached his first, Jair whooped.

Mayli moaned as she dragged her sore feet, a blister breaking. "I let you win."

He sat and waited expectantly. "Sure you did."

Per the rules of their game, Mayli helped push Jair's throne closer to the table like a servant, rousing a pompous grin on his face. She lifted a napkin and placed it on his lap. "Your Highness," she cooed.

Her father laughed. "Ah, how I love seeing you home, and already back to your ways."

Mayli walked by her father and kissed him on the cheek. "It is good to be home."

He peered up with adoring eyes. "All cleaned up. You look so beautiful now."

"Was I not before?" Mayli challenged with narrowed eyes.

He patted her hand. "You're just more beautiful every moment I spend with you."

Mayli slipped from his touch and continued to her own seat. "Then I best never leave here again in fear of growing ugly," she said, scooting in with effort. It suddenly came easily as Charli helped with the last push before taking his position.

A low rumble chuckled from her father. "Oh, Little Bird. If only I could keep you in this nest. But you're meant to fly from it."

"I think I've done enough flying for a while." Mayli took up her fork but paused, noticing the unusual spread. Served before them was a light soup, cooked goat, and a dish of rice. She looked over the table trying to spy the curry to pour over. Seeing a tray with a lid she opened it. Inside, were layers of flatbread. *Has our old cook died since I left? What is this?*

Bakhari pulled a piece onto his plate and let it soak into his soup. "That's right. You have yet to tell us about your adventure! I know Jair will be eager to hear all about the Cad Islands." He munched on the soggy bread.

"You were at the Cads?" Jair's boyish face lit with wonder. A grain of rice fell from his lip.

"Yes." Mayli selected a piece of bread and put the lid back. "And it wasn't as daring as you made it out to be."

"But weren't there pirates?"

"Yes."

He leaned in, eyes sparking. "Did they talk funny?"

"Yar," Mayli mocked, tearing a piece off and dipping it into the soup as her father had done.

Jair's fists shook in excitement. "Then you must have seen all sorts of strange characters!"

Mayli chuckled at the memory of the man with the llamas and his unique song, the large fellow strapped in belts, and of course the man in red. "Yes, all sorts. People dressed in whatever outfits they liked. It was a very colorful town, incorporating all cultures." She took a bite, tasting nothing but hot water, yeast, and a bite of cayenne pepper. Despite her father's willingness to eat it without complaint, Mayli set it down, unfinished.

Jair threw a few shadow punches across the table. "Well, I bet you saw sword fights and brawls in the street?"

Mayli shook her head, picking up her spoon to explore her other options. She turned over the pile of rice. The white grains looked and smelled to her usual liking. "I didn't see any."

"No?" He rested his wrists on the corner of the table, utensils pointed in the air. "Are you sure you went to the right island?"

"Yes, and it was a unique and freeing place, Jair. There were performers, blends of food, and fun music. Shops offered almost anything you could think of. The Cad Islands were actually quite pleasant and reminded me of the Festival of Gezmek."

He blinked, disappointed. "Did you even see the King of the Cads?"

"King? I didn't think the islands were a kingdom."

Jair slumped. "Don't you listen to any of my tales?"

"Um... I try not to."

Jair raised his knife into the air like a sword. "The King of the Cads is said to be one of the last nobles of Gezmek. He's notorious and vicious, but stands for freedom and power, which is why the Cads are so diverse."

Bakhari seized the small blade from the young prince. "He's not really a king, Jair. Marks Thielen anointed himself when the capital in Gezmek fell, claiming the Cads as his kingdom. But the islands aren't large enough to be considered such, and so I and the other kingdoms have refused to acknowledge his claim."

Jair settled down. "Yeah, well that didn't stop him from ruling over the locals and patrolling the seas to ensure they had a right to live."

"True..." Bakhari looked at Mayli. "And so began the Cad Islands and all the stories your brother raves about."

"I see..." She blinked in thought. "Well, I did stay at an old inn called Thielen's Lodge. But it was run down. Nothing someone who thought themselves as a king would claim."

"He likely owns it like he does much of the land..." said Jair, biting into his meal.

Chewing, Bakhari dipped his bread again. "Damgard, what was your account while being there?"

Charli stepped from his position at the bottom of the dais and addressed the king. "Marks Thielen is rumored to be dead. The performers were just pickpockets, using entertainment as a ruse. Many shops sold forgeries or stolen goods. I saw a merchant set fire to his competition's shop when it lured over his patrons for better prices. There were rings to bet on fights—both man and beast. Nomads peddled rumors, and whores did their practice in the open."

Jair's face resumed its eye-widening fascination.

Charli changed his focus from Bakhari to Jair. "In search of your sister, Arkello and I killed Shadowen Thieves in the dark alleyways. No one batted an eye at the blood we spilled. It may not be the adventure you've imagined, Prince Jair, but it was no place for royalty."

"That is for certain," agreed Bakhari. "Thank you, Sir Charli, for your bravery in finding my daughter and rescuing her from such disorder."

Charli bowed and resumed his post.

"Where is Arkello anyway?" asked Jair, looking around. "I haven't seen him yet."

"He's...on an expedition. Parted ways after I was found," Mayli said, unsure if it was a lie or not.

Charli eyed her with a flicker of resentment.

Bakhari raised his glass. "Well, let's hope he finds what he's after this time. Perhaps he has a sister for you, Jair."

Mayli looked at her brother. Under his layer of perfect makeup and a forced smile, a familiar expression hid: despair.

Mayli played with the food on her plate. "Father? Why can we not consider other nobles like before?"

He lifted his eyes for only a moment. "Would you rather rule alongside a kingdom or a small plot of land?"

She paused to consider the question, twisting her spoon in his hands. "I suppose a kingdom has more power, but you and Mother wed, and she wasn't royal."

"Times were different. We had the King of Vatan to keep us whole. Now that we are on our own, we must seek to unite through the strongest alliances."

"But there are so few kingdoms and royals," said Jair. "If we look beyond the ringed crest, then Mayli wouldn't have to marry Gavin, and I would have more options."

"Absolutely not!" Bakhari beat down on the table. Glass rattled, and the plates seemed to hop, spilling a few grains of rice to the colorful tile surface. He lifted his fist and pointed a finger from Jair to Mayli. "You both will marry royalty and bring honor and power to Ammos. Is that clear?"

Mayli's shoulders sunk.

Jair mindlessly spun a bracelet on his wrist. "That doesn't mean you're going to let King Briar court her again, does it Father?"

"Never," Bakhari proclaimed.

"Wait?" Mayli's jaw dropped. "Did you say, *King* Briar?"

"Oh." Jair blinked. "I suppose you haven't heard..."

"No!" She stared between her brother and father. "What happened?"

Her father's lip snarled. "King Olivar Colte of Dregs and his sister are said to have died of fever. A bit too convenient for my taste." He shoveled a bite of bread into his mouth.

"This can't be, Briar was..." Mayli damned her mouth closed.

"A Densen fraud, yes, but his mother's Dreggen blood is still within him."

Mayli shook her head. She'd only just left Briar's side over a week ago, hugging him goodbye and thanking him for his efforts in rescuing her. He'd rushed to her aid when Alden had alerted him and even brought her a dress. He'd shielded her in the small house when Brimleyn thugs came. He gave them safe entry into Dregs past the Hiorean knights, then secured passage on a ship set to Ammos. Most outstanding though was he hadn't tried to flirt as he once had, even smiling when he saw her cuddle with Alden. *He'd grown. Matured. He cared about his people, Alden, and his cousin. He cares about me, too...* Mayli realized. She eased into her lush seat, pondering the possibility that Briar could be a rival suitor to contend with Gavin if it came down to it. "Briar is king..." she said aloud as if it would help make sense of the sudden transition of power.

"Do not fret, Little Bird. He is of little concern. His people are already rioting over him ignoring my demands."

Mayli cocked her head. "What demands, Father?"

"Handing that monster over, of course."

"Colin?"

"Who else?"

Mayli shook her head. "But Briar would never do that. He would rather endure hardships than hand over his cousin. He's proved that for the last three years serving as guard captain. You don't give up that much of yourself to protect the guilty."

"You would if they were family," argued her father. "Would you surrender your brother if he was accused of murder?"

Mayli gave her brother a sly smile. "I'd have him arrested if he was accused of stealing my lipstick again."

"Hey!" Jair covered his red mouth. "I only borrowed it!"

"Guards!" Mayli teased, calling over her shoulder to Charli.

"Mayli..." her father scolded.

"What?"

"Do not joke."

She shrugged. "Who says I was?"

Bakhari shook his head. "Regardless, King Briar needs to take the murder of a queen seriously if he expects our cooperation. But instead of giving up Colin, he foolishly chose to end our trade agreement."

Jair shook his head. "But Father, don't we need their goods too? This food doesn't taste right without their dairy or vegetables."

Mayli stared at her plate. She realized then why the meal

looked and tasted so off. *No rich butter curry, no yogurt, no carrots... No cream for tea.* Having no stomach for her father's politics, Mayli scooted her plate away. "This is awful."

"I am sorry, we are still experimenting with different recipes." Bakhari wiped his mouth with a cloth napkin.

Mayli swirled her finger around the strange cuisine. "If the trading ban has already affected the palace, how will our people eat? How will our livestock? Without lumber how will we expand or build new ships to fish? And his people are innocent; they are likely suffering too."

Her father looked over her with fondness. "You bring up such fair concerns, but your worry is unnecessary. Unlike the trials we faced that summer, this is temporary. Soon we will have everything we want."

"Even chocolate-dipped fruit?" asked Jair.

"We could have chocolate-dipped whatever!" he laughed, pinching the prince's cheek.

Mayli relaxed. "So you will be considering lifting this ban?"

Bakhari took up his fork again, resuming the meal. "No need. Goods from Hiore will be on their way, and King Briar will have to find other means of enriching his people."

Already more exhausted than she ever felt from her travels, Mayli stood from the table. "I'm going back to my room."

"Mayli, you didn't even touch your food," Bakhari exclaimed, clashing his spoon to his bowl.

"It has left a foul taste." Mayli scurried to rise and before her father could catch her arm, she fled.

CHAPTER TWELVE

SHOOT TRUE

Feathers scattered as Mayli released another bird on a journey to Briar in Dregs. She watched it twist and flutter as it disappeared into the setting sun.

Turning from the balcony, Mayli walked past a cart of dirtied dishes. Midway through the day, Lidia had brought lunch: a plate of rice and meat-stuffed rolls. It took care of Mayli's hunger but again lacked a creamy sauce. She'd rather have wild rice and rabbit. Despite being full, she still craved satisfaction. Taking her bow and quiver, Mayli swung her door open.

"Good afternoon, Your Highness."

Holding onto her door's handle, Mayli blinked as a guard shifted to address her with a bow. It wasn't Charli.

Although the bulk seemed similar, this guard was a bit shorter, nearly her height. He kept a single sword and stood stoutly. His dark complexion blended in with the shadows. Sensing familiarity in his eyes, Mayli moved her lips trying to form a memory of his name. "Um... Kre... Ka—"

"Keegan Gatemen." He touched his shoulder in introduction and gave another formal bow.

"That's it!" She looked around him. "Where's Charli?"

"I do not know where he may be at this moment, but Damgard is on break." His voice was clipped and formal, offering no sense of friendship.

"So you'll be my escort until he's back?"

He nodded, eyes averted as if looking at her would earn him castration.

Mayli inwardly laughed. *Father likely gave him the same warning he gave Charli.* Sighing, she walked past. "I'm not going to bite."

"I am sure of that," he said.

"Unless you want me to..." Mayli played, if only just to see him squirm.

"I have no interest in such things with you."

Mayli mocked hurt. "Ouch..."

"I did not mean that as a jeer, Your Highness." His stiff footsteps trailed behind as they descended the steps.

"I know, *Korbin.*"

"It's Keegan."

Mayli reached the bottom. "I know," she said, wrapping around the corner with a trill of giggles.

His steps followed. "Are you going to the range?"

Mayli lifted and shook her bow. "That's why I have this..."

"Then, allow me to lead you." Keegan picked up his pace, shuffling by her to be in front.

Mayli paused, half-amused by his professionalism. "I know the way."

He stopped and touched his hand to his shoulder respectfully as he faced her. "That is true, but I just don't wish for any more surprises. I failed you once, it won't happen again."

Rolling her eyes, Mayli continued. "No one is going to kidnap me from my own home, Karl."

Keegan sighed. "Of course, Your Highness... Lead on..."

Mayli proceeded down the hall, past rusting iron gates, and into a sun-crisped courtyard. Farther she went; through an arbor, down the hill, around a watchtower, and finally to where three terraced yards made up the archery range. Each had several targets shaped like men and a shaded shelter to shoot from, complete with supplies. Guards patrolled the wall overlooking the seascape beyond. Despite the familiar heat blowing from the desert, it couldn't warm the ice in her veins.

Mayli set her feet in position and faced the range. The bow felt complete in her grip—an extension of herself. Another limb, or perhaps her heart. Releasing a breath, Mayli whipped an arrow from her quiver and secured it to the string. Without much thought, she raised it, pulled back, and loosed.

A satisfying *thwack* struck the center of the dummy's head.

Again, she repeated the motion. Again she hit the target. The actions were visceral, crafted by years of practice and frustration in order to find a sense of fulfillment. She hit again. Inside the palace, she'd be judged should she let loose a single tear, so Mayli took to loosing arrows to relieve her heart, thick with mourning. *Thwack.* Nearly every day she had visited the range and in time had perfected her form. Strengthened her arms. Honed her vision. When she practiced, everything around her became like a dream. After countless sessions, the act took little concentration, as if she were sending each troubling thought from her head and into her target. For years, she imagined the dummy as Colin, but today the figure had no identity. Just an emptiness she craved to fill. She sent another volley.

Center. Center. Center.

Mayli traced her thumb along the rim of her quiver. Finding it empty, she collected her arrows and repeated the motions as the sun continued to fall and sweat broke on her brow.

"Back at it already?"

Mayli startled, nearly releasing her arrow prematurely. She

turned to scold Charli for sneaking up, but a bouquet of white roses filled her vision in endless beauty. A sweet floral scent emitted. She blinked, looking around the arrangement to see Charli's charming smile. "Are those for me?"

"Well, Keegan didn't seem impressed." Charli thumbed backward where Keegan walked back to the palace. "So I suppose you can have them in his stead."

Mayli huffed a laugh then turned to aim at her target. She released her arrow, crowding it with the others lodged in the dummy's head.

"Ah. Nice grouping as always, Princess."

"I'm afraid so."

"There's no need to be afraid of such impressive talents. I have none in this regard."

"Prove it." Mayli extended her arm, offering him the bow in exchange for the flowers. She hugged the thorn-plucked bouquet, inhaling the soothing, fragrant perfume.

Charli took an arrow from her quiver and readied his stance. He pulled, held, then released. It struck the thatched wall beyond. "See?" Frowning, he drew another.

Mayli watched as he held his aim again before letting another fly. This one hit slightly closer, just grazing the dummy's shoulder. She rubbed hers. "It's not talent. It is skill."

"So says the natural expert." He winked.

She pointed his gaze back to the target. "Don't hesitate after you draw, just loose, keeping in mind where you want to strike. Shoot true."

Shrugging, Charli pulled the bow once more and immediately let the arrow fly, striking the target's red-painted heart.

"See!" Mayli clapped, careful not to damage the roses. "You did it!"

He smiled. "After three tries. And look at you, fierce as ever."

Mayli eyed the red center of the dummy's head she'd struck

over and over, remembering the blood she spilled. She swallowed, recalling the results of what her skills had earned. *Two deaths.* The thief, Paige, had chased her wordlessly through the forest like a reaver hunting prey. When Mayli had come to a stream, too wide for her to cross, she had no option but to turn and strike. Like in practice, the arrow had flown without thought. A gut intuition. Another day at the range. Another target. Just a way to release her fears. When she watched the woman fall back—dead—the reality of what she'd done had shaken her. Killing Reyn was just as easy.

"You okay?" Charli set the bow aside and stepped to her. "If I've done something to offend you, Princess, tell me."

Mayli shook her head. "What makes you think that?" she asked part accusation, part genuine curiosity.

"You've been avoiding me since the Cads."

Mayli sighed. "I haven't been avoiding you..." She lifted the flowers to her nose, hiding her lying smile within.

"Locking yourself in your room and denying me isn't avoiding?" he challenged.

"I'm sorry. It's not you. I just needed time to process what I'd gone through." She touched one of the petals, admiring the faintest blush of pink breaking the skin as if it were as embarrassed as she.

"I understand, Princess. But after everything, I would have thought you might..." He sucked in a breath through a hopeful grin. "I don't know."

"Thought I might what?"

He stepped in. "Still considered me as someone to confide in."

She furrowed her brow. "You are."

"Then is it about Arkello? Because, Princess, I'm not mad at you. He made his choice. Going into the desert has risks, no matter how well-versed he was with it. At least now I have a lead on where to go with a full crew. And he was right about the kanavaur eggs... Selling those to Mr. Vaurus gave me enough to hire a team. And with your father's reward, I'll have everything ready to send them in."

Mayli cocked her head. "Are you going after Arkello?"

"I—" Charli chuckled and stood a bit taller. "Yes. I can't just leave my friend there, now can I?"

"That's...relieving," Mayli lied. "But I wasn't concerned about him."

"Oh? What has you prickling that poor man down there then?" He gestured toward her target.

Heart thundering, she picked at dirt still clinging under her nails. "Well..."

"Colin?" he guessed.

"Not quite..."

"Briar then? Don't worry, your father is making the right decision. Starving him out this way will expose his weakness, and then we can demand anything we want from him."

Mayli glared. "That's cruel."

"It is politics, Princess. If we don't make the first move, he will."

"That's only to assume he craves war."

"He harbors your mother's killer." Charli lifted a finger to point. "He threatens you every day he doesn't oblige this generous peace offering."

Mayli turned from Charli. "I'm not threatened by Briar. I'm more concerned about what I've done."

"What you've done?" Charli laughed. "Princess, nothing you do could be classified as intimidating."

"I killed people."

"The lives lost in war are not on your hands, but on Colin's."

She stared at the straw target. "No, like, I have personally killed people."

Charli dipped his head. "Excuse me, *what*?" He chuckled.

"It isn't a joke, Charli. I killed a woman and a man. Both Shadowen Thieves." She blinked to look at him.

Wrinkles waved over his brow. His eyes searched her own. "To escape?"

"Yes. They were going to kill me or..." She swallowed, unable to bring herself to the idea of what Reyn would have done to her had Alden not allowed her to escape her binds by throwing his dagger to her. According to the man's journal and his accounts with Kira... Mayli took a deep breath, casting the images away. "I had to do things I didn't think possible."

"Everyone is capable of more than they believe. But it takes strength to harness that power. Seeing you here with your bow shows me you're a true Ammosian fighter. One who I greatly admire..." He leaned in, chewing his lip while eyeing hers.

She raised the bouquet. "Don't..."

"Don't what?" he laughed, parting the flowers.

"Kiss me."

"Why not?"

"So Father won't kill you."

His grin cocked even further to the side. "Don't think Bakhari's warning will stop me from wooing you," he said.

She pushed the flowers back with a laugh. "I'm not the one that needs wooing."

Charli took a step back, taking the bouquet with him as he mocked a return to the throne room. "Then I best deliver these to the king!" He waved them like a knight's token.

Giggling, Mayli chased him. "Stop!"

Charli obeyed, turning and nearly bumping into her. A step closer, he plucked a single rose from the bouquet and lifted the flower. "I'll never stop loving you, Princess."

She'd frowned at the rich attempt to resume what once was. Had nothing gone amok in the past month, Mayli believed she would have fallen right back into his distraction. Unlike archery, Charli soothed not only her mind but her body as well. His passion overruled her father's command—perhaps her own. She couldn't blame him, she'd been the one to first push her advances, twist, and conform his loyalty to the kingdom to be hers alone. While she saw their relationship as a friendship that served also as a lustful indulgence, she never allowed love to become part of the equation. He, however, could not tame his feelings, it seemed. "Loving me?" she asked.

Charli tucked the flower in her hair, thumb caressing her cheek. "Yes."

"Charli, I—"

He then lowered to grip her chin and suddenly sealed his mouth onto hers.

Mayli felt her face flush as a twist of deceit and repulsion as shame set in again. Quickly, she pressed both hands to his breastplate, jerking her head away and having sucked in a lost breath. "You need to stop."

His eyes went wide in surprise as he followed her gaze. "I gave you privacy on the ship because I thought you were ill. But now after I brought you home, after becoming knighted, and having earned my rightful place back at your side... *Princess,* I thought you would be glad to be with me?"

"And I am, but...you're still my guard, Charli. You're lucky Father didn't sever your crest."

"You know he wouldn't have," he chuckled and pushed his chest out with pride and bravado.

"But he will if you disrespect us again, which you are!" Mayli pushed from him, embarrassed that he clung so close after she had told him off. She eyed the patrolling guards, but beyond the shaded pavilion, none paid them any attention. "We can't keep playing these games..."

"Games?" Charli closed the gap once more. "I wasn't under the impression that is what this has been all these years."

"Of course it was..." Mayli cast her gaze away, saddened for them both. "We knew all along nothing would become of us. It was all in good fun."

"Then why stop the fun?" His hand toured her backside, stirring memories of days untamed. "Do I not make you happy?"

"Of course you do... Which is why it needs to end before Father rips us apart again." Mayli held her position, ensuring Charli knew it was his place to adjust and move—not hers. She lifted her chin with authority and raised the bouquet of white flowers he still held between them. Their delicate beauty—a barrier. "I need you at my side, protecting me but not suffocating me while I focus on life around me...because, like these flowers, I need space to breathe in order to thrive."

Charli looked down to observe her metaphor. The once crisp roses were now bruised, bent, and wilted. A few petals lay around their feet in the dirt. His steel-toed boots shifted back.

The heartbreak in his eyes wavered between duty and passion. His arm drooped, tipping the flowers to the ground. Slowly, they began to slip. One by one, they fell like a discarded dream. With his empty hand, Charli raised it to his crested shoulder and bowed. "Your Highness."

CHAPTER THIRTEEN

A KINGDOM'S WORTH

"There you are!"

Alden glanced over his shoulder. Kira's dress swished with each thrown leg as she ran to meet him from the adjoining hall. Sneering, he continued his march. "Like you ever have a problem knowing where to find me."

She slowed to match his lumbering stride. "I thought I'd give you some privacy after the announcement. I know how you get."

"How do I get, Kira?" Alden snapped.

"Cranky."

He threw her a sour look. "And ya think I shouldn't be after what Bri did?" he asked, walking past the common area and into the hall leading towards Briar's office.

"Didn't say that," Kira said. "But I know this annexation of Brimley into Dregs has hit a tender spot. Briar feels terrible."

Alden fidgeted with his helm's strap, anger mudding the movements. "Oh, he does, does he? So terrible that he stole my kingdom without giving me the common decency of a notice beforehand?" Finally freeing the heavy metal from his head, Alden shook his hair out. Greasy wisps hung over his eyes.

"Come on. He told me he thought you were going to be in your quarters so he could discuss it privately with you." Kira grabbed his arm, slowing him. "And didn't he say he'd sign Brimley back to you after you clear your name?"

He jerked away. "Yeah! Only after I asked. And he called me *Colin* and asked me to *trust* him," he hissed over his shoulder.

"So?"

"So!" Alden spun to face Kira. She stumbled, nearly bumping into his chest from his sudden halt. Her round eyes stared up with concern. *She's trying to reason with me, not defend him.* Tempering his rage, Alden blew out a long sigh through the nose. "So...I've never *not* trusted him before this. Why would he ask me to now? Why use my birth name? And why not call on me 'till now?"

"Those are good questions..." Kira bobbed her head. Then, like old times, she brushed her fingers through his bangs, clearing them from his view. Her long nails gently and lovingly massaged his scalp as if knowing the thoughts troubling him needed to ease. "Have you considered that Briar is over-whelmed? That since the announcement, he's barely made time to be with anyone, even me, or more surprisingly his horse?"

Alden shook his head ever so slightly as to not shake her touches away.

She continued to soothe. "You know he's busy dealing with this transition of power, earning the nobles' respect, and trying to bring peace between both your people. As you saw how the Brimleyns were treated—that union won't be so easily made by a nice speech and claim of land. And now this trading ban with Ammos and managing what supplies we have to keep the nobles happy has just amplified all of that pressure. Not to mention the Shadowens may still be lurking."

Alden closed his eyes. "You're right."

"Mmhmm," she hummed, cradling his face. "So ya think

Briar really wanted to add more stress into his life by taking in a whole other kingdom and enraging you in the process?"

"No."

"Right, because it's a lot of responsibility to manage. You understand what that does to one's mind."

"Yeah..."

She brought her hand down to touch his right shoulder. She squeezed it. "And has Briar ever done anything to hurt you before?"

His head shook.

"And...is your name Colin?"

He nodded.

She gripped both shoulders. "So, you can't assume he's trying to hurt you."

Looking back at her, he sighed. She spoke truth and reason, grounding him as the knot of anxiety let free. "I suppose you're right."

She smirked, knowingly. "When am I not?"

He chuckled. "Rarely."

"Mmhmm, so you should relax about all this," Kira said, rubbing Alden's arms.

He let her sway him, helping to further loosen the tension. Rolling his head, Alden lowered it to rest on the top of hers. He pulled Kira's warm body against his, melting away knots he couldn't work out on his own. Her usual peppered vanilla fragrance she wore filled his nose, and his worries eased completely.

He missed this; these tender moments of their beloved friendship he'd grown to count on over the last few years. They had kept him going, even through the hardest times, knowing that despite everything, love and happiness were still somewhat tangible. However, over the last few weeks, he'd been deprived of even the simplest of her gestures—given all to

Briar. It made the overwhelming responsibilities he carried become nearly unbearable. Still, right now, it was him Kira chose to seek out, not Briar. He hugged her tighter. "Thank you for always taking the time to talk me down... A slap would have been quicker."

Kira stepped from his embrace and shook an open palm. "I can still arrange that?"

Laughing, he shook his head. "My mind is abuzz as it is. The effort would be wasted."

"Hmm, shame." Kira recoiled her fingers. "Next time..."

Alden turned around. At the end of the hall, a stone triangle frame encased two double doors. Beyond them, an unknown fate awaited in Briar's office. He hesitated as if he were approaching his father's study.

Kira playfully pushed his back. "Go on. Trust your cousin."

Princess Mayli Drake of Ammos arrived safely home by the escort of her guard, Sir Charli Damgard. Information leading to the arrest and conviction of those responsible for her kidnapping, including; The Shadowen Thieves Guild members, one thousand gold; Pierz, the guild leader, five-thousand gold; and Prince Colin Densen of Brimley, fifteen-thousand gold. Any other leads to the arrest will be compensated accordingly.

Rubbing his face, Briar tossed the letter onto his desk. Another two letters recently received by carrier bird sat before him. Each were adorned with a white feather and orange wax marked with the princess's emblem. Written with long silky script, they were each addressed to him, but one was noted for Alden.

He reached for his own and broke open the seal. Despite the

cracked wax, the envelope still held tight, wrapped in complicated folds. He tugged and wiggled, nearly tearing it as he worked to unwrap the puzzle. Finally solving it, he flicked the paper wide.

King Briar,

I'm home. Thank you for your help getting me here. I am forever in your debt, as well as Alden's. I hope he received my letter as well?

I hear you are king now! Living in the tallest tower in the castle must be a change for you after living in that loft. Is William liking the change? Though, I suppose he was already spoiled as much as a horse could be.

I've just learned my father has restricted trade with you! I'm sorry. That is unfair. I knew you wouldn't turn in Colin—even if he's guilty. And honestly, I can no longer blame you. I would never give up the people I love, no matter how much wrong they've done.

Briar sighed.

I will do my best to find out what I can. How grand would that be if we could unite our families and bring peace to Vatan?

Your friend,
Mayli Drake

A knock came from the door. "Your Majesty, Alden of Brimley has arrived," said a steward.

Briar pushed both letters aside. "Allow him in."

Alden stepped past the steward, hardly waiting for the invitation. Alden's scrunched brow as angry as Dean's made the similarities to his grandfather uncanny. When the door clicked shut, Alden bent into a deep and theatrical bow. "You summoned for me, Your Maj—"

"Stop... Stop with the formality." Briar stood and hurried forward, pleased to be in like company where a casual departure from his desk wouldn't be classified as undignified. His hand gripped Alden's shoulder, pulling him up with a light shake. "There's no need for that. We are family."

Alden brushed him off, resuming his snide act. "Then you could come see me like one. Not demand my presence."

Briar frowned. "Asking you here was just convenient... I'm sorry if it was inconsiderate. I've been busy."

"Then there's nothing to apologize for. Being king has you managing a hundred different things. I am but one of those."

"Alden..." Briar walked back to his desk and sat in his leather wing-back chair. He rapped his fingers on the polished wood, looking around the foreign room. Even after being crowned king and having replaced furniture, the staff, and art, like his kingdom the new office still didn't feel like his. The long hall-like room was daunting. Boisterous. It set a tone of potency he didn't have. He sighed. "I never expected this responsibility. Nor did I want to take anything from you."

"Yet here we are." Yanking back a wood-arm chair, Alden sunk in and tossed his guard helmet on the desk. It spiraled into a cluster of papers until the open face stared at Briar.

Frowning, Briar removed his crown and rested it on top of the helm. "Yet here we are."

They both stared at the unit.

"Ya know..." Briar leaned back. "Dean just wanted to joust. Thought giving people a show could help them forget their worries enough to keep smiling. And it worked. It didn't even matter what kingdom they were from or who challenged him, the crowds cheered because he offered them something to believe in; a common man could win nobility then rear a royal family. My father wanted to be like him, and I strived to be like my father. To inspire and be admired for my valor."

"So ya did. Earned joust champion and kept the title for years." Alden gestured at the art installation behind him.

Briar glanced at the collage. An assortment of all things yellow and black such as stones, stained glass, bulbous gems, scraps of metal, swords, fabric, hats, broken crockery, wood carvings, wagon wheels, and other miscellaneous remnants of Dreg's history were arranged in a large herringbone pattern across the back wall. The art seemed to reflect his mind—just as fragmented despite having some sense of structure. He spotted the broken lance that threw him from his horse at the last Festival of Gezmek, ending his undefeated winning streak. *Olivar would have that displayed...* Turning his back on it, Briar snarled. "Yeah. Until Sir Stridan took that title."

"And now you've taken mine."

Keeping his fingers together, Briar spread them wide as he sucked in a breath. "You're still an heir. Still a prince. Still my cousin..."

"Then what's your point?" Alden snapped.

"My point, Alden, is that unfortunately, neither of us have been granted the luxuries of our preferred lives."

"But you're making these choices."

Patience tested, Briar pressed his lips into a line, then leaned in. "What option other than to turn you in was there for me to make? Would you rather me do that? Or do nothing and continue to deny our people a kingdom of power and security because you're insulted?"

Alden looked away. "No."

"Then you can agree that taking Brimley isn't some kind of attack?"

He shrugged. "I dunno."

Briar groaned, unable to reason with his cousin. *It's like he's drunk again. But worse, cause he's sober...* His eyes fell upon the letter bound with Princess Mayli's seal. He lifted it to Alden. "This came for you."

Dark eyes widened enough for a spark of hope to ignite inside. Alden's chest grew large. Jaw trembled. Unable to hold back his excitement, he snatched Mayli's letter from Briar's hand and tugged at the string. The wax snapped open. He expertly unfolded the complicated paper and darted his eyes across the princess's words. His lips twitched to a smile, then wavered. He sighed. Then he let his arm bend down.

Their eyes met and Briar rubbed his chin. "What did she say?"

"Arkello is dead."

"*What?*" Briar raised from his seat, bending across the desk to look at the letter.

Alden instead pocketed it. "She says that, but I'm not buying it. She said he was on their ship and took them to the desert...where reavers then attacked."

"Reavers?" Briar sat back in his chair. "I thought they were a myth?"

"They are. Trod, one of the Shadowens—"

Briar raised a finger. "He's the one who wants you dead because he thinks you killed Paige?"

"I think they *all* want me dead, but yes, especially him. From what I've gathered, he was a nomad whose party wandered too deep into the desert about three years back. They fought, but he managed to capture one—her. Paige."

Briar blinked. "Paige was from Gezmek?"

Alden bunched his shoulders. "She refused to talk, and Trod was reserved so I couldn't confirm if their story was founded in reality or nomadic folklore. The tales only began circulating when Arkello resurfaced from Gezmek. But her ability to see well in the dark was enough for me to suspect it to be true."

"That's certainly an option."

"I need to consider all if I'm to find evidence to pin on Arkello. Maybe Mayli will find something now that she's looking... We need to solve this conspiracy, Bri. I want my kingdom back."

He'll never let what happened in Brimley go, Briar realized, tapping his finger to the headpieces. The crown adjusted ever so slightly fitting more snugly on the helmet as if knowing its place. Satisfied, he pulled his hands back and wove his fingers together. "I know how much you care. Which is why you should go back home."

"To Brimley?" Alden blinked as if being pulled from a dream. "You just gave me a room here."

"And now you'll have a room there."

"Is that an order?"

"No." He frowned, shaking his head nonchalantly. "I only assumed you'd want to go back and help with the restoration of the castle. Ya know, be a part of the process?" Briar scraped open a drawer and ruffled through some papers.

"I guess..." Alden sat more snugly in his chair, although he still looked uncomfortable. "But what about the murder? The kidnapping?"

"We have more eyes working to find out the truth than ever. You don't have to carry the brunt of that responsibility anymore. I have things under control here and maybe you'll learn what's important there." Finding a blank sheet, Briar pulled it out and began writing. After signing his name he folded it into thirds. Yellow pooled as he poured wax from a small candle-heated kettle. Briar then pinched a mound of gold fleck from a tray. He twisted his fingers, letting the metal glitter down into the wax. He stamped it with the royal crest of Dregs then handed it across the desk. "This will give you access into the castle without showing crest. You'll be addressed as Alden of Brimley and working under Lord Dean. I'm giving Earl access too."

Alden frantically waved his hand. "Wait, wait, wait. You've made Granda lord of *my* castle?" He squinted as if he hadn't heard right.

Briar closed his eyes. *Always the victim, Alden still can't see past his entitlement to what really matters. He's defeated—wounded almost beyond repair. Perhaps he already is...* Briar adjusted his pose to sit more upright, his leather chair moaning for him. "It was his land to begin with. He built Brimley Castle around his farm and raised our fathers there. Of course, I honored Dean with the title of lord."

"Why not me?" Alden tapped at his chest. "I am king!"

"Claim that all you like, Col, but you are still just a prince."

His glare intensified. "My tattoo may not show I'm a king, but you know it's my right. Your father said so. That why you're doing all this? To make sure I don't ruin your new reign?"

Briar scoffed, shaking his head to the ceiling. He fell forward, meeting Alden's cynical eyes. "Why do you see me as a threat all of a sudden?"

"Same reason you see me as one." Alden snatched Briar's crown off the helmet and raised it to look through. Framed like a painting in the gold circlet, his stern glower shattered through the broken mask he displayed.

He isn't beyond repair, Briar thought. *He's only just shed everything that had broken him. He's raw. Vulnerable. Scared.* Touching his hand to his shoulder, Briar dipped, silently pledging himself.

Alden watched the submissive act as if not expecting it. Looking from the crown to Briar, he lowered his arm. Slowly, he placed it on Briar's head. "Fine. I'll get out of your way, *Your Majesty.*" He snatched the letter.

"Bah." Briar captured the crown before it slipped off. "Colin, we are on the same side here!"

"Stop calling me that!" Just before leaving, Alden stopped and looked at a painting hung on the wall. His fingers twitched at the knife at his side. Making a fist instead, he continued out the door, leaving his first painting still hanging on the wall. "And take that down."

Kira jumped as Alden pushed through the doors, the joints nearly cracking despite their industrial hold. His snarl was just as unhinged.

"Whoa, you look even more cranky."

Alden pushed past her, shaking his head. "I knew not to trust him."

"What?" Kira watched the door click shut. She hesitated, wanting to burst into the study and demand Briar undo whatever he'd just done. However, she knew Alden. Knew his temper and self-pitying attitude. Bunching her dress, she rushed after her friend. "What happened?"

"Briar has no respect for me at all. He has my painting hung when I specifically told him to get rid of it."

"Huh?"

Alden looked at her a moment then shook his head, stomping away. "Doesn't matter. He's kicked me out."

"Kicked you out?"

He waved a letter above his head. "Mayli is home. I've heard rumors my reward has doubled, so she clearly still hates me— as Colin. Still, I hear my name chanted in the streets for my capture from protesters... I'm a liability and a threat, so Briar is sending me and Squirrel to Brimley where Granda is now lord of my freakin' castle, free to boss me around. Despite being a king, I have no control over anything. Not even my own life."

"Come on. You're acting rashly."

"Ya think?" Alden started up the stairs, hand gripping the railing pulling himself higher. Arriving at the landing, Alden pointed. "Hey, Squirrel. Pack up, then ready Emory and a horse for yourself. We are leaving."

Squirrel stepped from Alden's door, a smile stretching. "Where?"

"I'll tell ya when we're there." Alden unlocked his door.

"All right! Adventure!" Squirrel spun then pointed at Kira as she topped the stairs. "You coming too?"

She shook her head.

"Aww."

Seeing Alden was already inside his room and closing the door on her, and most likely itching to lock it, Kira rushed to slip inside.

Alden ignored her intrusion—a lesson learnt after countless tries that never ended in his favor. He started picking up his unusual mess. Books, papers, boxes, notes, and piles of clothes still busied his room. Rek lounged in a dresser drawer, half pulled out. Kira counted at least four—six—mugs of tea left out. Some still held liquid. A plate with a half-eaten cucumber sandwich sat on his bed. Flies buzzed.

Kira picked up his brown woolen cloak from the floor. "You've become as messy as Briar."

Alden took it from her and wrapped it around himself. "Yeah, well I guess like him, I have a lot overwhelming me. Only it's not something I can celebrate." He grabbed a large leather bag, set it on the bed, and started folding clothes into it.

"He's not celebrating anything."

"Just wait," Alden sneered.

Finding his favorite tabard crumpled and thrown in the

corner, Kira went to collect it. She pulled it taut, doing her best to smooth the wrinkles out. A heavy odor wafted as if he'd worn it for a week straight. *Not a bad smell,* she thought, handing it to him. "Will you be gone long?"

Dark lashes cloaked his eyes as he looked at the offering. He grabbed it, taking her hand as well. Alden then let his deep brown eyes fall over her body. Slow, sensuous, and never in a way he'd openly let her see before. A rousing tightness swelled in her belly as he stepped nearer, his thumb brushing against her knuckles. "Not sure. But maybe, Ki, you could come with me?" His voice was soft—pleading.

"I don't think—"

"You'll have more than my sweater to sleep with then..." Closer, he came, tossing the tabard aside. "I'll keep you warm."

"Alden..." Without having to reach out, her fingers pressed against his chest as he moved nearer. She shook nervously, not out of fear of anything he would do, but of what selfish desires she might indulge in. Bask in the heat he promised. Sleep in the arms he offered. Already she was in her true king's room. In his space. His smell. His embrace. She could finally be in his bed. His life... Realizing he was nearing for a kiss, she closed her eyes. *I must do anything for him, even if it means heartbreak.* Before they touched, Kira willed her desires away to speak against his lips. "You're making me uncomfortable."

For a moment, he hovered. Their closeness stilling all time. Then, to Kira's relief, he released his hands from her arms. His body from her palms. His face from hers. His heart...

Kira's tore with him as he stepped further back. Having air to breathe, she swallowed a fresh gulp.

"Kira, I—" His voice wavered.

She raised her hand between them. "Don't."

"I can't just abandon everything we had..."

"We didn't have anything."

"We had each other."

Kira frowned deeply. "Not when there's Princess Mayli." She peered up at him.

"I'll never have her. But Ki, I love ya. So much. You've kept me alive in more ways than one." He took a step forward, reaching. "And I know you've felt the same for me..."

Kira stepped back. Brow furrowed in worry and shame, Alden stopped, looking as devastated as she felt. She shook her head. "Even so, that time has passed so you don't have the right to come back and resume our bonded night after you left and I was forced to move on from it. Yes, I still care for you. Yes, I still want to be around to help with your mission to reclaim your home and honor. But, Alden, you need to accept that I am committed to Briar now, and I love him. A lot, actually." She rubbed her hands.

He studied her, eyes holding hers. "Already you're so convinced he's who you would rather be with?"

"Yes." She touched the jewels of Gezmek laced around her neck. "And he loves me too."

Eyes following the action, Alden sneered. "Of course, ya think he does. He'll adorn any woman who offers him time in bed with gifts and gold to keep 'em around, making up for his unsuitability."

"Alden!"

"Or did ya already know that before ya got crested, and ensured he got crowned? What? So you could be queen?"

"Hey!"

"You're such a great actress, Kira, I wouldn't be surprised if you are still working for Pierz. I guess then fucking Briar was just part—"

Kira slapped his face.

Alden stumbled back from the fierce blow. He put his hand

on his cheek, then checked it. Feeling the pain rouse, he looked back at Kira with an open mouth.

She pointed. "You asked for that."

He rubbed his face again. Unable to wipe away the red mark of humiliation, he covered his brow. "You're right. I'm sorry."

"Are you?" She raised her brow.

He nodded, eyes downcast.

"Good because we are *all done.* So stop thinking we are something more than friends and live up to your oath, *Colin.*"

He peered up in shock.

"And Briar and me?" Kira took a step forward, fist flexing. "I couldn't care less if he found all the lost treasures of Gezmek and gave them to me, I love him for him. King or not. Just as I had you. I don't seek to be a queen. Damnit, Alden, I didn't even wanna be noble! I didn't plan this, but I'm flattered you'd think I could. Truth is, I have found my stage, and I'm enjoying it. I'm enjoying him, the dresses, the respect. And why shouldn't I?"

"You should be happy..." he said, voice soft.

"That's right. So please don't make this any harder on us."

"I was trying to make it easier..."

"You think that constantly pushing your boundary with me will make me dismiss a man who accepted and trusted me immediately? Or that professing your jealousy in front of him the other day somehow was okay? How is that easier for everyone and not just you?"

"It...isn't." He sighed, voice now heavy. "I know it's not fair. I damn myself every moment for not coming forward when I see you two together thinking that could have been us. I was too scared to lose the only thing good in my life if you turned on me. But now I see I have anyway."

"You haven't lost me, I'm still your friend, Alden. Besides, I'm not the only good thing..." Kira gestured at a drawing on his easel. Well-rendered lines illustrated long black hair whipping in the wind, feathers flying all around, a silken scarf slipping, and hands falling from her face. "You have Mayli."

"That's a bit of an optimistic assessment, Kira." He turned the art piece around. "I lied to her just the same and worry I've done far worse."

Kira folded her arms. "Well, after your travels with her, I have to believe you two formed something stronger than what we ever had. And that will overpower any misconceptions."

"How?" He scoffed. Lips gaping, he looked around in wonder. "What if I am a murderer? I can't remember if..."

"Even if..." Kira grabbed him firmly at the shoulders. "As stubborn and dense and sometimes rude as you may be, you're worth loving and forgiving for the efforts you put forth to right your wrongs. And if she can't see that, then she's not worth your love."

His mouth opened to argue, but it hung wordlessly.

Kira lifted her hand to close it for him. "Alden. Keep fighting, but let this jealousy and contempt you have for your cousin go. He's a good man. You know that. And if I find anything to suggest otherwise, I will let you know. I may be committed to him, but I'm still pledged to you. My king." She cupped his face.

The scratch of his beard raked across her palm as he nodded. His lips pressed into a deep, regretful frown. "I don't deserve a friend like you, Kira."

"You deserve a kingdom's worth of friends like me. I hope you find them in Brimley. I'll make them for you in Dregs." Rising on her toes, she kissed his cheek. "Now go, so I can be your Shadow Seeker."

CHAPTER FOURTEEN

A PIERCED HEART

"Ah, there's my Little Bird!" Bakhari said, taking his hands from the wood railing. Dressed in his brightest orange suit and cape, he spread his arms out wide.

"Here I am..." Mayli said, lifting the hem of the long gown Lidia insisted she wear over her sandals to hide her sores. Carefully, she descended the tiled stairway. She paused seeing a white sand strider, saddled with a pavilion and silk canopy adorned with long ribbons as if they were about to partake in a parade. As it was brought to the dock for them to board, the giant bird fluffed its feathers and extended its long neck upon seeing her. Mayli lifted her hand, gesturing around. "Father, what is this?"

Her father met her at the base of the steps, frowning deeply. He took her hands, leading her to stand by his side. "After the other day, I reflected on how troubled you were by your excursion and how much things have changed in your absence. So after keeping to your room, I thought it would serve well for you to accompany me to the showroom at the coliseum. Lidia mentioned you wanted some new dresses."

"The coliseum, Father? Doesn't Mr. Vaurus visit us with his silks?"

"Yes..." He leaned in, quieting his voice. "But when it involves commissioning the remains of your mother's dress into another scarf, I like to see matters handled more personally."

Mayli touched her neck where a yellow-orange scarf accented her pearlescent dress. While it was beautiful and looked similar to her old one, it didn't offer the sentiment. "You mean I could have the same scarf made?"

With a promising smile, he placed his hand on her shoulder and squeezed firmly. "Of course."

Mayli hugged her father, squeezing him tight. "Thank you!"

He patted her back. "Certainly." He raised his hand in summoning, and a servant opened the gate leading to the sand strider.

Mayli crossed a small bridge and stepped aboard. Her silent shadow, Sir Charli, trailed behind followed by her father and Madam Nive. Two archers joined them in the pavilion as they took their seats. Mayli kept to the middle, daring not to look over the edge as the strider rose to its full height, towering over the horsemen who guarded below with flagged spears. A man below tugged a silk-braided leash, leading them down the winding hill from Upper Ward to Lower Ward, then past the curtain wall and into the city below. Immediately, a gathering formed in the streets.

Mayli looked down at the people with a practiced smile. They waved to her, calling her name and praising the king and Sir Charli for their valiant efforts. There were drums and bells, clapping and cheering. The chorus of attention after weeks of hiding in the shadows with an enemy afoot had Mayli hesitant to lift her hand. And seeing the hunger and poverty lingering in her people's eyes made her feel ashamed for living so lavishly. Mayli settled back and looked to her father. "There are so many people out. Was an announcement of our travels into town made?"

Bakhari patted Mayli's leg. "I could not refuse them from knowing. They were devastated after learning of your mishap, so to see you home and safe shows we are a kingdom that does not fall. Now show some gratitude and wave."

Feeling the love and adoration of her people as well as the peace, protection, and ease of being home, Mayli tossed a wave. The crowd cried out and whistled, swooning over her as if she alone were giving them hope.

She wished she could feel as confident.

A few overly excited children, dressed in rags and dirt, rushed under the guards' defenses to get a closer look. Instinctively protective, the strider fluffed her feathers and hissed them away with a snap of its long narrow beak.

"Lady, be nice," Mayli cooed, stroking the bird's velvet-like feathers.

Lady curled her neck, forming a perfect "S" casting Mayli in its shade and protection. Cautious, round eyes stayed wide while her beak chittered nervously, observing the wild commotion in the streets as guards gathered into a tighter formation, warning back any others who dared venture closer. Offering a sympathetic smile, Mayli waved her admirers goodbye.

After parading down the street, and her hand well-shaken, the sand strider's handler tugged at the rope. The giant bird knelt, lowering into the shade of the coliseum. Mayli looked up to admire the central building of Ammos that seemed to compete with the palace for elegance. Two-story marble pillars stood tall. Intricate carvings lined the window frames, doors, and awnings upon the stucco walls. Several men cloaked in the most exquisite silk robes imaginable guarded a pair of doors just as grand.

Sir Charli rose from his seat on the platform and unlatched a staircase. After letting it fold down, he stood formally beside it. Eyes forward but averted from her.

Since the archery range, Charli had pulled back from their previous closeness. Instead of spending his off time with her, he'd taken leave elsewhere. When he was on duty, especially when in view of others like now, he acted as the perfect guard. When alone with her, he kept his speech clipped. While she appreciated his respect, Mayli missed his charming smiles, jokes, and curious conversations.

She missed her one friend.

Realizing he wouldn't meet her eyes, Mayli looked away and shifted out of her seat, following after her father and Madam Nive.

"Watch your step, Princess," cautioned Charli. "It is still high."

Now with attention called to the narrow staircase, Mayli hesitated. Even with Lady lowered, the steps were steep and as long as a lance. She looked up, waiting for Charli's outstretched hand to help guide her, but it remained at his side as if helping her would be inappropriate. Clinging to confidence, Mayli took a delicate step on the steep incline. The distance still tightened her chest, yet reluctantly, she descended, doing her best to not let her fear of heights deter her from moving on. A moment later, she met the dirt road below without incident and smiled. *I don't need him.*

Her father clenched tightly to a metal case embossed with swirling lines of feathers around the Ammosian Crest. He pointed with it toward the building. "Let us get your new scarf made." He walked forward, and it took no show of crest or announcement for the two stylish guards to swing the large doors open for their king.

Following, Mayli paused at the array of garments greeting her in the showroom. Usually, Mr. Vaurus would visit the castle, arms draped with several limited colors and patterns to choose from. Never had she thought there were more than what he offered, but here in the tall marble room, the choices seemed endless. The brilliant sheens spanned from the brightest whites to the deepest blacks and nearly all colors of the rainbow— minus blue. Aside from the variety of dyes, there were dresses formed in styles never previously presented to her. She touched one, admiring the simplicity. Black, long skirt, U-shaped collar. It was sleeveless aside from a wrap of fabric that would hang just under the shoulder's crest.

"Mayli, over here there are dresses in your style." Her father raised the hem of an intricate frock adorned in an embroidered chiffon.

Looking back at the display ahead of her, Mayli took the simple dress from its hanger. "This is my style." She put it to herself as if trying it on. Smiling, she looked at Charli expecting his approving wink.

Stationed at the door, his attention was focused on an adjoining hallway, as uninterested as Keegan might be. *For the better, I guess.*

Frowning, Mayli continued through the shop. She selected a few other gowns of varying looks, sticking mostly to blacks and gray; however, a striking orange ball gown with blooming frills did not escape her. She laid them all out on the kiosk just as a familiar tall, white-bearded man hurried through the hall.

"Your Majesty!" Mr. Vaurus exclaimed with a grand bow. He pivoted. "And the brave Royal Highness!"

Mayli smiled. "Hello, Mr. Vaurus."

Her father greeted the man as he rose, patting him on the shoulder where a layer of silk parkled against the noble crest of Ammos when the light hit it ever so. "Taji. You look as fashionable as ever!"

"Aye, so do you! As humbled as I am by this royal visit, I am curious why I was not requested at the palace? Surely I could have brought these to you." Mr. Vaurus eyed the garments Mayli had selected and his lips faltered. Doing his best to uphold a polite smile, he folded one off to the side. "We can tailor anything for you, Princess. Perhaps we design that one in a bright color?"

"Black is fine." She lifted a finger. "But let's add a hood."

"A hood?"

Mayli framed her face. "Yes, wide and droopy so it lies on my shoulders while it's up?"

"If you wish it..." Mr. Vaurus flicked a smile, but as he turned, his eyes went wide in astonishment.

Bakhari chuckled awkwardly then tapped the case at his side. "Taji, I have come to discuss a special project with you..."

"Ah..." Mr. Vaurus waved him to follow down the hall. "Privacy then. Come, come."

Her father turned. "Mayli, why don't you continue shopping for some dresses."

"Can't I come with?" She stepped forward to catch his arm. "I want to see her dress."

Bakhari's eyes sorrowed.

"Please? I'd love to have a say in how my scarf will be made."

Glancing at the case in his hand he sighed. "I suppose you are old enough... Okay, Little Bird, but you must promise me to say nothing of this. Not even to your brother."

Mayli cocked her head, brow furrowing. "Okay?"

"Promise?"

She shook her head with finite assertion. "I promise."

Nodding, Bakhari put his hand on Mayli's back and helped her follow Mr. Vaurus. The hall was tall, nearly two stories, and arched at the top. They passed many doors until they paused at one near the end. While Bakhari let Madam Nive join them, he motioned for Charli to remain outside, closing the door on him.

Unlike the pristine appeal of the lobby, showroom, and grand hall, the office revealed the mind of a busy craftsman. Papers, letters, spools of fabric, dyes, and a tray of black needles with a matching set of scissors lay scattered about. Mr. Vaurus hurried to clear his cluttered table. He lit a gas lamp then shut the curtains, clouding the room in a dark warm tone. A faint sulfuric odor hung in the air mixed with the smell of old books.

Bakhari gingerly lifted a bottle to examine. A pearlescent oil substance swirled inside, faint sparkles of purple catching in the light. "Arkello's ill-timed absence will not be an issue I hope?"

"No, Sire. Thankfully, Sir Charli Damgard has provided me with fresh eggs. Seems he is quite capable of finding treasures. And while Arkello excels in milking kanavaurs and has no qualms taking the coin to sit down in the pits with those monsters, I do possess the knowledge. Thankfully though, this bottle of toxin is more than enough for the job." He took it from the king and set it gently back in place.

"Good." Bakhari set the case on the table. He withdrew a key in the shape of an arrowhead and inserted it into the hole. After a turn one way, then the other with a push and back, the lid popped open.

Like the yawning morning, gold light shimmered around a fold of orange fabric. Mayli's eyes watered seeing her mother's nightgown. Feather-woven embroidery, diamonds, and fine silk all shone like treasures. The last outfit she had seen her mother wear...

Something tapped at Mayli's side. A handkerchief lay in her father's hand, his kind eyes doing their best to offer a smile. She tugged the fabric from his hand and dabbed her eyes, not at all surprised she'd already let tears fall. Sniffing, Mayli wiped her nose and adjusted to recollect herself.

Mr. Vaurus gently pulled Queen Margaret's nightgown from its case and laid it across the table. At the bottom, a long stretch was missing—having been used for Mayli's lost scarf. He stroked it, smoothing out wrinkles. "Yes, it looks like I can cut another from this. Although, to dodge the...*blemish*...it will need to be a tad bit thinner if Her Highness wishes to keep the same length. Or it can be shorter." The man's hand gestured over a thread-splitting tear.

A tear? Mayli's eyes widened, noting a curious dark red stain circling it. *Blood?* She stared harder, realizing the placement was centered in the chest. *Into the heart.* Pointing at the marking, Mayli looked at her father. "I don't understand, Father. Why is this dress damaged...and bloodsoaked?"

Bakhari closed his eyes and sighed deep.

A heaviness set in. "Wait, are you saying her throat wasn't slit, but she was stabbed *through* silk?"

Bakhari waved her down, looking around guiltily. "Quiet."

"Father! How is that even possible? Silk is impenetrable without—" Mayli looked at the jar her father had examined. "*Kanavaur Toxins*..."

"This is why I was hesitant to bring you along..." He turned her at the shoulder, leading her out. "You needn't know such things."

Mayli pulled free from his lead and snatched the bottle from the table. "Father, why was this kept secret from me...or the public? This is evidence to her murder!" She shook it in his face, rousing the toxin's glow.

"To keep our enemies from discovering the vulnerability of our silks, and to do so we must keep our voices down." He grabbed her hand, stealing the bottle.

"Who knows?" Mayli's tone remained elevated.

"The Densens, of course."

"Besides them?" She leaned in, eyes searching.

"Well everyone here." Her father gestured around the four of them. "Madam Nive, as she was who found Margaret. The Vaurus family and the workers here. And now you."

"The workers?" Mayli turned around as if to see them beyond the walls. Each a potential threat. "Why?"

Mr. Vaurus cleared his throat. "You see, Your Highness, it requires the use of toxins to coat a pin or scissors to cut and sew the Ammosian Silks. Without a bit of shared knowledge, our wares cannot be produced. Rest assured that you are in no danger among them—all my workers are trusted nobles who have pledged an oath of silence regarding its technique for the good of the kingdom."

The odor Arkello's kanavaur had emitted when it glowed flared back in her memory, linking her to the smell lingering in the room. So pungent and strong that it could weaken its silk eggs. Likely her skin had Arkello not intervened. *He helped me then, yet kept no pledge talking about the toxin so openly with me. And...he's a Densen. He has no respect for Ammos as a kingdom and said himself he'd do whatever it takes.* Reminded once more of Alden's warning, Mayli stilled. *What if "whatever it takes" means hiring thieves to kidnap me and rouse a reward from Father... Or worse: Killing Mother since she denied him support as the heir to Vatan?* Staring at the gash in her mother's dress, Mayli put her hand to her mouth. "I think I'm going to throw up."

Bakhari waved a hand at Mr. Vaurus. "Close that up, will you? You've made your assessment."

Mr. Vaurus bowed. "Yes, Your Majesty. I'll have the scarf made in a few days." He shut and locked the case.

Mayli held her hand out. "I don't think I want another cut from that anymore."

Bakhari pulled at her arm. "Come, Little Bird. This was far too much excitement for you after such an ordeal—I apologize. I shouldn't have let you see that. Let's return you home to rest."

Mayli walked with her father into the lobby. "It's fine Father, I'm glad you did. Although I doubt sleep will come easily."

"Then I will have Lidia bring you some dune ale to sip."

Madam Nive offered a maternal frown as she moved to open the door for them.

"Thank you..." Mayli said, stepping out to be beside Charli. He remained stationed as Mr. Vaurus, and Madam Nive walked back to the showroom. A moment passed in silence before Mayli looked up at her guard. "Charli?"

He ignored her.

"Char... Can we go to Lower Ward later?" she asked under a whisper.

His brow raised as he met her gaze. "You want *me* to take you?"

"Well, yes. You're my guard."

"So is Keegan. Ask him; my shift is over after this." He looked away.

"But..." Mayli touched Charli's arm, his skin warm and muscles firm. "I need you."

Charli cocked his head, a twinkle catching in his eye. "Why me, Princess?"

"Because..." Mayli swallowed her guilt for casting him aside before. *He's trying so hard to be what I need. And how can he if I don't open up?* She glanced at her father as he pushed aside all the clothes she had picked out, save for the orange ball gown. *I promised Father I wouldn't speak of the dress, but I need someone to talk with and help sort out these challenging thoughts. Someone other than a straw man to bury my frustrations into.* She stepped closer. "I need to get into Arkello's house."

"Arkello?" Charli looked to the side. His mother's watchful eyes caught his before looking at the king, as if reminding him to behave. Charli put his hand on the small of her back, leading Mayli into the lobby, offering privacy and full focus on her. "Why?"

Mayli looked him straight in the eye and kept her voice low. "Charli, I still want to confide in you. As *friends.* So if I tell you something, do you swear you will keep it between us?"

"Have I ever made you doubt I wouldn't?" he asked. His honest smile offered all his sincerity.

"Never..."

"Okay. Go on then."

Mayli picked at her nail. "I'm starting to believe, Colin was framed."

He scoffed, chuckling rudely.

Mayli whacked his chest. "Don't laugh. I'm serious."

He laughed again, looking down on her. "First you're defending Briar and now this? Princess, your time in the north has subjected you to conspiracy theories. Perhaps you're looking too deep into things."

"No. I'm not looking deep enough!"

His face balled with pity.

Tossing her head to the dome ceiling, Mayli walked in a circle, leading her into a private nook with a small tiled fountain in the wall. She groaned sitting on its ledge. She looked up as Charli followed. "Look, Alden has been searching for years in the guild and has found nothing, but maybe that's because he has been looking in the wrong places. Which is why I want to look into Arkello..."

"Who is Alden?" Charli folded his arms.

Mayli bit her lip. *Oops.*

"The guild..." Charli rubbed his chin. "Was he one of the thieves? Is this why you're so conflicted? Is he the one planting these troubling thoughts? Princess..."

"No! Well, yes. I suppose..." She dipped her finger in the fountain, welcoming the touch of the cool water to settle her nerves. "He's had me thinking about the war from the Brimleyn's point of view."

"That's dangerous, Princess. Their perspective is skewed."

"So is ours!" she snapped, flicking water at him.

"Okay then," Charli said, raising his hands. "What more can you tell me about the thieves? Maybe start with this *Alden* fellow."

Mayli closed her eyes, picturing Alden's melancholic stare. His dark, worried eyes seemingly begged her to let him remain in the shadows. Speaking his name had already broken his trust. The thought of hurting him more than what he'd endured pulled at her heart.

The light caress of Charli's voice tickled her ear. "Remember, you can tell me anything. Especially if you believe this will reveal who knows the truth of your mother's murder..."

Mayli looked at her friend finding his determined focus. *Speaking out could very well aid in Alden's recovery. I can at least tell Charli.* Mayli took a deep breath. "Alden was a Shadowen," she admitted.

"And was he old? Young? Where is he from?"

"Does it matter?"

"Every detail matters." He sat beside her.

Mayli sighed and wove her fingers together and started playing with her nails. "Just a little older than me, I think."

Charli waited for more, eyebrow arching. When she shrugged innocently he smirked. "I know you pay too close attention to men to note only that."

"Only if I think they are handsome." Mayli dipped her head so he wouldn't see her blush from her deceit.

"Fair enough." He folded his arms as if making a conclusion. "So, Alden is a typical brim-nose runt. Meaning he most likely has brown hair and pale skin if he's stuck to the shadows."

She winced at his accuracy. "Yep..."

"Do you know what rank he had among the thieves?"

"Shadow Seeker." She tapped her fingers together. "Usually he was one to observe, draw, and take notes."

"An artist then? He the one who drew you?"

"Yeah..."

"So you *do* like him."

Mayli opened her mouth to protest, but Charli's knowing gaze couldn't be argued with. She gave in to a smile. "He had qualities I admired..."

"Sure..." Charli cleared his throat. "What was an artist doing on a high-risk mission to kidnap royalty then, do you think?"

"He said it was so I'd be taken without harm. You see, he's not a thug like the rest. He was sympathetic but strong enough to do the job."

"I am relieved to know they considered your safety while endangering your life..."

"Alden *saved* my life."

He scoffed. "Saved you?"

"He's not just a thief in the guild. He was an undercover spy. He went rogue."

"For who?" Charli growled.

Mayli nodded and kept her voice under a whisper. "Briar."

"Br—*What*?" Anger flooded Charli's pale eyes to black. He rashly pulled her to standing along with him. "You cannot be talking with him of all people! It's no wonder you're so confused!"

"Just listen!" She yanked her arm from his tight hold. Pained, she rubbed it. "Briar and Alden have been working all this time to try to solve who killed Mother! That's why instead of going forward with the guild's orders *Alden* rescued me and took me to Brimley."

"Rescued you to Brimley..." Charli's gaze narrowed. "Do you hear yourself? Sounds like this was the plan all along."

"It's not like that!" Mayli waved her hand. "They said they weren't involved!"

He raised a brow. "Tsk, and you believed a Densen lie?"

Her heart clenched, giving way to the thought. *Could it have been?* She considered it for only a moment before the genuine look of shock on Alden's face upon seeing her Ammosian Crest while in the carriage formed clearly in her mind. She shook her head. "Alden had no idea I was the Shadowen's target."

"Mayli—"

"And when they came for us, Alden protected me with his life. He was my ally! So I killed those thieves to save not just my life—but *his*. He was injured so I had to hunt, cook, scavenge, and keep busy, all the while caring for him..."

A jealous rage flared in his eyes. "You cared for your enemy?"

"Well I wasn't going to let him die after he did the same for me," Mayli said.

"You don't know his intentions."

"Yes I do," she said confidently.

"Do you?" He cocked his head.

"They were to get me home, and look where I am!" Mayli spread her arms wide.

"I brought you home, Princess." He tapped his chest then pointed outward. "He took you to the Cads."

"No thanks to the draclynn." Mayli put her hands on her hips.

He blinked, shaking his head. "I thought you were joking about that."

"Alden killed it—not Scraggs. I took a shot too, blinding one eye. Anyway, the damage to *The Lucky Fish* and its crew forced us to take refuge in the Cads to undergo repairs. That's when I found you! I wanted Alden to come and claim a reward, but he refused and asked to remain anonymous out of fear of our retaliation."

"Too bad." Charli cracked his knuckles.

Mayli touched his shoulder. "He and Briar are not our enemies."

"So they have you think. Remember how deceitful the Densens can be. Briar is now conveniently king, so he likely planned to kidnap you from the start and kept it from his spy to secure belief."

Mayli furrowed her brow at the idea. "Don't you think Briar would have hired a more impressive accomplice? Or more of them?"

"Perhaps it was all an act, Princess."

"An act?" She scoffed. "He nearly died!"

"Perhaps he should have."

"Charli!"

"I'm just saying"—his voice took on an empathetic tone—"that while you are considering more possibilities like Arkello somehow being involved, you mustn't exclude what King Briar, his spy, and his cousin may be planning."

"I *am* keeping an open mind..."

"Good. Because you were so hurt the last time they lied. I would hate to see you subjected to such trials again, but know I'll always be here for you when they do." He reached forward.

"I know, thank you." Mayli took a step back, touching his

arm to block his approach. "So help settle my ease and get me into Arkello's apartment."

He shook his head. "You're asking a lot, Princess. Arkello has considered me his closest friend since I found him dying in the sand drifts. Now he is dead or lost again, and you want me to help you break into his home because you suspect he had something to do with your mother's murder. Don't you think I would have suspected such claims?"

"If he is responsible, I think he could befriend us and keep a secret like that from you. He could be a fraud after all. It was his idea to go into the desert knowing the risks. What if he knew that marker meant reavers were there and they were men in suits? His men? That he wanted to take me back to Gezmek and use me as blackmail or something? What if he hired the thieves too, Charli?"

Charli's face took on a stoic expression. "Those who take advantage of one's good faith are the most desperate to keep something hidden..."

"So you'll take me?"

"No. You're letting your imagination go wild. You saw the reavers. The blood. Many died, most likely even him too, which is why I had to man the ship nearly by myself to get you home safe. Do you really think I would have left him otherwise?"

Guilt flowing, Mayli hunched her shoulders, shaking her head. "No, I know you're honorable. But we also saw that he knows how silk can be cut."

"What does that matter?"

Mayli cupped her hands in front of her chest. She lifted a finger to her lips. "Charli, what I saw behind Mr. Vaurus's door just now was more than just mother's nightgown. What I saw was the dress she was *murdered* in. Stabbed through her heart. Through *silk*. Just like the kanavaur egg."

Charli's eyes went wide, nostrils flaring.

"Mr. Vaurus mentioned they coat scissors and needles with kanavaur toxin to craft their silks. Arkello knows that secret."

Charli closed his eyes as if pained. His chest grew large as he took in a deep breath, then looked at her as he released it. "I understand your concern now. Give me a few days, Princess, and I will open Arkello's home so you may find the answers you seek. All will be resolved."

CHAPTER FIFTEEN

THE GUEST

Sun winked through the thinning forest, warming Alden's cold thoughts since leaving Dregs. Kira had made her choice. So had Briar. To them, his time to rule was saved for a later date, and in all honesty, he couldn't blame them.

If he wanted, he could have stepped forward to rule. To forget the accusations cast upon him and foster a kingdom. There were plenty who did see him as innocent. The Brimleyn refugees caravanning with them proved as much. They could have created a militia and fought to defend his name. But Alden knew it would only end in more bloodshed. The way their enemies continued to harass them, burning their homes, refusing their business, and humiliating them was proof enough. His reign would have been limited, and it wouldn't have solved the murder or proven anything other than his greed. Alden honored himself and his people enough to acknowledge that now, despite his desires.

As the forest began to wane, Alden looked from the newly trampled road hugging the Draclynn River to the sandstone bluff ahead. Above it, dark stone walls crowned its plateau. Turrets still armored all but one far-off corner. Where the great tower once stood as tall as the sun, rubble now flowed to the beach. Each stone—a grave marking Brimley's demise.

The castle looks how I feel. Defeated.

"Brimley?" Squirrel slowed his horse.

Alden sighed, leaning back on Emory to match pace. "Yes," he said, surprised by how choked he sounded.

Squirrel looked over his shoulder as if not realizing the journey with a mass of other Brimleyn refugees, signs pointing towards Brimley Castle, and the thick forest were not clues enough. He walked his horse closer to Alden's, nearly bumping their stirrups. "Why?"

"I suppose to further my studies on who killed Mayli's mother and who hired the guild to take her." Alden frowned further. The likelihood he'd learn anything more than what he'd already known slimmed by the day. But another try back where it began was worth investigating. Besides, this time Mayli wasn't lingering, he wasn't wounded, and he had friends loyal to the cause. Alden reached across, tapping Squirrel on his arm. "Maybe with your keen eyes, I might find something."

Squirrel squinted. "What will happen if we find out what really happened with Queen Margaret?"

"Then whoever was involved will face justice..."

Squirrel stared at Alden, his face long and worrisome. However, the look didn't last enough for Alden to question as he clamped his jaw up forming a toothy grin. "To Brimley then!" he cheered, leading his horse forward while pointing.

Ahead, a town he hardly recognized was blistering with life. Sheep ran through a field of newly pitched tents. Children laughed. People sang. In the distance, a ring of hammers clambered against steaks and nails as foundations of new homes, businesses, shops, inns, and farms were being built from the ash. While it all promised hope and unity, seeing the yellow paint invading his homeland still had Alden shiver in the light.

A couple of men paused from digging a trench to look up as he passed.

Alden dipped his chin, ensuring his hood was indeed cloaking his face. Despite announcements of Princess Mayli's safe return, rumors marking him responsible for the kidnapping still spread. His bounty grew by the day. *Fifteen thousand gold,* he scoffed.

"Hello!" said Squirrel, waving widely. His pink cloak seemed to glow, drawing the attention of other workers around.

The men smiled, greeting him with their own energized toss of their hands in greeting.

Alden relaxed, remembering that an exchange of a wave was as common as seeing a tree in Brimley. Sure he would gain more attention if he didn't engage, Alden raised his hand. "Good Afternoon," he braved to say.

"And a good evening," one replied before stomping his shovel back into the ground, resuming his work.

Alden continued to greet other townsfolk as he passed by. He smiled at a group of farmers, dipped his chin at a traveling merchant, and then laughed with five children who followed behind as Squirrel made funny faces. Even a charming man offered him a wink and then turned his head in admiration as he continued. For the first time in years, Alden felt a glimmer of his old life as a prince—riding through town, gracing his people with his presence. They showed excitement and pride in the land they tilled. Though today they had no idea it was him, the energy given seemed to offer the same bond of community.

Alden's hand stilled in the air as he instantly regretted having raised it to the next approaching group. It was led by a knight, dressed in a long, purple, velvet cape riding an armored white horse. Alden lost his short-lived smile.

She halted them in their path. "Nick. I am surprised to see

you in Brimley. I thought you and Emma were set to settle in Dregs?"

"Hello, Madam Veridia. You have a good memory of names..." Alden glanced at Squirrel, making sure the boy took note of the alias Veridia knew him by. However, Squirrel's gaze was distant, once again downcast.

"I must if I am to do my job." Veridia looked behind Alden where instead of the princess, his cat, Rek, slept curled in a wooden cage. "Where is Emma?"

Alden cleared his throat and shifted his standing in the saddle. "She cares not for Brimley. When I was assigned here, we had to part ways."

"I understand. Duty to your king comes first." She eyed the sketchbook dangling at his side by a leather strap. Pages flipped open in the wind revealing drawings Alden had paused to capture along their travel. "I see you're an artist. May I take a look?"

Having nothing to hide other than messy lines, Alden handed it over.

Veridia flipped through. "You have a wide range of skills, Nick. Portraits, animals, the wild, architecture..."

"The subject changes, not my eyes."

She studied a page. "When we last met, you'd mentioned the Shadowen Thieves Guild."

Squirrel's attention drew back, and he blinked rapidly as if noticing Veridia for the first time.

Alden bunched the reins in his hand but crossed his other hand over casually to conceal his tension. "What of it?"

"King Briar gave me a folder containing sketches of thieves after we'd met. Your style is uncanny." She closed the sketchbook and handed it back.

Accepting it, Alden swallowed a nervous lump, unable to deny her observations. "Yes. I spied on the guild. But when it became too dangerous, I left with Emma. Which is when Briar took us in."

"Wise choice. We had heard there was some suspicious activity here and came to investigate. With your notes and illustrations, we were able to identify this recent corpse." She beckoned her fingers. "Maybe you can help confirm."

A servant leading a donkey with a cart rolled beside them. The smell of decay that wafted made Reyn's presence known without the servant needing to present the man's face. Still, he did, exposing the tangle of stringy black hair, hallowed blank eyes, and teeth stained as yellow as his rotting flesh.

"Reyn," Alden said, putting a hand to his nose to smother the disgust.

Veridia waved her hand, and the servant covered the body and urged the donkey to the back of the group. The knight looked at Alden more sternly. "So you knew them well."

"Well enough to know he deserved that fate."

"Did you know they were planning the kidnapping?"

"No," he said with confidence. *Not a lie.*

"I see." Veridia took a red folder from a pouch at her side and pulled out a drawing. She flipped it around and extended her arm. "I found this among the remains. Who is it?"

Short hair framed a boxy face while a long braid pointed down the length of an exposed body, sprawled and legs spread. Agony hung in his heart. He swallowed deep, looking at the page but willing himself not to see the drawing he'd been forced to draw of Kira.

Still, the vision was burned in after Reyn had interrupted a casual drawing session between them. Reyn and his goons had circled. Knives drawn. Alden's charcoal stick had been no match against them. Kira had froze, as she always did when Reyn asserted himself. Both helpless, Alden was made to watch as they disrobed his partner. Reyn had shouted commands for

Alden to draw every mark. Every scar. Every mole, freckle, dimple, and weave of her braid. All so he could have her forever. It had been one of the most realistic portraits—one his father would be proud to see. But for Alden, there wasn't a day that he didn't regret drawing it.

Alden forced his gaze down the path, wishing to be dismissed by Veridia's questioning and memory of that dreadful day. "I don't know," he lied.

"You don't know?" repeated Veridia. She flicked it back to herself, eyes looking up and down the form. "It's drawn in your style, is it not?"

"A model he made me draw last year," Alden admitted. "Unfortunately, I'm not as good at remembering names as you are. Now, if you'll excuse me, I must be going."

"A model?" Veridia stepped her horse back as Alden attempted to ride. "You seem to know her."

Emory grunted with Alden as Squirrel moved his small bay mare between them. Despite their size, common apparel, and pink cloak, his guard-like stance held weight. "He answered your query, madam. Be on your way, we all have places to be."

Veridia blinked at the young boy. As did Alden, impressed by his confident authority.

"Very well," she said, leading her horse onto the path. "Continue your good work."

Alden dipped his chin at Veridia, refusing to touch his arm in honor of her, just as she had refused them. As the Hiorean troop moved along, Squirrel stared up at Alden. Feeling the question burn he frowned at the boy. "She'll be fine."

"Well, yeah, but why did Reyn have that? Why did you—"

"Like Kira, I didn't have a choice," Alden said breathlessly, continuing Emory forward. "Reyn took what he wanted and did things like that to hold power over us. Doesn't surprise me he kept such leverage over her on his person."

Squirrel followed, the sound of his horse reaching for low-hanging leaves crunching behind.

Following the trail, Alden cast his eyes down on his hands as they fidgeted on the reins. *He's really dead.* The idea was almost so surreal, that without having seen the body he hadn't quite grasped the reality of it. That he and Kira were free. At least from him. There were now his friends to consider, no longer bound by duty and loyalty to not touch her. *She's safe with Briar,* Alden reassured himself.

"Oie, hold!" called an authoritative voice. A knight took his hand from Emory's nose. He hooked his grip to the hilt of his sword and shook his head. "Only the crested or workforce with a laborer's seal may enter."

Alden leaned back on Emory, realizing she had been in control since the castle was in view. Like a memorized path, she'd walked them to the gatehouse, nearly inviting herself in.

"Are you crested, or do you have such papers?" asked the knight.

Alden stared at the barricade keeping him from his home. Gleaming in the sun's low beam, the man's right pauldron revealed an etched crest: the draclynn of Dregs, representing the river's delta with the sea monster's curling tentacles. Despite the Dreggen marking, a blue undercoat padded his wares. Alden smiled. *A loyal Brimleyn.* Pulling an envelope from his pocket, he offered it. "I have a letter from the king, granting me entrance."

The knight took the letter. Pursing his lips, he examined the blue Brimleyn seal. His golden eyebrow rose behind the rim of his helm. "The king you say?"

"That's right."

"Hmm." The knight slipped a finger under the paper. The wax snapped and with a shake, the letter unfolded. After reading, the scrutiny in the knight's eyes fell back to Alden. "*Alden of*

Brimley, as the sketch below will confirm, is exempt from showing crest and shall be welcomed to the castle as if he were I. Your King, Colin Densen."

Alden pointed to his face and smirked as he had in the mirror while drawing his portrait.

The knight frowned, unamused. "Sorry, I won't be able to grant you access with this forgery."

"Forgery?" Alden sunk in posture, chuckling under his breath. "I assure you, it is not."

"Doesn't matter if you did manage to get a letter and portrait done from Prince Colin. Brimley Castle is part of the kingdom of Dregs now." He pointed up. The hiss of yellow and black banners snapped traitorously overhead as if mocking Alden's stripped status. "Briar Densen is king and without a letter from him or Lord Dean, I cannot allow you in. But if you like, I can direct you to the Stride-On Inn down the road where you will be most welcomed, Alden of Brimley."

Alden felt as though his tattooed crest caught fire as rage ignited at the reminder that nothing was his. He grit his teeth. "So I hear... Yet, you still wear Brimleyn colors."

The knight looked at his shirt, frowned, then waved Alden's letter for him to take it. "I have my orders. If you are not noble but still wish to come inside, you may also sign up over there and can come back with a worker's permit once it's been approved and stamped by the appropriate authority." He pointed to a freshly constructed building where a line of people gathered.

Shaking his head, Alden exchanged his own letter with Briar's from his pouch. "Here."

Suspicion rose in the knight's eyes. Hesitantly, he accepted.

"I assure you, that is Briar's royal seal." Alden tapped. "Stamped in pure yellow ocher wax sprinkled with real gold fleck. Watched him press it myself."

The knight lifted it. A beam of sun caught, and the seal sparkled. "So it does. Why didn't you lead with this?"

Alden rubbed his nose, looking over the castle. "I was hoping there would be some loyalty left."

"I am being loyal to my vow, to His Majesty, Briar Densen, the rightful heir of these lands and—"

"Yeah, yeah. I get it."

The knight stared. After a moment he broke open the letter and flipped it up. His eyes raced back and forth as he read. "Alden, it says here you're here to work directly under Lord Dean?"

Under him... Alden sneered. "Yes."

The knight looked back at the letter, reading further, then paused to look at Squirrel. "And this is the Earl of Brimley? I thought he was...older. You his son or something?"

"I am Squirrel. Briar calls me Earl. Does that make me one?" He looked at Alden with genuine curiosity.

Alden managed a small smile at the boy's innocence. "Unfortunately not, but maybe in time." He winked.

"Well, Alden and Earl, welcome to Brimley." The knight stepped aside, waving his arm for the makeshift wooden gate to open.

With Squirrel at his side, he entered Brimley Castle's bailey. Workers hung on walls from ropes, clipping vines as if giving the castle a fresh shave. Goats roamed, trimming the tall grass in meandering pathways. A few men pulled saplings from the middle of the road, lifting them into a wagon for transplanting. A catapult still sat abandoned, a harsh reminder of their failed war.

A whinny echoed within the walls, calling Alden and Emory's attention to the stable. A gray horse peeked her head out from a stall door, mouth full of dried clover. It was Fawn,

Dean's old mare, and Emory's mother. The horse bobbed her head in greeting—her snack flying into the air.

Dismounting, Alden chuckled. "Let's hope my greeting with family is just as pleasant as yours, Emmy," he whispered in Emory's ear while giving her a good scratch.

Squirrel, still mounted, had his eyes fixated on the knight as the gate closed, sealing them in.

"Already fantasizing about being a knight now?" Alden mused. "If you wanted to squire for him, I'm sure you could reach rank quickly."

Squirrel blinked his focus back. "No. I don't like him."

Alden huffed, shrugging. "Can't blame ya. He's a bit of a jock, eh?"

Squirrel nodded.

"Well, would you mind being my squire then and tend to the horses?" Alden handed Emory's reins over.

Squirrel coiled them in his hand. "Okay."

"Thanks, bud. You can stable Emory with Fawn over there." He pointed. "And once you're done, bring our things inside. Including Rek. I'll meet you in the grand hall in half a turn."

"You betcha!"

Breaking away, Alden's smile crumbled as he reached the castle. Two large doors bore down on him as if passing judgment, the sounds of war still ringing in his ear. Evidence of the siege was etched into the walls: missing mortar, gashes in the wood from swords, and chipped corners. Blood still stained where combat had been heaviest. Alden put his hand to a large gash, whispering a silent apology. Breathing in what he hoped could be forgiveness, Alden gripped the handle and pulled.

Sophisticated, but not grand, the foyer brought Alden in like a hug. Brimley didn't flaunt large open rooms or tall stone pillars declaring superiority like Dregs did. Instead, it came from much more humble beginnings. Worn wainscoting climbed halfway up the walls that were lined with murals painted by his father at the top. Sand dunes in the foreground and an endless forest beyond illustrated his family's journey from Gezmek to here. Ahead, made of sun-bleached sandstone, was the original barn. Once used to latch cattle, iron pegs now held torches illuminating the tall room in golden light. Alden followed a fresh yellow carpet lining the granite tile floor, uncaring if his boots dirtied the foreign color. Before he could pull the dusty old doors open himself, they flung wide.

"Uff." Alden started back, touching his nose where it had been slammed.

A servant gasped. "I'm sorry! Oh! Milord!" Shaking in fright, he bowed, spilling rolls of parchment from his arms to the floor.

Alden kept his hand over his face, masking his features. "Milord?"

The young man braved a glance up. "You are not bound with a worker's tie. I assume you're noble? If so, I am *so* sorry!" He trembled.

Alden looked at the yellow ribbon bound to the servant's right arm. Instead of a crest, a hammer and brush crossed in black ink. "Oh. Yeah. I'm here to work too. Only just arrived." On the floor, a roll of paper continued to uncoil. It stopped at his feet. Alden picked it up and offered it back.

Tired eyes softened with relief as the servant stuffed the scroll back under his arms. "You won't want Lord Dean to catch ya without one. My mistake on the first day! Had a stern talking to and was investigated thoroughly to make sure I wasn't a spy or some such nonsense."

"I can imagine." Alden looked around. "So, where is he?"

"His Lordship is in the study." He bobbed his head back.

"Thank you." Alden stepped forward.

"Oh, I wouldn't recommend seeing him just yet..." The

servant halted him with a wave of his arm. "He is in an awful mood."

Alden mused a grin. "When isn't he?"

The servant smirked. "So you've worked for Lord Dean before?"

"My whole life."

"Really?" His eyes grew round. "You served under the royal family before?"

Alden rubbed his right arm. "Something like that."

"Wow! My parents did too. After Lord Dean discovered that during my talking to, he promoted me to this job." He shrugged a stack of parchment back in order.

"Your parents served as royal servants?" asked Alden.

"Yeah! Fredrik and Penna. Maybe you knew them?"

"Uh..." Alden shifted his gaze, remembering exactly who his family's personal servants had been. While Penna had passed in the war, Fredrik now served Briar. "Yeah. Good folks. They had to put up with a lot, thanks to the princes."

He laughed. "They came home with the funniest stories! Once, Briar had intended to gift his girlfriend a beautiful white horse, and just before it was presented in the great hall, Prince Dominick let it wallow in mud. Da said it would have been funny if he hadn't been the one to clean up afterward. I always wished I could have met them. Seemed so funny. But I was too young to come into the castle. Had to adore them from afar, ya know?"

Alden's smile grew, as did a blooming admiration for the young man. Much like his own attire, he wore layers of tan and brown, leaving his wavy black hair to draw all the attention to his soft-featured face. "What's your name?"

"Trip." He wove his hand through the papers to touch his bound shoulder and bow.

"Call me Alden."

"Allen, Pleased to meet ya!"

"Alden," he corrected. "Like, *all done*."

"Oh! Sorry, I never get names right..." He scratched his head.

Alden grabbed a scroll before it fell from Trip's grasp. "What are those for?" He helped secure it.

"Thanks. I'm delivering them to the artist's room..."

Alden raised his brow. With it, came his lips. "Artist?"

"Yes, I'm his personal servant. He's staying in the fallen tower's base. Dean had already restored a few rooms in the inner hall but made his room a priority. Maybe the light is better?"

"It does get the best sun," Alden agreed.

Trip looked out a window and cringed. "Which is setting! I gotta go deliver these! It was a pleasure to meet cha, Alden!"

Alden laughed. "Okay, I'll see ya around. And don't worry about the creases. They can be ironed flat."

Seeing hard folds pressed into the papers, Trip blushed. "Oh no!"

"It's really no big deal—"

"I need to go fix this! Good luck with Lord Dean," he called, jogging to the servant's quarters.

"Bye..." he said to a closing door.

Sweet lad. Perhaps Kira was right—I would find more friends here...

The soothing scent of lavender candles caressed Alden's still throbbing nose. As if called, he turned to enter the grand hall from where Trip had come. Spanning the upper half of the arched barn, blue light glimmered from a stained-glass mural of his family's crest.

He walked through the light, closing his eyes for a moment to bask in the tranquility. Knowing the exact number of steps, he opened his eyes just before meeting the royal table. Beautiful bushy white hydrangeas bloomed from a crystal vase. His mother's favorite. He smiled at the bouquet until the foul lines caught his attention on the natural stone walls beyond, the graffiti mocking him and his kingdom.

Shying his head before reading the insults, Alden sulked through the room to the back hall. He let memory guide his feet to the study door. To his surprise, one of Briar's twin royal guards stood at attention. *He must have assigned him to Dean. Or maybe me?*

With both Sir Exten and Sir Tarek aware of his identity, Alden never had a problem moving by them. So, he knocked on the door while inviting himself in.

The room glowed with crisp light from floor-to-ceiling windows. Spiraling wood pillars separated each pane of glass. Like trees, they led to the ceiling where thick beams reached like branches. Between each were leaf-textured panels, continuing the illusion of nature within. The windows framed a garden of blue cornflowers and lavender. He sighed at the memory of picking tea with his mother.

"Get out." Dean stood.

A stranger sat in a chair, back-facing the door. They tugged a black silk scarf around their head as if Alden had brought in the cold. Gloved hands and arms disappeared into long, loose sleeves of a well-tailored robe. A studded belt hugged tightly around their thin body. No weapons were visible. Alden stared, waiting for the stranger to rise to leave from Dean's command.

"You." Dean lifted his finger. "Now."

Alden pointed at himself and scoffed. "I've only just arrived and already ya wanna throw me out. Typical." Alden walked further in.

The stranger weakly stood, gripping a cane to help rise. Leaning into Dean, he whispered. Eyes on Alden, Dean nodded. A stiff hesitation hung in the room—a heaviness Alden couldn't discern. Turning from Dean and keeping their head bowed from

Alden's view, the stranger walked past, cane clicking along the wood floor with his limp.

Thankfully ignored, Alden sat where they had been.

"What are you doing here?" Dean began brushing the pile of papers into one stack.

Alden found and handed one over—a drawing of the farm before the stone barn was encased and restructured into the manor it was today. "This is home, isn't it?"

"You always assume you're welcome..." Dean snatched it from him. "You think I want to see you here after everything?"

Shame dipped Alden's head. He spied the original concept of the castle set at the top of a pile. Its work was loose and lacked refinement, but held all the wonder and promise of a noble ruler. His father, King Liam, had illustrated it shortly after being crested and granted the land to rule from the other kingdoms. Alden gently shifted through the others in the stack. Unlike the original, these were newly done and carefully rendered. Not a single stray line or misaligned mark blemished the page. Just like days he would stand before an easel with his father watching the master pull the world around him, the drawings seemed to come alive. Everything had been carefully measured, including blue ghost lines of what the building's current state was. The repairs and reconstruction introduced were simple but elegant, accentuating as if badges of honor. Still, some areas hadn't been addressed, like the tower. "These are beautiful, who drew them?" Alden lifted one up.

"Someone with far more respect for the Densen name than you," snapped Dean.

Alden's brows rose. Glaring, he pressed his finger firmly on the table, pinning the stack of drawings. "I have sacrificed everything to be here."

"That's for damn sure." Dean glared back.

Alden worked to keep his voice hushed, yet firm. "Look, I'm not here to argue. I'm here to help."

"Oh, *now*, you decide to step up. What, so you can capitalize on your cousin's good fortune and support?"

"I've been helping!"

"Bullshit. You abandoned your responsibility to rule the day you were too cowardly to accept what you'd done."

"I'm not a coward," Alden hissed. "Or a murderer."

"You are. We had the chance to avoid all this drama and save lives had you just gone to trial."

Alden's heart raced. "Da said their trial is a death sentence! We needed evidence. So that's what I've been working to collect all these years!" he yelled.

Dean tugged at the sketch. "Oh good. I'm sure you have plenty to share then and clear this mess up."

Seeing the original drawing tear, Alden let go, gut turning as if he'd just insulted his father. He swallowed. "I don't."

Dean sneered at the rip then placed the paper aside. He leaned in, challenging Alden with a deep scowl. "And what do you do instead? Show up to my mill dressed like a thug with that whore of a prin—"

"Don't ever insult her."

Dean's nostrils flared. "Then perhaps I'll just insult you." He clenched his hand into a fist as if to hit him like when he was young.

Alden stood and shifted into a readied stance. "Try."

Dean looked up and down his defense then laughed. "You really think being my grandson grants you unconditional respect?"

Alden shook his head. "No. But being your king does."

Dean rose his fist and pointed at Alden's face. "You are not my king."

Heat flared behind Alden's neck at Dean's traitorous words.

"You may be lord and crested but remember you're not of royal blood. *I am*. So just because Briar temporarily claimed this land as Dregs doesn't mean I am not still king of Brimley. I will not be stripped of virtue."

Dean scoffed. "Colin, what makes you feel so entitled?"

"My royal crest," he said with definition.

A withering smile hit Dean's lips. "You think I was suddenly given respect when I won nobility? That ink has mystical properties, boy?"

Alden shook his head, feeling childish for his answer. "No."

"That's right. I earned it when I gave of myself to honor the true kings of Vatan. I carried your father and his brother across dunes to save them. I fought for them at every corner until we arrived home on my piss poor farm where I built a kingdom from nothing but the seed of hope that they could bring the kingdoms together once more. Respect, Colin, is awarded to those who show valor. Like your cousin."

"You think I haven't shown that?"

"No. All I've seen from you is arrogance, selfishness, misery —" Dean opened his mouth to lecture more but a calm, cheerful hum echoed from the gallery hall.

A plump woman in a frilled tan dress opened the door. Her short gray hair was permed in a wave that curled around her ear. Tied at her waist was an apron dusted in flour. A plate of several swirled dough rolls topped with a glaze of caramel and pecans steamed from a plate in her hands. Her song ceased upon seeing Alden, and her face bloomed with even more joy.

Alden smiled back. "Gran..."

"My boy!" With eager steps, Mary trotted to Alden. She set the plate aside and wrapped heavy arms around him—soft and consuming like an overstuffed quilt.

Missing it terribly, Alden accepted the warm hug. Mary layered a few sloppy kisses on his cheeks then pulled back. Her hands rubbed Alden's arms then squeezed taking note of his strong biceps.

He flexed for her to admire.

"Wow..." She patted the firm muscle. After looking him up and down she frowned. "Don't you eat anymore?"

Alden laughed, amused yet not surprised by her comment. Freeing himself from her grasp, he placed his hands on his hips and shrugged. "Occasionally."

"Occasionally isn't good enough! It's no wonder you are thin as sticks now!"

"Well, I can manage myself better than when I looked like one of your sticky buns. Not that I am complaining." He glanced at the plate. One roll was already missing, and Dean was shamelessly biting into the treat.

"And still you are just as sweet as them." Mary kissed Alden's cheek one last time. Breaking away, she took hold of his thick beard. "But this, my, it's like you're all grown up. Even since we saw you just over a month ago or so, you've changed into a whole different person."

"I have."

Dean huffed, licking his thumb free of caramel. "Is there yet another name you expect us to call you then?"

Alden bit his tongue before firing up an argument by saying *'yes. Your Majesty'* but instead he said, "No."

Mary lifted a roll. "Please have one. Or a dozen like you used to!"

"One will do." Taking her offering, Alden closed his eyes as he bit in. The sweet, homey flavors triggered warm memories of sneaking off as a child to snatch the first batch pulled from the oven. Or, as a teen, stealing the whole tray with Briar and Dominick until their bellies popped buttons. Despite the happy moment, Alden set the roll down, too sweet for him to bear after his most recent memory of enjoying one with Princess Mayli at the abandoned cabin.

His grandmother's hand cupped his and squeezed. Her face asked, '*are you okay?*'

Unsure, Alden dropped his head to look at their clasped hands. Mary's were wrinkled, yet strong from a lifetime of work. She had kneaded dough, tended livestock, busied around the castle, cared for him, his brother, father, mother, brother, uncle, cousin, Dean, their daughter, stray children, cats...everyone. She'd done it all despite having servants offering her help —a habit of a nurturing lifestyle she couldn't break.

Alden twitched a smile, but his lips fell into a frown seeing his own worn hands. In recent years, they acquired scuffs along knuckles, cuts, calluses, and scars. His nails were chipped and dirty. Unlike Mary, his life wasn't one of generosity, but one of arrogance, selfishness, and misery as Dean observed. "As you said, I'm a different person."

"But you are still my sweet king." She pinched his tight cheek.

Alden looked at Dean. "Most don't see me that way."

Mary waved her hand in front of her husband. "Never mind what this old man can or can't see. He can hardly tell me apart from portraits on the wall."

"That why he's always glaring?" Alden prodded.

"My eyes are just fine." Dean walked around the table and kissed Mary. He lifted his gaze to Alden, displaying his classic glower. "I'll send servants to ready one of the rooms in the inner hall."

"The inner hall?" Alden blinked.

"Unless you'd rather sleep in the servant's quarters? Or even better, the stables?"

"Uh, no, but I do have a friend who would need a simple bed... But I thought there was a room in the tower for me?"

"That's off-limits to you."

"*Off-limits?*" Alden shook his head, aghast.

"That's right." Dean folded his arms. "And you will not disturb us or the artist in the tower."

"Artist? Wait, you *hired* an artist?"

"You saw his work, and I'm sure you made a very poor impression barging in as you did."

"That's who you were talking with?" Alden thumbed at the door where the stranger had left.

"Yes, and you will honor his privacy and work."

Mary stepped forward and lifted a drawing from the table. "Dean, you know he needs more help than just from Trip. Surely Alden's input and drawing skills would be valued? Perhaps if they worked together it would do them both well." She placed her hand on his shoulder.

"No."

"But Dean, he's—"

"The decision is made, and we will all respect it. You hear that, Colin?" Dean thrust his finger in Alden's face.

Alden soured at the use of his given name. "Yes, Your Lordship."

"Don't give me that tone."

Alden put his hands up. "I gave none!"

"Bullshit. I see right through your masked lies. Disrespect me again, and I will have you shipped straight to Ammos. Save us all a headache since you're too much of a coward to do it yourself." He waved his hand dismissively.

"Dean Wilkus!" snapped Mary.

Alden worked to present a calm facade, but inside his heart thundered knowing the fury sculpting his grandfather's face was genuine. It had been the same damning scowl he'd given Alden just after the war. Their endless arguing inevitably ended with Alden being tossed out of the mill they later hid in, quite literally. Not even Mary could sway Dean's decision then. Nor could she now if he decided to further ruin him. Alden lowered his eyes and placed his hand to his shoulder in respect. He retired his tone. "Yes, Your Lordship." His heart pinched in pain, finally accepting Brimley Castle was indeed his grandfather's to rule under Briar—not his. *Not yet.*

"Good. Now, if you are so desperate to help with your artistic skills, start by erasing the rubbish from the main hall. We are all tired of living in your wake of destruction." Walking to leave, Dean plucked another sticky bun off the tray and stuffed it in his mouth.

Alden flinched as the door slammed shut.

Mary rubbed her hand along Alden's back. "He doesn't mean it."

"I'll clean the hall. It's fine."

"Not that. About sending you to Ammos."

Alden looked at her. "What makes you so sure?"

"Alden." Mary paused. "You still wish to go by that?"

He nodded, smiling at the respect she still honored him with. "I do. I'm Alden now, and will be forever."

"Colin or Alden, you're a Densen. No matter how many towers fall, or kingdoms are beaten or buried, your lineage, time and time again, grows from a humble seed to a tree providing life and shelter for all. And that, Alden, is why I know he'd never truly extradite you." Mary traced her finger along where his Brimleyn crest lay hidden under his sleeve, contouring the lines of the oak knowing exactly where it lay. "We all make mistakes, but one moment doesn't define us forever. It is how we respond in the aftermath that does."

Alden peered at her. "You believe that?"

"Of course. Think of how you helped bring that princess home. You had every right to let the guild have her for her ruthlessness. But you risked your life—your identity—for an enemy." Mary gripped his chin, shaking him from the blaze of regret. "She won't forget your heroism."

"What the Princess of Ammos thinks of me is irrelevant."

"Hmph." Mary tapped his cheek in mock slap then pointed. "You may look grown and mature now, but what you know of love is still juvenile."

"What makes you think we are still in love?"

Round and rosy cheeks smiled knowingly. "Briar told me of the bond you two shared. Even that night in the mill, I sensed a connection. Not many share that—not even your Granda and I, or your father to our daughter, and I was happy to say Liam and Lily were quite close. Mayli's love for you is why I know you are not the monster you fear to be."

Alden tried to look away, but his grandmother pulled him into her embrace. Squeezing tight, she locked him in. Needing the comfort, Alden lowered his head onto her shoulder, breathing in her familiar sweet dough scent. He squeezed back. "Thank you, Gran..."

Mary pulled away. Her smile, wide and honest, wavered. "The truth of your character will show Vatan why you will be the best king it has ever had. Understand?" She gave him a light shake.

Alden bobbed his head, loose at first then firm, catching her words. *She said king.* He nodded. "I think so."

"Good. Now, go clear the lies others have painted of you."

CHAPTER SIXTEEN

SHADOW SEEKER

"Briar Densen!"

Briar threw his head up, feeling his shaggy hair flying into the air. His eyes widened, then pinched with irritation seeing the door burst open from a kick of legs throwing a blue dress like a tidal wave. "Kira, I am in a meeting."

The two nobles seated across from him craned their necks to look at her.

She didn't seem to care that they were scowling, or about Exten filing in after her as she came striding forth. "You've been in meetings nonstop for days. It's time we had one."

The nobles noted her flexing hands and purposeful march. Turning back toward him, they stood. "We can conclude, Your Majesty. You are now well aware of our concerns regarding the continued break-ins on Ideal Avenue and what that means for our contributions."

Kira slipped in between the nobles as if they weren't there and pressed her knuckles into the desk. "Looks like you have an opening."

Briar closed his eyes, taking in a collected breath. He opened them to meet his guests' attention and tipped his chin towards the door in dismissal. They bowed and left the office, murmuring under their breath as they passed Exten, "No wonder our homes are being ransacked. He's lost all control if his guards can't even hold back a single woman."

As the door closed Briar met Kira's gaze. "You can't do that," he said while gathering papers and shuffling them into an unorganized pile.

"But I did. Now, will you spend some time with me? I'm bored out of my wits with Alden and Squirrel gone. I was hoping to pull loose gossip, but no one wants to talk politics, and those who do are too tight-lipped to confess any biases against you. I can't tell who is friend or foe."

"It is common practice among the nobles to treat everyone as a friend until they prove otherwise."

"Funny. It's the opposite among thieves."

Briar dropped the pile of papers on top of an unkempt stack, touching a finger to it as it began to sag to the side. "Look, Kira, I have so much going on... From managing Brimley to Dregs, my uncle's messes, William's needs, the noble's entitlement, and the commoner's struggles... I'm in over my head. I don't have time to—"

Kira leaned into his field of vision. "To what?" she pouted, squishing her breasts for him.

"—to, *uh*..." His gaze caught right where she lured him. *It has been a few days since we...* Wincing, he drew himself away. "Sorry, Kira. I can't. There's just too much on my plate."

She huffed upward, making her bangs flutter as she pushed off the desk. "Well, you know I like to eat. How can I help?"

Briar looked at her. "You want to help in court?"

"Yes!"

"You won't like what's on the menu..."

"Try me," she grinned.

"Which pattern do you prefer, Lady Kira?"

Kira reached out, uncaring which she pointed at. "That one."

Fredrik cleared his throat with a polite cough. "Stripes are a bold choice. Surely, I would have expected you to select floral."

Kira rolled her face across her palm, smooshing her cheek. Her lip quirked less so from the movement and more to do with Fredrik's spread of decor presented before her. As if she were at a street fair, boards were tacked with sketches, flowers, fabric swatches, and a novel's worth of notes rested upon easels. *All for a simple ball.* She grabbed the black and yellow chevron napkin from Fredrik and stroked it as if her choice had been intentional. "It's nearing winter. Floral makes no sense. Why would I choose that?"

"Because you are such a budding presence in the castle." He offered a yellow flowery doily.

Kira took it, thumbing over the loops and ties. "I don't know, does it really match me that well?" Bored, she put it on her head as if it were a hat.

Fredrik's lips quaked as he fought to correct her. Closing his mouth he smiled politely—a look Kira had trouble discerning whether genuine or mocking.

She sat up straight, embracing the look as a few noblewomen walked by. They eyed her, whispering among themselves.

Rolling her eyes, Kira assessed a table displaying options of dishware, from crystal to porcelain, and a sampling of foods of assorted flavors and aesthetics. All lovely, no doubt, and the noblewomen would have likely been eager to design and organize a ball, but the task was a waste of time when more pressing matters were at hand. *Briar should have tasked me with figuring out who's behind those break-ins on Ideal Avenue. Not arranging a damn ball.* Blinking back to the old man with a polite smile, she laced her voice with interest. "Fredrik."

"Yes, milady," he cooed, the smell of pipe smoke wafting as he lit up.

Kira held her breath a moment before speaking. She blinked, slow. "If I am to unite our people, I need more than just fancy drapes and place settings. We need culture. Music."

"Ah!" Fredrik raised a bony finger, shaking it once. "I have just the troupe. The Riffkin Lads. They've been playing here in Dregs for—"

"Perhaps as an opening act, but this ball needs something fresh. Perhaps someone with an accent. Someone with both Dreggen and Brimleyn ties..."

The old man's face had frozen from being interrupted, but it wrinkled up into a grin at her proposal. "A splendid idea. Whom do you have in mind?"

Kira thought for a moment. She hadn't sought folk song and dance in years but knew from her time on the road that most taverns offered the opportunity for such entertainers. Looking out the window of the sitting room, she smiled. "Surely I can find some talent in town."

"I shall send servants out to post flyers and recruit so that they may audition for you here." Fredrik waved to a servant at the door.

Kira stood. "No, no. That won't be necessary. I prefer to have an honest listen when they aren't fighting to make an impression." She began toward the door.

"Lady Kira!" cried Fredrik as he fled the table and hobbled after her. "Lady Kira, wait. It is not customary for the nobility of the castle to frequent the city. Lest I explain what's been happening with the Binx & Drink ever since His Majesty's appearance."

"I'm not a king; such repercussions do not follow me," Kira said while also noting the noblewomen were now wearing doilies on their heads, stolen from under vases. *Or perhaps they do.*

"Lady Kira..." Fredrik's weathered lungs wheezed as he shuffled after. "You cannot just go out on your own."

Kira whirled. "Am I a prisoner here?"

He skidded to a halt, hands outstretched as if he had intended to grab her. Fingers recoiled in. "Kings, no."

"Am I in danger out there?" She thumbed backward.

"I would hope not."

"Then I'm going out," Kira said, turning about to walk faster than the old man's steps could keep up with.

"But you still haven't picked out all the aesthetics for the ball!" he cried in desperation.

"Black and yellow stripes, crystal table sets, ivy-hugged columns, bigleaf hydrangeas, and yellow calla lilies. Serve brim tea, cider, wild rice, walleye fillets, butternut squash soup, and fruit salad," Kira listed. She walked a few paces before calling over her shoulder once more. "And cinnamon-apple doughnuts!"

Fredrik stood in place, scribbling notes in a small mole-skin pad. "A wonderful selection!" he replied, true appreciation ringing in his tone.

After fleeing the castle and exploring the city streets, Kira came to an eatery with grand columns and a steepled roof. She angled her ear, expecting the sounds of a crowd, laughter, or conversation—the jolly kind not filled with stiff noble politeness—but she was met with only the occasional clang of dishware.

Through the window, a handful of patrons had their luncheon with plenty of tables around them to spare. A platform in the back where musicians might play sat empty aside from a lone piano.

Moving along, Kira searched for the next venue; however, inn after inn, tavern after tavern, she found an emptiness to each. Help-wanted signs hung outside of shops, and the bed and breakfasts had signs in their windows for vacancy, as did a few apartments.

Many had moved to Brimley for the promise of new life and free housing in exchange for work to rebuild. In their absence, the cobbled streets were well-swept. Flower gardens were manicured, and shining carriages rolled by without protest. Even polished trash bins were free from stench or the homeless burrowing inside. However, the husk of a ship, burnt and drowned in the harbor, and shops with boarded-up windows along with graffiti begging for Colin's head still noted the serious grievances brewing in the kingdom.

I have to help expose who our enemies are before anything more comes to ruin.

After touring another songless establishment, Kira leaned against its wall. She huffed. "Lousy town. Even Colville had more entertainment," she said, kicking a rock across the road.

The stone rolled down the slight decline, clicking and bouncing until it landed before a shop. Above its door, a sign illustrated a dress and scissors dancing. The windows had wooden mannequins, posed in the same waltz. Both figures were dressed in loose ribbons, high-cut fronts, and tall leather boots. Both mimicked an assembly of looks she'd worn without much thought.

Hands reached forward and added a hat to one.

A doily.

Kira pushed off the wall and sauntered over. Pressing her

hand to the door, a bell chimed—the most musical note she'd heard all day.

"Lady Kira!" exclaimed the clothier, pins wiggling in her lips as she spoke. She finished pinning the hat to a horsehair wig and stepped down from the display. "Welcome to The Waltzing Thread. It is so good to see you again. Your advice from the meeting earlier this week has had business booming regardless of silk."

Kira noted the four other nobles within the store. One stood before a trifold mirror, examining herself in a dress matching the mannequin. The other two browsed a selection of fabrics while flicking their eyes to Kira at each turn of linen. "I see... And remind me of the advice that was so inspiring," Kira asked the clothier.

"Creativity. Of which you yield so much."

Kira walked to the mannequin, lifting a loose ribbon. To her surprise, it was not one stray tie, but an intricate weave of many, curling around in shimmering waves. She looked up spying the doily—only the headpiece wasn't a napkin, but a properly designed hat complete with a tie and brim. Kira pulled the hat from the mannequin and placed it on her head. Light and purposeful, it fit snugly. "I am flattered by everyone mirroring me, but I see much more beautiful attire from other well-known and more beautiful nobles. Why is it that they want to be me?"

"Either everyone wants to look like the lady who can favor a king, or impress him enough to catch his eye." The clothier relieved a pin from the hat and tucked her bangs to the side. "Like so."

Kira looked in the mirror. Rather than lying flat like the cloth she'd thrown on just to tease, the hat gave volume to her hair with the slight bob at the top.

Whispers from the corner grew. Kira turned her head

enough to see the nobles from the peripheral of her view. *I could suggest they wear nothing but a turnip, and I'm sure they'd oblige.* "It is impressive how you transform what I do into something much more elegant. What is your name?"

"Mrs. Chausmer." She touched her shoulder and bowed with grace.

Kira mimicked the introduction.

Turning to face her, Kira offered a polite smile. "Mrs. Chausmer, I am glad to see your business continues to thrive during this prolonged absence of goods. Other establishments have not been as fortunate."

Frowning, she nodded. "With Brimley being a beacon for new life, it seems many more than just Brimleyns have ventured west. I've lost clients too."

"I hadn't thought the new land would draw in Dreggens as well," said Kira. "I've only seen discontent from them toward Brimley."

"A shame so many have held onto such grievances, really. Like my competitor, Mr. Garbsen. His shop is just before Ideal Avenue and draws in much of the nobility but has a flag displayed refusing to design or sell to Brimleyns."

"So it doesn't bother you that the king chooses to protect Prince Colin?"

"Not at all!" Mrs. Chausmer shook her hand in dismissal then pointed. "I say good on the man to take care of his family and own people before giving into demands."

Lips quirking, Kira leaned closer to Mrs. Chausmer. "How would you like working directly with me for the attire for the upcoming ball? I know everything that's going into its design, and I am sure the attention your shop will get knowing it has something *I* designed will pay off."

The women in the corner stilled like statues while Mrs. Chausmer's eyes lit with excitement. "I'd say I'd be honored!"

Kira lifted a finger. "In exchange, you wouldn't mind putting up a Brimleyn flag in the window below the Dreggen one? To show your support?"

"It would be my honor!"

Kira grinned. "And do you like gossiping?"

Her lip spiraled into a devious grin. "My lady, by fan and fashion I do consider myself a herald and a hush."

"Good." She spoke even softer, whispering details of her plan. Together they designed a perfect style with yellow and black stripes, leather, and pockets before moving on to the next shop to relay similar yet different designs to Mr. Garbsen.

Hours later and satisfied her scheme to expose those disloyal would work, Kira crossed a bridge entering a street lined with three-story estates. Each home was painted bright yellow, accented with black trim, and lit by oil streetlights. The neighborhood was one of Dreg's many islansds, giving water access to each home, complete with private docks and boats. Some even had private stables or servants' quarters. As desirable as the estates looked, none offered the safety and security the nobles living inside likely assumed for living on a street called Ideal Avenue.

Any one of these could be a thief's dream. No wonder they are having trouble.

Kira rubbed her hands while watching sprawling white puffs wave from each chimney along the seemingly ideal avenue, keeping the noble occupants warm as a storm threatened invasion from the west. All but one. She walked to it, admiring the stone turret and timber framing. Beyond a small rose garden, a diamond-leaded window offered a glimpse inside where floor-to-ceiling books surrounded a formal desk.

"This one must be it," said a familiar voice in the distance. One she often heard alongside Reyn's company. Ricky.

Kira crept to the house's gate. She looked one way. Then the other. Concluding no one was watching, she popped it open and slipped inside the alleyway, following the voices.

"It's gorgeous," replied a feminine voice. Jual. It didn't surprise Kira she was paired with Ricky. She was a younger woman who followed Reyn's crew, eager for attention. Starstruck by their authority, she was oblivious to the harm they caused, just as she had once been. Kira hated to see the cycle repeat. Jual hummed. "You think Pierz knows what's going on?"

"Pierz may seem with it, but I bet he's as clueless as the rest of us," said Ricky. A door creaked open. "Which is why we are waiting on word of what to do in Brimley. In the meantime, we need to figure out what's going on with Kira. Unfortunately, I don't think any of those brim-nose punks have the worth to pay us back what they took."

"Maybe this will?"

"Hey, that is fancy."

Something shattered. They laughed, the sound fading as they moved further into the house.

Kira bunched her dress in her hands and pulled it overhead. Tossing the fine fabric to the dirty ground she drew her knife. Finding the service door the thieves had just entered still unlocked, and voices now distant, Kira slipped in. She entered a marble-coated kitchen that looked more like a grand palace than a place to cook food. Ignoring a bowl of chocolates, Kira snuck beside a pass-through in the wall. She peered out of wooden blinds, finding a dining room where a litter of porcelain sparkled on the floor.

Listening for signs of the thieves, Kira tiptoed from the kitchen. The manor was huge, with ceilings so high Kira doubted they could be reached even if she jumped. Much of the furniture was cloaked in white cloth, protecting it from dust. Columns held each corner of the room, providing just enough cover to hide behind. She found the grand entry where a large "H" inlayed in the tile greeted her. *Tacky,* Kira thought. *All this room and no one to live in it.*

The sound of pages being rifled through tugged at Kira's ears, and she scurried to hide behind an iron statue of a knight. Peeking into the next room, she saw Ricky and Jual touring the library.

Ricky sat at the desk and threw his feet up as if he owned the place. "I could get used to living here."

Jual traced her hands over a series of blue-spined books. "If Pierz ever pays us, let's."

Heart beating, Kira fixed her grip on her knife and crept against the wall. She could hear Jual making her rounds nearby. As she saw her foot appear in the door where she hid, Kira spun into the open room. She grabbed a bundle of Jual's coat and raised her knife. "Guards, I found them! This way!" Kira called in fake summons.

Jual yelped, falling into Kira's clutches. "Help! Ricky, I've been caught!"

With no other exit and likely worried about being surrounded, Ricky, to Kira's relief, instead threw himself out the window. Glass shattered as he stumbled into the front lawn.

Jual continued to buck and squirm in Kira's hold. Annoyed, Kira raised both of Jual's arms and pinned them above the girl with one of her own. Leaning into Jual's back, Kira touched her blade into a soft opening under her armpit. "Quit it, you know you're not stronger than me."

"Kira?" Jual's voice turned friendly as she stilled.

"Jual."

She tucked her head over her shoulder, whisking blonde

hair aside. Meeting Kira's eyes, her own grew bright. "Wow! It is you! I thought I was doomed! They said you were captured."

"That's true. But I escaped."

Jual laughed awkwardly. "Of course, you escaped, you're amazing."

"Also true."

She squirmed. "Let me go and we can catch up. I have so many questions."

"No." Kira's grip tightened. "But you're gonna give me answers."

"Kira?" Jual blinked. "I don't understand... Why are you treating me like an enemy? Aren't we friends?"

Kira scoffed. "I wouldn't call us that after you watched me suffer under Reyn."

"Suffer?" She shook her head in surprise. "I saw how much attention he gave to you. I was always so jealous."

"Ha!" Kira clenched her teeth. "Believe me, you didn't want his attention. Or Ricky's. They are the worst kinds of men."

Jual turned her head and scoffed. "Sounds like you're the jealous one."

"Mmm. Yeah, actually. I wish Reyn had abandoned me like Ricky just did. You're lucky."

Light and distant sounds of people gathering outside spilled in from the broken window. A diamond pane fell. Jual's shoulders drooped and her voice fell. "He's coming back..."

"Sure." Smiling, Kira turned Jual to face her and grinned. "We'll just wait here and chat till he or the guards do."

"Pierz said you may be a traitor..." She pouted.

"Which reminds me. Where is our lovely leader?"

Jual held her breath.

"Don't make this hard..." Kira tested, tracing her blade to Jual's belly.

Jual looked from the knife to Kira, to the broken window, then back at Kira. She sighed. "Colville."

"Ah yes. Back at the Cantwell Inn." Kira cozied closer, knocking her elbow to the wall and holding her head. "Did you know, Jual, I used to work there? Before the guild took it over?"

Hair flew as the girl shook her head.

"Back before all of this my brother and I traveled, inn to inn, putting on plays."

"Really?"

Kira leaned back slightly. It had been nearly five years since she had. Five years since her brother's untimely death. She leaned in, eyes glaring. "I used to, and it was that kind of attention that made Reyn convince Pierz that the Cantwell Inn would be the best location for a thieves' lair. Blind with love like you, I ignored his overbearing presence, his demand of me. I thought his concern was cute. That the first time he hit me, I deserved it. The second—still my fault. He made sure I knew it was. And in truth, it had been. I'd saddled up with that goon unaware that he'd sentenced my brother to his grave and myself to an abuser as they killed or displaced anyone unfit or unwilling to join the guild."

Jual's eyes had sorrowed, her fighting spirit gone. Quivering lips and the look of understanding and pain showed she had sampled the abuse Kira had experienced. "I'm sorry..."

Kira closed her eyes, not needing her sympathy. "Look. You have time to leave Ricky and even the guild if you wish. And if you want to be friends with me and the king of Dregs, you're going to help us expose them." Kira let the girl go.

Jual rubbed her wrists. Looking down, she swallowed, then met Kira's gaze. "What do you need to know?"

Kira smiled. "I need to know which business is being converted into a thieves' den here in Dregs."

"I... I don't know." She shied away.

"Jual, you can tell me. You don't need to be afraid of them anymore. Ricky can't hurt you."

She peered up with tears in her eyes. "What about the guild? They are hunting you. They'll hunt me too."

"I can protect you."

"How?"

Fingers steady, Kira unbuttoned her shoulder, exposing her Dreggen crest for the first time. "Jual. I'm noble. I can ensure your safety. Just as I have with Alden and Squirrel."

The girl's chest swelled as she laughed a sigh of relief. "Squirrel is okay?"

Kira smiled. "Yes."

Wiping her eye, Jual nodded. "Okay. I'll tell you. Although, I'm surprised you don't already know."

"Oh?" Kira raised a brow.

"Yeah, they..." Her face drained to white as her smile fell.

"They wha—"

The taste of iron sprinkled Kira's lips as warm blood splashed. Jual's body slumped, falling into Kira's arms. Blinking past droplets, Kira saw an arrow shaft adorned with yellow and black fletching protruding from the girl's head. "Fuck!" She scurried to a wall, heart racing.

A march of footsteps thundered. Armor clanged. Kira peeked out to see iron-clad guards gathered outside stomping through the rose garden. Several hurried through the window, knocking away more of the glass panel. They drew their swords and pointed them at Kira, the archer following behind.

She rolled her head and raised her hands. "Great."

The head of a tall man weaved through the crowd outside. He ducked under the window and met them in the library. His black and yellow tabard tailored in a V-cut, like Briar once wore, stood out amongst his companions. The captain of the guard's eyes widened at the sight. "Kira."

"Thomas." She wiped her face.

"I didn't know you were here. We nearly shot you, too." He plucked the arrow from Jual. Blood oozed out, soiling an Ammosian silk rug with a steady flow. "What are you doing?"

"Your job, apparently." Kira stepped from the body. "Although, I'd say I'm making much better work of it. I bet you had no idea this vacant house would be a target if Ricky hadn't crashed through that window."

"We have had our eye on your home for quite some time."

"Well maybe—" Kira paused, cocking her head. "*My* home?"

"This is the Harlow Estate. *Your* estate, Kira Harlow."

"What?"

Thomas stepped closer. "Did Briar never show you?" he whispered, eyes on the other guards flowing in to do a sweep of the house.

"He showed me my deed, but I never thought..." Kira looked around the grandeur with awe-struck appreciation. Every piece of furniture was exquisite, every display item made of gold, silver, or antique wood. She stared at the "H" on the floor once more. *Harlow...* She blinked back at Thomas. "This is really mine?"

"Yes."

She shook her head, unable to accept it. "But I'm no lady..." she said, buttoning up her sleeve.

"Perhaps if you called on us instead, you would still be dressed as one. Where is your dress?"

Kira crossed her arms and sassed her hip to the side. "I couldn't imagine bloodying up such fine stitchery...so I threw it in an alley." She smirked.

Thomas shook his head. "You shouldn't be getting your hands dirty in Shadowen activity anymore."

"Do you want to find who's behind all these disturbances or not?"

He closed his mouth in a wave. "Yes. Which is why I've brought *her*..."

A short but sturdy Hiorean knight with blonde hair cropped just under her ears stepped into the room. Her lips pursed as she surveyed the scene. The knight looked at Kira then pulled a red folder from a pouch. Licking her finger, she started flicking through pages. "What's your name?"

Kira shook her head back to attention and swallowed. "Kira Harlow."

She paused and looked up. "You're noble?" Her eyes dipped up and down her attire.

"That's what the surname implies," she said in a sarcastic tone.

"She lives here," informed Thomas.

The knight took a step in, observing the house. "It doesn't look lived in."

"I've only just returned," Kira said.

"How old are you?"

"Uh, twenty-four."

"Your hair"—the knight motioned above her head—"aside from your braid, has it been shorter?"

Kira touched the strands tickling her jaw. "It wouldn't have reached this length otherwise... You ever had longer hair?"

"No."

Hioreans may be an impressive sight, but damn if they aren't socially abrasive. Kira folded her arms. "And who are you?"

"Madam Veridia of Ironmere." She hardly bowed.

Kira examined the knight. She had fine fittings, immaculate armor, and a pose that shone with a rich upbringing. "You're a knight, but *not* noble?"

"No. Not yet. But that doesn't stop me from fulfilling Prince Gavin's commands. Like finding those responsible for his fiancée's disappearance." She continued to flip through the papers in her folder, then tapped. "This one here. She's a Shadowen."

Kira held her breath, fingers tightening around her knife. She noticed Veridia's longsword, unclipped to her side. Her mind whipped through the scenario of how to unsheathe it and tangle with the knight's cape just in time to bolt the way she came, but as Veridia stepped to observe Jual, Kira relaxed her stance. "Or was... Keeping her alive for interrogation would've been nice." She tossed a glare at the archer.

He shifted uncomfortably.

Waving to Thomas, Veridia handed over a drawing. It was made with quick, confident lines—fluid but informative. They expressed the girl's upturned nose, buck teeth, and slight freckling. A few notes were jotted on the side as well as other angles of her and a sketch of the stiletto she carried.

Kira's heart pounded. *That's Alden's style. I remember watching him draw that...*

As Veridia began sifting through the other papers, Kira saw portraits of Trod, Ricky, several others, and even Pierz. At each woman, she paused to look back at Kira.

Swallowing tightly, Kira looked at Thomas.

Catching her concern, Thomas stepped between them. "Madam Veridia. It seems you have made your assessment. Perhaps we can meet up with the patrol in search of the suspect who fled across the river?"

Veridia tucked the folder into her satchel. "Very well." She offered him a slight bow and left with the other guards.

Thomas remained. Once they were alone, and the yard cleared from onlookers, he shifted his attention to Kira. Closing the distance, he unbuttoned his cape and offered it. "Please, allow me to escort you back to the castle," he said, voice like melting ice.

"No, thanks." She dodged around him.

"Kira..."

"No. Last time you escorted me somewhere I was instead thrown to the fate of a monster. I'd rather walk alone, thank you." She went to the doorway.

Thomas sighed. "At least change into a dress... King Briar would—"

Kira spun on her heel. "*Briar* wouldn't care what I wore."

"No, but he would be furious if he knew you were out here associating with the Shadowens."

"Associat—" Kira sucked in a breath through her nose and closed her eyes. She fluttered them back open, taming her growl. "I was interrogating *Jual*. She was just a young girl who didn't know what she was getting mixed up with. Big difference as she nearly gave me the answer to where to find their leader. More than you or that knight have done in over a month. Train your men not to kill next time and we might learn something."

"Good thing you're still alive then."

Kira pointed her knife. "I'm not a Shadowen anymore."

He eyed it. "Well, you're not exactly noble either."

Kira grit her teeth. "Fuck you, Thomas. You knew exactly who I would become when you threw me to King Olivar. So don't act so mighty."

Thomas frowned. "I'm not. I'm just saying, being caught up with them can be dangerous. As you've learned."

Kira spun her knife masterfully around her fingers. "I wasn't in danger until you arrived."

"I respect your abilities, Lady Kira, but you have to see what it would look like if the nobles recognized you running amok in thieving attire. Walking around like that"—he gestured to her from head to foot—"will draw you more attention than you would want. Perhaps it worked in the shadows, but you're in the light now."

Kira looked over the dark layers she wore. Mud coated her boots. While her corset was new, she used it to tuck her breasts in place during battle, rather than boost them up for allure. And her new hat she'd inspired Mrs. Chausmer to make, had a red stain. After seeing how quickly influenced the people could be, she knew he was right. *Blood isn't a good look.*

"Now, you may stay here, as it is your home, or come back to the castle. Either way, guards are on watch."

"Are you suggesting they've been following me this whole time?"

"Yes."

Her back tightened at the idea. She hadn't noticed any trails, although Black-Coats did seem to tour every street. They had known to watch her house, even if she knew nothing of it. *Perhaps Briar really does have things under control.* She sighed. "Okay. You can take me back."

William shook his long black mane, sprinkling Briar with soapy water. Wiping his face, he laughed. "Hey now, I know it's been a while, but I'm not the one needing a bath here..." Stepping from his horse, Briar grabbed the bottom of his tunic and pulled his wet shirt overhead.

Giggles and dove-like coos echoed within the nearby well.

Briar glanced over his shoulder, spying the flock of noble-women. As if spending the day gossiping by the stables had been their original intent, they had sauntered over ever since Briar had begun his horse's grooming. The three of them sat on the well, each wearing blooming gowns. One adjusted a ridiculous hat that looked more like a doily. Another squished her corset around her breasts, claiming Briar's attention until the last crossed her legs, letting the high-cut fabric slip and expose the flesh of her thighs. More giggles.

Ringing out his shirt, he smiled and offered them a display of his well-formed biceps.

"Oh, so you do live outside your office."

Briar spun. "Kira?"

She eyed him and then the women. "I must have helped alleviate some time."

"You've done wonders." He grinned bright and hugged her, glad his muscles and body could be more than just admired by wishful eyes. He stroked her hair but then pulled away, feeling something sticky cling to his fingers. Mud dirtied his palm. Furrowing his brow, Briar looked Kira up and down, aghast. "Did you get into it with Evelyn again?"

"Nope."

"Then why are you so dirty?" He pulled another clod from her hair.

Long lashes swooped up. "Is that a question of my nature, or my dress?"

Briar closed his eyes as his lips broke a smile. "Maybe both?" He pressed his thumbs into her waist, earning a happy squeal.

Kira pawed his hand away, self-consciously brushing her hair smooth. "You can't expect pretty braids and tight pulled ribbons all the time." Her eyes began drifting toward the women again.

Stepping in, he tossed his head, throwing droplets just as William had. "Well, perhaps you just need a bath too."

Kira playfully shielded herself as if a great wave was coming down the Draclynn River. "Stop!" she sang.

He did, closing his arms around her once more, uncaring about the grime. Making up for the days lost to ruling, he layered on a series of kisses, from her forehead to her temple, her cheek, and then her lips. He paused over them. "I do adore you."

"Briar." Kira's voice turned serious. Foreheads touching she stared into his eyes. "Did you ever share the drawings Alden had done of me?"

Heat escaping him, Briar released Kira and took a step back. He glanced at the well, seeing the noblewomen were gone. He grabbed a brush and resumed washing William's hindquarter. "No. Alden never let me keep any drawings of you. I had to memorize your beauty instead." He peered back at Kira with a wink.

Smiling only slightly, her shoulders relaxed. Walking to William's head, she scratched his black nose. "I only ask because I ran into a Hiorean knight who had a folder of his drawings. Of Shadowens. She looked at me all judgingly and asked questions like I was in that folder, Briar."

He let out a breath and paused his scrubbing. "Veridia."

"So you know her."

Briar nodded, resuming. "She makes herself seem smarter than she is. Don't worry, she would't have any drawings of you or Squirrel, just the rest of the guild."

"Truly?"

"Believe me." Briar put his elbow to William's back, holding his head as he leaned against the massive animal. "Veridia wouldn't be able to make any correlation with you. Mayli was literally sitting behind Alden on his saddle when she was asking us about Her Highness's whereabouts. She's just intrusive and annoying. And not that good of a sword fighter at that. You've got nothing to worry about."

Kira let out a long sigh. "Good."

"Where did you bump into Veridia, anyway?"

"Nowhere important." Kira twisted her braid between her

fingers, acting innocent, but Briar was learning her acts. As he continued to stare, waiting, she bit her nail. "I may have snuck off to Ideal Avenue to investigate the break-ins."

Briar raised his brow. "How did you know about those?"

"Your meeting with the nobles. They mentioned there being trouble there. I knew then there was a good chance they could be Shadowens." Kira slipped under William's neck to the other side, hiding behind his bulk. "I expected you to task me on that rather than a ball."

Briar tossed his brush into a water bucket and followed her. "You assumed all that from an offhand comment?"

She leaned against the barn. "A lot can be heard from what is unsaid."

Briar sighed. "I suppose that explains the mud in your hair then?"

She shied away, and he could hardly muster a stern glare.

"Well, did you find anything interesting on Ideal Avenue?"

"I found the Harlow Estate." She rubbed her shoulder. "*My* estate."

"Yours?" Briar raised his chin, holding in his glee. "I thought you didn't want it."

Kira let her hand fall, letting it dangle at her side. She stared at him a moment, then shrugged. "It is beautiful but lacks security. I caught a couple of Shadowens sneaking in."

"Caught them?"

"Eh... Not exactly. You see, Jual *died*...and Ricky took off."

Briar leaned his head in. "You killed her? Don't you think keeping them alive—"

"I didn't!" Kira pushed off the wall and walked from him. "And don't you think I know that?"

Left staring at the old wood siding, Briar shut his mouth.

"You should teach your guards that. Had they not been so

pull-happy, Jual would have told me which establishment they've turned into their Dreggen den."

He looked at her. "They are establishing a base here?"

Kira sat on a hay bale. "Naturally."

Briar shifted uncomfortably. "Well, do you have any idea where?"

"Anywhere. The one Alden and I worked at was an inn. There's one in Basevein called Waypoint. Their latest one is Thielen's Lodge in the Cads. I've heard rumors of there being an apothecary in Ammos. And I guess before the town of Brimley burned they used the Balding Tree Tavern."

Mouth falling open, Briar shook his head. "No way. Col and I used to sneak out and get drunk there."

"I know. I've heard stories. Something about how you used to dress like old women?"

Briar flushed with embarrassment. "His idea."

Kira chuckled for a moment but then her face turned hard. "As I walked through town, I noticed most establishments were short-staffed. So tell your guards to look out for businesses that are busy or thriving. Normally, they will be killing off and stealing their positions. If they are lucky, maybe be recruited like I was when they took over the Cantwell Inn. I can thank Reyn for at least one thing, even if he'd made my life a living nightmare afterward."

Briar grit his teeth. "This is my kingdom. My city. I won't let shadows darken it, or any other innocent lives. I'll find where they are hiding, Kira." He sat beside her on the hay.

"I know..." She leaned into him. "I realize how much your guards have been active now."

Briar took her hand. "I told you I had things under control."

"I guess I'm just not used to this type of real power around me. In the guild, I always felt like someone had eyes on me, but when things turned bad it was never the hero watching. Not until Alden. And even then, we were hardly safe. He could only do so much." She peered up at him, squeezing his hand. "It hasn't been until you that I truly feel protected."

"We will always be there for you, Kira." He hugged his arm around her, and she laid her head on his chest. He swayed her gently, brushing his hand through her hair. It touched the wet again, and he glanced down to look. He realized then it wasn't mud, but blood. Clenching his fist and pulling her tighter, he sighed. "But you shouldn't need to put yourself into danger anymore. I'll put notices on potential dens for my guards to investigate. Meanwhile, you're supposed to be planning a ball, aren't you?"

"It's all taken care of." She began bobbing her head back and forth, extending her legs out as she listed. "From the decorations to the food, to the outfits. The guestlist. The schedule. Games... Ask Fredrik. I was just on my way to tell him I'd decided on some music when I saw you free from captivity."

Briar grinned with pride. "Planning a ball and hunting Shadows, all within a day's work?"

"The day isn't over, I still have to tend to the king." Kira grabbed a sponge from the bucket. She put it to his chest and squeezed water from it, wetting him. "If he has time..."

CHAPTER SEVENTEEN

THE KING'S BLADE

"Did you get access to Arkello's residence?" Mayli whispered to Charli as soon as Keegan had left his watch.

Charli grinned, exposing an iron key from his pocket. "I'm a royal guard, Princess. I can go nearly everywhere."

"Everywhere but my room." Mayli tapped his chest, pushing him from the threshold of her door.

"I've never needed a key for that..." He smirked. "Now, shall we see what secrets this unlocks?"

She hopped out, meeting him at his side. "Yes!"

"What secrets?" Jair slipped from his room, brushing his waxed hair back as he leaned against the frame. His smile— smug. "You're not going on another adventure without me, are you, Sis?"

Mayli folded her arms. "You just want to chaperone Charli and me again."

"That, or maybe I miss you?" Shimmering gold-painted eyes fluttered while he pouted his orange-red lips down.

Mayli cawed. "You just miss pestering me, you mean. And

stop stealing my lipstick. That color is special, and I don't have much left."

"She was my mother too." He shrugged off the doorframe. Inserting himself between Charli and her, Jair offered the stick back. "You got everything she had, the least you could do is share."

Mayli frowned. All too consumed in her own grief, Mayli hadn't considered how anyone else, like her brother, was managing. Least of all she didn't think about the implications that happened across Vatan with the kingdom of Brimley and their people. She never once regarded how her mother's death hung heavily on even Colin's shoulders. She sighed. "Sorry, Jair. It does look nice on you. You can keep it."

"Really? Thanks!" He pocketed the lipstick. "Now what are you two up to? Nothing gross I hope."

"If I say yes, will you leave us alone?"

"Princess," said Charli. "I think having Jair help with this would be good."

"Help with what?" Jair looked from Mayli to Charli, then back.

Mayli motioned him along. "Finding out who is causing Vatan such grief."

Winding down the steps terracing the cliff, Mayli smiled at nobles relaxing in their quaint patios in Upper Ward. Arches surrounded them with flowered vines sprawling across like curtains. Tranquil babbles of water flowed from fountains built beside the more wealthy estates. With Charli following in step behind Mayli and Jair, they continued down the steep incline, until the grand decor lessened to the more simple dwellings of Lower Ward. Despite the shift in class, these dwellings still displayed a radiance befitting the palace grounds.

As they neared the curtain wall and the grand gated entrance, Mayli paused. "I thought we were going to Arkello's house."

Charli stopped in front of a large building with three doors to individual units. Above each were small balconies just large enough to step outside to capture the view overlooking Sandwater Bay. Charli gestured at the entrance to the center unit. "We are."

"This is where he lives? I didn't realize the prince was this far down the hill and in a center apartment..." She looked down the street. "Another block and we'd be in town."

"Is Arkello back?" asked Jair as they approached his door. He pointed at the lock as Charli inserted the key. "Wait, why do you have Arkello's key? Are we breaking in?"

"Yes."

"We are?" His voice rose with excitement, then he huddled down. "Why are we breaking in?"

Because..." Mayli listened to the heavy device click free. "I think Arkello has some secrets about Mother's murder I'd like to uncover."

"You suspect Arkello? Wh-wh-why him?" Jair stuttered, inching forward with her as she pushed the door open. "He's been like a brother to me."

"Annoying and always in your business?" Mayli joked.

"No, never! I was the one always seeing what he was up to! He was always happy to have me around to tell stories about Gezmek. He taught me so much."

"Maybe there's a more sinister reason for that," suggested Charli as he thrust open the arched oak door.

As soon as Mayli stepped inside, a deep fragrance met her. She sniffed for a hint of toxin, but only inhaled a rich scent of old wood and long-abandoned parchment. Dust fluttered in a beam of sun blazing through the open door. Quietly, it rested on the mosaic floor. Mayli coughed. "It's like a cave in here..."

"As a man who is used to living underground, I think he found solace in that." Charli stepped in and found an oil lamp to light. He took it from the wall and led the light down a tight hallway.

Mayli followed until they arrived in an open room with a large work table. Coils of paper stuck out from baskets while others were sprawled out to display maps and diagrams held down by crystals, bones, goggles, and miscellaneous crockery. A kitchenette on the far wall acted as a continued workspace with stacks of books and papers, as well as dried herbs and jars of spices.

Jair walked in a circle, taking in everything with awe. "This place is amazing!"

"It's a little creepy," Mayli noted, pulling a curtain from the back window. Despite it being drawn, little light poured in from the narrow alleyway.

"Wow..." Jair gasped, hurrying up a ladder. A moment later more light shone into the room as the sound of chains scraping over an iron rod cast away the remaining shadows. "May, you should come up here."

Mayli eyed the sharp incline. "What did you find?"

"Just come see!"

She swirled her hand above her head. "Toss whatever it is down."

"It's just a simple ladder! Get up here."

Fear keeps you alive, as long as you believe you can overcome it. Arkello's words rang in Mayli's mind. Remembering she'd mastered the steps from the sand strider just fine, she took the ladder one step at a time. To her surprise, she reached the loft with a steady heart rate. Pulling herself up, she stood and stepped from the edge with pride. *I did it!*

When she looked up, something a hundred times more frightening than heights stormed her body. A black mass of feathers, teeth, and a menacing set of hallowed eyes stared back at her. *Reaver!* She screamed, taking a step back, wavering on the edge of the ladder.

Feeling her gut drop as she anticipated the fall, she winced.

Before she continued further, her brother caught her arm. "Oh, you should see your face!" Jair laughed, pulling her to standing.

Mayli breathed heavily, holding her heart. "Jair, you will kill me one of these days."

"Oh come on, it was funny!" He shook a feathered skull at her.

"No, it was not." Mayli backed away, nearing the ladder once more. She looked at where she nearly fell and smiled with relief seeing Charli climbing. "There you are. I'm starting to wonder if you're deliberately allowing me to fall prey to monsters."

He gave her a sympathetic smile, then pulled himself onto the loft. "Your brother is no monster, Princess."

"Arguable." Mayli raised her hand to present the nightmare as Jair threw the hood of a silk cloak back and tucked the skull of a sand strider under his arm. Mayli's shoulders drooped. "Wait. That wasn't a costume?"

"No, Arkello has got a bunch of specimens here!" He set the head back in a pile of bones.

"Well, it looked just like the reavers we saw in the desert."

"The desert?" Jair's face bloomed with fascination. He rushed to Mayli, squatting to be level with her. "Tell me all about it! Was it hot? Did it melt skin? Did you get buried by sand? And you saw reavers? What were they like?"

"Jair!" Mayli snapped. "Not every adventure is a mission of grandeur! Yes, it was arid, but those *things* were terrifying. So, if you scare me again I will throw you over the edge and blame that on Arkello."

He flashed his tongue.

She stuck hers out in reply.

Chuckling, Charli walked between them to a desk littered with papers. Unlike Briar's or even Mr. Vaurus's, it held some sense of organization. Numbers marked the top of each page as if made to go inside a book. Fine linework with near-perfect detail captured *The Rotting Barge* masterfully. However, it was free from the rot, displaying only luxury. Its masts were bracketed with brass, siding painted red and white—its sails striped similarly with the crest of Vatan painted in gold spanning wide. In the margin were notes about renovations, including costs, materials, and the estimated time of completion.

Charli tapped at the captain's quarters, drawn with taller roofs to accommodate larger windows. "Say, that's a good idea he's got. I think I'll make that adjustment to *Her Lady Damgard*."

Mayli rolled her eyes, finding another drawing of it in its current shape: moss, missing timbers, and all. "I didn't know Arkello was an artist. It looks as if I were looking at it in real life."

"Yeah, and a better one than that Alden fellow," Charli said.

"Who is Alden?" asked Jair.

"A friend," Mayli answered with a simple smile.

"Oh... A *friend*," Jair teased with a knowing poke to her side.

Charli continued to rummage through Arkello's things. "Alden is not your friend, Princess. Just like Arkello may not be ours." He lifted a glass jar filled with clear liquid. Oily orbs clung to a brush attached to the lid inside. He shook it and Mayli's vision was captivated by a bright white glow, just like the kanavaur had in the desert.

"Whoa!" exclaimed Jair. "What is that?"

"This, Jair, is what your sister was looking for..." Charli gave the bottle a stronger shake to make it glow brighter. "Shall we test and find out if this is what killed your mother?"

Clenching her hands to her chest, Mayli nodded.

Jair looked between them. "What are you saying? She was stabbed, not poisoned?"

"Give me your knife, Jair, and I'll show you," Mayli said, pulling off her purple scarf.

Charli put his hand out, stopping the prince before he could pull out his small thumb blade. "It would be safer if I use my own blade instead and you give me the silk, Princess. I don't want you two getting hurt."

Handing him her scarf, Mayli sighed. "Always the protector."

Charli winked and laid the silk on the table. Next, he unscrewed the bottle of toxin. Mayli coughed as a swoosh of pungent alcohol-like odor invaded the air.

Jair stepped back, covering his nose and mouth. "That smells worse than dune ale."

"That is because dune ale is made from unhatched kanavaur eggs," said Charli as he pulled the cap up with the brush, dripping with sappy liquid. "Their toxins must ferment."

Mayli about gagged. "I'm never drinking that again."

Keeping his hand steady, Charli withdrew a short knife horizontally from across his belt. He exchanged a quick look with Mayli before carefully applying a generous stroke of toxin from the crossguard to the point.

A crackle like burning ashes tickled Mayli's ears as the two made contact.

"It's reacting!" Jair said excitedly as the blade glowed. "This is amazing!"

Charli said nothing as he led the blade to the silk. Pressing the tip down, he dragged. As if it were made of nothing but paper, the Ammosian Silk split. The wood table underneath became exposed with a carved line.

Jair snatched the cloth and peered into the hole. "I can't believe it! Mayli, you knew about this?" His finger wiggled through.

"We only just learned about it the other day."

He wiggled his arms. "This is so exciting!"

"Jair!" Mayli snapped, stealing her scarf back. "This isn't exciting! Father showed me Mother's dress... She died wearing our silks. *Stabbed* through her heart."

He shrunk. "W-W-What?"

"Arkello did it," Mayli said, staring at the mythical glow of Charli's knife.

"All this proves is what we already knew: that Arkello knows how the toxins work," said Charli. "But we still don't have any evidence to expose him being responsible, for the murder or your kidnapping. Meanwhile, Madam Nive was the last to see Colin leave her room. I trust what my mother saw."

"Someone nimble like Arkello still could have crept into her room! The way you two fought proved his ability, and—"

The glow subsided and they all looked at the blade Charli had used to cut the silk.

It no longer shone.

Instead, there was darkness.

"Wow..." gasped Jair. "The metal looks like the night sky now!"

No, thought Mayli. *That blade looks like Alden's...*

Jair held the silk taut in offering. "Can it still cut?"

Charli pressed the dark tip to the fabric, but the silk held strong. "Seems it is only temporary, but the blade is now tarnished. Shame. I liked this one."

Mayli couldn't stop looking at the swirls of lavender forming on the dark surface. "I feel sick," she said.

Charli sheathed the knife and put the cap back on the toxin. "Yeah, the odor is a bit intoxicating. Let's get you two back to your room." He put his hand to her back, urging her along.

Nodding, Mayli crept to the ladder. The wood shook with each step down, but the height seemed like nothing compared to the depths of fear she felt stretching. Her lip trembled as she walked through Arkello's dark apartment. Shadow shapes seemed to move and watch her as if she were in a dream. *It can't mean what I think...*

Charli continued to lead Mayli and Jair back to the palace and eventually to her room. Hardly giving him or Jair a farewell, she cowered inside, and locked the door. Her feet led her to the vanity. She sat.

After what seemed like hours, Mayli finally opened the bottom drawer. There sat Alden's dagger. The memory of the King's Blade her mother once showed her carved back into her mind, mirroring its shape. However, leather bound the curved grip and a black blade hid in the dark. The weapon seemed innocent enough aside from a piece of leather that dangled free, daring her to unwind the truth.

Mayli shook her head, squinting her eyes hard as she picked it up. *Please don't be true,* she pleaded to the weapon. Rubbing her face with a breath of confidence, she lifted her chin and the knife. She took hold of the frayed leather. *Alden would have said.* The strap loosened. *He's been searching for who's responsible...* She used her nail to tug. *He said he didn't do it...* She bit at hardened knots. Pulled at loose binds. *Didn't he?* Mayli didn't stop uncovering every detail until the entirety of the weapon was exposed.

Beautiful blue jewels sparkled. Etchings of sand dunes and names of past kings were scribed in silver and gold. Every detail matched her memory, aside from the blade's color. Stained black from the toxins which helped end her mother's life. It was, without a doubt, the King's Blade.

No...

Tears poured.

It can't be...

Her arms shook.

She let her head hang from the weight of too many deceptions—too many lies. *Alden lied... And for him to hold me. Kiss me!* Her heart stretched and tore in every direction, feeling as though it were being stabbed through again and again—just like her mother's had.

Mayli dropped the murder weapon. It crashed back into the drawer seeming to scream with her as Mayli threw her hands to cover her mouth.

Alden... Oh Alle...

Her stomach ached, repelling the absurdity that her rogue was to blame. "You murderer," she cursed, but then his voice came to her mind: *You would kill if you were trying to survive or protect someone you love. That doesn't make you a murderer.* To settle her unease, Mayli shook her head trying to recall more words Alden had said trying to stress Colin's innocence.

That he and Colin weren't on good terms.

That she should consider someone else might be responsible.

That assassins could hide in the brightest shadows.

That they were on the hunt to find who was responsible—who hired the hit.

That Colin held her in the utmost regard and still truly loved her.

Or how Alden's guilt weighed him down when it came to their intimacy. Nearly every look he gave had been cast with sad eyes—shameful eyes. She swallowed, recalling his vague note on her drawing hoping for her forgiveness one day.

We all had it wrong, Mayli realized.

Alden did it.

Alden was the hired assassin who killed my mother...
No wonder they were so adamant that...
That...
Mayli covered her mouth. "Oh no..."

Colin is innocent.

CHAPTER EIGHTEEN

A FRESH START

Murderer.

Alden scrubbed harder at the stone. His muscles ached and back strained. The sour stench of vinegar teased his nose. Dirt and grime blackened his nails. Suds formed. His grip intensified, as did the clench of his teeth. When still the red-stained word continued to mock him after each desperate pass of his coarse brush, Alden cried out and tossed it across the stone floor.

Listening to it clatter, Alden pressed his hands to the wall and let his head dangle.

"Why not just sand the wood, and paint the stone?"

Alden looked under his arms seeing Trip pick up the discarded brush. "That's not a bad idea, but I can't do that."

Trip met him at his side looking at the sudsy mess. "Why?"

Alden slid from the wall and gestured around the room. "Anything that doesn't honor the original farm is like a direct assault against Dean."

"So he really expects you to scrub all this away?" Trip put

his hand on a marked stone as if soothing a wounded animal. "It's stained too deep."

Alden looked down the hall. Squirrel sat perched high on a ladder. Rek prowled the ledge beside him, dusting beams with his tail. Already halfway done with the north side of the grand hall, he'd made fine progress sanding graffiti from the wood posts. Alden frowned at his own progression—not much more than an arm's length and still the words mocked him.

"It's not like the stone is being taken away," said Trip.

"I suppose you're right..." Alden looked back at the servant. "One can't erase the past, but they can build on top of it."

Trip grinned at the wall. "I think paint will look good, and Lord Dean will just have to agree."

"You're right." Alden turned and swooped his arm. "Ey, Squirrel, come 'ere."

Moving down the ladder, Squirrel shook his hair, raising a bloom of sawdust as he landed at the bottom. His nose twitched before he sneezed and hurried over.

"Squirrel?" Trip stepped back at his arrival. "That's a funny name."

Squirrel looked him up and down. "What's yours?"

"Trip."

"That's a funny name too."

Trip mused a quiet laugh as if unsure whether he was offended or amused. He glanced at Alden for a brief moment before looking back at Squirrel. "Come on. What is your real name?"

Squirrel's lips twitched, doing their best to keep smiling. "Squirrel."

Alden grabbed his friend's shoulder, turning him from Trip's curiosity, sure the boy either didn't know his past or wish to remember it. "Hey, bud, there's a cart of painting supplies in the storage room beside the servants' hall. Ya know, next to where we took your things? Could ya wheel it out for us?"

"Wheely cart. Got it." With an eager nod, Squirrel dashed away.

"He's cute," said Trip.

Alden nodded. "That's a word for it."

Trip took a few steps back with a smile on his face and hands on his hips as if admiring the wall like a work of art. "I can't wait to see this wall clean so when Prince Colin arrives he won't need to feel so shunned."

Alden swished his finger around the room. "You don't find him responsible?"

Trip tossed his head, black hair flying. "Absolutely not. He may have been a prankster, but a murderer? No way."

Ease settled in Alden's shoulders, giving room enough in his chest to laugh. "That's a refreshing perspective to hear."

"You're right about that. I'm so glad to know most everyone in the castle here shares it. I don't need to talk in whispers about my alliance anymore, ya know?"

Alden nodded once. "Yep."

"Speaking of, I wanted to ask..." Trip stepped closer. "You mentioned you worked for the royal family before. Were you here during the battle?"

Alden closed his eyes as the panicked sounds of the day hit. There had been so much shouting. Crying. The metal scrape of swords clashing. Hoofbeats and arrows whizzing. The crash of stones against the tower sent by the Hiorean trebuchets made his heart race as the memory beat. "I—" He shuddered. It had been Trip's father, Fredrik, who had nobly held the door as the tower was assaulted. He ushered Dean, Mary, Prince Jamus, Briar, and Colin out before the tower began to crumble. Stones shattered. A thunderous crack split his ears. The grip of his brother's hand—lost. When he blinked past the cloud of dust, a bright sky and open air blew over him.

The tower had fallen.

His parents and brother along with it.

Prince Jamus had grabbed him then, dragging him from the devastation. Moments passed that Colin couldn't recall—too much a blur, too in shock of what he'd just seen. What he'd just lost.

They were in the stables then. Mary and was fixing tack with Briar, while Dean watched the door. Just beyond there were the sounds of battle. Jamus knelt on one knee and took both of Colin's shoulders, giving a shake. "Colin, you'll be king soon. The legacy of Vatan rides with you. And right now, you're not safe. So, take this and go with your Granda and stay low until we can resolve what happened with the queen." Jamus placed a bundle in his hands.

"We know what happened," grumbled Dean, pointing. "And right there is proof. If you and your brother are set on protecting Vatan you should cast that thing into a blaze. Not give it to the one responsible!"

Jamus glared. "The King's Blade is Colin's regardless of what you believe has been done. It will stay in the family."

Colin picked at a corner and pulled the fabric aside. Inside was a sabered dagger adorned in jewels save but one. *The King's Blade?* Colin rubbed his nail along the blade, flaking away dried blood. Still, the blade remained stained dark as midnight. Heart thundering, Colin turned around to gaze through a stall window at the absence of the tower. The room he lived in. The home he shared. His parents. Gone. *Because of me?*

"But Da..." Briar walked Excelsior, Jamus's black warhorse, to him. "You're the eldest heir, wouldn't that make you king?"

Jamus stood, checking his saber was secure on his belt. "I'm not accepting that my brother is dead just yet, son. I am going into battle to find him among the rubble, just as he did for me in Gezmek. I cannot guarantee either of us will return. If we don't, that responsibility will fall onto Colin, so you must continue to protect your cousin at all costs."

"But—"

A volley of Ammosian arrows hissed overhead. They struck the ground like hail racing towards them. Dean threw his shield up, collecting several as he protected Colin. A scream rang from above just before a man crashed into the stable's roof, spooking all the horses but Excelsior. More shouts erupted just beyond the gate as Hiorean troops neared.

Jamus shook Briar. "Pledge it, son!"

Tears streamed down Briar's face. "I will keep King Colin safe. I promise, Da."

Colin paled. *King Colin?* Hearing it, the reality of everything struck him like a rock from the tower landing in his gut.

"Good." Jamus hugged Briar then placed the reins into his hands. "Here, take William and ride with Dean, Mary, and Colin."

"William?"

Jamus rubbed the horse's large head and patted its neck. "He's your horse now, Son, and with it comes a new name to honor King Liam. Now, go!"

A warm touch graced Alden's arm, rousing him from the past.

"Hey..." said Trip, voice soothing.

Alden looked at the young man's green eyes pained with regret.

"Sorry." Trip frowned. "I should know better than to ask... But, you see, I lost my mother then, and I just keep asking people because I'm desperate to try to find any last memories of her."

Alden's gut turned, gnawing at the rocks of guilt he could

never quite digest. He knew exactly where and how Trip's mother died. Crushed by the same tower his own had. The same trauma. Same past. Alden closed his eyes, finding darkness. Within it, however, kinder memories grew. He could see his own mother's sweet smile, feel her long fingernails trace along his back as he read a book while they cuddled. Even his father, often stern and serious, Alden found a memory of pride as the king showed off one of his first paintings to the court—the one Briar refused to take down. Finding it in him to smile, Alden looked back at Trip. "You have enough memories within you already. Let those be what you seek."

Trip took his hand away and brought it to his ear to play with a small silver ring. "I suppose you're right. Besides, I'm sure she was honoring her king."

Alden leaned his crested arm against the wall, ignoring the foul names pushing back at him. "If she was anything like you, I believe she was."

Shying away, Trip blushed. "Anyway, I can't take credit for the paint. Art suggested it earlier." He handed the scrub brush back.

"Art?"

"Yeah. I call him Art, the artist?"

"Now that's a funny name."

"No more than Squirrel," teased Trip.

Alden chuckled, dipping his head to shake his mind. "Ya know, it would be great to meet him. It's not often I meet other artists." He pushed from the wall.

"Don't expect to. And besides me, the lord and lady, and that scary royal guard at the tower, he doesn't show face. Quite literally."

"Why's that?" Alden stepped closer.

Trip leaned in, tapping his cheeks. "It's all marked up!"

"What, like scarred?"

An echoing creak sounded through the hall as the main doors opened.

Trip sunk in posture, sucking his lips together. "Ope... He's here." He ducked behind Alden, pressing small hands to his back.

"The artist?" Alden faced the doorway. Instead of seeing a dark-cloaked man, the knight from the gatehouse strode into the hall. His gait was wide, prideful. His presence, demanding. Plucking off his helm, a blond mane was let free. He shook it, and strands fell around his steel gorget like a gold chain.

"Oh..." moaned Trip.

Alden looked down at the young man. Adoration sparkled in his eyes as he stared dreamily at the knight. Alden hicked a laugh. "I thought you said knights were scary?"

"Royal ones. Not..." He licked his lip. "*Him.*"

Armored clanked together as the knight continued forth. Pausing at a table of snacks, a charming dimple formed in his cheek. Plucking an olive and roll of sliced meat, he popped it in his mouth. He turned to look around the room then paused his chewing, seeing them stare.

"Oh no, no, no, no..." Trip stole Alden's brush back and tucked his head into the wall. Vigorously, he began scrubbing.

Alden huffed. Despite the knight's sculpted appeal, his strict personality at the gate was enough for Alden to dismiss him as enjoyable company. He turned his back to focus on Trip. "Why are you so shy toward a bloke like him?" He bobbed his head back.

"Because he's—oh! Right here." He squeaked.

The knight walked over with his hands on hips, nodding approvingly as if admiring a great work of art. "Nice to see the mockery being cleared away."

Alden sighed. He folded his arms and faced the man with a

sneer despite the welcoming words. "Hope that applies to me as well."

"Ah. Alden, was it? Our start was rough, and I realized I didn't properly introduce myself. Forgive me. My name is Sir Stridan Lance." He placed his hand to his shoulder then bowed.

Blinking with surprise, Alden glanced at Trip who was beet red in the face. *No wonder he's bashful. This man is a legend.* Retiring his snide for his own star-struck appreciation, Alden grinned with genuine pleasure and bowed back. "Sir Stridan. It's an honor. I should have suspected you would be here."

The knight waved his hand. "Please, I am nothing special. Just a man with a sword and once a lance."

Alden lifted. "Yet it was that lance which earned you your noble name. I saw the joust. Not every man can bring royalty to the ground."

Stridan looked away, rubbing his crested arm. "Lucky hit," he said, managing a smile.

"Maybe." Alden frowned, knowing they both knew the win was ill-won when Evelyn had hired Shadowens to sabotage Briar's saddle. "I haven't seen your name listed in tournaments for a year or so, nor has your presence been noted with the nobility. Where have you been in recent years?"

Stridan worked at removing his arm guards. "My time was better spent helping Brimleyn refugees than catering to those who already had a life of ease."

"Really? How so?"

He pulled the armor free and tugged at his gloves. "The land I inherited with my title was more than any one person should have, so I built a small commune where they live under my protection."

"That's admirable."

"The common people are where my heart lies, having been one myself."

A soft, delightful whimper mewled around them. At first, Alden looked up, expecting Rek to be touring the rafters above. When he saw his cat lounged on Squirrel's ladder with eyes closed, Alden looked down to see Trip, sunk into the wall, cradling the brush and looking on in fascination at the knight. When Stridan also caught notice, the servant tensed.

Trip's eyes flicked to an unmarked stone. "Wow. Look at that. Clean! Okay, Alden, I better help Squirrel get us the paint... I think I saw him go to the kitchen instead..." Scrub brush still clinging to his chest, Trip backed away. Spinning on his heel, he trotted to the servants' hall, giving fleeting glances back every few steps.

Stridan blinked. "Something I said?"

"He's got a thing about knights." Alden winked.

"Ah... I don't blame him. Most are jocks."

Alden held his laugh for having assumed him one. "So, what of your village now?"

"Mostly cleared out. Hearing Brimley was being restored most followed me back here picking up hammers and shovels to rebuild what once was. We started with the Stride-On Inn, of course."

"A loyal following."

"They ought to be."

Screechy wheels pierced the grand hall as Squirrel pushed in a wood cart splattered with an assortment of colors. White paint dripped from barrels as they rattled. A canvas tarp trailed behind. He stopped short, seeing the knight.

Alden sighed. "I best get back to work."

Stridan set his armor on a table and rolled up his sleeves, exposing wide muscles. "I'd love to help."

"That's kind, but this is my mess to clean." Alden grabbed a thick horsehair brush from Squirrel before the boy combed it through his hair.

"Nonsense, you didn't disgrace these walls." Stridan took the brush and dipped its bristles into paint. "Everyone who is here believes in a fresh start."

Alden watched as in one long swipe, Sir Stridan erased the word Alden had spent the last three years trying to scrub away. *Coward.*

Arms sore, Alden dropped the brush and stepped back to observe the completed work. Despite the dark of night, the great hall still glowed brightly from oil lamps, their light reflecting off white walls. Wood beams now seemed to pop and were held with sturdy support. Dust and grime had vanished with each painted stroke, leaving the room cleansed from its past. Inhaling, Alden leaned back, taking it all in. "It's the first time I feel like I can breathe in here."

Stridan wiped his hands on a cloth. "We did a good job."

Alden looked at the floor where Squirrel rested, coiled like a cat with Rek on his back. "Some more than others."

"He did a fair amount. The servant boy, however... I believe I scared him off for good. Perhaps I should offer him an apology next time I see him, but first I'd like to offer one to you."

"Me?" Alden wiped his hands on a paint-free spot on his tunic. "What for?"

"Refusing you entry per Colin's request. Had it been my own land, I would have welcomed you in. Any friend of his is one of mine."

Alden rose a brow. "You stand by Colin too?"

"Of course." Stridan touched his shoulder. "Although my ink and this kingdom is now Dreggen, he's still my prince first."

Alden studied Stridan carefully. "You also don't believe he's the murderer?"

"You think I form opinions based on scribbles on walls?" He

gestured around the now-clean room. Stridan stepped closer, hushing his voice. "Besides, Prince Colin went out of his way to try to save me from what he thought was a bad marriage. He needn't have done that when so much of his own life was troubled. Although my plans turned on their head, I owe him a great deal of respect. Which is why I felt it my duty to serve him in any way possible."

"Like giving homes to the refugees." Alden bobbed his head.

"And pledging my services here so that he may have one too."

Alden's chest unwound another knot feeling lighter knowing he had another true ally. "Glad you took Colin's letter to heart then."

"Look, again, I'm sorry I couldn't let you in with his word."

"That was no jest," said Alden. "I was referring to last year regarding Evelyn rigging the joust. She was wrong to doubt you and didn't deserve a man of your virtue."

Sir Stridan's cheerful knightly pride and demeanor hardened. "You know about all of that?"

"I was the one who found out and relayed the information." Alden gave a coy smile. "Besides. We are big fans. Couldn't let you marry a wench like her."

Stridan pinched his lips, stifling a frown. Closing his eyes, he took a deep breath. Then he leaned back, rousing his smile once more with a chuckle. "Fans? Please. You know I would have lost that joust if not for Evelyn's schemes. It would have been me lying in the dirt, still a commoner."

"I am not so sure of that. It was by no scheme you got so far to begin with. Briar was nervous to face you, admitting fearing a loss. Even had he not been thrown off William, his lance didn't strike you. It was still a win."

Stridan nodded. "It is an honor to know they think of me so highly."

"Doubt Briar would have allowed you a position guarding Brimley had he not."

"I suppose you are right." Stridan watched as the main doors opened. Several curious nobles peeked their heads in to observe the makeover. Large grins lifted their cheeks, and their eyes lit, pointing at the white walls and raw posts. Smiling along with them, Stridan looked back at Alden. "So, will Prince Colin be coming back after the renovations are complete?"

Shying his head from the gathering mass, Alden pushed their work cart towards the servant's door. "Not yet. Not till the murder is solved does he feel right to show face."

"Sensible. Well, if there's anything I can do to help, let 'em know that I pledge myself to the cause."

"Thank you, Sir Stridan. I'm glad to know there are friends we can count on here."

He bowed and dismissed himself.

A loud yawn sprawled from Squirrel as he stretched awake from his curl on the floor.

"Sleep well?" Alden asked, bending to pet Rek.

Blinking, Squirrel looked around. He offered a lazy grin, smacking his mouth. Then, noticing the gathering entering the hall, he pushed from the floor and hurried to Alden's side, nearly butting up against him with wide eyes.

Alden patted him. "It's fine," he said, more in reassurance to himself than to Squirrel, as an elder nobleman Alden recognized glanced their way. His eyes swept over them without thought as he stared in fascination at the fresh paint behind him.

A thief, a guard, or a servant, no one thinks beyond what they see other than what is painted. Maybe someday, the layers on my canvas will be enough to earn back their smiles when they see who I am and what I've become.

"Sweet kings!" exclaimed Dean.

Alden turned around, seeing Dean take two slow steps into the great hall. His mouth lay open, gaping at the room as his head swiveled. His brow worked in waves, from shock to awe. When his gaze landed on Alden, it hardened to sheer anger.

"Aw, fuck." Alden turned his back and grabbed the paint cart. He pushed it toward the servant's hall, pretending he hadn't just been spotted. It creaked loudly as if loyal to the lord of the castle.

Short yet loud footsteps beat on the tile floor. As they neared, Alden let out a sigh and stopped, dropping his head. He turned just as Dean met him, nearly a foot away.

"You," Dean growled, pointing a stubby finger in his face and shook it. "What did you do?"

Squaring his shoulders, Alden lifted his chin. "What you asked."

Dean leaned closer, gesturing at the wall. "This is not what I asked for!"

Alden inclined his head. "It's not?"

"No!"

"Did you want the walls painted blue instead?" He thumbed backward. "I will happily get that out and paint it all again. I'm afraid all the yellow was used up around town."

Dean slapped Alden's hand down. "How is it that whenever you offer help, you seem to only make matters worse?"

Cupping his hand, Alden looked down. "I—"

"You were supposed to restore this room to what it was before you came along."

Shame crept up his face. Noticing the crowd forming to watch, Alden dipped his head. "I tried that..."

"Obviously not well enough, but I suppose, like you, it's past salvaging now."

Alden flashed his eyes up, letting his brow dip low to glare.

"Don't you dare look at me like that. Mary may not believe

that I will, but I'd be damned if I let one more mistake keep me from sending you to where you belong."

Alden continued the look in challenge. Sensing Squirrel's unease behind him and the hushed conversation rousing from the crowd, Alden forced his eyes closed. Gritting his teeth, he placed his hand over his hidden crest and bowed. "Yes, Your Lordship. My apologies." He kept low until he felt the crowd move on.

"Good. Now, who is this pup behind you?"

Alden rose, looking at Squirrel. The boy stood firm at his side. "This is my friend, Earl," Alden offered, sure Dean would throw a fit to learn they called him Squirrel.

"He know what a fuck up you are?"

"Not exactly," Alden murmured.

"Then he's not exactly your friend, now is he?"

Squirrel glowered. Even beyond the dotting of paint accompanying his freckles and hair dusted with sawdust, a die-hard look of loyalty seemed to flash in his eyes. "Friendship is determined by a belief in the other. It is you, Your Lordship, who is not his friend," he said.

Alden smirked.

Dean laughed. "The pup has a bark."

"And a bite," growled Squirrel.

Both Dean and Alden looked at him in surprise. Dean formed his brows low then glared at Alden. "You best keep this one leashed."

"He'll behave." Alden pressed on Squirrel's back. Thankfully, he took the cue and bowed.

Dean turned his back on the gesture, crossing his arms. Overlooking the room once more, he began to nod. "For what it's worth. William would approve of what's been done." His tone sounded sincere, apologetic even.

Alden looked at Dean. Perhaps it was the way the warm

light bounced in the room more brightly, or the soft, clean tone of white creating a simple backdrop, but for once since the war, his grandfather looked unruffled. Peaceful even. The moment, however, was brief as Dean clapped his jaw tight and walked off, mumbling something.

"What was that?" Alden asked, easing forward.

"I said that you did a good job."

CHAPTER NINETEEN

INFLUENCE

Briar felt as though he was inside a bee's hive as the great hall buzzed with activity. Bold black and yellow lines cascaded down the windows, sprawled across the floor, crisscrossed over tabletops, and were woven around every guest.

Kira wore the same outfit as the other guests, but even in a room of mirrors, Briar had no trouble spotting her beauty. Her hips filled the side split gown. Her breasts perked up in a corset which seemed to add more volume than he ever imagined. She wore boots and a yellow crocheted hat. She, for once, let her hair hang loose, free from braids. Short layers she'd been working to grow out curled around her boxy chin, accenting her cheekbones. Unlike the ring of noblewomen she laughed and chatted with, doing their best to honor the unique look, Kira stood with genuine confidence and comfort.

As if knowing he was staring, Kira looked at him. Black-painted lips smirked along with her dark eyeliner as she winked.

Briar let out an unstable breath and walked over. The other ladies straightened their posture, attempting to lure his eyes away from Kira, but they were only shadows in Kira's light.

Grinning, he took her by the arm and pulled her behind a pillar, claiming a private moment. "You look lovely..." he said, letting his eyes drift over her.

Kira rubbed his arm. "As do you, Your Majesty."

Briar looked upon his pure yellow ensemble save for his black cape. He brushed his sleeve and huffed. "It seems I've missed the memo to wear stripes."

"Nonsense." Kira waved her hand before folding it into her arms. "You're secure enough to not feel obligated to any others' standards. Unlike everyone else here."

Briar tilted his head over his shoulder. He watched as the women Kira had been chatting with were working to untie their complicated braids. "Are you annoyed by them?"

Kira spread her hair in three parts and began weaving it back into a braid. "Hardly. I find their obsession amusing."

"Oh?" Smirking, Briar leaned against the pillar and folded his arms. "How so?"

"Well, it makes them easy to predict." She pointed to the women who were now scrambling to fix their loosened braids having seen Kira begin her weave.

Briar chuckled. "I see. So it's a game."

"Not quite. It's actually political." Kira let go of her hair and traced her hands down her body, movements Briar watched with privilege. "You see, I designed this outfit and as expected, everyone had to have it."

Briar smirked, reaching to follow her fingers as they reached the hem. "You're right. I, too, may need this dress..." He gripped the fabric.

Kira took his hands. "Stay focused tonight. While they all think they have the same design as I, there are major differences."

Briar assessed the crowd. Lords and ladies alike had some sort of black and yellow linework stitched into their design. He shook his head. "I can't tell. And don't let this be some joke about how I see colors differently."

Her lips quirked to one side, forming a deep and mischievous dimple. "It's not. Black stripes on their sleeves will identify anyone who is not in support of your cousin."

"Really?" His brows shot up as he readdressed the crowd. Then frowned. "Everyone has black stripes."

Kira traced her fingers up her arm where yellow ringed around her shoulder like a tribute to Dregs. To him. "I know, but those with yellow over their crest are loyal."

Briar's teeth clenched, starting to see the subtle difference. While most he knew he could trust wore yellow, others he had suspected to be against him, surprisingly wore the same pattern. He smiled until he saw a few of his drinking buddies capped in black. Turning back to Kira, Briar shook his head. "You're incredibly clever, Kira, but many could be misidentified."

"Which is why I visited the two most renowned clothiers in Dregs and gave them much different design instructions. You see, Mrs. Chausmer displayed a Brimleyn flag in her shop window, showing support to you and Colin, while Mr. Garbsen had a sign banning them. The people sorted themselves out with where they felt comfortable spending their coin."

"Astounding..."

"Isn't it? Who knew I could be so influential?" Kira said as the music picked up.

Briar curled his lips into an adoring smile and looked upon her, admiring the proud glow she possessed. "You made quite a profound influence on me in just one day. I'm not surprised in the least." Leaning in, he pressed his lips to hers and led her out to dance.

The party continued just as Kira had expected. Music from The Riffkin Lads—who she accepted as per Fredrik's request when she found no others to fit the bill—played a jolly tune. Everyone danced, feasted, and enjoyed the dinner featuring Brimleyn cuisine. The decorations were hung, and her plan to oust those disloyal was working.

Kira eyed the tree displaying apple doughnuts throughout the night, but each time she made an attempt to sneak over, another noble stole her into a conversation, complimenting her on a well-done event. She offered pleasant banter to yellow-striped guests and spoke with deeper interest with those wrapped in black, picking up on cues of disloyalty to their king. She'd relay the information to Briar and the guards after the night was over. Finally left to her own, Kira took the last few steps to the dessert table. However, not even a half, quarter, or bite of doughnut remained—hardly even crumbs. She watched as a servant grabbed the empty display and cleared the table.

Pleasant hums from beside her teased Kira's ears. Glancing over, she saw orange hair, halfway braided and laid across one black shoulder. Arm raised to her mouth, the woman held the last doughnut with a delicate bite taken out.

Kira sneered. "Are you enjoying that, Evelyn?"

The woman stiffened, then slowly squared off to look at Kira. With sugar still sprinkled on her red-painted lips, Evelyn soured. "I was..."

Kira looked closer at her outfit. Like everyone, she stood with a black and yellow striped gown. However, her right sleeve unexpectedly brandished yellow for loyalty while the other started black. The whole gown was a patchwork of mismatched pieces of fabric, some velvet, some linen, with wide and inconsistent stitches holding it all together. "That's an interesting dress. Where did you have it made?"

Evelyn tucked a stray thread into her sleeve. "You're asking me about my clothes?"

"Well, it seems to be a popular subject here and—"

"I'm not interested in small talk with you, Lady Kira." Setting the nearly untouched doughnut down, she walked from the table.

Kira eyed the pastry, tempting to take it for herself, but as heavy boots followed the baroness, Kira watched as an older Yellow-Coat guard shadowed her. Quickening her step to match, Kira met Evelyn at her side. "Then how 'bout a big talk?"

Evelyn glared at her. Looking beyond she shook her head. "Where is your guard?"

"Unlike you, I don't need a chaperone."

"I'm happy for Marvin's protection," Evelyn said, looking at the Yellow-Coat as he dipped his head.

"I'm sure you'd rather have a knight's attention. Shame Sir Stridan isn't here to turn you down again."

Evelyn's lip snarled in disgust. "He's the last person I'd want around."

Kira arched a brow.

"Really though, where is...? Alden was his name?" Her smile turned insidious.

"He was reassigned to Brimley." Kira shrugged. "Probably off guarding someone else important."

"So it's true..."

"What?"

"Oh nothing." Evelyn lifted her head with prestige. "It is impressive for a Yellow-Coat to have such clearance. Don't you think?"

Kira shrugged. "He's good at what he does."

"I have yet to see that. But I do find it curious that you also haven't been in court long."

"As part Brimleyn, I chose to live among them in Colville after the war," said Kira, relaying her scripted lines. "Briar would visit often and when he became king he invited me to move in."

"So you claim to be a refugee? No wonder he has a soft spot for you. I couldn't imagine any other reason."

"No, I'm sure you couldn't." Kira rubbed her fingers at the side of her hem, itching to touch her dagger. Needing a change of conversation, she offered a civil grin, pretending to be polite. "So, at the meeting last week, you brought up concerns about people's ability to have enough coin to be clothed and fed."

"What of it?"

"It was very thoughtful. Seems like living outside the castle has humbled you."

"I've always been humble."

Kira snorted.

Evelyn pivoted her next step, pausing Kira in her path. "You think being a baroness automatically offers a life of grandeur?" she asked, ignoring how her guard hovered.

"Um. Yeah," Kira said confidently. "You are at a party in a castle. It doesn't get much better than that. You're welcome for that invite, by the way."

"Invite or not, being titled doesn't matter when your mother gambles away everything. Including her land, husband, and life."

Kira pressed her judgmental lips flat. "Oh. I didn't know—"

"Don't act like you care. No one has." Evelyn turned to look at the occupied throne. A gathering of women surrounded Briar, laughing as he told a tale with wide gestures. "Least not Briar. I'm sure you've realized that yourself."

"Well, after what's gone on between you, I can see why he's not fond of you."

Evelyn whirled. "I've done nothing but be loyal to him!"

"Loyal?" Kira scoffed. "You think breaking up with him after his lineage was questioned was being loyal?"

"He ended it with *me!*"

"Yeah, after you were so unsupportive. Just like how you insulted his rule in the market."

"I was only challenging him to see the world for what it is."

Kira twisted her lips and swayed her hip, placing her hand on it. "Right. And I'm sure hiring the Shadowens to humiliate him was just a way of challenging Briar too."

Evelyn tapped her chest. "I never did such a thing. Stridan, he..." Her arm drooped.

"He what?" Kira crossed her arms.

"Never mind." She shied her face. "He's just as much a noble as you are."

Kira stepped in, hands lowering hold of her hips. "What did you say?"

"Nothing... Just sometimes Briar is too innocent to notice when he's being deceived." Her eyes flicked Kira up and down.

"You should talk."

"And you should leave!" snapped Evelyn.

"Maybe *you* should leave, Evelyn," said Briar, voice stern and kingly.

Kira stepped back at his approach, but his hand came around her waist, securing her to him. His blue eyes were ice, glaring down at Evelyn.

The baroness fumbled her lips, unable to speak. She looked at Kira, then Briar, then all around as a crowd formed. Sucking in a wavering breath, she twirled, tears flying from her.

Once gone, Briar sighed deeply. "When will she learn?"

Kira rubbed her shoulder. "I think she has. She said something about my nobility in relation to Sir Stridan," she whispered.

"She must think you earned it under unfair advantage."

"Well, she's right."

"In this case, I will agree," said Briar, placing his hand over hers to halt her constant rub of her shoulder.

Kira looked up, sorrowing her eyes. "What do you mean?"

His glimmered back as he tried to offer her a smile. "You should have been crested for your heroism and dedication to the throne, not under the circumstances my uncle subjected you to." Cupping her cheek, Briar kissed her forehead.

CHAPTER TWENTY
LITTLE BIRD

May,

> *Every day closer to your visit, I feel the sun warmer on my skin. You—a—Gezm—treasure. Soon we will hold each oth—the heat between us enough to—family. Vatan—*
> *—together.*

I love you,
> *Colin*

A tear fell, breaking off charred pieces of the only remaining proof of Colin's love. Mayli wiped her face, unable to forgive herself for ever doubting him. For turning on him. Her love. She'd never wanted to accept he was responsible. His words *were* proof. But, as time went on, her family adamant, and letters mostly all burnt, she'd forgotten his devotion and began to believe the horrors everyone spoke. Her mother was dead—that she had to accept that no matter what. As grief moved in, blind anger roused. Her judgment fogged. With a broken heart and too weak to even lift from her bed, she commanded the attack. She destroyed Brimley. Destroyed Colin. All with the power of a few words.

Gently, Mayli placed the fragile letter in her lap, careful not to further damage what was given to her.

I'd truly forgotten who he was.

Mayli willed herself to remember the bond between them. How letters were being sent every few days. The flapping of wings coming to her balcony had become a symphony to the rhythm of her life. She'd dance out of bed, feed the bird a treat, collect his letter, and rush to the tallest tower in the palace. Four flights. Sixty-six steps. The view spanned over all of Ammos, the Desert of Gezmek, the sea. And when she squinted, she pretended she could see Brimley over the horizon. Pretended Colin was there reading it to her.

She recalled his declarations. Like how he wanted nothing more than to hold her hands and take part in all her favorite dances. He had made it a mission to master them, and expressed how he learned to enjoy the balls with her in mind. In an effort to further connect, he said he'd once taken up the bow and arrow. However, after months of practicing, he admitted how terrible he was at it. A few too many stray arrows had found themselves lodged in the side of the chicken coop. Mayli suspected that was why Colin often asked what her favorite foods were. She'd joke if he'd struck another hen and suggested a poultry dish. Days later, he'd report in, expressing his love for the flavors. Then, he'd send back his own versions of the dish, introducing a Brimleyn fusion, and naming it after one of the hens, like Layna's Spiced Wild Rice. While she enjoyed his humor, she rarely was able to enjoy his recipes as many Brimleyn foods were far too sparse and expensive to import to Ammos. Even for royalty.

The last letter Mayli received from Colin was one of his

most heartfelt, and although the letter had become lost in the wind, his words stayed with her.

May,

I assume you've heard. I'm so sorry for your loss. I can't even bear to write this fearing what you are feeling. If there is anything you know true of me, believe this: I am no murderer. Yes, I was drunk. Yes, I was upset. But no, I would never hurt you, or anyone you love. Please know this. My respect for you is too great, which is why I know I couldn't have committed such an act.

I will find who has committed this injustice and I'll die on my sword to uphold that oath.

With sympathy,
Colin

Footsteps had reached her ears after reading his confusing letter that hot summer day. "Mayli," her father had said. His voice had sounded spent, but not from the climb of stairs. It was wounded. Weak. Nothing like how a king's voice should sound.

Mayli had turned from the northern view. "Father? What happened in Brimley? Colin's letter doesn't make any sense." She held it between both hands.

Bakhari's lips quivered. Tears she'd never seen him shed aside from cries of laughter spilled down his face. "Your mother...*she*..."

With sympathy? Mayli recalled, looking back at Colin's letter she read his words again, focusing on *murderer.*

"She's dead, Little Bird..."

The words struck her so hard, Mayli stepped backward, bumping into the balcony. Colin's letter slipped from her trembling fingers, and she spun, clinging to the railing to find support. "Dead?"

"Yes," her father said. "Prince Colin killed her."

The expansive view overwhelmed her, and she looked down, gasping for air. The great height seemed to deepen. Spin. The waves crashing upon the rocky shore rose as if to grab at her. Sea mist grew, consuming her vision. Her heart raced. Her stomach twisted. The altitude and constant barrage of waves seemed to intensify. Nauseated from it all, Mayli retched.

Clearing her mind from the memory, Mayli tightened her hand around the railing. She blinked, realizing she'd come to stand at the edge with a calm heart. The crash of waves broke beneath her and without much thought, Mayli looked down to watch. For once, her stomach didn't twist. Her heart didn't hurt. The waters shimmered brighter as ships sailed to and from port.

A brisk breeze blew over the balcony's edge. The charred page fluttered in her hand. More ashen edges broke away, flying into the air and over the balcony's edge. She looked at the letter, seeing Colin's name was now missing. To Mayli's relief, '*I love you*' remained.

With a smile, Mayli folded the letter and placed it back in her pouch. She looked down at the caged bird she'd brought with her. Its long white wings stretched as it sat waiting for flight. A blue vest hugged its small body, already equipped with two envelopes. Unlatching the lock, Mayli pulled the door open and reached for the bird.

Hesitantly, it hopped on her fingers.

"It's been a while since you've flown. Do you remember the way?" Mayli asked, raising the bird to her face.

It trilled then peeped five times. Brimley.

Mayli nodded, then she rose and swung her arm into the

air. Feathers came loose, and Mayli clutched her hands to her chest, watching the little bird fly free over Vatan, unafraid of the heights or distance it must endure.

CHAPTER TWENTY-ONE

THE FUTURE OF VATAN

"Only those who do not seek the truth are liars, and cowards do not sacrifice everything," a deep voice echoed through Alden's mind, stirring him in his sleep.

"Even so, it doesn't matter what you do," another growled. "The boy is guilty."

Alden turned over in his bed, willing his nightmare to change.

"He is no boy. He is your prince," the first declared. "And someday your king."

Like the morning haze, the dream faded as Alden blinked awake. Sleepy eyes played tricks as he worked to form images in the dark. He blinked groggily, and the form of a black mass with two pointed ears formed at his side. Rek. Petting his cat, Alden looked past, observing the lower-class room. It was small with worn furniture. Stacked stone built the walls. Blue rugs carpeted the floors. Murals of ivy were painted on the ceiling like moulding and patches were recently mended.

Eyes heavy, he drifted through memories, lingering on the worst. He recalled embarrassing remarks, foolish mistakes, and times he let his family down. He rewatched the tower fall, his grandfather throw him from the mill, and even bursting in on the princess's carriage. He mulled over each moment he drew blood or hurt someone even remotely, everyone but Queen Margaret. Despite his efforts, Alden failed time after time to recall the night of her murder. Alden rolled to face the wall. *Enough with the nightmares,* he urged himself, rolling over to cling to a pillow. With something soft to hold on to, Alden sought good thoughts—like how the princess's warm body had hugged against him...

"Alden?"

"Yes, Princess?"

"I'm cold."

Rain had hammered outside, beating on the roof of the small shack, matching the beat of his heart. Dark and stormy air blew in through the floorboards like secrets whispered upon his neck.

Horses stirred. Briar slept. They didn't.

Wrapping his arm around the forbidden princess, Alden pulled Mayli into his embrace. "Is this better?" he murmured.

Taking his hand, Mayli nestled her head on his right bicep as if using the crest of his kingdom as a pillow. "Yes," she breathed while brushing her rear into his waist.

Something soft. Teasing. Begging.

The rest of the environment fell away as Alden's memory slipped into a fantasy. He pulled the princess closer, letting her feel what she had roused beneath.

Something hard. Honest. Generous.

She moved against him, calling out his name—his real name. *"Colin..."*

Silencing her, he kissed her mouth and took the princess in his arms. Touching her endlessly. Warming her inside and out.

Mayli purred—strange and feline. Then, a spread of needle-like pricks cut into his face as she slapped him.

Wincing awake, Alden yelped. His cat lay on his pillow, tail swishing back and forth. Purring continued. He peeled the black paw off his cheek and flipped to his back. "Let me sleep, Rek."

Rek marched his heavy weight onto Alden's chest, gut, shoulder, and then neared his face. "Roww." He bit and tugged at his hair.

Grumbling, Alden opened his eyes. "Okay! I hear ya." Alden waved his arm above his head, sending his cat to the floor as he rolled forward.

Birds sang a happy morning melody on the window's ledge as if calling him to the new day. The glass was clear and free from cracks as, like the wall, it too had been recently replaced. Through it, Alden watched logs float down the river and collect at a dock. Men hauled the lumber ashore where others collected it to replace tents with solid foundations. The hammering of nails and calls of work played like a symphony with the birds.

Alden rubbed his eyes, yawning, wishing to wake in an easier time. One where the calming wave of blue flags of Brimley promised hope. Where there was no war or a fight for justice. To nights where nightmares and restless thoughts didn't haunt him, to when he wrote love letters to a woman he greatly admired. A woman who might never again be his.

Alden squeezed a pillow into his begging lap and exhaled a long lonesome breath. "Oh, May... I shouldn't even dream of you."

Rek clawed at the door, making it rattle.

"Always so impatient for breakfast, aren't cha?" Alden swung his legs from the bed, tossed the pillow aside, and stood. "You're gonna get plump if you stay in that kitchen with Gran for too long. Believe me."

"Rea! Reaaa," cried Rek as he ran to Alden, dancing circles around his legs as if excited by the idea.

Hopping on one leg to avoid stepping on him, Alden grabbed the door's handle and yanked it open. "Get ou—" Alden froze.

"Oh... Hello," Squirrel said from several feet away.

Feeling a draft chase across his bare skin, Alden thrust his tattooed arm behind the door, ensuring his crest stayed hidden. He looked at the floor where his tunic now lay. *Did I seriously strip in my sleep? This isn't healthy.* Thankfully, Squirrel's gaze had fallen to Rek as the cat did circles around his legs.

"Have you been guarding my door?" Alden asked.

"Sorry, no." He bent to pet Rek. "I've been busy but then Lord Dean asked me to summon you. I was about to knock."

"Summon me?" Alden kept the door open a crack and peered through. "Really? Is he angry? I patched a few holes I thought needed mending and touched up some murals I saw had flaked without permission. And I did clean a room he hadn't specifically requested be done, but it looked worn so—"

"Um, I don't think it has to do with the work we have done. I think he's been enjoying all the other changes since the grand hall was painted. Which is why he's asked for your help with something he says only you can do, so he sent me."

Alden blinked at the thought. *He approves?* Sighing out a small laugh, Alden nodded to Squirrel. "I'll be on my way then. Thanks, bud."

After shutting the door, Alden grabbed his discarded shirt off the floor and pulled it overhead, cursing himself for being so careless even if he weren't conscious. *Maybe I sleepwalk and that's why I can't remember the murder?* he mused to himself as he stomped into his boots. Shaking his head, Alden tied his wool cloak around his neck and flipped his hood overhead. Dressed and decent, he opened the door.

Sensing movement, Alden gazed to the left, finding a slim

figure at the end of the dark hall. Shrouded in darkness, his eyes were unseen, but Alden knew they were looking into his own.

The artist.

He hadn't seen him since walking in on his meeting with Dean. He kept to his room, hiding behind a locked door and a knight. For a moment, Alden waited for the man to move into the light or introduce himself. But he only stared back from within the shadow, the tension growing.

Rek meowed, drawing their attention downward. Alden's cat nuzzled and circled the stranger as if they'd been friends forever. Although, as Alden watched, the artist took a piece of food from his pocket and dropped it on the floor to feed Rek, and Alden knew that's all it would take to gain the feline's trust.

He's gonna be a spoiled little prince.

Art's cane wavered as he limped into the base of the tower and retreated into his room. He held the door open just long enough for Rek to join him inside and sit beside Trip who was preparing a canvas.

Sighing, Alden continued down the hall and made his way down the steps to Dean's study. He reached for the handle but hesitated. Clutching his hand into a fist, he raised it higher and knocked.

"Who's there?" asked Dean from beyond.

"Me."

Footsteps approached, and the door swung open. Wrapped in his blue robe, Dean welcomed him with a curt nod. "Glad to know you can be respectful."

Ignoring the jab, Alden entered. "You wanted my help?"

Dean closed the door and walked back to his desk. Taking a seat he gestured at the one across from him.

Alden sat.

Dean placed his elbows on the surface and began tapping

his fingertips together. He kept his eyes downcast. Time seemed to linger. Finally, he spoke. "I want to apologize."

Alden cocked his head. "Apologize? For...when you yelled at me 'bout painting the great hall?"

"No."

"For making me wear this stupid worker's tie?" He tugged at the yellow band.

"No."

"For kicking me outta your mill a couple years ago?"

"No."

"For...accusing me of murder?"

"Nope."

Alden sighed. "I could go on...so maybe you inform me what you'd like to apologize for." He folded his arms.

Dean grumbled. "After some...*reflection*...I realize you have been doing your best to make amends. Painting the walls, scrubbing stones, sanding wood. You've cleared out the debris and managed to salvage what you could. Trip has expressed appreciation for your tips in art. And Mary has noted how you've even helped cook on occasion and assist her with kitchen duties. Though she does wish you would eat more."

Alden looked away.

"With what you've done, the castle hasn't looked this good in a long while. It's clean. Organized. You've proved maturity I didn't realize you had, even if I do not agree with your methods or entitled attitude."

"Thanks?"

"What I mean to say, *Alden*..." he choked out. "Is that I am sorry for not supporting you when you needed it most. You are family, and that alone should grant you honor, and certainly more than what I've given you over the years. I've taken my anger and shame for not better protecting William and Jamus out on you, and that is my own burden to carry—not yours."

A great tension released in Alden's back. His shoulders drooped. "Thank you," he said sincerely.

"While we still may never see eye to eye on some issues regarding the past, we can come together to construct your future. But first, this came for you." Dean pulled a letter from a drawer.

"What's that?"

"A letter from Ammos."

"Ammos?"

"Yeah." Dean lifted his arm. Tiny flecks of gold shimmered in the finely blended and smooth parchment as he passed the letter through a beam of light. Stamped in orange wax and a white feather just like before, was the royal Ammosian Crest.

May...

Taking and lifting the letter to his nose, Alden breathed in. His eyes closed as the captivating aroma of spice perfuming her letter brought forth memories from when they had once courted. Each letter had been heartfelt. True. Honest. His time spent with the princess getting her home had proved it. He hated that he couldn't offer her the same.

Her last letter had spoken of how she missed him since parting in the Cad Islands. How she had come to turn her perspective around—see things from the shadows. She'd promised to search for truth. *Was this it?*

With trembling fingers, Alden tugged at each puzzle-like fold with ease. Flicking it open, Alden paused, seeing his name.

Colin,

He narrowed his eyes. *She's writing to...me?* Shaking his head, Alden continued.

Hi.

*It's been a while. I'd ask how you are but, I can only imagine;
not well. That's my fault, and I'm so, so very sorry. You've lost so
much because I wouldn't listen, and my actions against you and
your kingdom were not fair. I realize that now.*

*I'm not writing to earn forgiveness. I can't reckon you would
ever pardon me after smearing your name. Rather, I am writing to
admit to something you've known... You're innocent.*

"I'm *what?*" Alden's heart accelerated as he reread the last
line. "Innocent!"

Dean huffed.

Ignoring the old man, Alden's smile continued to grow. He
stood from the chair and began pacing the room, fingers tightening around the paper as he read on with hungry eyes.

*After discovering he'd given me the King's Blade, I realized a hired
assassin killed my mother: Alden of Brimley.*

Alden froze.

His throat clenched.

Breathing stopped.

Slowly, he lowered the letter and blinked to look up. Exhal-
ing, Alden sat in the nearest chair and put his hand to his forehead. He leaned in to hold it as a low chuckle started within
him, developing into a chaotic laugh. His head fell back, eyes
watering in both amusement and absolute pity for himself.

"Something funny?" asked Dean, still seated at the desk.

Alden gave him an absent grin. "She's got me all figured
out."

"That so?" Dean shuffled through a few papers, without
meeting his gaze.

Alden looked out the window, gazing upon the flower
garden. *What do I do with this? She likely hates me more than ever.*

A breeze swept over the field, and a loose leaf tapped the window. He looked at the letter in his hand where it would have landed if not for the glass. Alden flicked the paper stiff and held his breath.

I'm sure you're aware of my recent abduction attempt from the Shadowen Thieves Guild. Alden was among them, and I assume had been in the past when he killed my mother. Despite the foul deed, I do not believe it was something he had a choice in but was rather forced to do by order of the guild. At least, that is my theory as he, along with your cousin, went above and beyond to grant me safe passage home while insisting someone was still to blame. The guilt and shame Alden carries is as large as his loyalty to you. I understand why neither you nor Briar had wanted to turn in such a friend.

I'd never ask for his head.

Alden let out an unsteady sigh. He wiped his eyes, fogging with tears as he read on.

Colin, I still cannot bear the thought of how wrong I've been. But be assured, I will do everything I can to make this right for you and Alden, even if you never wish to hear from me again.

Best wishes,
May

PS
I'm glad to hear Brimley is being restored. It was as lovely as you always described.

PSS
Sorry for breaking a few extra things while I was there.

Alden laid the letter down and closed his eyes, taking it all in. His heart skipped beats in a fluttering dance much like after every letter she'd written him.

"Well?" asked Dean.

Calming his breathing, Alden looked at his grandfather. The man held a hard expression as if waiting for the opportunity to scowl. Alden sat up. "She doesn't hate me."

"Is that so?"

"Mayli discovered the King's Blade, so now she thinks I'm innocent because...I'm guilty." Alden furrowed his brow for a moment but resolved it with a curious twist of his forehead.

Dean said nothing.

"At least she is now considering the guild had its hand in this—not me." Alden stood from the chair and started pacing, twisting his hands as he worked out his thoughts. "Pierz is definitely involved since he orchestrated the kidnapping. Did he have Margaret assassinated too? And why? Does he find Ammosian rule threatening? Who else does?"

Dean leaned back in his chair, resting his elbows on the arms and threading his fingers together. He began rocking. "Alden."

Alden turned to face him. "What if—"

"Colin."

Alden's mouth hung open. He attempted to speak a few times as thoughts battled to be said. He managed it closed, swallowed, and asked, "What?"

"Sit down." Dean looked at the chair in front of him.

Alden eyed it as if it were a spider's web. That if he sat, he'd be caught, wound up, and devoured. "Why?"

"Because it is time we had this talk."

Alden closed his fingers around the hem of his sleeves, rubbing the ends nervously. "About?"

"Just sit."

Compelled, Alden sunk into the wingback chair. "Granda?" He hated how his voice sounded small.

Dean moved aside a letter, the same intricate fold signature of Mayli. It lay undone. Read. He took in a deep breath and regarded Alden with a sympathetic look in his eyes. "Don't you see what you're doing?"

Alden looked back and forth. "No?"

"Manipulating not only her...but yourself. And she's figured it all out."

Alden tossed his head back with a groan. "Look—"

"I was never sure who was more delusional," Dean interrupted. "Her or you, but I guess that's clear now."

Alden clenched his jaw.

"Let me just ask you one thing," said Dean.

"Go 'head."

He stared at Alden, forming the deep crease in his forehead. "How important is Vatan to you?"

Alden narrowed his eyes, feeling his own brow pinch. "Incredibly."

"Good. Then it is time you face facts. Hard ones. Ones your father has worked so diligently to keep hidden, but the world has had enough of this game of lies and coddling. Watching you run around, creating a cyclone of destruction in your wake..." Dean stood, drawing a hand through his thinning white hair. "It's gone on too long. We are all exhausted."

"Look, I'm sorry if I've come across as abrasive, I—"

"It's not about that, boy. I'm not punishing you." Dean stepped aside and caught his hand on the wall. He rubbed the hardened stone as if trying to soothe the history it kept secret. "I'm giving you the answer you've been seeking because you will not let this mystery rest."

"What haven't you told me?" Alden managed to stand, walking around Dean. He stopped an arms-length behind and dipped his head to find Dean's eyes. They were glazed, surrounded by a million wrinkles, this time not of anger but pain and sympathy. "Granda...?"

He faced him, taking a step in to grip Alden's shoulder. "You must promise me one thing. Promise me you stay here." His grip tightened.

"In Brimley?"

"Yes. It needs you. *We* need you. And you've proven yourself dependable. Don't throw everything you've worked for away."

"What are you trying to say?" Alden's voice rose.

Dean lowered his head, his demeanor weak. "What I've always been trying to convince you of."

Alden pulled away. His heart raced in his chest as if it were climbing up his throat with the bile he was working to keep at bay. Alden took a step back. Then another. He shook his finger. "No...that's not what you're saying."

Dean remained calm. "It is."

"No. Mayli just said I'm innocent. I—"

"She also learned you're not. And *that's* the truth."

Alden's shoulders drooped. *No...*

"I found you passed out in the stairwell after the alarm had sounded. Blood on your hands...face. That damn knife in your clutches."

Alden waved his hand, laughing as his world began to turn in on itself like he was stuck in another bad dream. Another timeline. Another delirium. "No. That's not what happened. Briar said I never saw the queen, that I went to bed—"

"I know what Briar said!" Dean snapped. "He was just as intoxicated and didn't want to get in trouble for leaving you. I brought you to your room and sent for your father and uncle. We all agreed with his plan to cover it up. William washed ya clean and returned ya to your room. Jamus kept the King's Blade hidden until he gave it back to you during the attack. It didn't matter as the queen's guard saw you leave last her room."

"But... I... You..." The world spun around him as if he were drunk again on his father's dune ale. That night had been a blur. Gone before he'd even remembered stepping into the queen's chambers. The possibility it was him had always been there. He just never wanted to fully admit it. Alden broke out a lost breath. "Really?"

"I'm sorry. You killed the Queen of Ammos. Intended to, or not." He patted his back with compassionate strokes.

All the tension and knots Alden had worked out in the last month pulled taut once more. His heart gripped his chest as if Dean's words and touch had struck him like a sword. The wound—too painful. Too deep. Alden snatched Dean's collar, shaking the old man. "I would have turned myself in had I known! We could have prevented the war!" he yelled, tears flying from his eyes.

Dean shoved Alden off and straightened his shirt. "Those warmongers would have fought us regardless of your sacrifice. Why do you think your father has fought so hard to paint your innocence and forced an oath on us all to keep you safe? Keeping our family whole was worth a roll of the dice."

"No... No, no, no, nooo! This can't be!" Crying out, Alden drove his face into his hands to try to ease the constant swirl. Blood pounded loudly through his body like battle drums. The intensity rose, and Alden covered his ears. "*I am a murderer!*"

Dean took Alden's wrists and brought his arms down to his sides. He dragged his hands up Alden's arms and gripped him by the shoulders applying tender pressure. "As are all kings."

Alden peered up.

"Colin, I've seen you proven to be a man. Strong. Capable. Even loving. You now understand life, its consequences, and how they can be overcome. Princess Mayli has grown too. So, it is time you let go of this vendetta against a shadow and accept your true identity."

"What?"

"Decide it now, boy. Either you're Alden, the king's renegade, or you're Colin, the future of Vatan. Which are you?"

CHAPTER TWENTY-TWO

THE KING'S RENEGADE

Another turn of sand passed since leaving Dean's study without answer. As rain transitioned to sleet, battering the windowpane and leaving icy clusters at its base, the morning had turned into night. Autumn into winter. Alden's tears were just as frozen—the time to pity himself was over. Still, salt remained on his lips. He bit them, drawing a more appropriate flavor—blood.

Unable to sit idle any longer, Alden turned from his constant study outside and rose from the bed. Leaving books, journals, notes, sketches, and weapons behind, he packed his bag, taking only enough clothes for a week. Rek had never returned. *I knew this day would come.*

Sighing, Alden slipped out the door. Walking the hall one last time, he let his feet lead him to the great hall. Dim blue light poured over him. Gentle and cool. Alden stepped from the stairs and entered as if it were a pool of dread as water dripped from the windows in sheets. Despite all the work he'd done painting the walls with feelings of hope, pride, and accomplishment, the truth still hid beneath.

I am a murderer, but at least I'll no longer be a coward.

Tucking his hood, Alden fled the castle—his home. His life. Tears once again started flowing but became nebulous as he stepped into the brewing storm, further drowning in his guilt. Alden resisted looking back. Resisted saying goodbye to Squirrel or even his grandparents, knowing that if he did he wouldn't have the strength to go forward and fulfill his oath.

Mud splashing, he burst into the stables. "Emmy..." he called.

The tussle of hay shifted in a stall. Slow and tired, Emory walked to greet him—loyal as ever. Seeing him, she squeaked pleasantly.

Alden hugged her large face, clinging tight. He kissed. "I don't deserve you, but let's take one last ride? Yeah?" He pulled away and stroked her rose dapple face. Hot air blew from her nose, heating him with just enough confidence to brush and prepare her for the journey.

"Poor weather to be out for a midnight ride."

Alden jumped, nearly dropping his saddle. His shoulders eased seeing a large blond man in a loose unbuttoned shirt, exposing a mountain range of muscles. "Sir Stridan, what are you doing here?"

The knight flicked a smile and cleared his throat. "Night rounds..." He finished securing his belt.

From the corner of Alden's eye, he saw the bare legs of Trip fly from the stables. *Oh.* Averting his gaze, Alden threw his saddle on Emory and adjusted it with the blanket beneath just under her shoulder. "Right."

Stepping in, Stridan grabbed the bridle and helped feed the bit into Emory's mouth. "Where are you going?"

"Far away from here." Alden pulled Emory's bangs from under the browband.

"Care for an escort?" He gestured to a large, spotted, black, draft horse with a white blaze and feathering on his lower legs. "Umbra is always ready for a good ride."

Alden pulled on the cinch straps. "No, thanks. I don't wanna keep ya from your *duties* more than I already have."

"The roads can be filled with bandits, and it is my duty as a knight to offer protection. Wouldn't want you to fall into the wrong hands. Besides, I owe you a debt for helping to inform me of Evelyn." Stridan covered his crested shoulder.

Alden sighed, the idea of highwaymen or thieves gutting him almost tempting. However, his purpose and promise would be defeated if he couldn't reach Ammos safely. Unable to deny Sir Stridan's offer, Alden nodded. "If ya wanna escort me to the harbor in Dregs, that would be fine."

"Great!" Stridan said, grabbing his saddle from a peg. "I have business there myself..."

The further they rode from Brimley, the lesser the storm had become. His mind had cleared along with the frozen rain as it softened to snow. The path had quieted in the fresh untrodden powder. His focus still. His heart—cold. Alden shivered as the checkpoint into Dregs came into view. Despite the illusion of peace, he knew even colder days were to come. And soon, death.

Bam.

Alden's head throbbed. His body ached. A pain intensified in his chest as he strained to catch his breath. Slush sucked between him and the ground as he rolled to the side. Alden wheezed, tasting icy soil as he tried to recapture lost breath.

Did I faint?

Emory whinnied.

Alden looked up, watching his horse circling back from losing her rider. Mane shaking, she whinnied again as if to laugh at his disposition. Then suddenly, she halted, nearly slipping on the wet ground. Ears high in alert, she swished her tail dramatically. Stomping, Emory twisted and bolted down the dawn-lit street.

"Emor—"

A force slammed Alden to a puddle, mouth swallowing mud. He squirmed, but the pressure between his shoulders held him firm. One wrist was taken, followed by the next. The coarse burn of rope strung them together. Struggling and gasping for air, Alden inhaled murky bubbles. His lungs ignited. Pain ripped in Alden's scalp as his hair was grasped, his head pulled back harshly to relieve him from drowning. He spat. Coughed. Sniffed, but inhaled the mud stuck in his nose.

Chuckling rumbled overhead. Boots crunched through an ice-capped puddle, splashing him. They stopped and squatted before him. Between the pair of legs, an ax swung like a pendulum. "Hello, Alden."

Alden closed his eyes, recognizing the man from the Shadowen Thieves Guild. "Ricky..."

"Ah, so you haven't forgotten about us!" Ricky said, looking around. "We were beginning to worry."

A burning pinch tugged at Alden's wrists as whoever held him pulled at the rope demanding him to stand. He obeyed, stumbling slightly. Rubbing his tongue along his gums, Alden freed a pocket of grit and spat. Mud and snow dripped from his hair and into his eyes. He wished to wipe it clean—the itch more irritating than the look on Ricky's smug face. With one eye squinted shut, he glanced down the street. The rising fog lightly masked three cloaked figures surrounding him. Morning light edged their ready blades. Lurking between two trees, Alden spotted another Shadowen holding a bow, fingers massaging the string at the ready.

Hoofbeats clopped behind. Alden turned to see Emory being

led by Sir Stridan. Hope rose in his chest until the knight said, "I got his horse."

Ricky clicked his ax into his belt. He shrugged it higher on his waist and grinned. "Good work, Stridan. Delivering this traitor really saved us the trip. Here's your reward." A fat coin purse flew to the knight.

Alden stared in disbelief, the bottom of his gut hollowing as Stridan pocketed the money. "You... *You're* allied with the guild?"

Sir Stridan smirked. "How else do ya think I was able to earn nobility so easily?"

Shoulders falling slack, Alden shook his head. "No... But Ev—"

"*Evelyn* was going to be my beautiful wife after Briar tossed her aside. She was heartbroken. Easy. Then you had to go inform Colin." Stridan walked close, sneering down at him. "She found the letter he wrote and started questioning my legitimacy. You ruined everything. Least she valued her life enough to keep quiet. Maybe you should have done the same."

Alden's teeth ground together as his cheeks burned with shame for harassing the baroness over the misunderstanding. "Guess so."

"Okay, boys. That's enough." Ricky spread his hands to part them. He pointed to a thief lying in wait. "Matt, take his horse and ride to Colville. Inform Pierz of our catch."

"My pleasure." Matt gripped Emory's wet saddle and pulled himself up to sit. With a fierce yank, he whipped the reins and called out.

Emory turned her head and stepped lazily to the side with a snort.

Matt attempted again, but still, Emory held position. He groaned, sneering at Alden. "She's as dumb as you!"

"I'm not sure that's the case..." Alden reserved a smirk.

Matt kicked his heel back, spurring the horse. "Go on you. Get!"

Neighing, Emory scampered. She shook her mane and reared, trying to send the foreign rider off.

Alden wiggled to break free of his own hold from Ricky as Emory and Matt fought for control. "Don't kick her!"

"How else am I to urge this useless beast to go?" He tugged on the reins, and Emory marched in backward circles, eyes wild and confused.

"Look, why not take me directly to Pierz? Emory responds to me. You can sit behind me with a knife at my back if you like."

"Ha. Tempting, but not happening." Ricky tsked a finger. "We have our orders, so you're hunkering down with us."

"Yeah, and if I have to walk all the way to Colville I doubt Ricky and your old buddies will be patient enough to keep that cute face of yours intact. So, Traitor, teach me how to..." Matt ducked as Emory led him under a low-hanging branch. "How to control this damn horse or I swear I'll make it into steak!"

Alden gulped as Matt drew a knife. "Don't."

The man touched the blade to Emory's delicate neck. "Then how do I stop?"

Laughing, Stridan called out. "To halt, try sitting further back in the seat."

Alden threw daggers from his eyes at Stridan. "You fucking, fraudulent asshole."

Stridan raised his hands, looking away without shame. "I draw the line when it comes to horses."

Releasing the tension, Matt lowered into the saddle and leaned back. Emory stopped. "Oh," he said in pleasant surprise.

Stridan winked at Alden then lifted his attention to Matt and Emory. "Now squeeze your legs to go forward. Yep. Now use the reins to glide against her neck to pressure her into the other direction."

Matt did as instructed, and Emory turned from Alden without question. Loyalty—like everyone else—gone. "Farewell," he said, sending Emory into a trot and fading into the morning fog toward Colville.

Stridan dragged his hand through his long blond hair, shaking out the snow. "Now, if you'll excuse me, I have places to be." He mounted Umbra with finesse and rode off.

Ricky took Alden's lead from the thief who held his back and yanked, pulling him along. He fixed Alden's cloak to hide his bonds and then pushed him along. "Luckily, I don't need special instructions to manage you. Let's go."

The surrounding thieves followed, keeping a guarded presence as Ricky led them into Dregs. His knife clung to Alden's side while his arm wrapped around him as if they were pals. No one paid them any mind. Not the commoners, nobles, nor the Black-Coat guards they passed. Alden didn't care. Nothing mattered anymore. He was a murderer. Deserving of this. Of the pain he'd soon receive. Of the fate that would follow. Pierz would learn his true identity and profit from selling him to Ammos. He'd get there one way or another. *So be it.*

Head down, Alden watched his feet turn and travel along a freshly shoveled walkway as Ricky led them to a building. Once on the deck, Alden looked up to see an old man sitting in a rocking chair with a quilted blanket draped across his lap. While he looked unthreatening, Alden knew the man was Lary, a Shadowen Guard who was to be respected for his speed and dexterity. He made no move as Ricky pushed through the door.

Warmth and dry comforts a thieves guild wasn't usually noted for greeted Alden, along with the heavy smell of fried meat, potatoes, and eggs. Large quilted chairs, striped black and yellow to honor the Dreggen flags, flanked a stacked river-rock fireplace. A man occupying one turned to watch as they funneled in. Mike. Several others shifted on their stools lining a center bar. Brock. Ebby. Wire. Some faces he didn't recognize, but none were friendly. At a table in the corner sat five more who didn't seem to notice and continued their game of Noble's Dice. Other patrons, blind to the dangers around them, continued their morning meals.

Hand on Alden's back, Ricky led him into a large private meeting room. It had a table, a wide bed, and space to mingle. Ricky kicked the back of Alden's knees, sending him to the floor. He hovered, as over the course of a half-turn, Shadowens entered one by one.

Despite his will to accept fate, Alden's heart raced. Several Shadows began circling like wolves, their snarls and howls taunting Alden's ears. He clenched his jaw and pressed his eyes shut in anticipation. Leather creaked. Knuckles cracked. Ricky held him as a woosh came, followed by a grunt from his own throat as someone drove a punch deep in his stomach.

He bent over, coughing.

With no time to recover, a smack to his face lifted him back up. Alden watched as the attacker dismissed themself, giving way for the next Shadow to carry out their assault. *A beating line. Perfect.* Turn by turn, they threw their punishment. Each hit was carefully placed to not make him pass out—a lesson learnt when Kira had been victim to such a line. Forced to engage, Alden had chosen to target her temple with full force, knocking her out of the nightmare. Unfortunately, no one here offered the same courtesy. *Why should they?* So Alden continued to take whacks, punches, and even knees and kicks to the body. His nose cracked. His tongue bled. Blood choked his throat. After being slapped across his cheek from the last in line, Alden lulled his head.

Ricky lifted Alden's chin, crooked smiling down on him. "You see how much we all missed you?"

CHAPTER TWENTY-THREE

PIERZ

The busy tavern quieted, heads turning to see who had entered. Briar paused in the doorway. Their cold looks sent shivers down his back more than the turn of the season had.

A muscled body with a round face padded by a thick beard stepped through the door just past Briar, stomping snow from his boots. Aside from a fine sword strapped to the man's right hip, he, too, kept his attire casual. Even without the armor, his guard looked to be a man not to be trifled with. Stripping off his hat, exposing short-trimmed black hair, Sir Exten nodded to Briar that it seemed safe.

Fixing a tuft of hair from his gray wig into a bonnet, Briar hoped the old-woman disguise was enough to grant him a proper ale undetected. Thirsty and tired, he shrugged his scarf higher around his neck. Wool scraped along his cheek as he offered a friendly smile.

Conversation roused, glasses clinked, and heads turned back to nurse their drinks. Freed from their attention, Briar walked in. He passed people without them giving him a second look. Eyes didn't follow. Neither praise nor gossip murmured in his wake.

Briar cozied into his favorite seat. The worn wood welcomed him in as the sticky surface caught on his leather sleeve like a great hug. Briar closed his eyes and inhaled deeply. Stale ale. Firewood. Charred ovens. *Serenity,* he thought. He needed this—a moment to relax. Be himself. Indulge in drink and life as it once was. One without the constant pressures from the kingdom.

Since the ball, Kira had helped expose over a dozen disloyal nobles. Some Briar had suspected, but there were others he had trusted that surprised him. Too many proved the kingdom's interests were not theirs. That they were lying in wait for Briar to reveal Colin's whereabouts in exchange for King Bakhari's reward and to rid the Densens of power. Briar felt sick knowing what secrets he'd already disclosed in court. Thankfully, despite his dismissal of them from his castle and court, they remained quiet. Threats of removing much more of their power and standing kept lips sealed.

The pungent scent of cheap liquor wafted as something wet splashed over Briar's side. "So awfully clumsy of me, milady!" said a man.

Briar closed his eyes, remembering his disguise. *Right...* He aged his voice. "It's fine..."

"No, no. My apologies!" Long brown hair smelling of smoke and dirt shook in Briar's face as hands were already patting him dry. Uncoordinated and tall, he bumped into the bar, splashing more booze from his cup.

Briar jumped to standing with a whine. "Come on, man..." Briar wiped his lap.

Exten stood with his hand on his sword.

"So sorry! So, so sorry!" The man backed away, raising his wet hands. "Let me buy you and your husband a drink."

"That isn't necessary." Briar shook his head at Sir Exten's menacing scowl. "Either of you."

"It is the least I could do... Here, have a...silver. Silver?" The drunkard blinked as if surprised by the sum. "Well, see? All better. Enough for a few ales and new clothes. It looks like you need it, Gran."

Wiping his coat, Briar settled back into his seat. "Will it pay for peace and privacy?" He eyed the man through a narrow gaze.

An embarrassed chuckle seeped from the man. "Oh, sure... I'll just be over here..." he said, backing into a serving girl, causing her to drop a serving platter. Glass shattered. Laughter erupted.

Briar ignored it, but Exten hovered at his side. Posture stiff and attention, focused. Patting his knight on his shoulder, Briar urged him around. "Relax, will you? If I had every man arrested who spilled a drink on me at this bar, there would be no one left in Dregs. Nobody suspects a thing," he said, rolling his eyes back to the bar.

"Your disguise ain't fooling me," said Binx, slamming two ales on the counter. "I smelt your smug pride as soon as you walked through the door."

"Ah, Binx!" Briar grinned, nestling back into his spot while slipping his hand around the stein. "How are you this fine evening?"

"Worse, knowing you're here. And dressed like those Brimleyn folk no less." Her eyes flicked up and down with a snarl. "What's with the wig?"

He sipped his ale with a smile. "Would you prefer I come in with my suit and crown?"

Binx folded her arms. "I'd prefer you not come at all."

"Come now, you love me. Look at all the business I gave you."

"Don't you take credit for my hard work. You've just brought problems. Nothing but scoundrels here."

Briar took a look around the tavern. Unlike the other taverns he'd passed along the walk here, the Binx & Drinx was full of life. Nearly every table was full. There were corners where a few people played Noble's Dice and others where harlots sat in laps. Meals were being had, and drinks were being drunk. From Fredrik's protest Briar had heard how the Binx boomed with activity since his last public visitation, but to see it in person was impressive. "I don't see a problem here. Unless you think being the most popular tavern in Dregs isn't in your favor. You're welcome."

"It is a problem when half my staff quits or leaves to Brimley and I'm stuck hiring girls like that." She nodded over her shoulder.

Briar leaned to view the woman who the drunkard had clashed with. Sensual curves shifted as she bent over the scatter of broken dishes, using bits of broken plates to scoop piles of mashed food back onto the serving tray. Her dress rode up ever so. "What's the problem?"

"Damn nobles don't know the first thing about catering to anyone but themselves, and I'm left with messes like this all day long."

"Noble?" Briar watched the woman more closely. As she finished picking up the last scraps she stood with the tray. Red hair slipped from her cowl as green eyes widened locking on him. *Evelyn?*

Flushing, the baroness pivoted and hurried across the room toward the kitchen.

Briar stood from the bar, taking his mug with him. "Excuse me…"

As Evelyn set the tray in the pass-through window, Briar

sank his elbow into the wall and held his head. "What are *you* doing here?" He grinned.

Evelyn grabbed a fresh tray and set the ready plates on it. "I could ask you the same thing," she whispered.

Swirling his ale, Briar looked down to watch the amber liquid twist. "Having a drink." He raised it to his lips and drank.

"Well, you should go have it back at the castle." Evelyn ducked under his arm to skirt past. "That wig isn't fooling anyone."

Turning, Briar followed. "Of all the places you could work, why choose my tavern?"

"This isn't yours," Evelyn called back.

Briar shrugged. "Technically, everything built in Dregs is mine."

Groaning as she shook her head, Evelyn quickened her step to a table of two rough-looking women. She smiled at them, despite their scowls, and handed them their meals. A copper tip was offered in exchange. She bowed and turned back to glare at Briar. "Because this place has paying customers. Now, give me a coin for my time or stop bothering me."

Grumbling, Briar felt around at his belt for his coin purse. "Fine. But don't expect this to get you anything more than a conversation. We both know you aren't—" His purse was gone.

"What?"

"I must have forgotten my purse." He looked at her guiltily.

"I don't have time for this." She stepped around him.

Briar stepped to the left, blocking her. "Wait. I haven't yet said what I wanted to talk to you about."

Evelyn shifted her hips impatiently. "Then say it already instead of harassing me, I need to make rent..."

"Leave Kira alone," Briar said, stern and definitive.

Evelyn scoffed, maneuvering around him to an empty table.

"Oh, Briar. When will you see that woman is not who you think she is?"

Briar hovered behind her as she started clearing dirty dishes. "I know exactly who she is, Evelyn."

Shaking her head, Evelyn laughed. "I don't think you do."

"Oh? Try me." Briar took a seat and rested his elbows on the table. He made a fist to rest his chin on. "See if I don't know."

Evelyn's eyes narrowed. They shifted across the tavern, as if in search, then landed on Briar once more. She leaned in and whispered. "Kira is a Shadowen thief."

"Was." Briar nodded.

Evelyn's eyes widened. "She also wasn't a noble!" she hissed.

"True." Briar lifted the stein to his lips and sipped.

Evelyn set the tray on the table and scooted a chair close to Briar. Taking a seat she said, "She killed your uncle!"

Breaking his lips from the ale, Briar sucked in a breath. "Ah, see, that is where you're wrong, Ev."

"I heard from a group of women the truth about your uncle's death. One named Eryn said how he died is being covered up. That Kira killed him and she's using you to become queen!"

Briar rubbed his head, trying to soothe Evelyn's cawing. "Conspiracy like that can lead to treachery, Evelyn. Best let it go."

"It's not a conspiracy! The girls showed me their burnt crests!"

"Yeah. I had their nobility revoked for being traitors. Do you want one to match?"

"You?"

"Me. And I know all about what happened with Olivar and his harem and the artist who crested them. Kira saved Eryn and the others. She was the only one who *didn't* kill Olivar. She sought me out for help. She's remained innocent, which is why I let her keep her nobility."

Evelyn rolled her neck. "Can't you see you're being played? Even if what you think is true, her guard, Alden, is also a Shadowen, and she's working with him!"

Briar laughed. "You really don't know anything. Alden has been working for *me*."

"So you think. These Shadowens, they are devious. Trusting them will land you in a ditch. You're stepping on unstable ground, Briar."

Briar downed the last of his ale and rose from the table. "Sometimes trenches need to be dug before footings can be set."

"You're insufferable!"

"Yeah? Well, so are you." He poked at her shoulder. "I don't need to see your stripes to know you aren't on my side."

She pawed him off. "Whatever that means. But, you'll see how wrong you are. I've almost proved it."

"I have everything under control, so I don't need you to prove anything, Evelyn. It is obvious you are just jealous." Briar walked towards Exten.

"I'm not jealous!" She chased after. "I'm trying to protect you!"

Sir Exten stepped in, blocking her from reaching him.

Continuing towards the door, Briar called over his shoulder. "Leave Kira alone, Ev. This is your last warning."

"You'll regret this, Briar!" Evelyn shouted.

Ignoring her, Briar whistled, summoning Exten back to him.

As Briar reached the door, it opened for him. He nodded to the stranger who held it. "Thank you."

"It is my pleasure," the man said, touching a gloved hand to his shoulder. His short blond hair, neatly combed to the side, held in place as he bowed while a black scarf remained hugged tightly around his narrow face. A puff of air slipped from it as he said, "Your Majesty."

Pausing, Briar looked the man up and down, trying to place him. While his attire was fine enough for nobility, made with silver finishings, rich black suede, and polished boots, he wasn't sure they had met before. Beside him stood a shorter figure. In contrast, he wore long layers of knitted gray wool. Unique zig-zag weaves of red and black left patterns that looked similar to dunes. His face was wrapped tight in a tan scarf, threaded with beads and charms. A sliver of dark skin was left to reveal only his eyes.

Noticing the surreal silence, Briar looked back into the tavern. All eyes were now on him. No one moved. No one, except Binx, who tapped her fingers on her wide arms—her glare hardening. Finding Evelyn, the baroness's face turned red. She spun and rushed into the back room. *She outed me...*

Offering a sheepish grin to the rest of the tavern, Briar raised his wig, gave it a shake goodbye, and dipped out the door.

Alden sat, hands bound behind his back and hitched to a wooden wall in the cellar of the Binx & Drinx. His body ached. Bruised muscles throbbed, and his split lip stung. His nose— broken. The pain, however, was meaningless compared to his shattered heart. The Shadowen's punishment for his treason against the guild was only a small sample of what he hoped to endure. He wanted the pain. The hurt. He deserved it. *I only hope I can give Mayli the satisfaction of executing me herself.*

Oh May...

A creak whined at the door.

"As promised…" Ricky said.

Lifting his head, Alden watched as a short figure crept down a steep staircase with calculated movements. Standing at the base with a stiff posture, the shadow lifted his chin. Lamplight bounced off a tan, smooth-shaved head. Darkness accentuated white glimmers of eyes as they stared down at him. Layers of linen and silk wrapped around his body in misaligned fashion. A growl rumbled.

"See you both in a half turn. *Alive.*"

Alden rattled his chains. "Wait! Ricky, don't leave me alone with—"

The door clicked shut.

A thunder grew in Alden's chest—his heart suddenly racing, mocking him for his willingness to accept pain. So foolish to think the consequences of his actions could come so easy for his crimes. Alden tensed. "Trod…"

Trod's chest expanded and contracted heavily as if the act of standing was too much. His knuckles clenched, and veins in his neck bulged, ready to burst, but somehow he kept his restraint.

Alden released a tight breath, hopeful the nomad could be reasoned with. "Look, we should talk."

"The only discussion to be had"—a strange flicker of light sparkled in Trod's hand as he fingered an object—"is with her."

Her? Alden looked around, wondering if another Shadow had slipped into the cellar, unseen. There were crates and barrels filled with wine and ale, shelves stocked with canned food, a broken stool, and baskets of potatoes, gourds, and onions, but nowhere to hide. There wasn't even a window to crawl through. Finding his gaze back on Trod, Alden tensed once more, unable to make out the item he held. He swallowed deep, but his parched throat provided little relief to the fear which ignited.

Trod took a step forward. "You killed her…"

Oh. Alden reared, trying to stand, but there was little slack in his restraints. He pressed into the wall, wishing he could slip between the cracks. "Well, that—"

Trod threw a left hook.

Blood flew as a scab on his cheek reopened. A dancing dark light twinkled in his mind.

"My Paige!"

Another burst of pain bloomed across his head.

"A treasure of the sands—*stolen*..."

Although the accusations were false, Alden endured the next punch, assuming responsibility. *At least I can still protect May from this beating.* He smiled.

Trod grabbed Alden's hair, yanking him as high as he could. "And for that, I take yours."

Alden flailed his feet, trying to gain purchase. He shook his head, despite the violent tugs against his scalp. "Wait, stop! Ricky said to leave me alive!"

"It makes no difference to me what *he* wants!" Trod brought his blade up, and Alden's eyes nearly crossed. The unusual weapon's edge was chiseled crystal, and its grip was carved from an antler. Colorful threads laced with beads and bones, binding the pieces together. Some of Paige's red hair was woven in. He saw a tooth. Its crude beauty made Alden's heart wrench. Trod tightened his hold, pulling Alden's head back, further exposing his neck to the blade. "Only what *she* wants."

"Trod. Please. Cut me, beat me. *Whatever*. Just...you can't kill me." Alden whimpered.

"You have no right to beg for your life." The crystal pressed in.

Alden swallowed as he felt blood trickle. "You're right. I don't. And, in a way, I'm not. But, Trod, you—you were a nomad. Right?" He eyed the man.

"Yes." Trod removed his blade, and Alden took a breath of

relief. It was short-lived as Trod brought the rugged point to his temple and pressed in, lightly carving a design.

Alden winced, grinding his teeth and fisting his nail into his palm to endure the pain. "So, you should oblige your king," he hissed through his teeth.

Trod shook his head. "My only obligation is to her." The blade came up as Trod looked Alden over with glazed eyes, wild and unseeing.

"Paige, right?" Alden closed one eye as Trod came back in, drawing the tip from his temple to his ear. "And she fought as a reaver to defend Gezmek and Vatan...for *her* king?"

"Yes."

Alden took a deep breath. "Listen, my name is not Alden. I am not a thief. I am *not* a coward."

"That is no matter of mine."

"It is!" Alden said. "Because..."

The carving continued harder and deeper than before.

Blood flowing and pain igniting, Alden snapped. "Because I am the son of Liam, the late king of Brimley and heir to King Edune, ruler of Vatan! I...I am her king, Trod. So stop!" he yelled.

Trod lowered his ethereal blade.

A moment of peace stilled between them.

Alden huffed. Sweat mixed with blood as it dripped into his mouth. Relief hit Alden's lips, having finally said it. He looked up, hopeful for acceptance, awe, or allegiance, but Trod's face remained stoic. "You can check my crest if you don't believe me."

The nomad lifted the knife to Alden's shoulder, teasing the fabric. "Art marked on men gives no precedence over our ruling. I serve no one but her. And she no longer serves anyone."

Heat burst in Alden's arm as the crystal effortlessly ripped through his sleeve and flesh. Whipping his head, Alden stared in disbelief at a large gash opened in the center of his royal crest. The tree of Brimley severed from the seed of Gezmek. Blood gushed, coating the elegant design in a thick coat of red.

Alden screamed.

Another slash ripped along his face, silencing him. *This is it.* He winced as the cut and pain intensified. *A journey lost.* Helpless tears flowed down Alden's face as Trod ruthlessly swiped the blade across his chest. *I'll be mutilated to the point no one will know who I am.* Trod slashed. *She'll never know her mother's true killer.* Trod carved. *My promise—a lie.*

May...

"Mayli..."

Warm blood drizzled down his face along with his tears. A numbing throb waded through him. Life seeming to fade, his ears rang and vision faded to white. He was sure the beating was continuing, but he couldn't bring his awareness to the moment. *Perhaps I'm already dead.* Everything was beyond the point of pain, leading him to moments of peace. Flashes of faces came vividly. Kira's came first. Smart and snarky, her smile was skewed and her big eyes gleamed. Moments of them holding the other in comfort over the years came. *Oh, how I could use your support now*, Alden thought. The loud and charming laugh of Briar echoed in his memory, stealing her away. He'd always been one to challenge Alden to become something more. *Efforts lost.* And Squirrel, his cheerful innocence blurred with his brother Dominick. *I'm sorry.* Visions of Dean and Mary stuck out. Despite everything, they loved and supported him, even if his grandfather preferred not to show it. The soothing voice of his grandmother hummed, but Alden could barely hear it. Then he saw his parents. William's stern words and serious face softened even at the hardest of times. Lily's small hands holding large books as she read their family's history, learning with him. Alden held on to the fading memories, wishing to have one last moment with them. He smiled as meows from his cat, Rek, came. Neighs from Emory. He hoped they would be happy with their new keepers. Other casual faces like Thomas, Bosun Scraggs, Mr. Gray, and the old lady who once sold him art supplies twinkled before him. All were beautiful people whom he'd let down. But the most honored face he wanted to see, the sweetest voice he wanted to hear, and the love he wanted to feel, Alden was unable to recall. "Mayli," he whispered again, wishing she could hear his apology. He wished to see her smiling eyes or listen to her rolling laughter. He cried, knowing he didn't even deserve her in his final moments.

Alden sagged to the cold, piss-stained, dirty floor. It became a welcome luxury as he breathed in what he assumed would be his last.

Distant sounds radiated. *Yelling? Who else is haunting my mind?* A muffled conversation continued, pulling Alden from his wavering consciousness. He peered out from one eye, the other too swollen to open. Trod was gone. The small room was empty, but the door at the top of the stairs lay open, exposing the kitchen. Somewhere, someone grunted, and there was a rustle of fabric, then metal. Someone called a command. Labored footsteps preceded the sound of a body being dragged.

Silence followed.

Eased by the moment of calm, Alden's eyes drifted downward searching for peace and death to finally come.

A startling moment later he was yanked from the floor and held against the wall. Light tapping on his cheeks roused him. Alden blinked, trying to recover his focus. Blue eyes and blond hair met him. "Bri?"

Knees cracked as the man bent to his level. He placed his hand over his masked mouth and tugged the face-covering off. Nose pointed, lips firm, and eyes sharp as daggers, the leader of the Shadowen Thieves Guild, shook his head.

The need to faint subsided as adrenaline kept Alden alert. "Pierz..." he managed to say.

Pierz flicked his eyes to Alden's shoulder. Alden looked too, but all he saw was blood. Carefully, Pierz pressed his palm flat to the mutilated crest and wiped the gash. Brows rose in disbelief as the design revealed itself. He removed his hand and looked back. "King Colin."

Alden continued to stare at his damaged pride. So fallen, he didn't even flinch as Pierz's warm and wet blood-coated hand cradled his face. Assertively, he lifted Alden's chin, forcing his gaze. Pierz studied him curiously as he thumbed the cut on his cheek, brushing away lingering bits of scab. Still, Alden sat forlorn. Defeated. Dying.

When he thought Pierz might growl, caw, or mock him, a smile broke open tight lips. "I don't know if I want to slap or kiss you."

Alden blinked, unsure what shocked him most: the guild leader *smiling* or the man's dilemma. Hesitantly, Alden furrowed his brow. "Preferably neither...?"

Pierz smiled more, exposing teeth. "Careful, you might get both," he said, letting go.

Alden's head dropped. Confused and exhausted, he watched without protest as Pierz took hold of Alden's sliced shirt. Fabric tore as he twisted and pulled, splitting weakened seams from Trod's attack. He tossed scraps aside and ripped more free. He used a knife to tear through protective stitching, filleting open the last to uncover Alden's pale skin. Pierz watched Alden's nervous breathing—his own just as labored.

Cheeks burning with shame, Alden pressed his lips together. He lay exposed for the first time to anyone but his family. Deep cuts wept. Welts from the beating line were bruised. His identity and sense of self—beaten.

Absently, Pierz pinched a bit of cloth and tossed it aside. It hadn't been hiding any wounds. "They sure did a number on you," he said.

Alden sighed, his voice weak. "I deserved it."

"I suppose to them, you did." Pierz rested his forearms on his legs, letting his hands dangle between. He cocked his head. "What were you doing in my guild, Colin?"

Alden spat blood to the side, keeping his aim clear from the guild leader's clean boots. He sniffed. "It doesn't matter anymore."

"It does to me."

Alden jerked forward, meeting Pierz at his face, but the man didn't flinch. Evoking all his pent-up rage, Alden yelled. "No, because I thought I'd find who killed Queen Margaret! But it was me! I killed Mayli's mother!" He slammed his head back against the wall, rattling wine bottles in their racks. Alden pressed his eyes shut from the explosion of pain. He waited, expecting another cut to tear into him. For the end. He readied himself for a fist to meet his rowdy smile or a knee to the gut. His punishment. Anything to deliver more pain for the hurt he'd caused Mayli and the thousands of lives throughout Vatan.

However, no violence followed—not even threats.

Instead, an unfamiliar sound from Pierz bloomed, genuine laughter.

Slowly, Alden lowered his head to watch the hysteria. Pierz's face, normally stoic and firm, was balled in amusement. Open-mouthed, his teeth sparked brightly with each laugh. Pierz closed his eyes, quieting to a chuckle. He exhaled in a pleased sigh, head shaking with brows lifted high. "Colin, if I know anything about you from the couple of years in my guild, it's that you're no murderer."

Alden swallowed all the deaths in his life he was directly responsible for. Margaret for one. Then there were a handful of people from working in the guild that came with the territory.

The thieves he killed to protect Mayli. Indirectly, he was responsible for countless others. They settled in his stomach like the stones that had fallen from his tower, destroying a kingdom. Alden lulled his head. "Regardless of what you may think... Queen Margaret's death is on my hands."

Pierz frowned, all sense of humor gone. "We do what is necessary." He unlatched a leather bag belted to his side. From it, he retrieved a metal case, waterskin, and a rag. He clicked it open, revealing a set of sharp tools in an orderly line. Suspended in the case's lid by leather straps were rows of bottles. Pierz's finger turned several to better read their labels. He selected one with green liquid.

Alden's heart thundered as his wariness of bottles spiked. *Would it eat at my skin? Mar me as Reyn did to Ki? Is it some kind of intoxicating brew like I used on May?* He swallowed a mouthful of blood. "I don't mean to beg—I have no right to after what I've done—but may I make a request?"

After uncorking the bottle, Pierz looked up. He stared in his way to say *go on*.

"Don't kill me."

Pierz blinked.

"Turn me in and leave me to the Ammosian's fate."

Pierz tilted his head.

"It will be worse than anything you could administer," Alden said. "I promise you."

"Why would I do that?"

Alden sighed. "My reward is worth more alive than dead. You'll more than make up the ransom I deprived you of from Mayli's kidnapping."

"You beg for your life, to end your life, *to help me?*" Pierz tested his brow.

"Something like that." Alden looked away. "Look, my life is

owed to Princess Mayli after I took her mother. She deserves to be the one to take mine."

Pierz popped the cork and offered it. "This won't kill you."

Alden narrowed his eyes. The bottle was simply designed. By Reyn's standards, it would be a common aid. Still, Alden cowered from it. "How can I trust what this is?"

Pierz leaned in, looking at him so closely that the flecks of gold mixed with the blue of his irises revealed themselves. "Have I ever lied to you?"

Alden opened his mouth, sure to have a list of examples of when Pierz lied—he was a guild leader after all. However, none came to mind. Mostly, Pierz dodged questions and punished those who pried too far. He rarely spoke, and when he did it wasn't to explain the intentions behind the assignments given, just the orders that needed to be followed. And never did he laugh or joke. Everything Pierz said had been the truth, in one manner or another. Alden shook his head. "Perhaps no more than me..."

Pierz brought it to Alden's mouth. "Then drink."

Accepting fate and too curious about the man's intentions, Alden allowed Pierz to pour in the liquid. From the sharp vinegar-based bite, Alden expected a vile or putrid flavor to follow, but it softened like sweet tea. A soothing melody of chamomile and ginger flowed with a strong curry-like spice nipping at the end. He coughed, having finally quenched his thirst and replaced the iron tinge.

Corking the empty bottle, Pierz sat back on his heels and returned it exactly from where it came. He selected another. Smaller and filled with a clear liquid. The bottle glugged as Pierz wet his rag. He set the bottle back and raised the damp cloth to Alden's right arm.

Like a thousand stabs, his shoulder stung violently as Pierz pressed into the wound. Alden's fists formed rocks, shaking them as the burn intensified. "Sweet kings...!" he hissed, trying to pull free.

Pinning him to the wall, Pierz held firm. "Relax. Breathe," he demanded.

Alden's heart pounded, unsure of the mental game the guild leader may be playing, but he worked to suck in calming breaths.

Oddly, the pain began to subside, easing his tremors. In its stead, a soft numbing settled. After a moment, Pierz backed off. He took the rag away, revealing a foamy sizzle along his gash.

Setting the rag aside, Pierz took out a spool of thread with a curved needle laced through the bind. He unwound a long selection and wetted the tip between his lips. Going cross-eyed, Pierz pushed the thread through the needle's eye. Strung, he used his finger to pinch Alden's skin together at the shoulder to align the tattoo. Alden expected a sharp prick as the needle pierced, but he felt nothing.

Free from pain, Alden watched with great appreciation and awe as his enemy took precious time and care in mending the design until the tree's trunk and lines of the shield were stitched perfectly together. He tied a knot, leaving a long tail of thread. A fresh scent of mint and leather wafted as Pierz leaned in. His mouth pressed against Alden's skin, and with a small nip and brush of lips, the excess thread was severed.

Alden exhaled.

Pierz rose, thumbing across his stitch-work with an unnervingly gentle touch. "We are much alike."

"I don't think so..." Alden said. "You're not a royal in hiding..."

Pierz huffed as if it were a joke.

A drop of blood fell from Alden's nose.

"Is your nose broken?" Asked Pierz

Alden sniffed as a heavy drain of blood threatened to escape. "Yeah..."

"Hold still," Pierz said, placing his thumbs along the bridge. Then, without warning, thrust to reset it.

"Fuck!" Alden bent forward, letting the blood spill as his head spun in dizzying spells.

"Well, killing Paige wasn't smart." Pierz held a strip of fabric under Alden's nose to catch the flow.

"I know," he muffled.

"But you had to save the princess." Pierz eased Alden against the wall.

"Yeah..."

Pierz checked the red-soiled rag and tossed it aside. "I told you, we are much alike."

"Says the man who kidnapped her."

"Did you not do the same?"

"For different reasons."

"Hm." Pierz pulled at Alden's skin, testing the severity of the worst cut. "This wound is long but thankfully not deep."

Worthy of a scar if I'm alive long enough to see it form, Alden thought.

Pierz then dabbed a new rag with the numbing ointment he'd used on the shoulder. "This will sting again," he warned.

Alden closed his eyes as the bite came. Gentle strokes tended to him, as if Pierz was wiping away more than just blood and grime. Then a numb prick struck around his cut and the stitches began to pull him back together. Once again, the care was well-given and undeserved.

Alden let a tear fall.

As Pierz neared the end of the gash, Alden looked out. "I know you don't like questions, but...why are you healing me like this?"

Pierz tugged the needle through and let his arm hang in the

air. He looked at it as if he himself wasn't sure. His head tilted to the left. "Well, to be honest, I expected to watch you die tonight." They caught each other's gaze.

Alden managed a smirk. "I won't hold that against you."

Pierz didn't return the look. Instead, he focused on finishing his last hook and tied the knot. He wiped his knuckle across the cut—no pain, no blood—then placed his hand low on Alden's waist. That, Alden felt. He sucked in nervously as Pierz lowered his head to Alden's chest. Once more, lips met skin as Pierz bit the tail threads off. Goosebumps rose as he spoke. "I hope to never see that."

"See what?" Alden asked, his voice an unsteady breath.

Pierz lifted his head to be level with his. Honest eyes shone back. "Your death."

Alden furrowed his brow. "So, you're not killing me?"

"As you mentioned, you're much too valuable for that."

"Ammos then." Alden sighed, almost in relief.

"Not that either." Pierz leaned in. "I have use for you, Your Majesty."

"If you think you can exploit me, or use me as ransom to hurt Mayli, I'll sooner kill myse—"

Pierz slapped him.

Wincing, Alden peered out from one eye.

Pierz glared hard, pointing. "Stop with these foolish and suicidal thoughts. I'm not allowing you to die."

"Please!" Alden pleaded. "Just sell me to Ammos! Mayli has to—"

Pierz pinned him to the wall. "You're in no position to make demands."

"Then make yours!" he yelled, shaking in his chains.

Alden flinched as Pierz brought the same hand he slapped him with to wipe Alden's cut cheek, catching a fresh drizzle of blood. Gently. He looked at it, frowning. Locking eyes with

Alden, he said, "You don't want to die, Colin. You just want the suffering to end."

Alden stopped struggling then. The man's words so validating, so profound he couldn't help but succumb to his hold. He peered up. Soft, blue eyes looked over him with an understanding and acceptance that Alden craved. "How?" he begged.

"By trusting me," he said.

Before Alden could argue, lips grazed his as Pierz laid on a kiss. It was given like a promise—true and heartfelt. As Alden trembled, Pierz pulled away leaving Alden's mouth open.

"Understood?" asked the guild leader.

Alden stared in a daze, nodding.

"Good." Pierz then put a rag to Alden's nose. Unlike the other that soothed his wounds, this smelled of sulfur and drove Alden into a dizzying sleep.

Oh shit...

CHAPTER TWENTY-FOUR

THE PROPOSAL

"Briar! Your Majesty...!" The scuffle of feet dusted the stone floor as Fredrik chased. "*Sire!*"

"I heard you the first time, Fredrik," Briar said, continuing toward the grand staircase without looking back. "What is it?"

"You've missed several meetings! Where have you been?"

"Drinking." Briar pulled off his wig dusted with snow and let it drop from his fingers. Shaking out his real hair, Briar started his climb back to his quarters.

Fredrik paused to collect his discarded wig. "Dressed as you are, please don't tell me you were off galavanting at the Binx & Drinx again?"

Briar made it to the first landing and looked back to see the old man using the railing to help hoist him along. *Is he going to follow me all the way up four flights?* Briar put his hands on his hips and shook his head. "I wasn't galavanting."

A deep sigh of relief blew from Fredrik as he paused for breath. "Good... Good..." He then continued.

"I was drinking."

"Sire..." Fredrik dusted his suit off and looked firmly at Briar as he reached the top. "I don't mean to keep pestering you and questioning your ways, but I have been hired by the king to do a job, one which I am honored to perform. So, if you wish to be seen as one there are expectations to be held. Which includes staying here and attending to the people."

Briar turned his back and walked alongside the inner balcony leading to the second staircase. "I've been tending to them all week. I'm entitled to a moment's peace, aren't I?" He lifted his hand and dropped it in irritation to catch the railing leading up.

Fredrik gestured below. "That is why we have the castle pub."

Briar snarled. "And be served whatever is trending? No thanks. Last time my drink came with a flower and a crab leg. I wanted ale."

"Then I shall have arrangements made for your favorite ale to be served here as well. No need to expose yourself to the commoners and ignore the nobles who have waited days to see you."

Stopping halfway up, Briar rubbed the bridge of his nose. "What did I miss?"

"Ah." Fredric rose on his toes and drew out a notebook, glee sparkling in his eyes at the task. He traced his boney finger down his notes. "The Hiorean trade ship arrived, ready to supply us with goods from Ammos. And building is on track in Brimley with renovations underway. Sir Stridan even came by to report he has dealt with a ruffian causing much of the problems. Being that Ideal Avenue hasn't reported any more disturbances, I'd say everything seems in order."

"Good. So, does anything need my attention?"

The old man's lip drooped as he searched the papers. "No, it does not appear so." He smiled and tucked the notebook away.

"Then I had no reason to waste my time in those meetings. Your write-up was enough. Good night." Briar removed his woolen coat and tossed it to Fredrik. He turned and continued up the stairs.

After two more flights, Briar reached the small flight to his chambers. He checked over his shoulder, just to make sure the old man didn't have the nerve to keep on following him. Hall empty, Briar ascended the stairs. Two guards clicked their heels to attention upon him reaching the top. Briar dipped his chin in respect, and one opened the door.

Once inside, a flash of movement darted towards him. He pivoted, catching Kira around the waist before she could tackle him.

"Got ya!" she said triumphantly, touching her sheathed knife to his side.

He laughed with her. "I knew it was you."

"One of these days it's not gonna be, and you'll end up tangled with an assassin."

"I seem to remember that's how we met." He pressed his lips to hers and held her more intimately.

Kira drove her fingers into his side, giving him a tickling squeeze. He giggled, freeing her from his mouth. She pushed on his chest, trying to escape. "You smell of horse and piss," she whined.

Briar let her go and began unbuttoning his tunic. "Yeah, I had Sir Exten escort me to the Binx for some drinks."

"Sounds nice," Kira said, dragging her feet as she sat at their desk. She put her fists to the surface and bent over, looking at scrolls and journals. "I've been here going through my paperwork."

Unfastening the last button, Briar let his shirt flow loose and met Kira at her side, hand on her shoulder. "So, you're finally looking into your new life."

"I have to make sure I'm not caught unawares by anything." She lifted a stack and scattered some in search. "I can't find that stamped and signed document registering me as noble."

"That is locked up in the archives," said Briar, scratching his neck. "Why do you need it?"

"Because I can't shake the feeling Evelyn knows I'm a fraud..."

"Ah. Yes." Briar scratched his chin. "I just saw her at the Binx."

Kira cocked her head, throwing Briar a perplexed look. "What is she doing there? Isn't a mangy tavern a bit beneath her?"

Briar laughed. "Working, apparently."

Kira frowned. "She did say her mother gambled away her dowry."

"Yeah." His chuckling continued.

"It's not exactly funny, Briar. She lost her family too."

Sobering his amusement, Briar frowned. "That is true. It is why she's so desperate to pull at rumors."

"What rumors?"

Briar offered a sheepish grin. "Well, She knows you were a Shadowen."

Kira pushed off the desk, her hair flying. "She *what?*"

"And she knows you weren't originally a noble." He clenched his teeth while scrunching his brow.

Her breath came away. "Briar..."

Briar shook his head in dismissal. "Relax. Everyone in court knows that Evelyn is jealous and will do anything to catch some attention. Her babblings are worthless. She made some declaration that you are only with me to become queen."

Kira scoffed.

Briar waved his hand. "She was only projecting her own game. It is fine."

"This doesn't sound fine! How did she find out I was a Shadowen?"

"She talked with Eryn. Turns out she and the other captured women are upset they didn't get to keep their nobility and promised dues after killing a king. They don't like that you, on the other hand, are with me, crest intact and riches saved."

Kira touched her arm. "Will they cause a problem for you?"

Briar sputtered his lips. "Psh, nah. I'll have them rounded up for breaking their oaths and starting a conspiracy. No one will hear of it."

"You can't lock them up again..."

"What would you have me do then? Have them executed?"

"No!" Kira sorted through the papers. Finding one, she handed it to Briar. "Give them this. It's more than enough for all of them."

Reading it, Briar arched his brow. "Your estate? Kira, do you have any idea how much value this property has?" He set it aside.

"It doesn't matter." Kira waved her hand at the paper. "I don't need it, and the house was never mine to begin with. If they are upset this should settle some discontent and hopefully put an end to their spreading of rumors and hate towards us. Besides, the women should have *something* for their mishandling."

Tapping his fingers together, Briar shrugged and spread them apart. "I thought keeping their lives was fair."

"You didn't even like your uncle, Briar!"

"It is the principle of the matter. One cannot live a life of freedom for such a deed. Why do you think Alden is how he is?"

"Only *he* didn't kill anyone!"

Briar closed his eyes and rubbed his face. Dropping his hands, he nodded. "Fine. But those women can't have your estate, Kira; they aren't noble anymore. It isn't allowed. But you can allow them residency with you as lady of the estate in exchange for their service."

"Can I give it to Evelyn to share with them then? She's noble."

For a moment, Briar looked over Kira. Her eyes were focused, brow narrowed with determination. A sprawl of papers and notes surrounded her. For all the darkness she endured in the guild, a pure heart still glowed brightly. He smiled. "You are so giving."

She shrugged. "When all you've known is a life where people take, the only thing you want to do is ensure no one is without."

"And even Evelyn? After everything she's done?"

"I've only heard what you and Alden have told me about her. And while I trust you both, I can't help but sympathize."

"Your willingness to forgive those who have caused strife is a power I do not possess. Once someone disrespects me, I no longer have the patience to humor them..."

"I, too, have my limit. But Evelyn, Eryn, and the other women...they are hurting. And if you won't help them, I will." Kira grabbed the deed to her estate.

"Kira." Briar grabbed her arm before she could leave.

"I'm going to help them," she repeated, her tone definite as her eyes challenged him.

"I know." Briar smiled. Gently, he pulled her into a hug. "I just wanted to say, you will make a wonderful queen. Even if that was your plan all along."

Kira relaxed in his arms. "Yep, ya got me all figured out."

"Let me guess. Brimleyn tea. Cream and sugar. Very hot?"

Hardly a step inside the tavern, Binx blocked Kira's entry holding a tray of emptied steins. A body-length apron splattered with grease and spots of ale hugged tight around her waist, looking small. Kira smiled at the barkeep. "Thank you for remembering, Binx. Tea would be lovely now that you have it."

"I make it a mission to remember what all my clients prefer. It's how I've stayed in business despite certain folk coming by and causing a scene."

"You mean Briar..."

Binx waggled a finger. "I warn you, that man is a menace, you'd do smart to steer clear if you don't want a broken heart or your life made into a mockery. My offer still stands if you wish to work for me instead."

"I'm not a working girl for Briar." Kira played with the pendant he'd gifted her. "It is as he said, I'm with him on my own accord."

Binx shrugged. "You've got strange and bold taste, honey. But so be it. Just know that being friends with royalty doesn't dismiss you from paying. Two copper." She held her wide palm out expectantly.

Kira put her hand in her pocket, searching.

"That will be on me," said a soft voice that made Kira cringe.

Seated at the bar, hood draped across his shoulders, face mask hung around his neck, was Pierz. *Oh no.* He rested his wineglass on the circle on the counter that Briar had worn. He sat exactly as Briar had, foot up and posture lax. *He must know that's Briar's favorite spot...*

Whipping her eyes from side to side, Kira took in the company within the Binx & Drinx. One by one, she picked out familiar faces, blending in by laughing and enjoying their time just as they had in the Cantwell Inn back in Colville. The ones she didn't know either scowled as recruits or were legitimate patrons who carried on without a care. Some Shadows had already secured positions within the tavern as servants and even the cook. *Would Binx be next? Or is she in on it?*

Feminine gossip arose near the stairs. While a few were the same whores who had waved at Briar before, deceptive thieves now mingled with the flock. Evelyn was among them. They made eye contact, both offering a glare as Kira's heart beat fast. *I was a fool to think she could be so innocent...* Kira put her hand to a slip in her dress, touching her hidden blade.

Binx huffed. "I don't care who is paying, as long as it is spent." Binx walked behind the bar and said something under her breath to Pierz. Giving her the coin, he mouthed something back with a charming smile as if he wasn't the most dangerous man to ever step foot inside her walls. Binx laughed and put a kettle on.

Kira swallowed as Pierz looked at the seat beside him. A silent command.

She worked to stay calm and collected—the actress she was trained to be—and slipped into the stool, not unaware of the privilege that it was. "Thank you."

"The pleasure is mine." He slowly lifted his gaze to her, looking her up and down as if seeing her for the first time. "You look truly regal."

"Gotta say," said Binx, eyeing them as she fetched a mug from the cabinet. "You sure you don't want the job? This one hasn't had an interest in any of my ladies, but you walk in and he lights up."

Pretending to blush, Kira played with her braid. "That so?"

Pierz lifted his glass. "They were not true ladies. Although, perhaps neither is this one?" A dimple formed while he sipped his wine.

Kira resisted touching her shoulder. *A threat? Does he know?* Kira looked back where Evelyn was, but the baroness was gone. *That rat.*

Binx hissed a laugh. "Perhaps you are the devious type after all."

Kira forced a smile. "I'm sure he is."

Pierz fondled his wine glass. "Shall we go to my room and find out? I promise I won't bite," Pierz's smooth voice said.

Heat sprawled up Kira's neck. Even knowing his seduction was an act, the danger was still real. Kira lifted from the seat and smiled at Binx. "I will be right back."

Pierz left his glass on Briar's marker and stood with her, offering his arm like a perfect escort, his dark suit and slick leathers aiding the look. His stern eyes and stiff demeanor told differently. With no choice but to follow through, Kira took his arm and allowed the Shadowen Guild Leader to usher her through the den of thieves.

At the end of a narrow hallway, two Elite Shadows guarded a door, Micah and Glendel. Their hollow gazes deterred Kira from trying anything. *I'll be okay,* Kira thought as he led her to them. *Briar knows I'm here.* A guard opened the door. *I can escape this...* Pierz shoved her inside. Kira quickly scanned the room, searching for escape and potential weapons. Windows were boarded. Furniture was heavy and boxy. A small table sat in the corner. Accessories were sparse. And a large bed sat unmade, sending chills down her spine. She was trapped.

"Kira." Pierz shut the door. "Why has it taken so long for you to report in?"

Kira blinked. Her mouth gaped. Realizing she was visibly caught off guard, she shook her head. "Has it?" she asked, accepting the role.

"It's been almost two months. You were expected a fortnight after the ambush in the Cads. I heard you got caught, but then Ricky said he saw you out on your own."

"Ya know, life has gotten a bit busy." Kira started touring the room. Tapping at her sides, she was gutted to find her blade missing. *Of course, he would lift it,* she thought, seeing Pierz twirl her missing dagger in his fingers.

"Really?" He followed slowly, keeping his distance as he watched her like a hawk. Calm. Ready. Observing every tell. "It wouldn't happen to be that you've been working for Briar all this time?"

"That's absurd." Kira sat in a chair, recalling when she'd battled for her freedom from King Olivar using the leg from one. "I'm spying on him—doing my job. Ya know, seeking shadows."

A cruel grin fell over her. "Are you? Because being crested is not something that is just done or so easily faked. Perhaps your nobility was a reward of service?" Pierz pointed to her shoulder with her blade.

"My nobility was earned, yes. By great acts in bed." Kira cozied into her seat, resuming the ease she had kept in the guild. She waved out a wrinkle covering her crest. "A bat of my eyes and he swallowed me whole. I'm sure the ladies who tend this tavern can attest to his...*willingness* to pay for lustful desires. Why wouldn't he accept an easy lay?"

Pierz pounded his fist on the table, jolting Kira's bones. "Cut the act."

"No, I—"

Pierz tapped his knuckle on the table with each step he took closer to her. "Why is it, Kira, that Reyn was so captivated by you?" He stopped right beside her and leaned against the table, crossing his ankles and folding his arms.

Kira hugged herself for a moment then let her arms hang. "He liked using my body," she admitted.

"Perhaps. But I don't think that was special to him."

Kira glared upward. "What would you know of attractive women?"

Pierz tsked. "Reyn liked you because he knew when you

were acting. He knew when you were being untrustworthy and how to control your act to get what he wanted."

Shame turned Kira's face away.

"Do you know why I like your performances, Lady Kira?"

She shifted her eyes to meet his through a window of hair.

Pierz pushed off the table and looked down at her. "Because they are so convincing."

"What do you want, Pierz?" Kira snapped.

"What do *you* want, Kira, you're the one who walked straight into a thieves den."

Questions swelled in her mind. *Who hired the guild to kidnap Mayli? What are you doing in Dregs? Is Evelyn part of the guild? Why am I not dead yet?* But instead, Kira raised her chin and asked, "Why did you never stop Reyn from assaulting me?"

"As I said, you were convincing. I didn't know how severe his abuse was until our mission in the Cads. You both hid it so well."

"Are you saying you would have stopped him sooner?"

"You really think I'm that cruel?"

"Yes."

As they stared each other down, the hiss of her teapot sang from the other room. Once it was silenced, Pierz turned his back on her and walked to the door. "Stay put while I fetch your tea like a good host."

Something nudged Alden's foot. His sides, face, nose, arms, and shoulder all came to life, reminding him of the beatings. A faint numb lingered like death, masking some of the pain. Too exhausted to face another assault, Alden let his mind slip back to his dreams, despite the terrors they held.

"Wake up."

Alden inhaled deeply as his body was dragged along the wall, manacles clanking. He blinked in confusion as a blanket fell from his shoulders to his lap, exposing his bare chest. Instinctively, his eyes flicked to his shoulder. They widened seeing his noble crest covered with a clean bandage. Another was wrapped around his chest.

"I have a proposal." Pierz loomed over him, dressed in his tight black leathers. He held a glass of dark red wine in each hand.

Foggy memories of Pierz tending to him sprouted. He'd been slapped. Alden blushed. And kissed.

"For a favor," Pierz continued. "I will make it so Mayli will no longer see you as an enemy. A drunken fool, maybe. But not an enemy. And maybe, in time, the princess and you could even be together as you've wanted."

"I can't do that knowing what I've done..." His stomach irked just thinking about even touching Mayli for his crime.

"Regardless, I will reveal who is responsible for the kidnapping and who still threatens her life."

"Aren't *you* that person?"

Pierz crouched, meeting Alden at eye level. Ignoring Alden's query, he continued, "Agree to my offer, and no one will hurt you or Mayli as long as we are allies."

Alden dipped his chin. "Allies?" he said as if he'd misheard.

"Yes. And I meant what was said this morning. I have no intention of seeing your death."

Alden studied Pierz's face, searching for tells, but per usual, he only offered a blank stare. Folding his legs, Alden worked to sit more upright and attentive. "And in return?"

"You give me a place in court."

Alden gawked. "You ask for nobility!"

"Is it not noble to save your king's life, his land, his people, lover, and his *honor?*"

"It's not that simple. Briar stripped everything from me. I —" He paused. Blinked. Cocked his head. "Did you just imply I am your *king?*"

"I did, Your Majesty." Pierz dipped his head and touched his shoulder in a formal greeting while not spilling either wine glass.

"Wait. You can't be serious."

Pierz stood straight. "Why not?" He nearly sounded offended.

"I dunno, you're..." Alden looked him up and down. "*You.* A guild leader. A rogue. A—"

"A loyal subject," Pierz supplied.

Alden pursed his lips. "Sure. Even so, I can't just give ya nobility, Pierz. Ya need, documents, land, coin, a qualified tattoo artist..."

"That didn't seem to be an issue for Kira *Harlow.*"

Alden's throat clenched.

"Tell me." Pierz swirled the wine, watching the vortex. "What would happen if the courts learned she, or you, were Shadowens?"

"Don't." Alden pulled at his shackles, struggling to break free. "Leave Ki outta this. Do ya hear me?"

"Such fierceness for someone in your predicament." Pierz smirked. "I've always liked that about you. Always willing to fight against the odds."

Alden glared. "What do you want?"

"I told you. A place in your court."

"I don't have a court!"

"Not yet." Pierz offered the glass of wine. "Now, do you accept my offer?"

"This is blackmail," Alden said through grinding teeth. "I told you I'd rather die."

"No, my king, not blackmail. That would mean an ultimatum."

Rattling his restraints, Alden growled. "Then what is this?"

With a deep sigh, Pierz set the drinks on a barrel. He reached forward. Alden jerked in anticipation for pain, but Pierz delivered none. Instead, a gentle hand grabbed him. His clean, crisp, minty scent filled the air as he pulled in for an embrace. Alden tensed at their awkward closeness, but after a tug and a click, his wrists felt light. *Freed?* Still, Pierz lingered, and Alden dared not move.

"You may leave, uncontested," Pierz whispered into his ear. "And continue on your death march to Ammos. Mayli will watch you die a coward. My guild will not go after you, nor will they bother Kira and Squirrel, seeing as they are loyal to you. As with King Briar."

Alden looked at the cellar door.

"Or..." Pierz stood, grabbing the wine glasses, and offered his proposal once more. "...we can be friends, and establish your rightful place on the throne, save your princess, and establish peace and unity once more across Vatan."

Alden stared at the tempting red liquid. Last he'd drank, he'd woken up a convicted man. Alcohol had sent him into a life of shadows, fear, and unbearable burdens. He'd made many mistakes along the way. Earned valuable lessons as well as friends—though he'd lost more. He had killed. Killed to defend himself, to survive, and to save those he cared for. Still, Alden now saw himself no better than what the world saw in him: a murderer. But today, Pierz of the Shadowen Thieves Guild, held vital information that would threaten Mayli even if he sacrificed himself.

Mustering the strength, Alden weakly stood. The fatigue

hung on him, and he swayed. Pierz moved to brace him, his support firm and strong. When Alden found balance, Pierz respectfully stepped back, leaving the glass outstretched. Accepting the proposal, Alden grumbled. "To friends..."

"To friends," Pierz agreed with an honest tone.

They both sipped.

Alden expected the dry scrape of wine to hit the roof of his mouth. For his nose to itch and the bitterness to assault his tongue. He waited for the stale taste of rot to linger on his breath. However, it never came. The drink was tart. Sweet. Alden pulled it back. "Cranberry juice?"

Pierz concluded his own intake. "You don't drink."

A long smile pulled at Alden's lips at Pierz's consideration. "I expected wine..."

"Yet you accepted anyway." Pierz toasted, a daring look residing on his face. "So now I know, King Colin, that you'll keep your promise."

He swallowed, unsure if this was one he could keep. His promise to Mayli still came first, and he understood the Ammosians more than Pierz. Death would come, but it would have to wait until after he hunted down who threatened her. *Can't fail a promise if I won't be around to fulfill it.* Alden met the toast again and finished the juice.

Pierz took Alden's empty glass and set it on the barrel beside his own. He grabbed a fold of clothes and tapped them to Alden's bare skin. "Put these on."

Accepting, Alden moved to the corner and shrugged the fresh cotton shirt on, wincing as the long sleeves brushed over his cuts. Sturdy trousers were next. Alden refrained from looking at Pierz as he stripped from his soiled wares and stepped into the fresh pair. Wool socks and his old boots remained.

"And this." Pierz held out his arm.

Alden took the heavy hooded leather jerkin and shrugged it on. To his pleasant surprise, Ammosian Silk graced his fingers as he threaded his arms through the sleeves. Lifting the forepart, Alden examined the luxurious lining. "Nice piece."

Pierz stepped in to help secure a buckle. "You look good."

"I look like you."

A boyish grin spread on Pierz's lips as he continued to assist. "Is that a compliment to yourself or to me?"

"Perhaps both."

"I told you we were much alike."

Alden looked to the side, shamed by the affinity.

Pierz reached for something in a pouch. "Before I forget, there's one more thing missing from your attire." Pierz stepped in and wrapped a scarf around Alden's neck.

Like a rising sun, orange silk glimmered in the dim light. Drawn to the glow, Alden lifted the fabric—hand shaking until it caressed its smooth surface. He let his fingers roll over folds, making the edges pop with an even brighter sheen. A faint flowery spice still lingered. *May.* Alden took the scarf in his hands as if it were the princess herself, hugging it to his face. "Where did you get this..." he asked with a shaky voice.

"Saw it caught in a tree just outside Theilen's Lodge. I knew immediately it was hers and that you two were near. Unfortunately, we were too late in finding you. Had we, we might have avoided this whole mess."

"What do you mean?"

Pierz clapped Alden on the back. "Come. There's someone eager to see you." Pierz stepped aside, letting Alden go first up the stone-carved stairs. The smell of the dank cellar shifted to a slightly burnt roast as he entered the kitchen. Through a window, Alden could see the main room of the tavern where guild members hung in every corner, casting him looks. A slam rattled Alden's bones. He turned, watching a chef with thick arms cut a leg of lamb with a butcher's knife. His eyes held Alden's in warning.

Pierz took his arm, pulling him from view. He steered him into the hallway toward a door guarded by two Elite Shadows —some of Pierz's most trusted men. He realized he wore the same jacket. They stepped aside allowing Pierz to open the door and invite Alden in.

One step forward and something sharp met Alden's throat. Before it could slice, training with Kira kicked in, and Alden drew his hand up, batting the attacker's arm away and twisted. Stepping to the side, he raised his fist, aiming to strike their shoulder. Better prepared, they grabbed on and pinned him to the wall, reminding his body of all the pain from earlier. "Pierz!" Alden cried, losing strength.

"Alden!?" gasped a known voice.

"Ki?" Alden opened his eyes.

Kira had a splintered chair leg at his neck. Breathless, she wrapped her arms around him and hugged. He hissed as his bruises tenderized. Kira pulled back, eyes wild, looking him all over. They paused on each scratch, welt, and bruise. Tears formed in her eyes, but they vaporized as she threw a glare at Pierz. "What did you do to him?" she yelled.

Pierz put his hands behind his back and stood tall. "Gave him what he deserved."

"Why you—" Kira moved to attack, chair leg raised once more.

Before she could, Alden stepped in front of her, blocking her catlike claws and weapon from attempting to tear through Pierz. "Kira. He didn't hurt me. *Kira!*" She kept advancing, but Alden lunged, hooking her in his embrace and enduring the pain.

Kira screamed. "Let me go! I'ma kill 'em!"

Alden held her. "Kira, stop it. He saved me from Trod and patched me up."

"Yes, careful you don't break open your stitches, Colin," Pierz said, walking into the room. "I apologize, Lady Kira, I forgot your tea. Hope this tall glass of a king will do."

Kira threw Alden a look. Her eyes bore into him, untrusting and hurt. "Alden! What the fuck, he knows who you are?"

He rubbed his face, avoiding the welts. "Yes, and he's offering to expose who hired him to kidnap May."

Kira shifted her weight, swaying her hip as her demeanor frayed. She eyed Pierz who sat patiently, fingers woven and resting on the table. "And you're *trusting* him?"

"I understand why you would be hesitant to trust me after our misunderstanding with Reyn." Pierz rolled his shoulders back. "But you have no other choice now, seeing as I'm the only one with the information on who kidnapped the Ammosian princess."

"And I suppose you want something for it," Kira accused through clenched teeth.

"That's already been negotiated."

Kira threw Alden a look. "What did you promise him?"

Alden ignored her, keeping his focus on Pierz. "Tell me who hired you."

Pierz smiled. "No one."

Kira exchanged a nervous glance with Alden.

"The choice was my own," Pierz added, casually leaning against the table.

"Why?" Alden asked hesitantly.

"Same reason you did."

"I rescued her... You—"

"Saved her from a fate you would honor me for preventing," Pierz concluded.

Kira scoffed. "You've gotta be kidding me. I know you're not some kind of hero, Pierz." She gestured at him.

Pierz looked at Kira. "Have you forgotten that I stepped in when you and Reyn were last intertwined but *you* were the one to assure me it was consensual? I do not threaten to wet my blades for the fun of it."

Kira felt her face burst with shame. "I needed him alive so Alden could be on the mission to help Mayli..."

"Then you should have let me spill his blood. You and Alden were already assigned on the mission. He fooled you. Next time, trust me."

Kira shied her face from both Alden and Pierz, hugging herself in.

Alden cleared his throat. "Pierz, what did you want with Mayli? What fate were you saving her from?"

"A forced marriage she knew nothing about."

"Shit..." Alden breathed, brushing a hand through his hair. "To Gavin?"

Pierz nodded.

Kira slid her hands to her hips. "While I agree, Mayli and Alden are a better suit than she and that ancient crown, why do you care about the affairs of royals matchmaking?"

Pierz folded his hands. "Because of the power each union holds. And Hiore is already tyrannical. They invaded Basevein and then Colville. They then offered to help destroy Brimley, forcing Ammos into so much debt they are now only left with Princess Mayli to offer. I can only guess Dregs will be next in their conquest. Which is why I am here to prohibit that and help you and your cousin fight back so the true heirs of Vatan can reclaim power. And in order to do that, I had to take possession of their most precious treasure."

"Mayli?"

Pierz gave a slow nod. "Alive of course, as I was hoping to

expose the horrors each kingdom has, start a rebellion, and overthrow the world order back to what it once was. Where there was freedom and an economy that works with its neighbors, not against."

"Like what we did in the Cads last year..." Alden said.

Kira shivered as if reliving the memory.

"Precisely, but on a bigger scale."

"And..." Alden began. "Where do Mayli and I fall into this?"

"Well, you would step up as the King of Vatan, of course. Unless you'd rather it be one of your cousins? I have yet to meet Arkello, but have admired Briar. And Mayli would live under your protection. She might still hate you, but she'd be free. So, you either help with my rebellion and restore Vatan, or allow Hiore to take what's rightfully yours."

"All at the price that you have a place in my court," Alden affirmed.

"Think of it as a perk."

"Don't trust him, Alden," Kira said, shaking her head. "Remember who we are talking with. Pierz, leader of the largest thieves guild in Vatan. We can do what he's saying without his help."

"Can you?" Pierz asked.

Alden closed his eyes. His head dipped slightly as if the swelling on his cheek weighed him down. He sighed. "Can I have a day to think on it?"

"Sure." Pierz stood and walked toward the door. "As I've told you, Colin, you're free to go."

"Just like that?" asked Kira

Pierz opened the door. "Just like that."

CHAPTER TWENTY-FIVE
ROGUE GUILD

Kira followed closely behind Alden, seething as Micah, one of Pierz's Elite Shadows, escorted them while the other, Glendel, stayed behind guarding his door. Alden wore one of their same coats—perfectly flexible leather that accented his muscled form yet had many pockets to slip stolen goods into and secret folds to conceal hidden daggers. He had given in to Pierz. Defended him. They acted like partners. She couldn't help but glare. "I thought you went to Brimley," she growled under her breath.

Alden turned his shoulder, exposing his face from his hood. A gash cratered a dark swell below his eye. Strange red cuts marked from his temple to his ear like a map. His lashes stayed lowered. "I did."

"Then why are you wrapped up with Pierz?"

"Why are you?"

"I didn't mean to." Kira leaned in. "I was looking for Evelyn."

"Evelyn?" Alden asked. "Why?"

"To give her the deed to my estate so she and the women Olivar kept could have a place to live."

Alden shook his head. "Trusting anything to Evelyn is fool-ish, Kira."

Kira picked up the pace to stay within whispering distance. "You're some kind of fool to trust anything Pierz can offer. And for what? Him to have access to your matters, *Colin?*" She whacked his arm.

Alden flinched as if she'd actually done damage. He took a deep breath and looked at the ceiling before coming to a stop at the end of the hall. "I'm doing this for Mayli."

Micah looked between them as if having heard everything. "Pierz is a man of his word. You're free to go." He offered the room.

"You sure about that?" Kira pressed.

His arm remained outstretched.

Alden took Kira's hand. "Let's go home, Ki." He dipped his head and strode into the tavern.

No more than a few feet in, someone began clapping, slow and methodical.

"Ah, hah! Here he is to grace us!" sang Ricky's voice as he walked to the center of the room. Goons followed in his wake around bar tables.

"Yeah, *see,*" mocked Kira in a low voice.

Alden cursed under his breath.

Micah calmly walked to greet Ricky. His bold presence cast the other guild members back, securing a safe boundary around Kira and Alden. When he met with Ricky, his eyes narrowed. "Move aside, Pierz's orders."

"Pierz's?" Ricky looked over Micah's shoulder. "And why is our good old guild leader not here to give that order himself? How do we know you're not trying to take this shiny pot of gold for yourself, Micah? Did your buddy spill the tag on his head?"

Micah poked a finger into Ricky's shoulder. "Your payout will be granted for finding him, but Alden and Kira are no

358

longer wanted by Pierz. They are both clear to go." He shoved Ricky aside.

Ricky laughed, sliding back into the crowd. "Ah. My bad to think your dog-like loyalty could be bought like Glendel's could. Please, allow them by...*Trod.*"

A rainbow of prisms glimmered across the room. Fragments of light emerged from the shadows with the nomad, a strange crystal blade in his hand. With it aimed at Alden, Trod charged.

Kira grabbed at Alden's coat, pulling him back before the deadly thing could swipe. However, the effort was unnecessary as Micah caught Trod's wrist.

With a fierce rage, Trod jerked. As the hold broke, Micah shoved the small man back. He crashed into a tall table sending salad flying from a wooden plate. Green leaves scattered around him. Vinaigrette dripped.

Trod vigorously scurried to his feet. He pointed his strange weapon to them, his anger rising and face reddening and yelled. "You deprive us of justice!"

"Justice? Pierz has promised you all will be paid," said Micah. "You all must just be patient."

Trod flung spinach leaves from his shaved head. "He killed Paige! Payment will be his life!" Yellow, plaque-ridden teeth crunched as Trod heaved.

Micah crossed his arms behind his back and lifted his chin. "And going against Pierz's orders will cost you yours." Kira watched him withdraw hidden blades.

"My war is not with you." Trod stepped back but raised his knife forward as if commanding an army. "It is with him. He is not only responsible for Paige's death, or our missed gold but many lives including the Ammosian queen's. He is not *Alden of Brimley...* He is *Prince Colin Densen of Brimley!*"

Micah turned, slow and calculated, his eyes narrowed on Alden's. "Colin?" he said with disbelief.

Ricky mocked a bow as he clicked his ax free. "Yes, quite a surprise! Had I known I was escorting royalty, I would have handled you with more elegance, Your Highness. *Apologies...*" Ricky's tongue hissed lies.

More Shadows freed their weapons, snarling like a pack of starved wolves. A few, Kira noticed, kept quiet, watching nervously between Alden and the Elite Shadow. One winked to them in reassurance then turned to ready an attack on one of the aggressors. *Some allies. Better than none. Where is Pierz?* Kira thought.

A floorboard creaked behind them, and Kira looked to see if it was him. Unfortunately, it was a few whispering guildsmen drawing weapons. "They are flanking..." she warned.

On cue, a man pounced. To Kira's relief, Micah spun and stepped in to defend. Blood spilled on the floor. He reached to take a hammer from the attacker's weakening hand. With it, he calmly stepped back, weapons now in both hands—one a bloodied dagger. A throwing knife was missing.

The man who had held the hammer coughed, and red flowed from his mouth. He skirted back, dragging heavy feet back until he tripped over the gargling man where Micah's thrown knife had found its mark.

Micah pointed the hammer at Trod. He looked at Ricky and the others. "Is this who you choose to lead you to your death? You think a nomad with such vengeful blind rage will carry this guild? Do you not have faith in our leader's reasoning to let King Colin go?"

"I seek not power," yelled Trod, raising his fist. "Only vengeance!"

The room erupted in agreement.

"Well, I will take the lead then, because Pierz is a fool," declared Ricky. "Fight and claim your reward, Shadows! Fifty-thousand gold is here for the taking!"

A storm of blades and leather formed before Kira's eyes. Trod rushed Alden, yelling to ensure his presence was known. Called to action, Micah jumped in, bringing down the hammer. The bludgeoning weapon struck Trod's muscled neck, throwing him to the floor. The man cried out, holding his shoulder.

Another charged with a sword out. It reached Alden, scraping along his side. Kira held her breath but saw a shimmer of silk as the leather split. Uninjured, Alden stepped back, his eyes wide in fear.

"Your Highness," called Micah, tossing the hammer to him. "Behind you."

Alden caught it and used the momentum to swing at his assailant. Something loud popped, and a spray of red chunks rained over the bar. Alden let the hammer fly to put his hand over his mouth, gagging as the Shadow's jaw ripped away.

Seeing Alden pale and fatigued, Kira pulled him along. A few loyalists circled with their backs to them, creating a safety net around as she helped him recover. Still, one by one they were picked off, leaving them nearly undefended as Ricky found passage, ax twirling.

A shattering of wood burst from the front door of the tavern, jolting all in the midst of battle. From the opening, moonlight glistened off an army of shining knights and purple capes. Longswords flared out like spikes on a porcupine, piercing any who stood in their way.

Kira smiled as Madame Veridia came through the door. Their eyes met, and she nodded for them to move aside. Kira nudged Alden. "Hey, we might just get outta this okay."

"We should leave," warned Alden.

"Oh? Well, I don't think that's an option anymore," Kira said as a wall of plate mail waded through the ranks of the shadows, positioning themselves at each door and window. Two met them, and Kira dropped her found weapon.

Some thieves were slain as they continued to fight while others submitted, accepting shackles as the Binx & Drinx was completely overtaken by purple and steel. Ricky was seized. Trod was chained. The sounds of battle subsided as swords were sheathed. Kira watched as the knights lined up the captured thieves against the wall, Micah among them.

Veridia walked to them, red folder in hand. She flipped a few pages back and pulled a sheet free. She huffed as if pleased with herself. Without showing the drawing to Alden or her, she walked past to the line of thieves, flashing the paper. "Do you know who this is?"

Ricky blinked in surprise then grinned wide. "I'd know those tits anywhere."

Tits?

Veridia nodded. "And is there anything missing from this drawing? It seems every detail was considered."

Eyes hooked on the page, Ricky sucked on his bleeding lip. "Nope. That is exactly right."

"And was she in the guild?"

"Longer than me."

"And what is her name?"

"Kira. She's right over there." He nosed in her direction.

Me?

"Kira..." Alden's voice escaped him like a broken promise. "I'm sorry."

She whipped her head to him. "Did you fucking creep on me?"

"No!" He looked at her, eyes hurt. "No... I didn't, but Reyn... Shit, Ki, don't ya remember?"

"Remember what?" Kira snapped.

"This," said Veridia. The crackle of paper waved in her face.

Kira didn't dare look as she kept her gaze locked on Alden. A sickening brew twisted in her gut, fearing the unknown memories Reyn had stripped from her. Her eyes watered as Alden's tears freely flowed. "Alden..."

"Ki..." Alden shook his head. "Don't."

Unable to resist, Kira looked. At her. Breasts out. Body whole. Legs spread. Her eyes were open and alert—awake—yet she did not remember posing like that for Alden. Ever.

Kira reached to steal it.

Veridia put the illustration back in the folder. "I want this one locked up with the rest. She's a Shadowen and illegitimate noble. Give Evelyn Allwell her reward."

A knight moved in to secure Kira. Screaming, she wiggled against their armored grip. They kept pace, carrying her as she balled her body. Unable to fight, her wrists were shackled, and a chain was threaded through, hooking her with the other thieves. She heaved, glaring at Alden. Despite the pain and hurt she felt for him having disrespected her body, even if it were by Reyn's demands, she offered a frowning smile. *At least he's still safe.*

"Hey," Ricky said to her right. "Pierz, our lovely guild leader, is locked up, just down the hall."

"You bastard!" growled Micah, shaking in his chains.

Veridia flicked two fingers, sending two knights down the hall. They reached the unguarded door, opened it, and rushed in. After a moment of listening to heavy footfalls, they exited. "It's empty."

Ricky chuckled. "I guess Glendel was loyal to him after all. Well, you gonna lock him up too then, aren't ya?" He nodded toward Alden.

Veridia looked from Ricky to Alden. "No. Nick is who spied on you to get these drawings."

"Nick?" Ricky laughed, as did several other thieves in line. "That, my pretty knight, is Colin Densen. Prince of Brimley."

"Don't lie," Kira bluffed.

Her attempt to claim his innocence was unheard as the knight beside Alden drew her sword and pointed it to his neck. Another knight tugged at his leather coat, working to expose his crest. A clasp broke, and an orange scarf peeked out. She pulled it free and handed it to Veridia.

"Princess Mayli's scarf?" Veridia folded it. "I do say, this look is not good on you."

Alden closed his eyes as the knights continued to unclasp more. He jerked his shoulder away. "Stop. I'm him. I am Colin."

"No..." breathed Kira.

Veridia grinned deeply. "Oh, how this will make my prince proud. Bring them to his ship."

Outstretching his hand, Briar dug through the sheets. Soft furs and plush pillows teased his search. A cold space remained beside him. "Kira?" Briar turned his head and opened his eyes, finding her already out of bed.

Yawning, Briar rubbed his eyes. "Are you going over your papers again..." he asked, looking out over their room.

It was empty.

The desk still had all her documents sprawled out. Her vanity had been cleaned from makeup. Curtains closed, the room remained dark and forbidding despite him knowing it was morning.

Hesitantly, Briar stepped onto the chilled floor. His feet touched clothes that he had discarded while making his way to bed without her, too tired to wait upon her return from speaking with Evelyn. He furrowed his brow. *Evelyn...*

Briar grabbed his shirt off the ground and pulled it overhead. He struggled with the clips and ties Kira usually assisted with. Stepping into his breeches and then his boots, letting them sit loosely around his legs, Briar walked to his door.

Sir Exten, suited once more in his plate, turned his chin to attention.

Hanging from the door frame, Briar looked down the hall, then back at Exten. "Did Kira come back last night?"

He shrugged.

"Right. Your shift just started again." Briar drew his hand through his hair, pulling it away from his face and put his crown on. "I'll have to talk to the guards on duty last night... Come."

Exten dipped his head and followed Briar down the stairs. Nearly halfway to the ground floor, Fredrik rushed from Briar's meeting room and bowed, nearly topping himself over from the rush.

"Your Majesty, finally, you're up! I—"

"Do you know where Kira is?" Briar interrupted, stopping to better tie his bootstrings.

"Not yet... I have only just concluded a meeting with Evelyn, and Madam Veridia has not honored us the time to speak and has already left."

Briar looked up. "Veridia?"

"Yes, Sire. Kira was arrested last night."

"Arrested!" Briar rose to tower over Fredrik, his fists pulsing. "What do you mean, Kira was arrested? Why wasn't I informed?"

"You asked not to be involved in meetings... I—"

"That doesn't pertain to emergencies!"

"Thomas has been in search, but it seems Evelyn Alwell had reported Kira Harlow to the Hiorean authorities, and they have already left port." Fredrik thumbed over his shoulder to the room he'd come from. "She's in the meeting room waiting to discuss something she insists is only meant for you. I had her wait until you were awake."

Briar brushed shoulders with Fredrik as he marched past. Flinging the door open he shouted. "Evelyn!"

The baroness jumped from her seat. Her hands trembled as she worked to bow. "Your Majesty."

Not allowing her to complete the action, Briar slapped her back into the chair. "How dare you."

Evelyn held her cheek with both hands. Her eyes watered. "Briar... I'm sorry!"

He pointed down at her. "I specifically told you to leave her alone... *But no.* You had to bring Hiore into this. Do you know how taxing their trials are? How this will affect everything we have been trying to do? You really had—"

"They captured Colin," she interrupted.

"Wha..."

Evelyn slowly stood, raising her small hands to grasp Briar's shirt. "I didn't know Alden was Colin or I would have never told the Shadowens where to find him. I thought he was scheming with Kira. And when she came by the Binx to talk with their leader like friends, I knew I had to do more. To protect *you*. I saw the knights and turned them in. I'm sorry... I'm sorry." She clung to him, burrowing her head into his chest.

Evelyn's sobbing continued as more excuses wept from her lips. Briar didn't hear any of it. He just stared out over her, eyes glazing over the fragmented mural behind her. *They have Kira and Colin?*

"Ow, Briar... You're hurting me."

His fingers continued to wrap around Evelyn's arms. He glared down at her. "And why shouldn't I?"

Eyes puffy and red she blinked away a rush of tears. Her pink lips wavered. "Because I've only been trying to help you I —Ow." She winced at his constant pressure.

"Help me?" Briar scoffed, releasing his fist as he resisted the urge to destroy her here. "You have been nothing but a thorn in my side since you wanted to believe I wasn't an heir to King Edune. You entitled prune even wanted me to turn in my cousin so we could still have a chance... Now you've done that *and* expect forgiveness? You took away the two people I love most thinking you could fill that void. I should have you killed for treason."

"Don't!" she cried. "*Please.*"

Sickened, Briar tossed Evelyn to the floor. "Do not grovel. There is nothing you can say or do to redeem yourself now." He whistled in summons.

Several Black-Coat guards rushed in, surrounding Evelyn. Briar watched with satisfaction as they clamped shackles to her wrists, chains down her back, and cuffs around her legs. One pulled her spread of red hair back and held her head up to look at him.

He ignored her pleading green eyes, focused on his guard. "Lock away this traitor. I never want to see her again."

The clink of steel and march of boots masked the baroness's shrieks of protest as the guards escorted her from the room.

Breathing heavy, Briar turned and pressed his knuckles into this desk. He pounded his fist. He screamed. Cursed. Then slowly, his head dipped, giving into a cry.

His crown slipped off.

Opening his eyes, he grabbed the fallen circlet. Holding it tightly, he said, "I need William."

CHAPTER TWENTY-SIX

THE GIFT

After days at sea and several more in port, chained to the cast of thieves caught at the Binx & Drinx, Alden sat by himself mulling over the past and dreading the future. The horrors, however, were no match to the grueling present as the tension between Alden and Kira grew. She hadn't looked his way since they had been brought on board. Hadn't muttered a word since he'd allowed himself to be captured. Thinking back, Alden realized Kira hadn't even offered anything friendly since discovering he had aligned with Pierz. Heart at its limits, Alden braved a glance, hoping to catch her stare.

She sat hunched over with knees folded to her chest and head down.

"Ki..." Alden said.

She shifted, looking behind herself as if running from his call.

"Kira."

Her shoulders bobbed as faint sobbing filled the ship's hull.

He watched. Witnessing the pain he'd caused. The deceit he'd planted. Alden watched as she shook uncontrollably because of the man he was. The monster he'd become. The killer. The fraud. Without a tear to shed for himself, Alden looked out the porthole, preparing himself. *This is only a small fraction of the pain I'll see on May...*

As if his thoughts of her had manifested it, from the sea rose an arid, rocky island out the porthole. Circling up the land were grand estates. Rows and clusters of trees with tall trunks and bushy fronds danced in the wind as if welcoming his entry. Crowned at the top, a dark stone wall surrounded a delicate, white sandstone fortress. Its elegant towers were arranged like arrows shooting true into the sky. Orange canopies Alden knew to be silk shaded every window, and long thin flags waved proudly upon each apex. Sunlight caught in the carved details, showing a padded armor-like design wrapping around each tower. Arches supported the halls, overhangs, towers, and walls. Even when there was seemingly nothing to reinforce, a scalloped curve added a beautiful and elegant design. No detail was spared in the construction of the Ammosian palace.

Alden's mouth hung open and dry of words. *It's more beautiful than I imagined.*

Port bells chimed, and crewmen worked above to lower the sails. The ship turned toward a wide stone bridge connecting the island to the mainland with boats of assorted shapes and sizes docked to it, though most were small due to the rarity of wood in the southern region. Many had long arms extending to a canoe where fish splashed in the netting hung between. A few elegant yachts that mimicked the elaborate carvings of the palace above sailed by, flaunting their wealth. One ship was exceptionally large, *Her Lady*—the Drake's royal ship. Nearby, *Her Lady Damgard* was tied to a stone dock leaving much to be desired with its flaking paint, rotting boards, and makeshift repairs. However, seeing the ship that Mayli had boarded with Charli Damgard in the Cads put Alden's heart at ease knowing she truly was home and he was on his way to see her one last time.

The ship he traveled on nestled next to a Hiorean galley. Its grandeur outshone all others with its robust beams, a trio of masts, and high-polished wood. As they came to a stop, Alden saw the name *Terminus* painted in bold and angled script.

Alden sighed. *Let it begin...*

After a long while, Veridia descended the steps. Two other Hiorean knights followed. Her eyes scanned the thieves, Kira, and then him. She smiled. More knights filed in. They continued to check the restraints of the other prisoners. Confirming all were still bound and accounted for, they took positions guarding. In unison, they called out.

Veridia pulled at Alden's chains. "Stand, Prince Colin."

As he hobbled to obey, a few Shadowens scoffed and howled at him, calling him a traitor, murderer, and brim-nose bastard. It was as if he were in the great hall of Brimley Castle, humiliated and shunned by a wall of hate. On his feet, Alden ignored their outrage. Having accepted the truth, they were unable to cast him down any longer. Instead, he listened for one voice: Kira's.

It remained silent.

Graceful footsteps pressed into the stairs as heeled, black leather boots embroidered with gold descended. They stopped at the bottom. "Is this him?" asked a deep and refined voice.

Veridia bowed low and submissively. "Yes, Your Royal Highness."

Alden peered up, working to focus on the man as shimmers of purple silk sparkled in the lone sunbeam falling into the ship's hull. A royal Hiorean crest peeked out from the suit's shoulder hole: a sword with a crowned top like mountain peaks and the three four-pointed stars of Vatan flanking its sides and sword's point. The hard angles and bold color seemed more powerful than the gentle lines and broken tree on Alden's own arm. Black hair, trimmed to perfection, lay neatly. His narrow but healthy face held a curious expression, looking Alden up and down as if unwilling to believe what he was seeing: a prince, dressed as a thief, and bruised like the dead, alive before him.

"Prince Colin," Gavin said, remaining upright.

"Prince Gavin," Alden addressed just the same.

There was a low murmur among the thieves as a hesitation rested in the room.

Gavin politely cleared his throat. "Hearing Madam Veridia and my knights had finally found you, I came straight away to meet you here in Ammos—even before seeing the princess." He stepped forward, his gait slow and cautious but not without confidence.

"I am honored," Alden said, keeping his gaze low. "Considering she's your fiancé."

His brow raised with suspicion. "Perhaps after this, she might finally be. Still, it is not honor I seek. It is truth and clarity. For years you've denied responsibility but now claim libel. This concerns me, as I cannot in good faith sentence an innocent man. However, it is said you have been involved in the Shadowen Thieves Guild and a conspirator of Princess Mayli's abduction. If there are any last words you wish to say to proclaim your truth, Colin Densen, speak them now."

Alden sensed Kira's head rise. Despite the temptation, Alden kept his mouth closed. He looked at Gavin, meeting his eyes. The contest held as if the prince of Hiore was genuinely waiting for a plea of innocence. Alden shook his head. "While I was undercover in the guild, I was involved in her kidnapping. However, when I realized it was Mayli, I went rogue to help return her home. Since then, I have realized I killed Queen Margaret and am now ready to accept retribution."

"No!" Kira's scream met Alden's ears like a heartwarming stab. She pulled at her restraints as if she could run over and fight back the words he'd just admitted. When the chains held, she collapsed to her knees and shook her head, pleading. "It had to have been an accident. Prince Gavin, please have mercy on him! He's no murderer."

Gavin slowly turned his head, small eyes honing in on her. "Who is that?" he asked Veridia.

"Her name is Kira. Or as she claims: Kira *Harlow*." Veridia pulled a ribbon to let Kira's window sleeve expose her fraudulent tattoo.

Gavin examined it. "It looks legitimate to me."

"An impressive imitation, I'll agree. However, the Harlow name died in the war, and she not only stole their name but their home. She was found at the scene of a break in there last week where she must have stolen the deed. She's a Shadowen thief like the rest here, responsible for Princess Mayli's kidnapping. Evelyn Alwell, the baroness who reported them, said Kira had seduced King Briar in order to spy for the guild." Veridia showed Gavin the deed to the Harlow Estate along with the sketch Alden had done. "This drawing links her further to the guild, having been found on another member and drawn—"

Face flushed seeing the explicit drawing, Gavin waved it out of his face. He looked at Kira. "This true?"

"While I was a Shadowen I never asked to be crested. When I left the guild to expose their wrongs, Briar honored me with nobility, and I have been loyal to him," breathed Kira. "As with Ald—*Colin*. Even if he somehow murdered Queen Margaret, he's changed. He's a good man. He—"

"I see that he is," interrupted Gavin, looking down on Alden. "Because only good men accept consequences when given the opportunity to flee."

Alden peered up. "I do have a request, Your Highness."

Gavin faced forward to address him. "I will hear it."

Alden swallowed. "Be good to Mayli."

"I have no other plans than to treat Her Highness with respect."

Alden closed his eyes, willing his heart to stay intact. "One more thing."

"Go on."

"Allow her to sentence me. I understand your trials are fair and just, but she deserves this from me the way she's wanted it."

Gavin's eyes narrowed before he blinked his concern free. "Very well. That was my intention after all. Veridia?"

The knight touched her shoulder. "Sire."

"Take them to Mr. Vaurus's dungeons and have them prepare for a trial and ceremony."

Veridia bowed. "Yes, Sire."

Looking back at Alden, Gavin placed his hand on his shoulder. It was gentle. Kind. Still, pain ignited despite the gentle touch. "May you die with dignity, Colin Densen."

Days had gone by with still no reply from Colin, Alden, Briar, or even Lord Dean. *Why?* Mayli wondered, hoping her letters had brought some peace. *Do they not trust me?* Mayli walked to her balcony, not doubting it. She'd been the reason for all their sorrows, then was too stubborn to listen to their pleas.

Colin... Are you so angry with me that you can't even accept my help?

The breeze blew, carrying cheers and music to Mayli's ears. It sounded like the Festival of Gezmek as activity gathered from the coliseum to two large ships, larger than any she'd ever seen.

Purple flags flew high, signifying their origins as Hiorean. Their arrival had been unscheduled and sent King Bakhari into a scurry to prepare the castle, including sending Mayli to her room to put on her very best to court with Prince Gavin of Hiore.

Not now. Not to Gavin. Not while I have the possibility of mending things with Colin.

"You need to control these waterworks, Mayli Drake. We can't be doing your makeup over again." Using the backside of her finger, Lidia dabbed Mayli's face free from tears. She then coiled a purple scarf around Mayli's neck. "You have an important man to impress. Gavin shouldn't need to see you in such despair. Courting should be done with smiles and a strong presence."

Mayli brought the scarf to her face as if to pat her face dry. Hiding inside it, she screamed silently. She steadied her anger and pulled the silk away. The foreign sheen stared back at her. Despite its beauty, it couldn't replace her lost scarf, even if it was cut from a fabric of sorrows. *I will free Colin from this burden, no matter the cost.*

"Ah!" Lidia stepped back and swooped her arms in display. "There's the strong and beautiful Princess of Ammos we know."

Faking a sniffle, Mayli dabbed her eye with the silk. "Yes, I just wish Mother were here..." she said, trying to sound frail.

"Oh..." Lidia cupped her hands around Mayli's shoulders. "As do I, dear. As do I."

Mayli embraced Lidia. The old woman's bones hugged back. Stepping away, Mayli offered the old woman a pleading smile. "Might I have a moment by myself? I don't want Gavin to see me like this." She wiped an invisible tear.

Lidia bowed. "Certainly. Be no longer than a half-turn." After flipping an hourglass over on her vanity, Lidia departed.

Alone, Mayli dipped her head to observe her overstitched

ball gown. The bright purple was nauseating. It rippled around her arms, neck, and feet. White feathers were stitched at the cuffs, making her hands itch as if she were wearing wool. Mayli found a ribbon on her back. Slowly, she tugged. The bow came free, and her corset loosened. Catching another, she pulled. The dress relaxed. Shaking her shoulders, Mayli stripped from her expectations.

Freed once more, Mayli rushed to her wardrobe and threw open the doors. She shifted through endless outfits she never wanted until she found the black dress. "Hello, again," Mayli said, bringing the shadowy silk to her skin.

Slipping it on, Mayli dressed herself—for herself. She added the corset but left it loose around her stomach enough to breathe. Unpinning her tight bun, her hair came down in waves, and she placed her arrowhead crown on top. Next, she applied a dusting of dark powder to her eyes, then lined them more heavily. Curious, she marked her lips with it as well.

A wave of strength and power surged through Mayli as she looked at herself in the mirror. "There is the beautiful Princess of Ammos I know. I just need one last thing." She opened the bottom drawer of her vanity.

The King's Blade stared up at her.

Swallowing, she reached. The jeweled handle felt cold in her hand, trying to convince her no amount of beauty could forgive the deed. Pulling the blade to her, Mayli clipped it to a belt then strung it around her corset. "Let's show Gavin who I really am." Seeing the hourglass long spent, Mayli took a confident breath and exited her room.

"Good day, Princess." Keegan met her with a bow, showing off his shaved tan scalp.

"Hardly. But it will be, Klide." Mayli looked over the balcony where the court was decorated with grandeur as if expecting days of celebration. Orange drapery wrapped around pillars overhung on trellises and stretched across the open air above where glass mosaic lanterns glowed.

In her black gown and the low light, she had enough cover to watch without her father or brother noticing. They stood waiting at the door, both dressed in their finest wears, as gussied up as she had been. A subtle glimmer of purple rippled in Bakhari's silk's orange sash as he talked with Madam Nive and Sir Dallion. Mayli frowned, not seeing Charli as part of their escort.

Pushing from the balcony, Mayli met with her family below. "I'm ready."

"Hey!" gawked Jair, eyes as dilated as a cat. "How come Mayli gets to wear that? All I'm allowed is a pocketknife."

Mayli tucked the King's Blade behind her back before her father could understand her brother's protest.

"Mayli!" Her father's chest grew as he stepped forward. "Where is the gown and scarf I had sent up?"

Mayli shrugged. "They weren't to my taste."

"Wearing that was not a suggestion... They were to honor Prince Gavin!" Bakhari rubbed his face with the tips of his fingers, careful not to upset his makeup. "I would ask you to change, but I am afraid we are already running late!"

"Shame..." Mayli rolled her eyes as she walked out the doors.

Upon reaching the grand foyer, guards snapped to attention. A handler pulled on a silk rope, commanding a sand strider to its knees so that its saddled platform lay level with the deck. Following her brother and father, Mayli boarded with their guards.

"Hurry along now!" her father called before he'd even sat. At his command, the strider rose, knocking him into his seat. He growled. "And be careful! Let us not fall victim to another ambush before my daughter meets Gavin again!"

Mayli sneered. "Why is Prince Gavin here, Father?"

"Does it matter?" said Jair. "We get to go to the coliseum for a show!"

Mayli blinked. "Really? I didn't think we could afford such events."

"Whatever gave you that idea?" Her father laughed self-consciously.

"Maybe because of how fragile we became when you cut trade with Dregs. Or how rundown the city is," said Mayli. "Or how we haven't hosted a party in years."

"I've declined parties for your comfort, Little Bird. I know how hard it was for you after your mother's passing. It has been a challenge for me as well to express joy."

"Then why now?"

"Because Prince Gavin is eager to meet you, and we owe Hiore a great deal. Now wave." He raised their hands high as they passed the first gathering of nobles ready to join in the parade.

Lips plastered into a stiff smile, Mayli offered her hand, resuming the role as princess. As the people waved back, their excitement faltered. Heads tilted and lips whispered into their neighbor's ears. Mayli sulked, curious as to what she'd done to offend, but upon hearing one mumble something about her attire, she looked self-consciously over herself.

Jair nudged her side. "I think you look cool. It is as if you've conquered the shadows themselves."

Mayli grinned. "Thank you, Jair."

Confidence reclaimed, Mayli waved and smiled at everyone passing, unafraid to express herself. The energy immediately changed, and her people waved her on once more. Cheers and pride in their kingdom encouraged them all the way to the coliseum where a large crowd was lining into the building.

Trumpets blared as two sets of heavy iron doors opened for

their arrival. In the arena, acrobats twirled, danced, and spun, streams of orange and purple silk flowing after them. Large desert cats jumped through hoops. A man with dual fire whips cracked them over and over. Jugglers tossed glowing orbs. *Kanavaur toxins,* Mayli realized.

Reaching the royal pavilion, the sand strider pivoted to dock with the second-story landing. Upon the gate opening, Mayli stepped out to take the hand of a guard.

"Princess," greeted a sultry voice.

Mayli threw her gaze up to meet Charli's pale eyes. While he wore his orange cape, he was free from his guard's uniform. Instead, he wore a matching suit nearly as embroidered as the king's. Still, he stood at attention and chin elevated as if on watch. Mayli sighed with relief and allowed him to help her onto the landing. "Charli! I'm so glad you're here. You always made such events tolerable."

"And how did I do that, Princess?" A devious glint in his eye winked at her.

With her father within earshot, Mayli blushed, knowing he knew exactly how Charli distracted her. "Laughter and good conversation." She winked.

His smug grin wavered. "Your outfit. It's..."

"It's what?" Mayli postured.

He scrunched his face, trying to smile. "Didn't Lidia help you get dressed?"

"She did... And then I helped myself," she said proudly.

"I could have helped..." Charli's eyes trailed down her body. A muscle in his jaw bulged and he reached for her side. "What are you doing with that knife—"

Before he could grab it, a large arm wrapped around Mayli's back. The smell of her father's sharp smoke cut the space between them. The king tested his brow at her, then glared at Charli. "Perhaps, Damgard, your free time should be spent courting eligible women." Her father nosed toward the stands.

Seated to the side of the shaded pavilion, sat Mayli's old friends. They wore fancy dresses, so detailed in embroidery that Mayli wondered if there was any original silk to show. All three averted their eyes after likely gossiping about her closeness with Charli or her dark apparel.

Mayli sighed. *It wouldn't have mattered had I smiled. They abandoned me long ago.* Tired of Mayli's tears and the talk of her mother's death, they worked to avoid her and made excuses to skip outings with her. Mayli looked at her clenched fist. Realizing she had true friendships, she extended her fingers one by one. *Charli, Briar, Al...* She hesitated to count Alden's name. She considered adding Colin's. Her head hurt. Her heart was torn. *I have fewer friends than even a rogue.*

Shaking her hand out, Mayli looked back to her father. "A couple of ladies from Lower Ward seem unfit for a man of Sir Charli's stature, don't you think, Father?"

"They would bear him crested children. That is enough for his family line to resume their standing in the palace. If that is what he intends." Her father glared at Charli. "Don't you agree, Damgard?"

"Perhaps." Charli glanced at Mayli. While his focus sharp and dominant, his voice came out as a velvet whisper. "But I do imagine there is someone better suited for me."

Mayli swallowed.

"Ah yes, I see a duchess from Hiore in the stands who would be ideal. Go honor her with your tales of heroism."

Charli bowed but instead walked to his mother.

Bakhari's grip tightened around Mayli, walking her to the steps of the dais. Releasing her to the throne, he scolded her. "You cannot keep being so familiar with your guards, Mayli."

"It wasn't like that!"

"Not from what I saw!" Jair crossed his arms, his brow and nose raised high.

"You don't know what you saw!" Mayli argued. She turned to her father. "Father, Charli is my friend, he—"

"We have gone through this. He isn't ranked high enough to fly with you..." Her father raised a fat finger and pointed as the gates to the arena opened once more. "But, ah, I now see the man who is."

Six Hiorean knights, each cloaked in purple strode in on white horses. They circled the arena in a gait that looked more like a dance than any style of riding she'd ever seen. They crossed in the middle, raising pikes adorned with orange tassels as a sand strider, draped in gold entered.

A herald riding alongside a man dressed in a purple silk suit tailored to present a muscular form lifted a small horn. It blared, calling the attention of anyone who hadn't noticed the grand entrance. He tucked it under his arm and stood stiffly as the strider paused in the middle of the arena. "His Royal Highness, Son of His Royal Majesty, Vron Henmury of Hiore, Ruler of the Northern Realm, and Protector of Vatan, Prince Gavin."

Mayli rose on her toes, looking past the handsome man on the strider in an attempt to spy Old Man Gavin come into the gates. But as the double doors closed and the crowd hushed, she noticed all attention was upon the central man. She looked too. His short black hair waved to the side, showing off a shaved hair design with sharp, angled lines, matching the crest of Hiore. Finding his neutral gaze locked upon her, Mayli's eyes widened, then her cheeks blushed as dimples bore in the man's cheeks. *Him?*

His strider came forward, docking alongside them. Once secure, Prince Gavin stepped forward, reaching the dais.

Armor clanged as a wall of knights stepped forward. They bent into a deep bow, gripping their right shoulder. The

Ammosian nobles gave the same respectful gesture. Mayli, Jair, and her father stood but remained upright—equals among royalty. But as gray eyes toured her as if assessing bought goods, Mayli couldn't help but get the feeling like she was expected to submit while in the prince's presence.

"Prince Gavin," King Bakhari began, stepping closer with hands spread wide. "We are honored to have you here on such a fine day. A wonderful surprise."

"I deeply regret the manner of our last attempt, so the honor is mine." A heavy Hiorean accent, much like steel meeting gravel, drew out the words as Gavin placed his hand to cover his royal crest inked on light skin. He rose, eyes focused on Mayli. "Princess Mayli. It is a shame we could not meet at my citadel."

"Hmm. Yes." Mayli cleared her throat, trying to maintain her headstrong composure. "I am glad you made it here without incident. I had quite the ordeal, falling prey to thieves no thanks to your kingdom's inability to protect me."

The nearby crowd gasped from her forward insult, and several nobles turned their heads to discuss.

Gavin raised both brows. "Indeed, you are correct, Your Highness. I hope what I bring for you today more than makes up for my shortcomings." Gavin touched his shoulder and turned as a servant ran over to help unclip his cloak.

"*Mayli!*" Bakhari grabbed her wrist, pivoting her. Fire seemed to crackle in his eyes. "That was wildly inappropriate."

The fierce hold felt as if it were burning her skin. "Father—"

"Do you not know how much I've worked to get you to this moment?" He jerked his chin out over the open arena. "You are so lucky Prince Gavin did not take offense. Do not disrespect him the same you do me. Understand?"

Mayli ripped herself free. "Understood..." she hissed.

"Good." Without another look at her, Bakhari took his seat

next to Jair. He tapped the boy's hand and pointed out over the arena, smiling as if nothing had happened.

Mayli drew her hands back up her arms and held herself. The ache of where her father had pressed still throbbed.

"Everything all right, Princess Mayli?" asked Gavin.

Mayli closed her eyes at Prince Gavin's voice. It was soft, kind, and given from a respectable distance. Without looking, she took her seat and nodded. "Yes, Your Highness."

"Gavin," he suggested, sitting beside her. "And, if you don't mind me saying, that dress accentuates your beauty."

A polite lie. Confidence tested, Mayli pressed her eyes harder shut. A tear still escaped. "You mean, I look beautiful in this dress?"

"That too. However, you were lovely to begin with."

Mayli sniffed, dabbing her eye. "Thank you, Your Highness."

"Again, Gavin is more than acceptable, but if you wish to address me formally, I will not pressure you again." He sat back in his chair.

Is he genuine? Curious, Mayli finally gazed upon *Old Man Gavin.* Only he didn't look as old as she'd envisioned. Mayli searched for a stray gray hair or peppering in his beard, but every strand was richly dark. His skin was pale but healthy and free from makeup. While a few creases were spreading from the crest of his eyes, they gave him a kind regard—one of someone accustomed to smiling. *He's beautiful,* she admitted and hated herself for it. She glared. "Why are you so perfect?"

Gavin's cheeks bunched forming a dimple in each, amplifying his good looks. He offered her a wry smile. "I'm hardly that, Mayli. But I will try for you." His jolly face subsided as he lifted a finger. On command, a Hiorean knight stepped forth. They bowed, presenting an iron box. Gavin took it and offered it to Mayli.

"What's this?"

"A present."

Mayli accepted the box. She rubbed the elaborate emboss-
ing, feeling the bumps and creases illustrating a mountainous
scene with wildflowers curling along the sides. Diamonds
sparkled at each corner. The box was a gift in itself, but a latch
shaped like a four-pointed star begged to be opened. Taking a
breath, she drew it upward.

The inside seemed to glow as light pooled in. Orange radiated, illuminating her skin and the world around her. A warm
breeze blew. Golden fibers shimmered. Her heart stopped realizing it was the same silk fabric her mother died in. She closed
her eyes and formed a grand frown. *Father would have that scarf
made for Gavin to flatter me with...* Knowing it wasn't his fault,
Mayli looked at the prince. "Thank you, Gavin."

"I know you've been in pursuit of justice since your mother
was taken. As have I." Prince Gavin lifted the new scarf from the
box, stroking its beauty. "So I hope by giving you this we can
mend what was lost."

Mayli lowered her eyes to watch Gavin coil the offensive
fabric around her. It was wrong. The wrong scarf, given by the
wrong man at the wrong time. But as he wrapped it a second
time, Mayli recognized the extra length Mr. Vaurus couldn't
promise, lay upon her. Its size was perfect. Complete. She
spread it in her hands, finding a familiar stain—now realizing it
was blood. "This *is* my old scarf..." she breathed.

A horn blew, drawing their attention to the arena. In the
middle stood a herald with a large cone to broadcast his voice.
"Lords and Ladies! Ammosians, our friends from the north,
nomads, and especially King Bakhari, Princess Mayli, Prince
Jair, and our esteemed guest Prince Gavin of Hiore, you have all
been invited to witness history!"

Cheering in the crowd erupted. Finding nerves crawling up
her back, Mayli swallowed. The bottom of her stomach turned,

feeling the edge of something amiss prodding. Still, she inched forward on her seat, eager to see.

"As tales of Her Highness's endeavors have reached the doors of your homes and filled glasses in taverns, many have been eager to know who was behind such terrors." The herald bent at the hip and pivoted to address everyone. The crowd grew restless under his coaxing. The man lifted. "And so, today, Prince Gavin of Hiore does not just honor our princess's promises of two kingdoms united, but of all. For Vatan."

"Kingdoms united?" Mayli repeated. She twisted to look at her father. A satisfied smile rested proudly on his face addressing everyone in the arena but her. Jair remained wide-eyed and focused as a far-off shriek sounded. Mayli's heart beat fast, and she spun to face Gavin. "What is this?"

"The gift you've always wanted."

CHAPTER TWENTY-SEVEN

TRIAL

M uted cheering thundered beyond the stone walls. Dirt fell from the ceiling as stomping above rumbled with excitement. Chains scratched along the floor as Kira and the other prisoners were escorted to a large door. Hearing the distant announcement, her heart raced fearing what was being said—what awaited not only her...but her king.

Ahead, Alden stood solemnly next to two Hiorean knights and several Ammosian guards. While Kira had pulled her wrists, twisted, bit, dug, and contorted to try to free herself, he gave no efforts to escape—he'd come willingly. Accepted—*no*—given up on everything he had tried to resolve over the last three years. Abandoning everything. Briar. Pierz. Her. Even Mayli. All so that he could *die*.

This wasn't honorable. It was shameful—cowardly.

"Don't look at me like that..." Alden said.

"Like what?" Kira sneered. She felt her lip uptick and nostrils flare.

"Like you hate me."

She lifted her chin. "Maybe I do."

Dark lashes cloaked Alden's eyes with acceptance, head

bowing to the floor. He sighed.

Kira's heart sank, her face smoothing out its hostility. She opened her mouth to take it back but only an unsure breath came through.

"Don't worry," Ricky crowed beside her. "I hate him too!"

A rally of agreement cheered from the other Shadowen prisoners. Kira glanced at them. They glared at Alden. A few shifted their hate to stare at her with just as much contempt. Trod stood in the corner, mumbling to himself. However, Micah looked at her hopefully and whispered, "Kira, you always get out of situations like this. Help."

"I can't." She showed her bleeding wrist, rubbed raw from the shackles. "Every time I move they get tighter."

"Well, what about your boyfriend?" asked Ricky. He flopped his head toward Alden. "Not you. You're worthless. I mean your cousin. King Briar! Surely *he* can help some of us out. Half of the guild members here weren't even on that mission with the Ammosian princess. We shouldn't be here!"

An Ammosian guard chuckled. "The only chance to be freed is to be the last one standing, as per the governing of Ammosian trial."

Ricky laughed, smiling down the line of Shadows. "Ha, easy then. I'll gut you saps in a matter of minutes." His amusement was accepted with soft chuckling from the guards. So much so, Ricky's cocky grin unsettled into an unsure snarl.

"No one is getting out of this alive," said a guard.

"I will," Kira promised.

The guard smirked. "I don't think you understand what you're up against here."

She looked around. "Sure I do. A few Shadows, one wild nomad, and a cowardly king." She looked right at Alden, hoping to rouse him to fight back.

He just frowned, accepting.

"The prince of Brimley won't be joining you this round," the guard said, pulling the doors open as trumpets blared outside.

Bright light stretched into the dungeon as if to grab them. Swirls of dust spun into the dry air, dancing with the music beyond. The chain went taut as it tugged at her ankles, shuffling her toward the open arena.

Kira held her breath, trying to keep collected. Sweat formed on her brow and pooled in her fists. She kept her chin up and eyes forward, but as she passed Alden, hearing his chains shake she couldn't help but give him one last look. "Colin..." she said in reassurance.

Eyes brightening at the call of his name, her king broke through the knight's hold. His hands took hers, and he pulled her from the line. She stumbled into him, and they fused together in a tight embrace.

Her chains yanked back.

Alden resisted, hanging onto her long enough to say, "Ki, I'm so sorry," into her ear before being beaten to the floor by the knights.

Kira screamed as they restrained him. Helpless to offer aid, she continued to be dragged away. The sounds of Alden's beating drummed behind her until the doors clicked shut.

Then, everything turned to silence.

Movement was all around her. Hands waved in the crowd. The sun beat down—too hot for winter. Guards escorted the other prisoners to every point of the hexagonal colosseum. Orange and purple flags whipped overhead. Following the distraction, Kira looked up where a wooden pavilion unparalleled to the rest branched out over the arena. It was adorned with masterful carvings and mosaic tile. An orange silk canopy shaded a sitting of nobles. In the shadows, she noticed a tan woman with flowing black hair tangled in an orange scarf. Princess Mayli Drake. *You bitch.* Kira glared.

"Hands please," requested a guard.

Kira blinked to see two guards at her side. Neither held their weapons at the ready, seemingly unaware that they were about to free her hands. Hands that would take hold of the polearm, knock it behind their knee, and spin. The one guard would fall while she—

Someone screamed from across the arena. Kira threw her attention over as a body fell to the ground: Micah's. Four arrows laced through. She took an unintended step back. "Shit."

The guard before her chuckled, pulling her back into place. "In case you were thinking of trying anything, there are archers stationed throughout." He lifted a finger and swirled.

Seeing looming white-coated figures with long orange feathers in their hats, Kira offered her hands. "I wasn't." She batted her eyes.

"Good." The guard brought a key to the shackles.

"Hey Kira," called Ricky.

She looked up, seeing him a few lances to her left, already unbound and unguarded. "What?" she snapped.

He gave her a snakish look. "Work with me to take out the others, or I'll make your end quite a display." He winked.

Kira threw her hand up, giving him a repulsive gesture. She blinked, seeing her wrists freed from their binds. Rubbing them, she turned to watch the guards disappear out a service door while a gate centered in the arena lifted.

"Fresh from the Desert of Gezmek and caught by your hero, Sir Charli Damgard," a voice called over the crowd, "comes a wild kanavaur, just a month old. But don't let its age fool you, this hatchling is vicious and hungry!"

Clicking and chittering echoed from inside the dark chamber. A brown segmented figure as tall as Kira crept forth, racing chills down her back. Coming into the light, clusters of red eyes blinked arrhythmically, seemingly taking note of everything around them. As the crowd gasped, it flinched, hissing out a spool of tendrils from around its beak.

Kira shuffled backward, nearly falling. "That's a hatchling?"

"So, let's see how these crooks fare!" concluded the herald with a blow of his horn.

As soon as the doors clicked shut, the kanavaur's chains were let free. Several Shadowens dove for each other while others went after the kanavaur. One plucked the arrows from Micah. They tossed them to the others and together they cornered it. As if afraid, the creature backed away, hissing.

Suddenly, Trod rushed to defend the creature, his battle cry following. He tackled the closest man, flailing fists. The kanavaur followed. Startled, the other Shadows halted, raising their arrows like spears. Although Trod was now just below it, the kanavaur avoided him and sent whips of glowing tendrils out at the two men. Each took a hit, flying back.

Trod stood, his back to the kanavaur. Together they marched toward their next group of Shadows.

Kira spun and rushed the pavilion protecting the royals. As she neared, archers drew their bows and pointed down at her. She skidded to a halt, dust blooming, and raised her hands. "Princess Mayli! Stop this!" she yelled, waving her arms.

Rocks crunched behind Kira, and she spun with fists up, finding Ricky's dark smile. "You think the princess is going to listen to you? Ha. Your acts may have fooled the Densens, but no one here gives a damn. Least of all, me. Now let me have a taste before you're wasted for kanavaur meat." He cracked his knuckles.

Seeing the hungry grin, Kira ran, uncaring how it made her chest burn and belly ache. The glow neared and she slowed, reaching the kanavaur. Up close, its size seemed to amplify. "Oh, sweet kings..."

Three bodies stained the sand red—limbs ripped from

them. One Shadowen remained fighting with Trod. The creature kept at a distance with its tendrils moving around Trod to aid in the attack. Inhaling deeply, Kira took her chances and joined the nomad.

For a moment Trod bared his teeth like a startled wild animal, but as Kira kicked back his assailant he refocused. Together, they assaulted the Shadow. Kira grabbed their collar, bringing them down. Trod stomped. They screamed, but the cry was choked out as a tendril wrapped around their neck.

Looking behind her, she saw the horror of the kanavaur just an arm's length away. One glossy eye was focused directly on her as if seeing her intentions. "Hello..." she cooed, despite her racing heart.

The eye darted to the left, and a whoosh of air blew past her. Bright light blinded her for a moment as a yelp from Ricky cried out. The swift breeze came back as the kanavaur retracted its tendril back around its beak. The eye fell back on her.

"Thanks," Kira said and turned her back on her new companion to face the threat.

Trod pulled an arrow from the neck of a Shadow. The body fell to the ground, gurgling. Kira hated that it wasn't Ricky. Instead, he stood a few feet away rubbing his arm where an acid-like burn bubbled from the kanavaur's attack. He looked at her, eyes seething with hate.

If Ricky dies first, Trod won't fight the kanavaur, and I will be left to face him alone, Kira realized. *Will the kanavaur pick sides?* Not wanting to find out, Kira lunged at Ricky. He stepped back, eyes blinking in surprise at her forward aggression. Catching himself, he redirected his next step toward her. Kira smiled as he threw a punch. Pivoting ever so slightly, she grabbed it and pulled, encouraging his momentum right into Trod.

The two stumbled, falling into the kanavaur. The creature sent all its tendrils out in surprise. Light burst. Both men screamed as it burned them in its glow. Rising on thin legs, it lifted Trod. For a moment, Kira thought it was going to free him, but as Trod flailed to break free, it opened its beak and crunched down.

Kira turned away, wincing at the sound of breaking bones. She could hear Ricky grunting as he tangled with the toxic tendrils, but his struggling slowed, and soon the only sound remaining was a worrisome chittering.

Kira didn't move.

She didn't look.

She stood there with hands balled and back taut.

Something wet and rubbery touched her shoulder through her open window sleeve. Kira opened one eye to see the kanavaur's tendril, holding her crest as if honoring her. The light had waned. Its vicious nerves settled. All eyes were on her —from the crowd's to the kanavaur's.

"I...won?"

The dark undertone of applause hit Alden like a thousand slaps to the face. *She's dead...* The shriek and cry of a kanavaur continued. *I killed her.* Alden let his head hang—the defeat too heavy. *Kira...*

Alden cowered as the celebration continued. His best friend. Gone. Their love. Destroyed. Every moment he spent with her, Alden had only invited her to her end. He knew the risk. Knew that because of who he was, anyone who stayed by his side was in danger. He'd been selfish.

The doors burst open as a horn blared. Through the yawling light, the excited voice of a herald amplified through the dungeon. "What a show! But prosecuting a few thieves responsible for the kidnapping is not all for today!" sang the herald. "No, Prince Gavin has brought our princess a most prudent present."

"You're up," said a guard, bringing him to his feet.

It took little effort for the guards to lead Alden forward. Still, he dragged his steps as his pride and will to live were left far behind in Brimley. Past the gate, he walked. Through bloodstains. Through suffering. A disembodied arm. A broken arrow. He kicked past Ammosian cheer flags and flowers, tossed down in celebration of Kira's death.

The guards stopped Alden in the middle of the arena. One tapped his face. "Wake up. You best give Her Highness a show. It is the least your sorry ass could do."

His cheeks numbed, tingling nervously as realization hit him. *Mayli is here...*

The herald called out from overhead. "I present to you, the one responsible for murdering our queen..."

The arena burst in outrage. Alden could feel the vibrations of hate coiling through him. He could feel Mayli's eyes upon him, watching with just as much spite.

Face her. Face her... Face...

Mayli rose from her seat. Slowly, timidly, the bearded man in the arena lifted his gaze. Bangs which had cloaked his eyes parted. Dark desolate eyes immediately found hers, and Mayli's heart sank. "No...! He turned on the guild to rescue me! He shouldn't be down there! He—" Mayli choked on her next words. *Is innocent? That isn't true. He had killed Mother. He...*

"Mayli," said Gavin. "I present, your mother's murderer."

They know? Mayli looked at Alden as guards were unshackling him. His eyes still held hers, offering condolences. *No. I can still fix this.* She shook her head. "That's a lie. It was an assassin. A Shadowen. Um... *Reyn!* He's who did it!" Mayli lied.

"Reyn?" repeated Gavin.

"Yes! I killed him when he taunted me with a confession and escaped. I didn't want to believe it because I was so sure Colin had done it!"

A Hiorean knight with blonde hair stepped in beside her prince. "I can confirm we found a Shadowen of that name dead in Brimley."

Mayli gasped. "Veridia! I met you at the checkpoint in Dregs! Remember? He called himself Nick, and me Emma... We were with Briar!"

Her brow furrowed, then it arched high. "Wait..."

Gavin turned, wide-eyed at Veridia. "You let her slip through your fingers?"

Her face flushed as she bent into a deep submissive bow. "I am sorry, Your Highness. I did not think the princess would be in the Densen's company so willingly!"

"Don't be mad at her." Mayli pulled at Gavin's sleeve. "I tricked her."

Gavin glared down at her. "Why?"

She slumped. "Because Briar and Alden were helping me. Alden isn't guilty. It was Reyn... Reyn killed Mother," she pleaded.

"Alden?"

"Yes!" Mayli pointed down at Alden. "Him!"

"You seem to be very confused, Mayli," said Gavin. "I think you've been manipulated by the Densens."

"No I haven't!" she stomped her foot.

"He confessed, Mayli. On his own. He wanted this."

"What?"

"Then let him die," commanded her father. He stood with

clenched knuckles and a glare so foul Mayli knew there was no convincing the king of anything else.

Tears flowed down Mayli's cheeks. "No..."

"This isn't going to get easier," said Gavin. "But I hope this helps heal some of the trauma you and your family have suffered."

"Prince Gavin is right, May," said Jair. He stepped forward and squeezed her hand. "He may have helped you... But he killed our mother."

Mayli held on to her brother's hand for sheer support and turned to face the man who risked everything to see her home safe. The man who fought thieves and monsters to keep her alive. Who lay by her side each night keeping her warm and comforted. Who had kissed her ever so softly. The man who tried to make up his wrongs, and now was taking full accountability. For her. For his king... "Alle..." she whimpered.

The guards were now removing the leather jacket he wore. Damage revealed itself. Bruises dotted his body. A bandage was wrapped around his torso. Blood stained it. The sleeves fell away, and Mayli saw the scars on his arms from his fight with Reyn, the stab wound in his side, and other blemishes from years in the guild. But most notably, Mayli caught notice of another wrap around his right shoulder.

Alden flinched but kept his eyes locked on her as the guards took the cloth bindings. He shuddered as they became unwound. Winced as it peeled off. And when he became fully exposed, he froze.

The guards left him. The crowd murmured.

Mayli stared into his glassy eyes. She didn't want to look away. Couldn't. She didn't want to catch sight of what she knew couldn't possibly be true. *There's no way... Alden can't be...* Swallowing that thought, Mayli shook her head. *He's innocent.*

"It is with great pleasure that I present to you today,"

continued the herald, "the trial of your most sought-after criminal. Kingdom destroyer, liar, drunkard, and murderer, Prince Colin Densen of Brimley."

"*No...*" Mayli whispered into her hand as she pressed it against her lips.

"And...without further ado. The judge of all! The mother beast you all know and love! Talia!"

The full set of large doors opened. Mayli could hear the chittering and hissing as the full-grown kanavaur entered the arena, but still, she kept her gaze on...

Colin.

He didn't turn to ready himself to fight. Didn't plea for his innocence. He hardly glanced at the kanavaur as its dark mass crept behind him. Instead, the prince knelt into a deep submissive bow. His hand came to his shoulder, covering the royal crest she still refused to address. He shook his head and said, "I am sorry, May."

Her father laughed, tapping Jair's shoulder as if it were all a big joke. "He begs for forgiveness! Ha! I can't wait to see him be ripped apart."

Mayli flew her gaze to Bakhari. "That's horrible!"

"*He's* horrible, Little Bird." Bakhari rubbed his hands together. "He's only getting what he deserves for killing my wife and abusing my daughter."

Whimpering, Mayli looked back down. Still, the prince of Brimley remained bowed. A glimmer of relief filled her, believing the kanavaur wouldn't find him a threat. From what she'd seen in the desert they were peaceful until provoked. And the hatchling had seen the thief from before protecting it and honored her with equal trust and respect. It gave Kira Harlow the right to keep her nobility. But as the old battle-worn kanavaur continued to creep toward Alden, it raised its mane of tendrils and screeched.

"Alden!" Mayli screamed, gripping the railing as a single tendril whipped out.

His body tumbled into the air before crashing into the dirt.

The crowd cheered, her father even louder. Even Jair whooped and hollered. Gavin remained quiet beside her.

Alden groaned. Coughed. Then he got to his knees, looked at her, and bowed again. She shook her head. *He's dying on his sword... Just as he promised.* The kanavaur sauntered after. *And the kanavaur knows he's guilty.* Mayli's nostrils flared. *No. I am not allowing him to die...* She looked to the side, spotting an archer keeping watch. Blood pumped through her, fueling her to move. She rushed the archer, grabbing the bow and arrow from his hands. He fought back a moment but seeing it was her he forfeited his weapon.

As quick as her training sessions, Mayli drew and loosed. The arrow struck true, piercing into a tendril reaching to whip. Mayli grinned as the kanavaur's cry amplified within the coliseum. Then a light brighter than the hatchlings bloomed. Mayli stared in awe as it intensified, changing from white to a bright violet hue.

A force pulled back on the bow. "Princess, give me that," demanded Charli.

Mayli tightened her grip. "No! That's Alden!" she screamed.

Charli tugged, bringing her ear to his lips. "See how he's fooled you? That's *Colin!*"

"I know!"

"So you know what you are doing is treasonous. Now let go of this foolishness, you're embarrassing yourself!"

"No, I won't let—" Mayli's hands slipped as Charli twisted the bow while he yanked. Losing balance, her legs hit the railing. The dry wood split. The crowd gasped. A moment later she was falling.

Falling.

Time slowed as she watched Charli, her father, brother, Madam Nive, and even Prince Gavin look over the edge where she'd broken through, expressions aghast. As she fell farther from them, she pressed her eyes shut in anticipation of the crash. For the drop to end. She awaited the hard ground. For her body to break. Death.

Falling.

The impact came, awkward and turbulent. A sprawl of arms crashed to the ground with her. A warm body cushioned her landing. Slick sweat glided them together as powerful muscles tightened, pulling her close. A faint masculine scent captured her along with the sweet undertone of lavender. Mayli breathed it in. She was alive. Dirty hair brushed against her face as he nuzzled into the nape of her neck. "May..." he moaned.

Mayli opened her eyes, finding herself safe with the most hated man in all of Vatan. "Alle..."

Alden shook his head. "You know that's not my name."

Mayli lifted her chin to gaze upon him. His beard had grown. Bruising discolored his nose which now had a slight bend to the ridge. Strange cuts lined his temple. Dirt smudged with sweat and blood over his brow. Still, the angles of his cheeks, chestnut hair, and dark kind eyes resembled everything she remembered of him. Mayli stroked his swollen cheek and delicately traced her thumb over a cut. "My rogue."

He huffed, closing his eyes as a pained smile formed. "That, I cannot deny."

The kanavaur screeched, breaking the illusion of a peaceful moment. Mayli looked out. The creature plucked the arrow she had delivered with another tendril. It snapped in its clutches and the pieces flew into the crowd. Legs stomping, the kanavaur pivoted to look at the broken railing, then all of its eyes narrowed in to look right at them.

"Alle..." Mayli clung to Alden.

"Get up."

As they stood, the arena began to rumble as the kanavaur beat the ground in furious succession. Mayli's heart raced just as quickly. Shouts and commands boomed. The crowd screamed.

Mayli took Alden's hand, but he shook it loose. He gestured toward the ladder folding down from the pavilion. "Princess, go to them. I'll keep it distracted," he said, rushing back into the arena. He waved his hands, hollering. The kanavaur reared as if startled by his sudden will to fight.

Calls for her name rang out overhead, trying to draw her to safety. Mayli didn't move as for the first time, her vision fell upon the royal Brimleyn crest and shield on Alden's arm as he raised his hands to the beast. A long cut drew across the design. Fresh stitches held it together as if he was worth forgiving. Her broken protector. Her rogue. Her prince. *Her love.*

"Mayli!" called Bakhari.

She looked overhead, seeing her father near the ladder waving his hand for her to come. Keegan was climbing down.

A light erupted from behind, and Mayli turned to see Alden tossing rocks at the beast. Tendrils aglow, the kanavaur tested the distance between them with quick whips. Alden moved closer, taunting it. Before he could sacrifice himself, Mayli rushed in. Her feet pounded dirt. Her hair whipped. The glow brightened. Sound muted. Her heart raced her to his side. Clasping Alden's crested arm, Mayli pulled just as a snap of tendrils whipped. They fell to the ground.

The crowd gasped as dirt exploded.

"What are you doing?" Alden yelled, getting to his hands and knees.

Heaving, Mayli pressed on her leg and lifted. She shuffled forward, positioning herself between Alden and the beast. As the kanavaur rose to its full height, chittering and hissing, she drew the King's Blade. "Not letting you die," she said, pointing it at the beast.

A uniform snap of bowstrings broke the air. From every direction, a volley of arrows rained down, darkening the sky.

Daylight seemed to come once more as the kanavaur lit its tendrils.

"Mayli!" Alden wrapped his arms protectively around her as a thundering storm beat all around them. Something thick and white sprayed into the air. Dust bloomed, then settled.

The crowd gasped.

Together they stood.

Mayli peered out, seeing a peppering of arrows. They had ripped precisely through the kanavaur's eyes, segmented shell, and prickly legs. They skewered its crown to its jaw. A leg was severed. With one last hiss, the kanavaur collapsed into the sand, tendrils flailing. They pulsed from purple to white, then subsided to a clear, lifeless cord.

Mayli and Alden breathed heavily. Both alive. Both together. She lifted her chin, finding his face a flurry of emotion. Her own bunched up, just as flustered. He smiled then frowned. She laughed, then cried. They shook their heads, then brought their foreheads together. They paused to just gaze upon one another, hands on each other's crests.

A swell in Mayli's chest felt too tight, bursting with the love she knew she shouldn't have for the man before her. "I hate you," she sniffed.

"I know." He stroked her hair, frowning. With a remorseful sigh, he peeled her off and stepped away.

An arrow suddenly struck dirt.

Startled, Mayli spun to check if the kanavaur was still alive. It lay still, eyes fading to white.

Another whiz sounded. Mayli twirled to find a second arrow had hit next to Alden. Closer.

Mayli's heart burst at the realization. "No!" She launched herself forward, taking Alden back in her arms. Then, they both screamed.

A hot pain erupted in her back. She squeezed Alden as the ache intensified. Blood wetted between them, pouring over his bare chest. She clung on, knowing that if she were to let go, more archers would loose their attack. "Alle..." she cried.

Alden's fingers traced up her back as blood poured down. They bumped into a shaft of wood protruding from her shoulder blade. She could feel it strung through her and into him, binding them. *He really would have died...* she realized.

"Why'd ya do that?" His voice cracked.

Lifting her head, she batted her wet lashes. "Because... I also love you?"

"Oh, May... Don't you understand? I did it. It was me. Colin. *I* killed your mother..."

"I understand."

"Then how..." He winced, shaking his head. Looking back at her, his eyes offered all the sympathy she knew he had. The honest regret he harbored. The love he always carried for her. The will to make things right. "How can you still love me?"

"Because..." She leaned in, enduring the pain in her chest and heart to place her lips to his, kissing softly. "I forgive you."

Alden's shoulders drooped. His whole body eased. A weight seemed to fall free from him as his breath hitched. "You *what?*"

The march of boots through sand surrounded them. Swords clanged and armor clashed. A whisper hushed through the crowd.

"Unhand the princess!" demanded Charli's deep voice.

Alden obediently lifted his hands skyward. Mayli sunk from the loss of support, watching the arrow's head pull from Alden's chest. Eyes quivering with horror, his gaze found the severity of her own wound. Disobeying orders, Alden took her back in his hold. His eyes then narrowed on her attire. "H-How did it go through your silk?" he asked, voice hoarse.

"I said, step back!" Charli ripped Alden away, tossing him into the arms of Keegan and several other guards.

Mayli cradled her arm and chased after. "Don't hurt him!"

Charli yanked the King's Blade from her hand and held her back. "You fell off a balcony and got hurt because of this man's lies and manipulation!"

"He saved me, and the kanavaur was dead by the time I was shot..." Mayli touched her collarbone where fibers of her dress had split from the arrow's dark tip. Her hand shook as she looked at the blood. A queasiness set in. "I think I need to sit."

"You need to go to the surgeon." Charli grabbed her scarf and tied it around her arm, creating a sling. With one arm wrapped around her waist, Charli pointed vigorously at Alden. "And you... While my steel will find your neck for touching my princess someday soon, the king has ordered you back to the dungeon. Take him away."

The guards pulled at Alden's arms, dragging him toward the gates he'd entered the arena from.

"No, stop!" Mayli pulled forward, but a spark of pain rolled down her back as Charli held her tight. Wincing, she fell into her guard's merciless hold as he escorted her in the opposite direction.

The further the distance between she and Alden grew, the harder it seemed for her to breathe. Just before entering through a gate, Mayli turned back. His chin rested upon his crested shoulder, watching her. Their gazes held. Smiles lifted. Breath filled her lungs once more and simultaneously they both mouthed, "I love you."

The series continues in

Book Three of The King's Renegade

VALOR

GLOSSARY OF TERMS AND NAMES

ALDEN: A rogue loyal to Brimley; artist

ALLE: Nickname given to Alden by Mayli

AMMOS: Large northern desert island kingdom that specializes in archery; colors are orange, white, and black

AMMOSIAN: People of Ammos

AMMOSIAN SILK: An armor-like silk made from kanavaur silk threads

ARKELLO DENSEN: Claims to be from Gezmek as the true heir of King Edune

BAKHARI DRAKE: King of Ammos

BASEVEIN: Town at the base of Mount Hiore; ruled under Hiore

BINX: Barkeep of the Binx & Drinx

BLACK-COAT: High-ranking guard of Dregs

BOSUN SCRAGGS: Captain of *The Lucky Fish*

BRIAR DENSEN: Prince of Brimley; Captain of the guard in Dregs; Colin's cousin; son of Jamus and Trish Densen

BRIM-NOSE: Insult given to Brimleyns

BRIM TEA: A black tea with lavender and vanilla that is served with cream; Alden adds orange peel to give it an Ammosian flare

BRIMLEY: Fallen kingdom in the western woods of Vatan; colors are blue, black, and gray

BRIMLEYN: People of Brimley

BROCK: Shadowen thief

CAD ISLANDS: A cluster of islands in Zollner's Bay near the southwestern tip of Vatan where pirates, thieves, and rogues take refuge in the bohemian life

CANTWELL INN: Hub for the Shadowen Thieves Guild located in the center of Colville

CARL: Yellow-Coat Guard of Dregs who later is promoted to lieutenant

CHARLI DAMGARD: Mayli Drake's personal guard

COLIN DENSEN: Outcast Prince of Brimley; accused of murdering Queen Margaret Drake of Ammos; Briar's cousin

COLVILLE: Mining and port town ruled under Hiore; northeast tip of Vatan

CLIDE VAURUS: Mercer; brother to Taji

DEAN WILKUS: Marshal of Brimley; miller after the war

DESERT OF GEZMEK: Huge desert spanning half of Vatan in the south

DOMINICK DENSEN: Colin's younger brother, also goes by Nick

DRACLYNN RIVER: River that flows from Lake Ironmere and runs south through Northern Vatan, connecting to Zollner's Bay

DRACLYNN: Sea monster covered in thick white scales with a wolf-like head, wing-like fins, and a long snake-like body that ends with many tentacles

DALLION DAMGARD: Royal Guard in Ammos; Charli's father

DREGS: Kingdom at the delta of the Draclynn River, consisting of many islands

DREGGEN: People of Dregs

DUNE ALE: An extremely potent liquor from Gezmek

EARL: Squirrel's new name, dubbed by Briar

EBBY: Shadowen thief

EDUNE: King of Vatan when Gezmek fell

ELITE SHADOW: A highly skilled member of the Shadowen Thieves Guild

EMMA: Mayli's alias

EMORY: Alden's horse

ERYN WRIGHT: Blacksmith from Brimley; leader of Olivar's harem

EVELYN ALLWELL: Baroness of Dregs; ex-lover to Briar Densen

EXTEN: One of Briar's royal knights

FAWN: Dean's horse; Emory's mother

FREDRIK: Briar's man-in-waiting; Trip's father

GALAVANT: Name of Jamus Densen's saber

GAVIN HENMURY: Prince of Hiore

GEZMEK: Lost kingdom buried underneath the traveling sand dunes in Ammos

GLENDEL: One of Pierz's Elite Shadows

HER LADY DAMGARD: Small ship Charli Damgard used to search for Mayli

HIORE: Kingdom ruling around the Crown Mountains; the towns of Colville and Basevein are under its control; known for their quality steel; colors are purple, black, and gray

HIOREAN: People of Hiore

IDEAL AVENUE: An avenue with noble estates in Dregs

JAIR DRAKE: Mayli's younger brother; Prince of Ammos

JAMUS DENSEN: Briar's Father; brother to King William; Prince of Brimley

JUAL: Shadowen thief

KANAVAUR: A large, ancient, crustacean-like desert creature with claws; has tentacle-like acidic jowls; lives in the sand; lays eggs; silk used for crafting

KEEGAN GATEMEN: Mayli's guard

KIRA HARLOW: Shadowen thief; shadow seeker; noble of Dregs

LARY: Shadowen thief

LIDIA: Mayli Drake's lady-in-waiting

LILY DENSEN: Late Queen of Brimley; Colin's mother; Dean and Mary's daughter

MATT: Shadowen thief

MARGARET DRAKE: Late Queen of Ammos; Mayli's mother

MARKS THIELEN: Said to be the King of the Cads

MARY WILKUS: Wife of Dean; baker

MARVIN: Yellow-Coat guard assigned to Evelyn

MAYLI DRAKE: Princess of Ammos

MICAH: One of Pierz's Elite Shadows

MIKE: Shadowen thief

MR. GARBSEN: Clothier in Dregs

MR. GREY: Old man who owns the Five Leaves tea shop in Colville

MRS. CHAUSMER: Clothier at the Waltzing Thread

NICK: Alden's alias

NIVE DAMGARD: Royal Guard in Ammos; Charli's mother

NOBLE'S DICE: Betting game using a twenty-sided die

OLIVAR COLTE: King of Dregs; Briar's uncle

PAIGE: Shadowen thief; pathfinder

PENNA: Trip's late mother; servant in Brimley

PIERZ: Leader of the Shadowen Thieves Guild

REAVER: A fabled creature of the desert

REK: Alden's one-eyed black cat with a white chin

REYNOLD: Shadowen Thieves Guild shadow commander; assassin; master of poisons; better known as Reyn (pronounced "Ren")

RICKY: Shadowen thief

SAND STRIDER: Large bird-like creatures used for riding in the desert

SANDWATER BAY: Bay between Ammos and the shore

SHADOW SEEKER: A Shadowen who gathers information

SHADOWEN THIEVES GUILD: Notorious thieves guild stationed at the Cantwell Inn in the center of Colville

SHADOWEN: Someone belonging to the Shadowen Thieves Guild

STRIDAN LANCE: Winner of the Bahar Festival earning nobility

SQUIRREL: Yellow-Coat guard

TALIA: Ammos's kanavaur

TAREK: One of Briar's royal knights

TAJI VAURUS: Kanavaur handler; mercer; clothier

THE ALBATROSS: Large galley ship owned by Briar Densen

THE BINX & DRINX: Tavern in Dregs

THE BRIM WAR: War against Brimley after their prince, Colin Densen, was accused of murdering Queen Margaret Drake of Ammos

THE FESTIVAL OF GEZMEK: A celebration that honors unity across Vatan, hosted between Ammos, Brimley, Dregs, and Hiore every three years

THE FIVE LEAVES: Mr. Grey's tea shop where Alden lived while in the guild

THE KING'S BLADE: A sabered dagger owned by King Edune and used in the murder of Queen Margaret

THE LUCKY FISH: Captain Bosun Scragg's ship

THE RIFFKIN LADS: Popular music group in Dregs

THE SEA MONSTER'S GRINN: Inn along the docks in the Cad Islands

THE WALTZING THREAD: Clothing shop in Dregs; owned by Mrs. Chausmer

THIELEN'S LODGE: Inn in the Cad Islands

THOMAS: Captain of the Guard in Dregs

TRIP: Servant in Brimley

TRISHA COLTE: Briar's late mother; married to Jamus Densen
TROD: Shadowen thief; nomad; traps specialist
UMBRA: Sir Stridan's horse
VALOR: Name of Briar's saber
VATAN: The country composed of the five small kingdoms of Ammos, Brimley, Dregs, and Hiore
VERIDIA: Hiorean knight
WAYPOINT: Inn in Basevein
WILLIAM DENSEN: King of Brimley
WILLIAM: Briar's black warhorse; named after King Liam when he passed in the war
WIRE: Shadowen thief
YELLOW-COAT: Common guard of Dregs

ACKNOWLEDGMENTS

BETA AND ALPHA READERS

Airic Fenn * Ariel Baker * Caitlin Crick Vaga * Caitlin Theriault *
Grace McNally * Jae Cooper * Jennifer Darnell * Jordan McLean
* Sara Jacintho-Schavz * SJ Raymond * Tiffany Moeung

SPECIAL THANKS

200 Rogues * Amy Elmore * Beth Hodgson * Chris Holmes *
Nikaya Chausmer * Johnny Ritenbaugh

DEDICATIONS

Pat Terry: Mum, you were the strongest person I knew. Thank you for your strength, courage, and creativity! You are still my hero.

Rest in Peace.

Chris Holmes: My hubby. You are always at my side to help ease my burdens and feel seen. Thank you for your patience, support, friendship, and understanding. Love you so much!

Dominic Pitera: My dear cousin, when I had you pose for my painting 'Burden' in 2014 I had no idea what we created would inspire so much. Thank you, I am forever grateful.

Thank you for reading Burden, Book Two of The King's Renegade. Any and all feedback on this debut novel is encouraged, so please take a moment to review on Amazon, Goodreads, and personal blogs.

Keep updated on social media!

www.theartofliz.com
www.Instagram.com/theartofliz
www.tiktok.com/@theartofliz
www.facebook.com/AuthorLsteinworth
www.twitter.com/Liz_Steinworth

Made in the USA
Monee, IL
29 May 2022